JOHN CARTER
of MARS

VOL. 2

JOHN CARTER
of MARS

VOL. 2

THUVIA, MAID *of* MARS
The CHESSMEN *of* MARS

FALL RIVER PRESS

New York

FALL RIVER PRESS

New York

An Imprint of Sterling Publishing
387 Park Avenue South
New York, NY 10016

This 2012 edition published by Fall River Press
Introduction © 2012 by Brian Stableford

ISBN 978-1-4351-3976-3 (print format)
ISBN 978-1-4351-3946-6 (ebook)

Distributed in Canada by Sterling Publishing
$^c/_o$ Canadian Manda Group, 165 Dufferin Street
Toronto, Ontario, Canada M6K 3H6
Distributed in the United Kingdom by GMC Distribution Services
Castle Place, 166 High Street, Lewes, East Sussex, England BN7 1XU
Distributed in Australia by Capricorn Link (Australia) Pty. Ltd.
P.O. Box 704, Windsor, NSW 2756, Australia

For information about custom editions, special sales, premium and corporate
purchases, please contact Sterling Special Sales at 800-805-5489 or
specialsales@sterlingpublishing.com

Manufactured in the United States of America

2 4 6 8 10 9 7 5 3 1

www.sterlingpublishing.com

CONTENTS

Introduction

When Edgar Rice Burroughs had completed his trilogy detailing the adventures of John Carter on the planet Mars, presented in its glorious entirety in *John Carter of Mars*, his initial project was complete. The trilogy proved so popular, however, that the pressure of reader demand soon forced him to return to the location. Fortunately, a planet is an exceedingly capacious fictional space, and a potentially inexhaustible source of marvels, so there was no danger that a sufficiently imaginative writer would run out of scope for the colorful adventures that were the chief stock-in-trade of the pulp magazines. Burroughs had already undertaken to extend his imagination more freely than anyone before him, and he was still perfectly able, and more than willing, to rejoice in the further exploitation of that freedom.

As with many writers extending popular series, Burroughs' first recourse was to move forward by a generation and allow the children of his original hero and heroine to take up the torch that the demands of narrative closure had caused their parents to set down. *Thuvia, Maid of Mars*, serialized in *All-Story Magazine* in 1916 and reprinted in book form in 1920, details the exploits of Carthoris, the worthy but callow son of John Carter and Dejah Thoris, who is framed for the kidnap of the eponymous heroine by the actual abductor, and forced to undertake a solo rescue mission. *The Chessmen of Mars*, which followed it in what had become *Argosy All-Story* in 1922, and was reprinted in book form the same year, featured Carthoris' spoiled but zestful sister Tara, who gets into trouble by virtue of her spirited recklessness, thus requiring a long pursuit and rescue by the young prince Gahan.

The plots driving the two narratives are standard devices of pulp melodrama, but Burroughs great strength as a storyteller, and the principal reason for his enormous popularity, was his ability to dress such conventional and elementary plots with an exotic décor that not only invigorated the relentless action but continually threw up unusual problems that no pulp hero had ever had to face before, thus injecting their thrills with a welcome dose of the unexpected. Once Burroughs had set this example, many other writers followed where he had led, always striving to match or outshine him, but there is a special interest, even for readers who have grown accustomed to the strategy, in exploring these pioneering ventures and participating in their development.

Although they were separated by a six-year gap in their initial production, occasioned by America's involvement in World War I and its aftermath, these two stories form a natural couple, not simply because of the carefully-skewed symmetry of their employment of the children of John Carter, but also because their story-lines mark out the crucial development in Burroughs' method that allowed him to maintain the series' energy. *Thuvia* resembles the initial trilogy in being relatively modest in its innovations, although it makes the most of the strange society of the Lotharians and the redeemed phantom warrior Kar Komak, but it lays solid groundwork for the more elaborate inventiveness of *Chessmen*, which adds more detail to the culture of magnificently bizarre kaldanes, and to the peculiar rituals of the land of Manator, where jetan—Martian chess—is played with living pieces.

Although the transition between the two novels is relatively seamless, seen from the viewpoint of today, it is perhaps worth bearing in mind that while Americans were involved in fighting World War I, and for some while thereafter, "escapist" fiction came to be viewed with a certain suspicion, as if it might qualify as a kind of mental cowardice. The mistrust in question was unjustified— relaxation is even more psychologically valuable in times of stress than when everything is going well—but the prejudice left its mark nevertheless, and *Thuvia* and *Chessmen* were therefore produced in significantly different intellectual climates, requiring an extra measure of determination in the latter story. This does show up in the narrative tone of the stories, and makes an interesting comparison, no matter whether readers prefer the more relaxed tone of *Thuvia* or the edgier agitation of *Chessmen*.

Edgar Rice Burrroughs was no exception to the general rule that any series of stories will eventually suffer the effects of the law of diminishing returns, coming to seem tried and routine, but he was always enthusiastic to explore his fantastic locations as fully as they warranted. Although the later volumes of a series cannot duplicate the novelty of the initial sequence, they can take on a compensating detail and richness, which not only renews the excitement of the readers' first encounter but continues to supply them with lavish rewards. The intermediate volumes of the Martian series fulfilled that role with an admirably gaudy verve, not only answering the demand for "more of the same" whipped up by the initial trilogy but maintaining and enhancing the appetite for further endeavors. There is nothing in the least tired about *Thuvia* and *Chessmen*, which are as wide awake as any action-adventure novel ever penned, and the scenarios through which their narrative traction draws the reader are by no means routine, even by comparison with all the imitations heaped up since 1922. These are tales best enjoyed when young, or when nostalgia has set in, but for those kinds of readers they retain their full value, and are now possessed of a precious kind of timelessness.

BRIAN STABLEFORD

Brian Stableford is the author of more than seventy-five books, including fifty novels and short fiction collections and the definitive critical studies *Glorious Perversity: The Decline and Fall of Literary Decadence*, *Scientific Romance in Britain: 1890–1950*, and *The Sociology of Science Fiction*.

THUVIA,
MAID *of* MARS

CONTENTS

I

CARTHORIS AND THUVIA

pon a massive bench of polished ersite beneath the gorgeous blooms of a giant pimalia a woman sat. Her shapely, sandaled foot tapped impatiently upon the jewel-strewn walk that wound beneath the stately sorapus trees across the scarlet sward of the royal gardens of Thuvan Dihn, Jeddak of Ptarth, as a dark-haired, red-skinned warrior bent low toward her, whispering heated words close to her ear.

"Ah, Thuvia of Ptarth," he cried, "you are cold even before the fiery blasts of my consuming love! No harder than your heart, nor colder is the hard, cold ersite of this thrice happy bench which supports your divine and fadeless form! Tell me, O Thuvia of Ptarth, that I may still hope—that though you do not love me now, yet someday, someday, my princess, I—"

The girl sprang to her feet with an exclamation of surprise and displeasure. Her queenly head was poised haughtily upon her smooth red shoulders. Her dark eyes looked angrily into those of the man.

"You forget yourself, and the customs of Barsoom, Astok," she said. "I have given you no right thus to address the daughter of Thuvan Dihn, nor have you won such a right."

The man reached suddenly forth and grasped her by the arm.

"You shall be my princess!" he cried. "By the breast of Issus, thou shalt, nor shall any other come between Astok, Prince of Dusar, and his heart's desire. Tell me that there is another, and I shall cut out his foul heart and fling it to the wild calots of the dead sea-bottoms!"

At a touch of the man's hand upon her flesh the girl went pallid beneath her coppery skin, for the persons of the royal women of the courts of Mars are held but little less than sacred. The act of Astok, Prince of Dusar, was profanation. There was no terror in the eyes of Thuvia of Ptarth—only horror for the thing the man had done and for its possible consequences.

"Release me." Her voice was level—frigid.

The man muttered incoherently and drew her roughly toward him.

"Release me!" she repeated sharply, "or I call the guard, and the Prince of Dusar knows what that will mean."

Quickly he threw his right arm about her shoulders and strove to draw her face to his lips. With a little cry she struck him full in the mouth with the massive bracelets that circled her free arm.

"Calot!" she exclaimed, and then: "The guard! The guard! Hasten in protection of the Princess of Ptarth!"

In answer to her call a dozen guardsmen came racing across the scarlet sward, their gleaming long-swords naked in the sun, the metal of their accouterments clanking against that of their leathern harness, and in their throats hoarse shouts of rage at the sight which met their eyes.

But before they had passed half across the royal garden to where Astok of Dusar still held the struggling girl in his grasp, another figure sprang from a cluster of dense foliage that half hid a golden fountain close at hand. A tall, straight youth he was, with black hair and keen grey eyes; broad of shoulder and narrow of hip; a clean-limbed fighting man. His skin was but faintly tinged with the copper color that marks the red men of Mars from the other races of the dying planet—he was like them, and yet there was a subtle difference greater even than that which lay in his lighter skin and his grey eyes.

6

There was a difference, too, in his movements. He came on in great leaps that carried him so swiftly over the ground that the speed of the guardsmen was as nothing by comparison.

Astok still clutched Thuvia's wrist as the young warrior confronted him. The newcomer wasted no time and he spoke but a single word.

"Calot!" he snapped, and then his clenched fist landed beneath the other's chin, lifting him high into the air and depositing him in a crumpled heap within the center of the pimalia bush beside the ersite bench.

Her champion turned toward the girl. "Kaor, Thuvia of Ptarth!" he cried. "It seems that fate timed my visit well."

"Kaor, Carthoris of Helium!" the princess returned the young man's greeting, "and what less could one expect of the son of such a sire?"

He bowed his acknowledgment of the compliment to his father, John Carter, Warlord of Mars. And then the guardsmen, panting from their charge, came up just as the Prince of Dusar, bleeding at the mouth, and with drawn sword, crawled from the entanglement of the pimalia.

Astok would have leaped to mortal combat with the son of Dejah Thoris, but the guardsmen pressed about him, preventing, though it was clearly evident that naught would have better pleased Carthoris of Helium.

"But say the word, Thuvia of Ptarth," he begged, "and naught will give me greater pleasure than meting to this fellow the punishment he has earned."

"It cannot be, Carthoris," she replied. "Even though he has forfeited all claim upon my consideration, yet is he the guest of the jeddak, my father, and to him alone may he account for the unpardonable act he has committed."

"As you say, Thuvia," replied the Heliumite. "But afterward he shall account to Carthoris, Prince of Helium, for this affront to the daughter of my father's friend." As he spoke, though, there burned in his eyes a fire that proclaimed a nearer, dearer cause for his championship of this glorious daughter of Barsoom.

The maid's cheek darkened beneath the satin of her transparent skin, and the eyes of Astok, Prince of Dusar, darkened, too, as he read that which passed unspoken between the two in the royal gardens of the jeddak.

"And thou to me," he snapped at Carthoris, answering the young man's challenge.

The guard still surrounded Astok. It was a difficult position for the young officer who commanded it. His prisoner was the son of a mighty jeddak; he was the guest of Thuvan Dihn—until but now an honored guest upon whom every royal dignity had been showered. To arrest him forcibly could mean naught else than war, and yet he had done that which in the eyes of the Ptarth warrior merited death.

The young man hesitated. He looked toward his princess. She, too, guessed all that hung upon the action of the coming moment. For many years Dusar and Ptarth had been at peace with each other. Their great merchant ships plied back and forth between the larger cities of the two nations. Even now, far above the gold-shot scarlet dome of the jeddak's palace, she could see the huge bulk of a giant freighter taking its majestic way through the thin Barsoomian air toward the west and Dusar.

By a word she might plunge these two mighty nations into a bloody conflict that would drain them of their bravest blood and their incalculable riches, leaving them all helpless against the inroads of their envious and less powerful neighbors, and at last a prey to the savage green hordes of the dead sea-bottoms.

No sense of fear influenced her decision, for fear is seldom known to the children of Mars. It was rather a sense of the responsibility that she, the daughter of their jeddak, felt for the welfare of her father's people.

"I called you, Padwar," she said to the lieutenant of the guard, "to protect the person of your princess, and to keep the peace that must not be violated within the royal gardens of the jeddak. That is all. You will escort me to the palace, and the Prince of Helium will accompany me."

Without another glance in the direction of Astok she turned, and taking Carthoris' proffered hand, moved slowly toward the massive marble pile that housed the ruler of Ptarth and his glittering court. On either side marched a file of guardsmen. Thus Thuvia of Ptarth found a way out of a dilemma, escaping the necessity of placing her father's royal guest under forcible restraint, and at the same time separating the two princes, who otherwise would have been at each other's throat the moment she and the guard had departed.

Beside the pimalia stood Astok, his dark eyes narrowed to mere slits of hate beneath his lowering brows as he watched the retreating forms of the woman who had aroused the fiercest passions of his nature and the man whom he now believed to be the one who stood between his love and its consummation.

As they disappeared within the structure Astok shrugged his shoulders, and with a murmured oath crossed the gardens toward another wing of the building where he and his retinue were housed.

That night he took formal leave of Thuvan Dihn, and though no mention was made of the happening within the garden, it was plain to see through the cold mask of the jeddak's courtesy that only the customs of royal hospitality restrained him from voicing the contempt he felt for the Prince of Dusar.

Carthoris was not present at the leave-taking, nor was Thuvia. The ceremony was as stiff and formal as court etiquette could make it, and when the last of the Dusarians clambered over the rail of the battleship that had brought them upon this fateful visit to the court of Ptarth, and the mighty engine of destruction had risen slowly from the ways of the landing-stage, a note of relief was apparent in the voice of Thuvan Dihn as he turned to one of his officers with a word of comment upon a subject foreign to that which had been uppermost in the minds of all for hours.

But, after all, was it so foreign?

"Inform Prince Sovan," he directed, "that it is our wish that the fleet which departed for Kaol this morning be recalled to cruise to the west of Ptarth."

As the warship, bearing Astok back to the court of his father, turned toward the west, Thuvia of Ptarth, sitting upon the same bench where the Prince of Dusar had affronted her, watched the twinkling lights of the craft growing smaller in the distance. Beside her, in the brilliant light of the nearer moon, sat Carthoris. His eyes were not upon the dim bulk of the battleship, but on the profile of the girl's upturned face.

"Thuvia," he whispered.

The girl turned her eyes toward his. His hand stole out to find hers, but she drew her own gently away.

"Thuvia of Ptarth, I love you!" cried the young warrior. "Tell me that it does not offend."

She shook her head sadly. "The love of Carthoris of Helium," she said simply, "could be naught but an honor to any woman; but you must not speak, my friend, of bestowing upon me that which I may not reciprocate."

The young man got slowly to his feet. His eyes were wide in astonishment. It never had occurred to the Prince of Helium that Thuvia of Ptarth might love another.

"But at Kadabra!" he exclaimed. "And later here at your father's court, what did you do, Thuvia of Ptarth, that might have warned me that you could not return my love?"

"And what did I do, Carthoris of Helium," she returned, "that might lead you to believe that I *did* return it?"

He paused in thought, and then shook his head. "Nothing,

Thuvia, that is true; yet I could have sworn you loved me. Indeed, you well knew how near to worship has been my love for you."

"And how might I know it, Carthoris?" she asked innocently. "Did you ever tell me as much? Ever before have words of love for me fallen from your lips?"

"But you *must* have known it!" he exclaimed. "I am like my father—witless in matters of the heart, and of a poor way with women; yet the jewels that strew these royal garden paths—the trees, the flowers, the sward—all must have read the love that has filled my heart since first my eyes were made new by imaging your perfect face and form; so how could you alone have been blind to it?"

"Do the maids of Helium pay court to their men?" asked Thuvia.

"You are playing with me!" exclaimed Carthoris. "Say that you are but playing, and that after all you love me, Thuvia!"

"I cannot tell you that, Carthoris, for I am promised to another."

Her tone was level, but was there not within it the hint of an infinite depth of sadness? Who may say?

"Promised to another?" Carthoris scarcely breathed the words. His face went almost white, and then his head came up as befitted him in whose veins flowed the blood of the overlord of a world.

"Carthoris of Helium wishes you every happiness with the man of your choice," he said. "With——" and then he hesitated, waiting for her to fill in the name.

"Kulan Tith, Jeddak of Kaol," she replied. "My father's friend and Ptarth's most puissant ally."

The young man looked at her intently for a moment before he spoke again.

"You love him, Thuvia of Ptarth?" he asked.

"I am promised to him," she replied simply.

He did not press her. "He is of Barsoom's noblest blood and mightiest fighters," mused Carthoris. "My father's friend and mine—would that it might have been another!" he muttered almost savagely.

What the girl thought was hidden by the mask of her expression, which was tinged only by a little shadow of sadness that might have been for Carthoris, herself, or for them both.

Carthoris of Helium did not ask, though he noted it, for his loyalty to Kulan Tith was the loyalty of the blood of John Carter of Virginia for a friend, greater than which could be no loyalty.

He raised a jewel-encrusted bit of the girl's magnificent trappings to his lips.

"To the honor and happiness of Kulan Tith and the priceless jewel that has been bestowed upon him," he said, and though his voice was husky there was the true ring of sincerity in it. "I told you that I loved you, Thuvia, before I knew that you were promised to another. I may not tell you it again, but I am glad that you know it, for there is no dishonor in it either to you or to Kulan Tith or to myself. My love is such that it may embrace as well Kulan Tith—if you love him." There was almost a question in the statement.

"I am promised to him," she replied.

Carthoris backed slowly away. He laid one hand upon his heart, the other upon the pommel of his long-sword.

"These are yours—always," he said. A moment later he had entered the palace, and was gone from the girl's sight.

Had he returned at once he would have found her prone upon the ersite bench, her face buried in her arms. Was she weeping? There was none to see.

Carthoris of Helium had come all unannounced to the court of his father's friend that day. He had come alone in a small flier, sure of the same welcome that always awaited him at Ptarth. As there had been no formality in his coming there was no need of formality in his going.

To Thuvan Dihn he explained that he had been but testing an invention of his own with which his flier was equipped—a clever improvement of the ordinary Martian air compass, which, when set for a certain destination, will remain constantly fixed thereon, making it only necessary to keep a vessel's prow always in the direction of the compass needle to reach any given point upon Barsoom by the shortest route.

Carthoris' improvement upon this consisted of an auxiliary device which steered the craft mechanically in the direction of the compass, and upon arrival directly over the point for which the compass was set, brought the craft to a standstill and lowered it, also automatically, to the ground.

"You readily discern the advantages of this invention," he was saying to Thuvan Dihn, who had accompanied him to the landing-stage upon the palace roof to inspect the compass and bid his young friend farewell.

A dozen officers of the court with several body servants were grouped behind the jeddak and his guest, eager listeners to the conversation—so eager on the part of one of the servants that he was twice rebuked by a noble for his forwardness in pushing himself ahead of his betters to view the intricate mechanism of the wonderful "controlling destination compass," as the thing was called.

"For example," continued Carthoris, "I have an all-night trip before me, as tonight. I set the pointer here upon the right-hand dial which represents the eastern hemisphere of Barsoom, so that the point rests upon the exact latitude and longitude of Helium. Then I start the engine, roll up in my sleeping silks and furs, and with lights burning, race through the air toward Helium, confident that at the appointed hour I shall drop gently toward the landing-stage upon my own palace, whether I am still asleep or no."

"Provided," suggested Thuvan Dihn, "you do not chance to collide with some other night wanderer in the meanwhile."

Carthoris smiled. "No danger of that," he replied. "See here," and he indicated a device at the right of the destination compass. "This is my 'obstruction evader,' as I call it. This visible device is the

13

switch which throws the mechanism on or off. The instrument itself is below deck, geared both to the steering apparatus and the control levers.

"It is quite simple, being nothing more than a radium generator diffusing radioactivity in all directions to a distance of a hundred yards or so from the flier. Should this enveloping force be interrupted in any direction a delicate instrument immediately apprehends the irregularity, at the same time imparting an impulse to a magnetic device which in turn actuates the steering mechanism, diverting the bow of the flier away from the obstacle until the craft's radioactivity sphere is no longer in contact with the obstruction, then she falls once more into her normal course. Should the disturbance approach from the rear, as in case of a faster-moving craft overhauling me, the mechanism actuates the speed control as well as the steering gear, and the flier shoots ahead and either up or down, as the oncoming vessel is upon a lower or higher plane than herself.

"In aggravated cases, that is when the obstructions are many, or of such a nature as to deflect the bow more than forty-five degrees in any direction, or when the craft has reached its destination and dropped to within a hundred yards of the ground, the mechanism brings her to a full stop, at the same time sounding a loud alarm which will instantly awaken the pilot. You see I have anticipated almost every contingency."

Thuvan Dihn smiled his appreciation of the marvelous device. The forward servant pushed almost to the flier's side. His eyes were narrowed to slits.

"All but one," he said.

The nobles looked at him in astonishment, and one of them grasped the fellow none too gently by the shoulder to push him back to his proper place. Carthoris raised his hand.

"Wait," he urged. "Let us hear what the man has to say—no creation of mortal mind is perfect. Perchance he has detected a weakness that it will be well to know at once. Come, my good fellow, and what may be the one contingency I have overlooked?"

As he spoke Carthoris observed the servant closely for the first time. He saw a man of giant stature and handsome, as are all those of the race of Martian red men; but the fellow's lips were thin and cruel, and across one cheek was the faint, white line of a sword-cut from the right temple to the corner of the mouth.

"Come," urged the Prince of Helium. "Speak!"

The man hesitated. It was evident that he regretted the temerity that had made him the center of interested observation. But at last, seeing no alternative, he spoke.

"It might be tampered with," he said, "by an enemy."

Carthoris drew a small key from his leathern pocket-pouch.

"Look at this," he said, handing it to the man. "If you know aught of locks, you will know that the mechanism which this unlooses is beyond the cunning of a picker of locks. It guards the vitals of the instrument from crafty tampering. Without it an enemy must half wreck the device to reach its heart, leaving his handiwork apparent to the most casual observer."

The servant took the key, glanced at it shrewdly, and then as he made to return it to Carthoris dropped it upon the marble flagging. Turning to look for it he planted the sole of his sandal full upon the glittering object. For an instant he bore all his weight upon the foot that covered the key, then he stepped back and with an exclamation as of pleasure that he had found it, stooped, recovered it, and returned it to the Heliumite. Then he dropped back to his station behind the nobles and was forgotten.

A moment later Carthoris had made his adieux to Thuvan Dihn and his nobles, and with lights twinkling had risen into the star-shot void of the Martian night.

II

SLAVERY

s the ruler of Ptarth, followed by his courtiers, descended from the landing-stage above the palace, the servants dropped into their places in the rear of their royal or noble masters, and behind the others one lingered to the last. Then quickly stooping he snatched the sandal from his right foot, slipping it into his pocket-pouch.

When the party had come to the lower levels, and the jeddak had dispersed them by a sign, none noticed that the forward fellow who had drawn so much attention to himself before the Prince of Helium departed, was no longer among the other servants.

To whose retinue he had been attached none had thought to inquire, for the followers of a Martian noble are many, coming and going at the whim of their master, so that a new face is scarcely ever questioned, as the fact that a man has passed within the palace walls is considered proof positive that his loyalty to the jeddak is beyond question, so rigid is the examination of each who seeks service with the nobles of the court.

A good rule that, and only relaxed by courtesy in favor of the retinue of visiting royalty from a friendly foreign power.

It was late in the morning of the next day that a giant serving man in the harness of the house of a great Ptarth noble passed out into the city from the palace gates. Along one broad avenue and then another he strode briskly until he had passed beyond the district of the nobles and had come to the place of shops. Here he sought a pretentious building that rose spirelike toward the heavens, its outer walls elaborately wrought with delicate carvings and intricate mosaics.

It was the Palace of Peace in which were housed the representatives of the foreign powers, or rather in which were located their embassies; for the ministers themselves dwelt in gorgeous palaces within the district occupied by the nobles.

Here the man sought the embassy of Dusar. A clerk arose questioningly as he entered, and at his request to have a word with the minister asked his credentials. The visitor slipped a plain metal armlet from above his elbow, and pointing to an inscription upon its inner surface, whispered a word or two to the clerk.

The latter's eyes went wide, and his attitude turned at once to one of deference. He bowed the stranger to a seat, and hastened to an inner room with the armlet in his hand. A moment later he reappeared and conducted the caller into the presence of the minister.

For a long time the two were closeted together, and when at last the giant serving man emerged from the inner office his expression was cast in a smile of sinister satisfaction. From the Palace of Peace he hurried directly to the palace of the Dusarian minister.

That night two swift fliers left the same palace top. One sped its rapid course toward Helium; the other—Thuvia of Ptarth strolled in the gardens of her father's palace, as was her nightly custom before retiring. Her silks and furs were drawn about her, for the air of Mars is chill after the sun has taken his quick plunge beneath the planet's western verge.

The girl's thoughts wandered from her impending nuptials, that would make her empress of Kaol, to the person of the trim young Heliumite who had laid his heart at her feet the preceding day.

Whether it was pity or regret that saddened her expression as she gazed toward the southern heavens where she had watched the lights of his flier disappear the previous night, it would be difficult to say.

So, too, is it impossible to conjecture just what her emotions may have been as she discerned the lights of a flier speeding rapidly out of the distance from that very direction, as though impelled toward her garden by the very intensity of the princess' thoughts.

She saw it circle lower above the palace until she was positive that it but hovered in preparation for a landing.

Presently the powerful rays of its searchlight shot downward from the bow. They fell upon the landing-stage for a brief instant, revealing the figures of the Ptarthian guard, picking into brilliant points of fire the gems upon their gorgeous harnesses.

Then the blazing eye swept onward across the burnished domes and graceful minarets, down into court and park and garden to pause at last upon the ersite bench and the girl standing there beside it, her face upturned full toward the flier.

For but an instant the searchlight halted upon Thuvia of Ptarth, then it was extinguished as suddenly as it had come to life. The flier passed on above her to disappear beyond a grove of lofty skeel trees that grew within the palace grounds.

The girl stood for sometime as it had left her, except that her head was bent and her eyes downcast in thought.

Who but Carthoris could it have been? She tried to feel anger that he should have returned thus, spying upon her; but she found it difficult to be angry with the young prince of Helium.

What mad caprice could have induced him so to transgress the etiquette of nations? For lesser things great powers had gone to war.

The princess in her was shocked and angered—but what of the girl!

And the guard—what of them? Evidently they, too, had been so much surprised by the unprecedented action of the stranger that they had not even challenged; but that they had no thought to let the thing go unnoticed was quickly evidenced by the skirring of motors upon the landing-stage and the quick shooting airward of a long-lined patrol boat.

Thuvia watched it dart swiftly eastward. So, too, did other eyes watch.

Within the dense shadows of the skeel grove, in a wide avenue beneath o'erspreading foliage, a flier hung a dozen feet above the ground. From its deck keen eyes watched the far-fanning searchlight of the patrol boat. No light shone from the enshadowed craft. Upon its deck was the silence of the tomb. Its crew of a half-dozen red warriors watched the lights of the patrol boat diminishing in the distance.

"The intellects of our ancestors are with us tonight," said one in a low tone.

"No plan ever carried better," returned another. "They did precisely as the prince foretold."

He who had first spoken turned toward the man who squatted before the control board.

"Now!" he whispered. There was no other order given. Every man upon the craft had evidently been well schooled in each detail of that night's work. Silently the dark hull crept beneath the cathedral arches of the dark and silent grove.

Thuvia of Ptarth, gazing toward the east, saw the blacker blot against the blackness of the trees as the craft topped the buttressed garden wall. She saw the dim bulk incline gently downward toward the scarlet sward of the garden.

She knew that men came not thus with honorable intent. Yet she did not cry aloud to alarm the nearby guardsmen, nor did she flee to the safety of the palace.

Why?

I can see her shrug her shapely shoulders in reply as she voices the age-old, universal answer of the woman: Because!

Scarce had the flier touched the ground when four men leaped from its deck. They ran forward toward the girl.

Still she made no sign of alarm, standing as though hypnotized. Or could it have been as one who awaited a welcome visitor?

Not until they were quite close to her did she move. Then the nearer moon, rising above the surrounding foliage, touched their faces, lighting all with the brilliancy of her silver rays.

Thuvia of Ptarth saw only strangers—warriors in the harness of Dusar. Now she took fright, but too late!

Before she could voice but a single cry, rough hands seized her. A heavy silken scarf was wound about her head. She was lifted in strong arms and borne to the deck of the flier. There was the sudden whirl of propellers, the rushing of air against her body, and, from far beneath the shouting and the challenge from the guard.

Racing toward the south another flier sped toward Helium. In its cabin a tall red man bent over the soft sole of an upturned sandal. With delicate instruments he measured the faint imprint of a small object which appeared there. Upon a pad beside him was the outline of a key, and here he noted the results of his measurements.

A smile played upon his lips as he completed his task and turned to one who waited at the opposite side of the table.

"The man is a genius," he remarked.

"Only a genius could have evolved such a lock as this is designed to spring. Here, take the sketch, Larok, and give all thine own genius full and unfettered freedom in reproducing it in metal."

The warrior-artificer bowed. "Man builds naught," he said, "that man may not destroy." Then he left the cabin with the sketch.

As dawn broke upon the lofty towers which mark the twin cities of Helium—the scarlet tower of one and the yellow tower of its sister—a flier floated lazily out of the north.

Upon its bow was emblazoned the signia of a lesser noble of a far city of the empire of Helium. Its leisurely approach and the evident confidence with which it moved across the city aroused no suspicion in the minds of the sleepy guard. Their round of duty nearly done, they had little thought beyond the coming of those who were to relieve them.

Peace reigned throughout Helium. Stagnant, emasculating peace. Helium had no enemies. There was naught to fear.

Without haste the nearest air patrol swung sluggishly about and approached the stranger. At easy speaking distance the officer upon her deck hailed the incoming craft.

The cheery "Kaor!" and the plausible explanation that the owner had come from distant parts for a few days of pleasure in gay Helium sufficed. The air-patrol boat sheered off, passing again upon its way. The stranger continued toward a public landing-stage, where she dropped into the ways and came to rest.

At about the same time a warrior entered her cabin.

"It is done, Vas Kor," he said, handing a small metal key to the tall noble who had just risen from his sleeping silks and furs.

"Good!" exclaimed the latter. "You must have worked upon it all during the night, Larok."

The warrior nodded.

"Now fetch me the Heliumetic metal you wrought somedays since," commanded Vas Kor.

This done, the warrior assisted his master to replace the handsome jeweled metal of his harness with the plainer ornaments of an ordinary fighting man of Helium, and with the insignia of the same house that appeared upon the bow of the flier.

Vas Kor breakfasted on board. Then he emerged upon the aerial dock, entered an elevator, and was borne quickly to the street below, where he was soon engulfed by the early morning throng of workers hastening to their daily duties.

Among them his warrior trappings were no more remarkable than is a pair of trousers upon Broadway. All Martian men are warriors, save those physically unable to bear arms. The tradesman and his clerk clank with their martial trappings as they pursue their vocations. The schoolboy, coming into the world, as he does, almost adult from the snowy shell that has encompassed his development for five long years, knows so little of life without a sword at his hip that he would feel the same discomfiture at going abroad unarmed that an Earth boy would experience in walking the streets knickerbockerless.

Vas Kor's destination lay in Greater Helium, which lies some seventy-five miles across the level plain from Lesser Helium. He had landed at the latter city because the air patrol is less suspicious and alert than that above the larger metropolis where lies the palace of the jeddak.

As he moved with the throng in the parklike canyon of the thoroughfare the life of an awakening Martian city was in evidence about him. Houses, raised high upon their slender metal columns for the night were dropping gently toward the ground. Among the flowers upon the scarlet sward which lies about the buildings children were already playing, and comely women laughing and chatting with their neighbors as they culled gorgeous blossoms for the vases within doors.

The pleasant "kaor" of the Barsoomian greeting fell continually upon the ears of the stranger as friends and neighbors took up the duties of a new day.

The district in which he had landed was residential—a district of merchants of the more prosperous sort. Everywhere were evidences of luxury and wealth. Slaves appeared upon every housetop with gorgeous silks and costly furs, laying them in the sun for airing. Jewel-encrusted women lolled even thus early upon the carven balconies before their sleeping apartments. Later in the day they would repair to the roofs when the slaves had arranged couches and pitched silken canopies to shade them from the sun.

Strains of inspiring music broke pleasantly from open windows, for the Martians have solved the problem of attuning the nerves pleasantly to the sudden transition from sleep to waking that proves so difficult a thing for most Earth folk.

Above him raced the long, light passenger fliers, plying, each in its proper plane, between the numerous landing-stages for internal passenger traffic. Landing-stages that tower high into the heavens are for the great international passenger liners. Freighters have other landing-stages at various lower levels, to within a couple of hundred feet of the ground; nor dare any flier rise or drop from one plane to another except in certain restricted districts where horizontal traffic is forbidden.

Along the close-cropped sward which paves the avenue ground fliers were moving in continuous lines in opposite directions. For the greater part they skimmed along the surface of the sward, soaring gracefully into the air at times to pass over a slower-going driver ahead, or at intersections, where the north and south traffic has the right of way and the east and west must rise above it.

From private hangars upon many a roof top fliers were darting into the line of traffic. Gay farewells and parting admonitions mingled with the whirring of motors and the subdued noises of the city.

Yet with all the swift movement and the countless thousands rushing hither and thither, the predominant suggestion was that of luxurious ease and soft noiselessness.

Martians dislike harsh, discordant clamor. The only loud noises they can abide are the martial sounds of war, the clash of arms, the collision of two mighty dreadnaughts of the air. To them there is no sweeter music than this.

At the intersection of two broad avenues Vas Kor descended from the street level to one of the great pneumatic stations of the city. Here he paid before a little wicket the fare to his destination with a couple of the dull, oval coins of Helium.

Beyond the gatekeeper he came to a slowly moving line of what to Earthly eyes would have appeared to be conical-nosed, eight-foot projectiles for some giant gun. In slow procession the things moved in single file along a grooved track. A half dozen attendants assisted passengers to enter, or directed these carriers to their proper destination.

Vas Kor approached one that was empty. Upon its nose was a dial and a pointer. He set the pointer for a certain station in Greater Helium, raised the arched lid of the thing, stepped in and lay down upon the upholstered bottom. An attendant closed the lid, which locked with a little click, and the carrier continued its slow way.

Presently it switched itself automatically to another track, to enter, a moment later, one of the series of dark-mouthed tubes.

The instant that its entire length was within the black aperture it sprang forward with the speed of a rifle ball. There was an instant of whizzing—a soft, though sudden, stop, and slowly the carrier emerged upon another platform, another attendant raised the lid and Vas Kor stepped out at the station beneath the center of Greater Helium, seventy-five miles from the point at which he had embarked.

Here he sought the street level, stepping immediately into a waiting ground flier. He spoke no word to the slave sitting in the driver's seat. It was evident that he had been expected, and that the fellow had received his instructions before his coming.

Scarcely had Vas Kor taken his seat when the flier went quickly into the fast-moving procession, turning presently from the broad and crowded avenue into a less congested street. Presently it left the thronged district behind to enter a section of small shops, where it stopped before the entrance to one which bore the sign of a dealer in foreign silks.

Vas Kor entered the low-ceiling room. A man at the far end motioned him toward an inner apartment, giving no further sign of recognition until he had passed in after the caller and closed the door.

Then he faced his visitor, saluting deferentially.

"Most noble—" he commenced, but Vas Kor silenced him with a gesture.

"No formalities," he said. "We must forget that I am aught other than your slave. If all has been as carefully carried out as it has been planned, we have no time to waste. Instead we should be upon our way to the slave market. Are you ready?"

The merchant nodded, and, turning to a great chest, produced the unemblazoned trappings of a slave. These Vas Kor immediately donned. Then the two passed from the shop through a rear door, traversed a winding alley to an avenue beyond, where they entered a flier which awaited them.

Five minutes later the merchant was leading his slave to the public market, where a great concourse of people filled the great open space in the center of which stood the slave block.

The crowds were enormous today, for Carthoris, Prince of Helium, was to be the principal bidder.

One by one the masters mounted the rostrum beside the slave block upon which stood their chattels. Briefly and clearly each recounted the virtues of his particular offering.

When all were done, the major-domo of the Prince of Helium recalled to the block such as had favorably impressed him. For such he had made a fair offer.

There was little haggling as to price, and none at all when Vas Kor was placed upon the block. His merchant-master accepted the first offer that was made for him, and thus a Dusarian noble entered the household of Carthoris.

III

TREACHERY

he day following the coming of Vas Kor to the palace of the Prince of Helium great excitement reigned throughout the twin cities, reaching its climax in the palace of Carthoris. Word had come of the abduction of Thuvia of Ptarth from her father's court, and with it the veiled hint that the Prince of Helium might be suspected of considerable knowledge of the act and the whereabouts of the princess.

In the council chamber of John Carter, Warlord of Mars, was Tardos Mors, Jeddak of Helium; Mors Kajak, his son, Jed of Lesser Helium; Carthoris, and a score of the great nobles of the empire.

"There must be no war between Ptarth and Helium, my son," said John Carter. "That you are innocent of the charge that has been placed against you by insinuation, we well know; but Thuvan Dihn must know it well, too.

"There is but one who may convince him, and that one be you. You must hasten at once to the court of Ptarth, and by your presence there as well as by your words assure him that his suspicions are groundless. Bear with you the authority of the Warlord of Barsoom, and of the Jeddak of Helium to offer every resource of the allied powers to assist Thuvan Dihn to recover his daughter and punish her abductors, whomsoever they may be.

"Go! I know that I do not need to urge upon you the necessity for haste."

Carthoris left the council chamber, and hastened to his palace.

Here slaves were busy in a moment setting things to rights for the departure of their master. Several worked about the swift flier that would bear the Prince of Helium rapidly toward Ptarth.

At last all was done. But two armed slaves remained on guard. The setting sun hung low above the horizon. In a moment darkness would envelop all.

One of the guardsmen, a giant of a fellow across whose right cheek there ran a thin scar from temple to mouth, approached his companion. His gaze was directed beyond and above his comrade. When he had come quite close he spoke.

"What strange craft is that?" he asked.

The other turned about quickly to gaze heavenward. Scarce was his back turned toward the giant than the short-sword of the latter was plunged beneath his left shoulder blade, straight through his heart.

Voiceless, the soldier sank in his tracks—stone dead. Quickly the murderer dragged the corpse into the black shadows within the hangar. Then he returned to the flier.

Drawing a cunningly wrought key from his pocket-pouch, he removed the cover of the right-hand dial of the controlling destination compass. For a moment he studied the construction of the mechanism beneath. Then he returned the dial to its place, set the pointer, and removed it again to note the resultant change in the position of the parts affected by the act.

A smile crossed his lips. With a pair of cutters he snipped off the projection which extended through the dial from the external pointer—now the latter might be moved to any point upon the dial without affecting the mechanism below. In other words, the eastern hemisphere dial was useless.

Now he turned his attention to the western dial. This he set upon a certain point. Afterward he removed the cover of this dial also, and with keen tool cut the steel finger from the under side of the pointer.

As quickly as possible he replaced the second dial cover, and resumed his place on guard. To all intents and purposes the compass was as efficient as before; but, as a matter of fact, the moving of the pointers upon the dials resulted now in no corresponding shift of the mechanism beneath—and the device was set, immovably, upon a destination of the slave's own choosing.

Presently came Carthoris, accompanied by but a handful of his gentlemen. He cast but a casual glance upon the single slave who stood guard. The fellow's thin, cruel lips, and the sword-cut that ran from temple to mouth aroused the suggestion of an unpleasant memory within him. He wondered where Saran Tal had found the man—then the matter faded from his thoughts, and in another moment the Prince of Helium was laughing and chatting with his companions, though below the surface his heart was cold with dread, for what contingencies confronted Thuvia of Ptarth he could not even guess.

First to his mind, naturally, had sprung the thought that Astok of Dusar had stolen the fair Ptarthian; but almost simultaneously with the report of the abduction had come news of the great fetes at Dusar in honor of the return of the jeddak's son to the court of his father.

It could not have been he, thought Carthoris, for on the very night that Thuvia was taken Astok had been in Dusar, and yet—He entered the flier, exchanging casual remarks with his companions as he unlocked the mechanism of the compass and set the pointer upon the capital city of Ptarth.

With a word of farewell he touched the button which controlled the repulsive rays, and as the flier rose lightly into the air, the engine purred in answer to the touch of his finger upon a second button, the propellers whirred as his hand drew back the speed lever, and Carthoris, Prince of Helium, was off into the gorgeous Martian night beneath the hurtling moons and the million stars.

Scarce had the flier found its speed ere the man, wrapping his sleeping silks and furs about him, stretched at full length upon the narrow deck to sleep.

But sleep did not come at once at his bidding.

Instead, his thoughts ran riot in his brain, driving sleep away. He recalled the words of Thuvia of Ptarth, words that had half assured him that she loved him; for when he had asked her if she loved Kulan Tith, she had answered only that she was promised to him.

Now he saw that her reply was open to more than a single construction. It might, of course, mean that she did not love Kulan Tith; and so, by inference, be taken to mean that she loved another.

But what assurance was there that the other was Carthoris of Helium?

The more he thought upon it the more positive he became that not only was there no assurance in her words that she loved him, but none either in any act of hers. No, the fact was, she did not love him. She loved another. She had not been abducted—she had fled willingly with her lover.

With such pleasant thoughts filling him alternately with despair and rage, Carthoris at last dropped into the sleep of utter mental exhaustion.

The breaking of the sudden dawn found him still asleep. His flier was rushing swiftly above a barren, ochre plain—the world-old bottom of a long-dead Martian sea.

In the distance rose low hills. Toward these the craft was headed. As it approached them, a great promontory might have been seen from its deck, stretching out into what had once been a mighty ocean, and circling back once more to enclose the forgotten harbor of a forgotten city, which still stretched back from its deserted quays, an imposing pile of wondrous architecture of a long-dead past.

The countless dismal windows, vacant and forlorn, stared, sightless, from their marble walls; the whole sad city taking on the semblance of scattered mounds of dead men's sun-bleached skulls—the casements having the appearance of eyeless sockets, the portals, grinning jaws.

Closer came the flier, but now its speed was diminishing—yet this was not Ptarth.

Above the central plaza it stopped, slowly settling Marsward. Within a hundred yards of the ground it came to rest, floating gently in the light air, and at the same instant an alarm sounded at the sleeper's ear.

Carthoris sprang to his feet. Below him he looked to see the teeming metropolis of Ptarth. Beside him, already, there should have been an air patrol.

He gazed about in bewildered astonishment. There indeed was a great city, but it was not Ptarth. No multitudes surged through its broad avenues. No signs of life broke the dead monotony of its deserted roof tops. No gorgeous silks, no priceless furs lent life and color to the cold marble and the gleaming ersite.

No patrol boat lay ready with its familiar challenge. Silent and empty lay the great city—empty and silent the surrounding air.

What had happened?

Carthoris examined the dial of his compass. The pointer was set upon Ptarth. Could the creature of his genius have thus betrayed him? He would not believe it.

Quickly he unlocked the cover, turning it back upon its hinge. A single glance showed him the truth, or at least a part of it—the steel projection that communicated the movement of the pointer upon the dial to the heart of the mechanism beneath had been severed.

Who could have done the thing—and why?

Carthoris could not hazard even a faint guess. But the thing now was to learn in what portion of the world he was, and then take up his interrupted journey once more.

If it had been the purpose of some enemy to delay him, he had succeeded well, thought Carthoris, as he unlocked the cover of the second dial the first having shown that its pointer had not been set at all.

Beneath the second dial he found the steel pin severed as in the other, but the controlling mechanism had first been set for a point upon the western hemisphere.

He had just time to judge his location roughly at some place southwest of Helium, and at a considerable distance from the twin cities, when he was startled by a woman's scream beneath him.

Leaning over the side of the flier, he saw what appeared to be a red woman being dragged across the plaza by a huge green warrior—one of those fierce, cruel denizens of the dead sea-bottoms and deserted cities of dying Mars.

Carthoris waited to see no more. Reaching for the control board, he sent his craft racing plummetlike toward the ground.

The green man was hurrying his captive toward a huge thoat that browsed upon the ochre vegetation of the once scarlet-gorgeous plaza. At the same instant a dozen red warriors leaped from the entrance of a nearby ersite palace, pursuing the abductor with naked swords and shouts of rageful warning.

Once the woman turned her face upward toward the falling flier, and in the single swift glance Carthoris saw that it was Thuvia of Ptarth!

IV

A GREEN MAN'S CAPTIVE

hen the light of day broke upon the little craft to whose deck the Princess of Ptarth had been snatched from her father's garden, Thuvia saw that the night had wrought a change in her abductors.

No longer did their trappings gleam with the metal of Dusar, but instead there was emblazoned there the insignia of the Prince of Helium.

The girl felt renewed hope, for she could not believe that in the heart of Carthoris could lie intent to harm her.

She spoke to the warrior squatting before the control board.

"Last night you wore the trappings of a Dusarian," she said. "Now your metal is that of Helium. What means it?"

The man looked at her with a grin.

"The Prince of Helium is no fool," he said.

Just then an officer emerged from the tiny cabin. He reprimanded the warrior for conversing with the prisoner, nor would he himself reply to any of her inquiries.

No harm was offered her during the journey, and so they came at last to their destination with the girl no wiser as to her abductors or their purpose than at first.

Here the flier settled slowly into the plaza of one of those mute monuments of Mars' dead and forgotten past—the deserted cities that fringe the sad ochre sea-bottoms where once rolled the mighty floods upon whose bosoms moved the maritime commerce of the peoples that are gone forever.

Thuvia of Ptarth was no stranger to such places. During her wanderings in search of the River Iss, that time she had set out upon what, for countless ages, had been the last, long pilgrimage of Martians, toward the Valley Dor, where lies the Lost Sea of Korus, she had encountered several of these sad reminders of the greatness and the glory of ancient Barsoom.

And again, during her flight from the temples of the Holy Therns with Tars Tarkas, Jeddak of Thark, she had seen them, with their weird and ghostly inmates, the great white apes of Barsoom.

She knew, too, that many of them were used now by the nomadic tribes of green men, but that among them all was no city that the red men did not shun, for without exception they stood amidst vast, waterless tracts, unsuited for the continued sustenance of the dominant race of Martians.

Why, then, should they be bringing her to such a place? There was but a single answer. Such was the nature of their work that they must needs seek the seclusion that a dead city afforded. The girl trembled at thought of her plight.

For two days her captors kept her within a huge palace that even in decay reflected the splendor of the age which its youth had known.

Just before dawn on the third day she had been aroused by the voices of two of her abductors.

"He should be here by dawn," one was saying. "Have her in readiness upon the plaza—else he will never land. The moment he finds that he is in a strange country he will turn about—methinks the prince's plan is weak in this one spot."

"There was no other way," replied the other. "It is wondrous work to get them both here at all, and even if we do not succeed in luring him to the ground, we shall have accomplished much."

Just then the speaker caught the eyes of Thuvia upon him,

revealed by the quick-moving patch of light cast by Thuria in her mad race through the heavens.

With a quick sign to the other, he ceased speaking, and advancing toward the girl, motioned her to rise. Then he led her out into the night toward the center of the great plaza.

"Stand here," he commanded, "until we come for you. We shall be watching, and should you attempt to escape it will go ill with you—much worse than death. Such are the prince's orders."

Then he turned and retraced his steps toward the palace, leaving her alone in the midst of the unseen terrors of the haunted city, for in truth these places are haunted in the belief of many Martians who still cling to an ancient superstition which teaches that the spirits of Holy Therns who die before their allotted one thousand years, pass, on occasions, into the bodies of the great white apes.

To Thuvia, however, the real danger of attack by one of these ferocious, manlike beasts was quite sufficient. She no longer believed in the weird soul transmigration that the therns had taught her before she was rescued from their clutches by John Carter; but she well knew the horrid fate that awaited her should one of the terrible beasts chance to spy her during its nocturnal prowlings.

What was that?

Surely she could not be mistaken. Something had moved, stealthily, in the shadow of one of the great monoliths that line the avenue where it entered the plaza opposite her!

Thar Ban, jed among the hordes of Torquas, rode swiftly across the ochre vegetation of the dead sea-bottom toward the ruins of ancient Aaanthor.

He had ridden far that night, and fast, for he had but come from the despoiling of the incubator of a neighboring green horde with which the hordes of Torquas were perpetually warring.

His giant thoat was far from jaded, yet it would be well, thought Thar Ban, to permit him to graze upon the ochre moss which grows to greater height within the protected courtyards of deserted cities, where the soil is richer than on the sea-bottoms, and the plants partly shaded from the sun during the cloudless Martian day.

Within the tiny stems of this dry-seeming plant is sufficient moisture for the needs of the huge bodies of the mighty thoats, which can exist for months without water, and for days without even the slight moisture which the ochre moss contains.

As Thar Ban rode noiselessly up the broad avenue which leads from the quays of Aaanthor to the great central plaza, he and his mount might have been mistaken for specters from a world of dreams, so grotesque the man and beast, so soundless the great thoat's padded, nailless feet upon the moss-grown flagging of the ancient pavement.

The man was a splendid specimen of his race. Fully fifteen feet towered his great height from sole to pate. The moonlight glistened against his glossy green hide, sparkling the jewels of his heavy harness and the ornaments that weighted his four muscular arms, while the upcurving tusks that protruded from his lower jaw gleamed white and terrible.

At the side of his thoat were slung his long radium rifle and his great, forty-foot, metal-shod spear, while from his own harness depended his long-sword and his short-sword, as well as his lesser weapons.

His protruding eyes and antennaelike ears were turning constantly hither and thither, for Thar Ban was yet in the country of the enemy, and, too, there was always the menace of the great white apes, which, John Carter was wont to say, are the only creatures that can arouse in the breasts of these fierce denizens of the dead sea-bottoms even the remotest semblance of fear.

As the rider neared the plaza, he reined suddenly in. His slender, tubular ears pointed rigidly forward. An unwonted sound had reached them. Voices! And where there were voices, outside of

Torquas, there, too, were enemies. All the world of wide Barsoom contained naught but enemies for the fierce Torquasians.

Thar Ban dismounted. Keeping in the shadows of the great monoliths that line the Avenue of Quays of sleeping Aaanthor, he approached the plaza. Directly behind him, as a hound at heel, came the slate-grey thoat, his white belly shadowed by his barrel, his vivid yellow feet merging into the yellow of the moss beneath them.

In the center of the plaza Thar Ban saw the figure of a red woman. A red warrior was conversing with her. Now the man turned and retraced his steps toward the palace at the opposite side of the plaza.

Thar Ban watched until he had disappeared within the yawning portal. Here was a captive worth having! Seldom did a female of their hereditary enemies fall to the lot of a green man. Thar Ban licked his thin lips.

Thuvia of Ptarth watched the shadow behind the monolith at the opening to the avenue opposite her. She hoped that it might be but the figment of an overwrought imagination.

But no! Now, clearly and distinctly, she saw it move. It came from behind the screening shelter of the ersite shaft.

The sudden light of the rising sun fell upon it. The girl trembled. The *thing* was a huge green warrior!

Swiftly it sprang toward her. She screamed and tried to flee; but she had scarce turned toward the palace when a giant hand fell upon her arm, she was whirled about, and half dragged, half carried toward a huge thoat that was slowly grazing out of the avenue's mouth on to the ochre moss of the plaza.

At the same instant she turned her face upward toward the whirring sound of something above her, and there she saw a swift flier dropping toward her, the head and shoulders of a man leaning far over the side; but the man's features were deeply shadowed, so that she did not recognize them.

Now from behind her came the shouts of her red abductors. They were racing madly after him who dared to steal what they already had stolen.

As Thar Ban reached the side of his mount he snatched his long radium rifle from its boot, and, wheeling, poured three shots into the oncoming red men.

Such is the uncanny marksmanship of these Martian savages that three red warriors dropped in their tracks as three projectiles exploded in their vitals.

The others halted, nor did they dare return the fire for fear of wounding the girl.

Then Thar Ban vaulted to the back of his thoat, Thuvia of Ptarth still in his arms, and with a savage cry of triumph disappeared down the black canyon of the Avenue of Quays between the sullen palaces of forgotten Aaanthor.

Carthoris' flier had not touched the ground before he had sprung from its deck to race after the swift thoat, whose eight long legs were sending it down the avenue at the rate of an express train; but the men of Dusar who still remained alive had no mind to permit so valuable a capture to escape them.

They had lost the girl. That would be a difficult thing to explain to Astok; but some leniency might be expected could they carry the Prince of Helium to their master instead.

So the three who remained set upon Carthoris with their long-swords, crying to him to surrender; but they might as successfully have cried aloud to Thuria to cease her mad hurtling through the Barsoomian sky, for Carthoris of Helium was a true son of the Warlord of Mars and his incomparable Dejah Thoris.

Carthoris' long-sword had been already in his hand as he leaped from the deck of the flier, so the instant that he realized the menace of the three red warriors, he wheeled to face them, meeting their onslaught as only John Carter himself might have done.

So swift his sword, so mighty and agile his half-earthly muscles, that one of his opponents was down, crimsoning the ochre moss with his life-blood, when he had scarce made a single pass at Carthoris.

Now the two remaining Dusarians rushed simultaneously upon the Heliumite. Three long-swords clashed and sparkled in the moonlight, until the great white apes, roused from their slumbers, crept to the lowering windows of the dead city to view the bloody scene beneath them.

Thrice was Carthoris touched, so that the red blood ran down his face, blinding him and dyeing his broad chest. With his free hand he wiped the gore from his eyes, and with the fighting smile of his father touching his lips, leaped upon his antagonists with renewed fury.

A single cut of his heavy sword severed the head of one of them, and then the other, backing away clear of that point of death, turned and fled toward the palace at his back.

Carthoris made no step to pursue. He had other concern than the meting of even well-deserved punishment to strange men who masqueraded in the metal of his own house, for he had seen that these men were tricked out in the insignia that marked his personal followers.

Turning quickly toward his flier, he was soon rising from the plaza in pursuit of Thar Ban.

The red warrior whom he had put to flight turned in the entrance to the palace, and, seeing Carthoris' intent, snatched a rifle from those that he and his fellows had left leaning against the wall as they had rushed out with drawn swords to prevent the theft of their prisoner.

Few red men are good shots, for the sword is their chosen weapon; so now as the Dusarian drew bead upon the rising flier, and touched the button upon his rifle's stock, it was more to chance than proficiency that he owed the partial success of his aim.

The projectile grazed the flier's side, the opaque coating breaking sufficiently to permit daylight to strike in upon the powder phial within the bullet's nose. There was a sharp explosion. Carthoris felt his craft reel drunkenly beneath him, and the engine stopped.

The momentum the air boat had gained carried her on over the city toward the sea-bottom beyond.

The red warrior in the plaza fired several more shots, none of which scored. Then a lofty minaret shut the drifting quarry from his view.

In the distance before him Carthoris could see the green warrior bearing Thuvia of Ptarth away upon his mighty thoat. The direction of his flight was toward the northwest of Aaanthor, where lay a mountainous country little known to red men.

The Heliumite now gave his attention to his injured craft. A close examination revealed the face that one of the buoyancy tanks had been punctured, but the engine itself was uninjured.

A splinter from the projectile had damaged one of the control levers beyond the possibility of repair outside a machine shop; but after considerable tinkering, Carthoris was able to propel his wounded flier at low speed, a rate which could not approach the rapid gait of the thoat, whose eight long, powerful legs carried it over the ochre vegetation of the dead sea-bottom at terrific speed.

The Prince of Helium chafed and fretted at the slowness of his pursuit, yet he was thankful that the damage was no worse, for now he could at least move more rapidly than on foot.

But even this meager satisfaction was soon to be denied him, for presently the flier commenced to sag toward the port and by the bow. The damage to the buoyancy tanks had evidently been more grievous than he had at first believed.

All the balance of that long day Carthoris crawled erratically through the still air, the bow of the flier sinking lower and lower, and the list to port becoming more and more alarming, until at last, near dark, he was floating almost bowdown, his harness buckled to a heavy deck ring to keep him from being precipitated to the ground below.

His forward movement was now confined to a slow drifting with the gentle breeze that blew out of the southeast, and when this died down with the setting of the sun, he let the flier sink gently to the mossy carpet beneath.

Far before him loomed the mountains toward which the green man had been fleeing when last he had seen him, and with dogged resolution the son of John Carter, endowed with the indomitable will of his mighty sire, took up the pursuit on foot.

All that night he forged ahead until, with the dawning of a new day, he entered the low foothills that guard the approach to the fastness of the mountains of Torquas.

Rugged, granitic walls towered before him. Nowhere could he discern an opening through the formidable barrier; yet somewhere into this inhospitable world of stone the green warrior had borne the woman of the red man's heart's desire.

Across the yielding moss of the sea-bottom there had been no spoor to follow, for the soft pads of the thoat but pressed down in his swift passage the resilient vegetation which sprang up again behind his fleeting feet, leaving no sign.

But here in the hills, where loose rock occasionally strewed the way; where black loam and wild flowers partially replaced the somber monotony of the waste places of the lowlands, Carthoris hoped to find some sign that would lead him in the right direction.

Yet, search as he would, the baffling mystery of the trail seemed likely to remain forever unsolved.

It was drawing toward the day's close once more when the keen eyes of the Heliumite discerned the tawny yellow of a sleek hide moving among the boulders several hundred yards to his left.

Crouching quickly behind a large rock, Carthoris watched

the thing before him. It was a huge banth, one of those savage Barsoomian lions that roam the desolate hills of the dying planet.

The creature's nose was close to the ground. It was evident that he was following the spoor of meat by scent.

As Carthoris watched him, a great hope leaped into the man's heart. Here, possibly, might lie the solution to the mystery he had been endeavoring to solve. This hungry carnivore, keen always for the flesh of man, might even now be trailing the two whom Carthoris sought.

Cautiously the youth crept out upon the trail of the man-eater. Along the foot of the perpendicular cliff the creature moved, sniffing at the invisible spoor, and now and then emitting the low moan of the hunting banth.

Carthoris had followed the creature for but a few minutes when it disappeared as suddenly and mysteriously as though dissolved into thin air.

The man leaped to his feet. Not again was he to be cheated as the man had cheated him. He sprang forward at a reckless pace to the spot at which he last had seen the great, skulking brute.

Before him loomed the sheer cliff, its face unbroken by any aperture into which the huge banth might have wormed its great carcass. Beside him was a small, flat boulder, not larger than the deck of a ten-man flier, nor standing to a greater height than twice his own stature.

Perhaps the banth was in hiding behind this? The brute might have discovered the man upon his trail, and even now be lying in wait for his easy prey.

Cautiously, with drawn long-sword, Carthoris crept around the corner of the rock. There was no banth there, but something which surprised him infinitely more than would the presence of twenty banths.

Before him yawned the mouth of a dark cave leading downward into the ground. Through this the banth must have disappeared. Was it his lair? Within its dark and forbidding interior might there not lurk not one but many of the fearsome creatures?

Carthoris did not know, nor, with the thought that had been spurring him onward upon the trail of the creature uppermost in his mind, did he much care; for into this gloomy cavern he was sure the banth had trailed the green man and his captive, and into it he, too, would follow, content to give his life in the service of the woman he loved.

Not an instant did he hesitate, nor yet did he advance rashly; but with ready sword and cautious steps, for the way was dark, he stole on. As he advanced, the obscurity became impenetrable blackness.

V

THE FAIR RACE

ownward along a smooth, broad floor led the strange tunnel, for such Carthoris was now convinced was the nature of the shaft he at first had thought but a cave.

Before him he could hear the occasional low moans of the banth, and presently from behind came a similar uncanny note. Another banth had entered the passageway on *his* trail!

His position was anything but pleasant. His eyes could not penetrate the darkness even to the distinguishing of his hand before his face, while the banths, he knew, could see quite well, though absence of light were utter.

No other sounds came to his ears than the dismal, bloodthirsty moanings of the beast ahead and the beast behind.

The tunnel had led straight, from where he had entered it beneath the side of the rock furthest from the unscalable cliffs, toward the mighty barrier that had baffled him so long.

Now it was running almost level, and presently he noted a gradual ascent.

The beast behind him was gaining upon him, crowding him perilously close upon the heels of the beast in front. Presently he should have to do battle with one, or both. More firmly he gripped his weapon.

Now he could hear the breathing of the banth at his heels. Not for much longer could he delay the encounter.

Long since he had become assured that the tunnel led beneath the cliffs to the opposite side of the barrier, and he had hoped that he might reach the moonlit open before being compelled to grapple with either of the monsters.

The sun had been setting as he entered the tunnel, and the way had been sufficiently long to assure him that darkness now reigned upon the world without. He glanced behind him. Blazing out of the darkness, seemingly not ten paces behind, glared two flaming points of fire. As the savage eyes met his, the beast emitted a frightful roar and then he charged.

To face that savage mountain of onrushing ferocity, to stand unshaken before the hideous fangs that he knew were bared in slavering blood-thirstiness, though he could not see them, required nerves of steel; but of such were the nerves of Carthoris of Helium.

He had the brute's eyes to guide his point, and, as true as the sword hand of his mighty sire, his guided the keen point to one of those blazing orbs, even as he leaped lightly to one side.

With a hideous scream of pain and rage, the wounded banth hurtled, clawing, past him. Then it turned to charge once more; but this time Carthoris saw but a single gleaming point of fiery hate directed upon him.

Again the needle point met its flashing target. Again the horrid cry of the stricken beast reverberated through the rocky tunnel, shocking in its torture-laden shrillness, deafening in its terrific volume.

But now, as it turned to charge again, the man had no guide whereby to direct his point. He heard the scraping of the padded feet upon the rocky floor. He knew the thing was charging down upon him once again, but he could see nothing.

Yet, if he could not see his antagonist, neither could his antagonist now see him.

Leaping, as he thought, to the exact center of the tunnel, he held his sword point ready on a line with the beast's chest. It was all that he could do, hoping that chance might send the point into the savage heart as he went down beneath the great body.

So quickly was the thing over that Carthoris could scarce believe his senses as the mighty body rushed madly past him. Either he had not placed himself in the center of the tunnel, or else the blinded banth had erred in its calculations.

However, the huge body missed him by a foot, and the creature continued on down the tunnel as though in pursuit of the prey that had eluded him.

Carthoris, too, followed the same direction, nor was it long before his heart was gladdened by the sight of the moonlit exit from the long, dark passage.

Before him lay a deep hollow, entirely surrounded by gigantic cliffs. The surface of the valley was dotted with enormous trees, a strange sight so far from a Martian waterway. The ground itself was clothed in brilliant scarlet sward, picked out with innumerable patches of gorgeous wild flowers.

Beneath the glorious effulgence of the two moons the scene was one of indescribable loveliness, tinged with the weirdness of strange enchantment.

For only an instant, however, did his gaze rest upon the natural beauties outspread before him. Almost immediately they were riveted upon the figure of a great banth standing across the carcass of a new-killed thoat.

The huge beast, his tawny mane bristling around his hideous head, kept his eyes fixed upon another banth that charged erratically hither and thither, with shrill screams of pain, and horrid roars of hate and rage.

Carthoris quickly guessed that the second brute was the one he had blinded during the fight in the tunnel, but it was the dead thoat that centered his interest more than either of the savage carnivores.

The harness was still upon the body of the huge Martian mount, and Carthoris could not doubt but that this was the very animal upon which the green warrior had borne away Thuvia of Ptarth.

But where were the rider and his prisoner? The Prince of Helium shuddered as he thought upon the probability of the fate that had overtaken them.

Human flesh is the food most craved by the fierce Barsoomian lion, whose great carcass and giant thews require enormous quantities of meat to sustain them.

Two human bodies would have but whetted the creature's appetite, and that he had killed and eaten the green man and the red girl seemed only too likely to Carthoris. He had left the carcass of the mighty thoat to be devoured after having consumed the more toothsome portion of his banquet.

Now the sightless banth, in its savage, aimless charging and counter-charging, had passed beyond the kill of its fellow, and there the light breeze that was blowing wafted the scent of new blood to its nostrils.

No longer were its movements erratic. With outstretched tail and foaming jaws it charged straight as an arrow, for the body of the thoat and the mighty creature of destruction that stood with forepaws upon the slate-grey side, waiting to defend its meat.

When the charging banth was twenty paces from the dead thoat the killer gave vent to its hideous challenge, and with a mighty spring leaped forward to meet it.

The battle that ensued awed even the warlike Barsoomian. The mad rending, the hideous and deafening roaring, the implacable savagery of the blood-stained beasts held him in the paralysis of fascination, and when it was over and the two creatures, their heads and shoulders torn to ribbons, lay with their dead jaws still buried in each other's bodies, Carthoris tore himself from the spell only by an effort of the will.

Hurrying to the side of the dead thoat, he searched for traces of the girl he feared had shared the thoat's fate, but nowhere could he discover anything to confirm his fears.

With slightly lightened heart he started out to explore the valley, but scarce a dozen steps had he taken when the glistening of a jeweled bauble lying on the sward caught his eye.

As he picked it up his first glance showed him that it was a woman's hair ornament, and emblazoned upon it was the insignia of the royal house of Ptarth.

But, sinister discovery, blood, still wet, splotched the magnificent jewels of the setting.

Carthoris half choked as the dire possibilities which the thing suggested presented themselves to his imagination. Yet he could not, would not believe it.

It was impossible that that radiant creature could have met so hideous an end. It was incredible that the glorious Thuvia should ever cease to be.

Upon his already jewel-encrusted harness, to the strap that crossed his great chest beneath which beat his loyal heart, Carthoris, Prince of Helium, fastened the gleaming thing that Thuvia of Ptarth had worn, and wearing, had made holy to the Heliumite.

Then he proceeded upon his way into the heart of the unknown valley.

For the most part the giant trees shut off his view to any but the most limited distances. Occasionally he caught glimpses of the towering hills that bounded the valley upon every side, and though they stood out clear beneath the light of the two moons, he knew that they were far off, and that the extent of the valley was immense.

For half the night he continued his search, until presently he was brought to a sudden halt by the distant sound of squealing thoats.

Guided by the noise of these habitually angry beasts, he stole forward through the trees until at last he came upon a level, treeless plain, in the center of which a mighty city reared its burnished domes and vividly colored towers.

About the walled city the red man saw a huge encampment of the green warriors of the dead sea-bottoms, and as he let his eyes rove carefully over the city he realized that here was no deserted metropolis of a dead past.

But what city could it be? His studies had taught him that in this little-explored portion of Barsoom the fierce tribe of Torquasian green men ruled supreme, and that as yet no red man had succeeded in piercing to the heart of their domain to return again to the world of civilization.

The men of Torquas had perfected huge guns with which their uncanny marksmanship had permitted them to repulse the few determined efforts that nearby red nations had made to explore their country by means of battle fleets of airships.

That he was within the boundary of Torquas, Carthoris was sure, but that there existed there such a wondrous city he never had dreamed, nor had the chronicles of the past even hinted at such a possibility, for the Torquasians were known to live, as did the other green men of Mars, within the deserted cities that dotted the dying planet, nor ever had any green horde built so much as a single edifice, other than the low-walled incubators where their young are hatched by the sun's heat.

The encircling camp of green warriors lay about five hundred yards from the city's walls. Between it and the city was no semblance of breastwork or other protection against rifle or cannon fire; yet distinctly now in the light of the rising sun Carthoris could see many figures moving along the summit of the high wall, and upon the roof tops beyond.

That they were beings like himself he was sure, though they were at too great distance from him for him to be positive that they were red men.

Almost immediately after sunrise the green warriors commenced firing upon the little figures upon the wall. To Carthoris' surprise the fire was not returned, but presently the last of the city's inhabitants had sought shelter from the weird marksmanship of the green men, and no further sign of life was visible beyond the wall.

Then Carthoris, keeping within the shelter of the trees that fringed the plain, began circling the rear of the besiegers' line, hoping against hope that somewhere he would obtain sight of Thuvia of Ptarth, for even now he could not believe that she was dead.

That he was not discovered was a miracle, for mounted warriors were constantly riding back and forth from the camp into the forest; but the long day wore on and still he continued his seemingly fruitless quest, until, near sunset, he came opposite a mighty gate in the city's western wall.

Here seemed to be the principal force of the attacking horde. Here a great platform had been erected whereon Carthoris could see squatting a huge green warrior, surrounded by others of his kind.

This, then, must be the notorious Hortan Gur, Jeddak of Torquas, the fierce old ogre of the southwestern hemisphere, as only for a jeddak are platforms raised in temporary camps or upon the march by the green hordes of Barsoom.

As the Heliumite watched he saw another green warrior push his way forward toward the rostrum. Beside him he dragged a captive, and as the surrounding warriors parted to let the two pass, Carthoris caught a fleeting glimpse of the prisoner.

His heart leaped in rejoicing. Thuvia of Ptarth still lived!

It was with difficulty that Carthoris restrained the impulse to rush forward to the side of the Ptarthian princess; but in the end his better judgment prevailed, for in the face of such odds he knew that he should have been but throwing away, uselessly, any future opportunity he might have to succor her.

He saw her dragged to the foot of the rostrum. He saw Hortan

Gur address her. He could not hear the creature's words, nor Thuvia's reply; but it must have angered the green monster, for Carthoris saw him leap toward the prisoner, striking her a cruel blow across the face with his metal-banded arm.

Then the son of John Carter, Jeddak of Jeddaks, Warlord of Barsoom, went mad. The old, blood-red haze through which his sire had glared at countless foes, floated before his eyes.

His half-Earthly muscles, responding quickly to his will, sent him in enormous leaps and bounds toward the green monster that had struck the woman he loved.

The Torquasians were not looking in the direction of the forest. All eyes had been upon the figures of the girl and their jeddak, and loud was the hideous laughter that rang out in appreciation of the wit of the green emperor's reply to his prisoner's appeal for liberty.

Carthoris had covered about half the distance between the forest and the green warriors, when a new factor succeeded in still further directing the attention of the latter from him.

Upon a high tower within the beleaguered city a man appeared. From his upturned mouth there issued a series of frightful shrieks; uncanny shrieks that swept, shrill and terrifying, across the city's walls, over the heads of the besiegers, and out across the forest to the uttermost confines of the valley.

Once, twice, thrice the fearsome sound smote upon the ears of the listening green men and then far, far off across the broad woods came sharp and clear from the distance an answering shriek.

It was but the first. From every point rose similar savage cries, until the world seemed to tremble to their reverberations.

The green warriors looked nervously this way and that. They knew not fear, as Earth men may know it; but in the face of the unusual their wonted self-assurance deserted them.

And then the great gate in the city wall opposite the platform of Hortan Gur swung suddenly wide. From it issued as strange a sight as Carthoris ever had witnessed, though at the moment he had time to cast but a single fleeting glance at the tall bowmen emerging through the portal behind their long, oval shields; to note their flowing auburn hair; and to realize that the growling things at their side were fierce Barsoomian lions.

Then he was in the midst of the astonished Torquasians. With drawn long-sword he was among them, and to Thuvia of Ptarth, whose startled eyes were the first to fall upon him, it seemed that she was looking upon John Carter himself, so strangely similar to the fighting of the father was that of the son.

Even to the famous fighting smile of the Virginian was the resemblance true. And the sword arm! Ah, the subtleness of it, and the speed!

All about was turmoil and confusion. Green warriors were leaping to the backs of their restive, squealing thoats. Calots were growling out their savage gutturals, whining to be at the throats of the oncoming foemen.

Thar Ban and another by the side of the rostrum had been the first to note the coming of Carthoris, and it was with them he battled for possession of the red girl, while the others hastened to meet the host advancing from the beleaguered city.

Carthoris sought both to defend Thuvia of Ptarth and reach the side of the hideous Hortan Gur that he might avenge the blow the creature had struck the girl.

He succeeded in reaching the rostrum, over the dead bodies of two warriors who had turned to join Thar Ban and his companion in repulsing this adventurous red man, just as Hortan Gur was about to leap from it to the back of his thoat.

The attention of the green warriors turned principally upon the bowmen advancing upon them from the city, and upon the savage banths that paced beside them—cruel beasts of war, infinitely more terrible than their own savage calots.

As Carthoris leaped to the rostrum he drew Thuvia up beside him, and then he turned upon the departing jeddak with an angry challenge and a sword thrust.

As the Heliumite's point pricked his green hide, Hortan Gur turned upon his adversary with a snarl, but at the same instant two of his chieftains called to him to hasten, for the charge of the fair-skinned inhabitants of the city was developing into a more serious matter than the Torquasians had anticipated.

Instead of remaining to battle with the red man, Hortan Gur promised him his attention after he had disposed of the presumptuous citizens of the walled city, and, leaping astride his thoat, galloped off to meet the rapidly advancing bowmen.

The other warriors quickly followed their jeddak, leaving Thuvia and Carthoris alone upon the platform.

Between them and the city raged a terrific battle. The fair-skinned warriors, armed only with their long bows and a kind of short-handled war-axe, were almost helpless beneath the savage mounted green men at close quarters; but at a distance their sharp arrows did fully as much execution as the radium projectiles of the green men.

But if the warriors themselves were outclassed, not so their savage companions, the fierce banths. Scarce had the two lines come together when hundreds of these appalling creatures had leaped among the Torquasians, dragging warriors from their thoats—dragging down the huge thoats themselves, and bringing consternation to all before them.

The numbers of the citizenry, too, was to their advantage, for it seemed that scarce a warrior fell but his place was taken by a score more, in such a constant stream did they pour from the city's great gate.

And so it came, what with the ferocity of the banths and the numbers of the bowmen, that at last the Torquasians fell back, until presently the platform upon which stood Carthoris and Thuvia lay directly in the center of the fight.

That neither was struck by a bullet or an arrow seemed a miracle to both; but at last the tide had rolled completely past them, so that they were alone between the fighters and the city, except for the dying and the dead, and a score or so of growling banths, less well trained than their fellows, who prowled among the corpses seeking meat.

To Carthoris the strangest part of the battle had been the terrific toll taken by the bowmen with their relatively puny weapons. Nowhere that he could see was there a single wounded green man, but the corpses of their dead lay thick upon the field of battle.

Death seemed to follow instantly the slightest pinprick of a bowman's arrow, nor apparently did one ever miss its goal. There could be but one explanation: the missiles were poison-tipped.

Presently the sounds of conflict died in the distant forest. Quiet reigned, broken only by the growling of the devouring banths. Carthoris turned toward Thuvia of Ptarth. As yet neither had spoken.

"Where are we, Thuvia?" he asked.

The girl looked at him questioningly. His very presence had seemed to proclaim a guilty knowledge of her abduction. How else might he have known the destination of the flier that brought her!

"Who should know better than the Prince of Helium?" she asked in return. "Did he not come hither of his own free will?"

"From Aaanthor I came voluntarily upon the trail of the green man who had stolen you, Thuvia," he replied; "but from the time I left Helium until I awoke above Aaanthor I thought myself bound for Ptarth.

"It had been intimated that I had guilty knowledge of your abduction," he explained simply, "and I was hastening to the jeddak, your father, to convince him of the falsity of the charge, and to give my service to your recovery. Before I left Helium someone tampered with my compass, so that it bore me to Aaanthor instead of to Ptarth. That is all. You believe me?"

"But the warriors who stole me from the garden!" she exclaimed. "After we arrived at Aaanthor they wore the metal of the Prince of Helium. When they took me they were trapped in Dusarian harness. There seemed but a single explanation. Whoever dared the outrage wished to put the onus upon another, should he be detected in the act; but once safely away from Ptarth he felt safe in having his minions return to their own harness."

"You believe that I did this thing, Thuvia?" he asked.

"Ah, Carthoris," she replied sadly, "I did not wish to believe it; but when everything pointed to you—even then I would not believe it."

"I did not do it, Thuvia," he said. "But let me be entirely honest with you. As much as I love your father, as much as I respect Kulan Tith, to whom you are betrothed, as well as I know the frightful consequences that must have followed such an act of mine, hurling into war, as it would, three of the greatest nations of Barsoom—yet, notwithstanding all this, I should not have hesitated to take you thus, Thuvia of Ptarth, had you even hinted that it would not have displeased *you*.

"But you did nothing of the kind, and so I am here, not in my own service, but in yours, and in the service of the man to whom you are promised, to save you for him, if it lies within the power of man to do so," he concluded, almost bitterly.

Thuvia of Ptarth looked into his face for several moments. Her breast was rising and falling as though to some resistless emotion. She half took a step toward him. Her lips parted as though to speak—swiftly and impetuously.

And then she conquered whatever had moved her.

"The future acts of the Prince of Helium," she said coldly, "must constitute the proof of his past honesty of purpose."

Carthoris was hurt by the girl's tone, as much as by the doubt as to his integrity which her words implied.

He had half hoped that she might hint that his love would be acceptable—certainly there was due him at least a little gratitude for his recent acts in her behalf; but the best he received was cold skepticism.

The Prince of Helium shrugged his broad shoulders. The girl noted it, and the little smile that touched his lips, so that it became her turn to be hurt.

Of course she had not meant to hurt him. He might have known that after what he had said she could not do anything to encourage him! But he need not have made his indifference quite so palpable. The men of Helium were noted for their gallantry— not for boorishness. Possibly it was the Earth blood that flowed in his veins.

How could she know that the shrug was but Carthoris' way of attempting, by physical effort, to cast blighting sorrow from his heart, or that the smile upon his lips was the fighting smile of his father with which the son gave outward evidence of the determination he had reached to submerge his own great love in his efforts to save Thuvia of Ptarth for another, because he believed that she loved this other!

He reverted to his original question.

"Where are we?" he asked. "I do not know."

"Nor I," replied the girl. "Those who stole me from Ptarth spoke among themselves of Aaanthor, so that I thought it possible that the ancient city to which they took me was that famous ruin; but where we may be now I have no idea."

"When the bowmen return we shall doubtless learn all that there is to know," said Carthoris. "Let us hope that they prove friendly. What race may they be? Only in the most ancient of our legends and in the mural paintings of the deserted cities of the dead sea-bottoms are depicted such a race of auburn-haired, fair-skinned people. Can it be that we have stumbled upon a surviving city of the past which all

Barsoom believes buried beneath the ages?"

Thuvia was looking toward the forest into which the green men and the pursuing bowmen had disappeared. From a great distance came the hideous cries of banths, and an occasional shot.

"It is strange that they do not return," said the girl.

"One would expect to see the wounded limping or being carried back to the city," replied Carthoris, with a puzzled frown. "But how about the wounded nearer the city? Have they carried them within?"

Both turned their eyes toward the field between them and the walled city, where the fighting had been most furious.

There were the banths, still growling about their hideous feast.

Carthoris looked at Thuvia in astonishment. Then he pointed toward the field.

"Where are they?" he whispered. *"What has become of their dead and wounded?"*

VI

THE JEDDAK OF LOTHAR

he girl looked her incredulity.

"They lay in piles," she murmured. "There were thousands of them but a minute ago."

"And now," continued Carthoris, "there remain but the banths and the carcasses of the green men."

"They must have sent forth and carried the dead bowmen away while we were talking," said the girl.

"It is impossible!" replied Carthoris. "Thousands of dead lay there upon the field but a moment since. It would have required many hours to have removed them. The thing is uncanny."

"I had hoped," said Thuvia, "that we might find an asylum with these fair-skinned people. Notwithstanding their valor upon the field of battle, they did not strike me as a ferocious or warlike people. I had been about to suggest that we seek entrance to the city, but now I scarce know if I care to venture among people whose dead vanish into thin air."

"Let us chance it," replied Carthoris. "We can be no worse off within their walls than without. Here we may fall prey to the banths or the no less fierce Torquasians. There, at least, we shall find beings molded after our own images.

"All that causes me to hesitate," he added, "is the danger of taking you past so many banths. A single sword would scarce prevail were even a couple of them to charge simultaneously."

"Do not fear on that score," replied the girl, smiling. "The banths will not harm us."

As she spoke she descended from the platform, and with Carthoris at her side stepped fearlessly out upon the bloody field in the direction of the walled city of mystery.

They had advanced but a short distance when a banth, looking up from its gory feast, descried them. With an angry roar the beast walked quickly in their direction, and at the sound of its voice a score of others followed its example.

Carthoris drew his long-sword. The girl stole a quick glance at his face. She saw the smile upon his lips, and it was as wine to sick nerves; for even upon warlike Barsoom where all men are brave, woman reacts quickly to quiet indifference to danger—to daredevil-try that is without bombast.

"You may return your sword," she said. "I told you that the banths would not harm us. Look!" and as she spoke she stepped quickly toward the nearest animal.

Carthoris would have leaped after her to protect her, but with a gesture she motioned him back. He heard her calling to the banths in a low, singsong voice that was half purr.

Instantly the great heads went up and all the wicked eyes were riveted upon the figure of the girl. Then, stealthily, they commenced moving toward her. She had stopped now and was standing waiting them.

One, closer to her than the others, hesitated. She spoke to him imperiously, as a master might speak to a refractory hound.

The great carnivore let its head droop, and with tail between its legs came slinking to the girl's feet, and after it came the others until she was entirely surrounded by the savage man-eaters.

Turning she led them to where Carthoris stood. They growled a little as they neared the man, but a few sharp words of command put them in their places.

"How do you do it?" exclaimed Carthoris.

"Your father once asked me that same question in the galleries of the Golden Cliffs within the Otz Mountains, beneath the temples of the therns. I could not answer him, nor can I answer you. I do not know whence comes my power over them, but ever since the day that Sator Throg threw me among them in the banth pit of the Holy Therns, and the great creatures fawned upon instead of devouring me, I ever have had the same strange power over them. They come at my call and do my bidding, even as the faithful Woola does the bidding of your mighty sire."

With a word the girl dispersed the fierce pack. Roaring, they returned to their interrupted feast, while Carthoris and Thuvia passed among them toward the walled city.

As they advanced the man looked with wonder upon the dead bodies of those of the green men that had not been devoured or mauled by the banths.

He called the girl's attention to them. No arrows protruded from the great carcasses. Nowhere upon any of them was the sign of mortal wound, nor even slightest scratch or abrasion.

Before the bowmen's dead had disappeared the corpses of the Torquasians had bristled with the deadly arrows of their foes. Where had the slender messengers of death departed? What unseen hand had plucked them from the bodies of the slain?

Despite himself Carthoris could scarce repress a shudder of apprehension as he glanced toward the silent city before them. No longer was sign of life visible upon wall or roof top. All was quiet—brooding, ominous quiet.

Yet he was sure that eyes watched them from somewhere behind that blank wall.

He glanced at Thuvia. She was advancing with wide eyes fixed upon the city gate. He looked in the direction of her gaze, but saw nothing.

His gaze upon her seemed to arouse her as from a lethargy. She glanced up at him, a quick, brave smile touching her lips, and then, as though the act was involuntary, she came close to his side and placed one of her hands in his.

He guessed that something within her that was beyond her conscious control was appealing to him for protection. He threw an arm about her, and thus they crossed the field. She did not draw away from him. It is doubtful that she realized that his arm was there, so engrossed was she in the mystery of the strange city before them.

They stopped before the gate. It was a mighty thing. From its construction Carthoris could but dimly speculate upon its unthinkable antiquity.

It was circular, closing a circular aperture, and the Heliumite knew from his study of ancient Barsoomian architecture that it rolled to one side, like a huge wheel, into an aperture in the wall.

Even such world-old cities as ancient Aaanthor were as yet undreamed of when the races lived that built such gates as these.

As he stood speculating upon the identity of this forgotten city, a voice spoke to them from above. Both looked up. There, leaning over the edge of the high wall, was a man.

His hair was auburn, his skin fair—fairer even than that of John Carter, the Virginian. His forehead was high, his eyes large and intelligent.

The language that he used was intelligible to the two below, yet there was a marked difference between it and their Barsoomian tongue.

"Who are you?" he asked. "And what do you here before the gate of Lothar?"

"We are friends," replied Carthoris. "This be the princess, Thuvia of Ptarth, who was captured by the Torquasian horde. I am Carthoris of Helium, Prince of the house of Tardos Mors, Jeddak of

Helium, and son of John Carter, Warlord of Mars, and of his wife, Dejah Thoris."

"'Ptarth'?" repeated the man. "'Helium'?" He shook his head. "I never have heard of these places, nor did I know that there dwelt upon Barsoom a race of thy strange color. Where may these cities lie, of which you speak? From our loftiest tower we have never seen another city than Lothar."

Carthoris pointed toward the northeast.

"In that direction lie Helium and Ptarth," he said. "Helium is over eight thousand haads from Lothar, while Ptarth lies nine thousand five hundred haads northeast of Helium."

Still the man shook his head.

"I know of nothing beyond the Lotharian hills," he said. "Naught may live there beside the hideous green hordes of Torquas. They have conquered all Barsoom except this single valley and the city of Lothar. Here we have defied them for countless ages, though periodically they renew their attempts to destroy us. From whence you come I cannot guess unless you be descended from the slaves the Torquasians captured in early times when they reduced the outer world to their vassalage; but we had heard that they destroyed all other races but their own."

Carthoris tried to explain that the Torquasians ruled but a relatively tiny part of the surface of Barsoom, and even this only because their domain held nothing to attract the red race; but the Lotharian could not seem to conceive of anything beyond the valley of Lothar other than a trackless waste peopled by the ferocious green hordes of Torquas.

After considerably parleying he consented to admit them to the city, and a moment later the wheellike gate rolled back within its niche, and Thuvia and Carthoris entered the city of Lothar.

All about them were evidences of fabulous wealth. The façades of the buildings fronting upon the avenue within the wall were richly carven, and about the windows and doors were ofttimes set foot-wide borders of precious stones, intricate mosaics, or tablets of beaten gold bearing bas-reliefs depicting what may have been bits of the history of this forgotten people.

He with whom they had conversed across the wall was in the avenue to receive them. About him were a hundred or more men of the same race. All were clothed in flowing robes and all were beardless.

Their attitude was more of fearful suspicion than antagonism. They followed the newcomers with their eyes; but spoke no word to them.

Carthoris could not but notice the fact that though the city had been but a short time before surrounded by a horde of bloodthirsty demons yet none of the citizens appeared to be armed, nor was there sign of soldiery about.

He wondered if all the fighting men had sallied forth in one supreme effort to rout the foe, leaving the city all unguarded. He asked their host.

The man smiled.

"No creature other than a score or so of our sacred banths has left Lothar today," he replied.

"But the soldiers—the bowmen!" exclaimed Carthoris. "We saw thousands emerge from this very gate, overwhelming the hordes of Torquas and putting them to rout with their deadly arrows and their fierce banths."

Still the man smiled his knowing smile.

"Look!" he cried, and pointed down a broad avenue before him.

Carthoris and Thuvia followed the direction indicated, and there, marching bravely in the sunlight, they saw advancing toward them a great army of bowmen.

"Ah!" exclaimed Thuvia. "They have returned through another gate, or perchance these be the troops that remained to defend the city?"

Again the fellow smiled his uncanny smile.

"There are no soldiers in Lothar," he said. "Look!"

Both Carthoris and Thuvia had turned toward him while he spoke, and now as they turned back again toward the advancing regiments their eyes went wide in astonishment, for the broad avenue before them was as deserted as the tomb.

"And those who marched out upon the hordes today?" whispered Carthoris. "They, too, were unreal?"

The man nodded.

"But their arrows slew the green warriors," insisted Thuvia.

"Let us go before Tario," replied the Lotharian. "He will tell you that which he deems it best you know. I might tell you too much."

"Who is Tario?" asked Carthoris.

"Jeddak of Lothar," replied the guide, leading them up the broad avenue down which they had but a moment since seen the phantom army marching.

For half an hour they walked along lovely avenues between the most gorgeous buildings that the two had ever seen. Few people were in evidence. Carthoris could not but note the deserted appearance of the mighty city.

At last they came to the royal palace. Carthoris saw it from a distance, and guessing the nature of the magnificent pile wondered that even here there should be so little sign of activity and life.

Not even a single guard was visible before the great entrance gate, nor in the gardens beyond, into which he could see, was there sign of the myriad life that pulses within the precincts of the royal estates of the red jeddaks.

"Here," said their guide, "is the palace of Tario."

As he spoke Carthoris again let his gaze rest upon the wondrous palace. With a startled exclamation he rubbed his eyes and looked again. No! He could not be mistaken. Before the massive gate stood a score of sentries. Within, the avenue leading to the main building was lined on either side by ranks of bowmen. The gardens were dotted with officers and soldiers moving quickly to and fro, as though bent upon the duties of the minute.

What manner of people were these who could conjure an army out of thin air? He glanced toward Thuvia. She, too, evidently had witnessed the transformation.

With a little shudder she pressed more closely toward him.

"What do you make of it?" she whispered. "It is most uncanny."

"I cannot account for it," replied Carthoris, "unless we have gone mad."

Carthoris turned quickly toward the Lotharian. The fellow was smiling broadly.

"I thought that you just said that there were no soldiers in Lothar," said the Heliumite, with a gesture toward the guardsmen. "What are these?"

"Ask Tario," replied the other. "We shall soon be before him."

Nor was it long before they entered a lofty chamber at one end of which a man reclined upon a rich couch that stood upon a high dais.

As the trio approached, the man turned dreamy eyes sleepily upon them. Twenty feet from the dais their conductor halted, and, whispering to Thuvia and Carthoris to follow his example, threw himself headlong to the floor. Then rising to hands and knees, he commenced crawling toward the foot of the throne, swinging his head to and fro and wiggling his body as you have seen a hound do when approaching its master.

Thuvia glanced quickly toward Carthoris. He was standing erect, with high-held head and arms folded across his broad chest. A haughty smile curved his lips.

The man upon the dais was eyeing him intently, and Carthoris of Helium was looking straight in the other's face.

"Who be these, Jav?" asked the man of him who crawled upon his belly along the floor.

"O Tario, most glorious Jeddak," replied Jav, "these be strangers who came with the hordes of Torquas to our gates, saying that they were prisoners of the green men. They tell strange tales of cities far beyond Lothar."

"Arise, Jav," commanded Tario, "and ask these two why they show not to Tario the respect that is his due."

Jav arose and faced the strangers. At sight of their erect positions his face went livid. He leaped toward them.

"Creatures!" he screamed. "Down! Down upon your bellies before the last of the jeddaks of Barsoom!"

VII

THE PHANTOM BOWMEN

s Jav leaped toward him Carthoris laid his hand upon the hilt of his long-sword. The Lotharian halted. The great apartment was empty save for the four at the dais, yet as Jav stepped back from the menace of the Heliumite's threatening attitude the latter found himself surrounded by a score of bowmen.

From whence had they sprung? Both Carthoris and Thuvia looked their astonishment.

Now the former's sword leaped from its scabbard, and at the same instant the bowmen drew back their slim shafts.

Tario had half raised himself upon one elbow. For the first time he saw the full figure of Thuvia, who had been concealed behind the person of Carthoris.

"Enough!" cried the jeddak, raising a protesting hand, but at that very instant the sword of the Heliumite cut viciously at its nearest antagonist.

As the keen edge reached its goal Carthoris let the point fall to the floor, as with wide eyes he stepped backward in consternation, throwing the back of his left hand across his brow. His steel had cut but empty air—his antagonist had vanished—there were no bowmen in the room!

"It is evident that these are strangers," said Tario to Jav. "Let us first determine that they knowingly affronted us before we take measures for punishment."

Then he turned to Carthoris, but ever his gaze wandered to the perfect lines of Thuvia's glorious figure, which the harness of a Barsoomian princess accentuated rather than concealed.

"Who are you," he asked, "who knows not the etiquette of the court of the last of jeddaks?"

"I am Carthoris, Prince of Helium," replied the Heliumite. "And this is Thuvia, Princess of Ptarth. In the courts of our fathers men do not prostrate themselves before royalty. Not since the First Born tore their immortal goddess limb from limb have men crawled upon their bellies to any throne upon Barsoom. Now think you that the daughter of one mighty jeddak and the son of another would so humiliate themselves?"

Tario looked at Carthoris for a long time. At last he spoke.

"There is no other jeddak upon Barsoom than Tario," he said. "There is no other race than that of Lothar, unless the hordes of Torquas may be dignified by such an appellation. Lotharians are white; your skins are red. There are no women left upon Barsoom. Your companion is a woman."

He half rose from the couch, leaning far forward and pointing an accusing finger at Carthoris.

"You are a lie!" he shrieked. "You are both lies, and you dare to come before Tario, last and mightiest of the jeddaks of Barsoom, and assert your reality. Someone shall pay well for this, Jav, and unless I mistake it is yourself who has dared thus flippantly to trifle with the good nature of your jeddak.

"Remove the man. Leave the woman. We shall see if both be lies. And later, Jav, you shall suffer for your temerity. There be few of us left, but—Komal must be fed. Go!"

Carthoris could see that Jav trembled as he prostrated himself once more before his ruler, and then, rising, turned toward the Prince of Helium.

"Come!" he said.

"And leave the Princess of Ptarth here alone?" cried Carthoris.

Jav brushed closely past him, whispering:

"Follow me—he cannot harm her, except to kill; and that he can do whether you remain or not. We had best go now—trust me."

Carthoris did not understand, but something in the urgency of the other's tone assured him, and so he turned away, but not without a glance toward Thuvia in which he attempted to make her understand that it was in her own interest that he left her.

For answer she turned her back full upon him, but not without first throwing him such a look of contempt that brought the scarlet to his cheek.

Then he hesitated, but Jav seized him by the wrist.

"Come!" he whispered. "Or he will have the bowmen upon you, and this time there will be no escape. Did you not see how futile is your steel against thin air!"

Carthoris turned unwillingly to follow. As the two left the room he turned to his companion.

"If I may not kill thin air," he asked, "how, then, shall I fear that thin air may kill me?"

"You saw the Torquasians fall before the bowmen?" asked Jav.

Carthoris nodded.

"So would you fall before them, and without one single chance for self-defense or revenge."

As they talked Jav led Carthoris to a small room in one of the numerous towers of the palace. Here were couches, and Jav bid the Heliumite be seated.

For several minutes the Lotharian eyed his prisoner, for such Carthoris now realized himself to be.

"I am half convinced that you are real," he said at last.

Carthoris laughed.

"Of course I am real," he said. "What caused you to doubt it? Can you not see me, feel me?"

"So may I see and feel the bowmen," replied Jav, "and yet we all know that they, at least, are not real."

Carthoris showed by the expression of his face his puzzlement at each new reference to the mysterious bowmen—the vanishing soldiery of Lothar.

"What, then, may they be?" he asked.

"You really do not know?" asked Jav.

Carthoris shook his head negatively.

"I can almost believe that you have told us the truth and that you are really from another part of Barsoom, or from another world. But tell me, in your own country have you no bowmen to strike terror to the hearts of the green hordesmen as they slay in company with the fierce banths of war?"

"We have soldiers," replied Carthoris. "We of the red race are all soldiers, but we have no bowmen to defend us, such as yours. We defend ourselves."

"You go out and get killed by your enemies!" cried Jav incredulously.

"Certainly," replied Carthoris. "How do the Lotharians?"

"You have seen," replied the other. "We send out our deathless archers—deathless because they are lifeless, existing only in the imaginations of our enemies. It is really our giant minds that defend us, sending out legions of imaginary warriors to materialize before the mind's eye of the foe.

"They see them—they see their bows drawn back—they see their slender arrows speed with unerring precision toward their hearts. And they die—killed by the power of suggestion."

"But the archers that are slain?" exclaimed Carthoris. "You call them deathless, and yet I saw their dead bodies piled high upon the battlefield. How may that be?"

"It is but to lend reality to the scene," replied Jav. "We picture many of our own defenders killed that the Torquasians may not

69

guess that there are really no flesh and blood creatures opposing them.

"Once that truth became implanted in their minds, it is the theory of many of us, no longer would they fall prey to the suggestion of the deadly arrows, for greater would be the suggestion of the truth, and the more powerful suggestion would prevail—it is law."

"And the banths?" questioned Carthoris. "They, too, were but creatures of suggestion?"

"Some of them were real," replied Jav. "Those that accompanied the archers in pursuit of the Torquasians were unreal. Like the archers, they never returned, but, having served their purpose, vanished with the bowmen when the rout of the enemy was assured.

"Those that remained about the field were real. Those we loosed as scavengers to devour the bodies of the dead of Torquas. This thing is demanded by the realists among us. I am a realist. Tario is an etherealist.

"The etherealists maintain that there is no such thing as matter—that all is mind. They say that none of us exists, except in the imagination of his fellows, other than as an intangible, invisible mentality.

"According to Tario, it is but necessary that we all unite in imagining that there are no dead Torquasians beneath our walls, and there will be none, nor any need of scavenging banths."

"You, then, do not hold Tario's beliefs?" asked Carthoris.

"In part only," replied the Lotharian. "I believe, in fact I know, that there are some truly ethereal creatures. Tario is one, I am convinced. He has no existence except in the imaginations of his people.

"Of course, it is the contention of all us realists that all etherealists are but figments of the imagination. They contend that no food is necessary, nor do they eat; but anyone of the most rudimentary intelligence must realize that food is a necessity to creatures having actual existence."

"Yes," agreed Carthoris, "not having eaten today I can readily agree with you."

"Ah, pardon me," exclaimed Jav. "Pray be seated and satisfy your hunger," and with a wave of his hand he indicated a bountifully laden table that had not been there an instant before he spoke. Of that Carthoris was positive, for he had searched the room diligently with his eyes several times.

"It is well," continued Jav, "that you did not fall into the hands of an etherealist. Then, indeed, would you have gone hungry."

"But," exclaimed Carthoris, "this is not real food—it was not here an instant since, and real food does not materialize out of thin air."

Jav looked hurt.

"There is no real food or water in Lothar," he said; "nor has there been for countless ages. Upon such as you now see before you have we existed since the dawn of history. Upon such, then, may you exist."

"But I thought you were a realist," exclaimed Carthoris.

"Indeed," cried Jav, "what more realistic than this bounteous feast? It is just here that we differ most from the etherealists. They claim that it is unnecessary to imagine food; but we have found that for the maintenance of life we must thrice daily sit down to hearty meals.

"The food that one eats is supposed to undergo certain chemical changes during the process of digestion and assimilation, the result, of course, being the rebuilding of wasted tissue.

"Now we all know that mind is all, though we may differ in the interpretation of its various manifestations. Tario maintains that there is no such thing as substance, all being created from the substanceless matter of the brain.

"We realists, however, know better. We know that mind has the power to maintain substance even though it may not be able to create substance—the latter is still an open question. And so we know that in order to maintain our physical bodies we must cause all our organs properly to function.

"This we accomplish by materializing food-thoughts, and by partaking of the food thus created. We chew, we swallow, we digest. All our organs function precisely as if we had partaken of material food. And what is the result? What must be the result? The chemical changes take place through both direct and indirect suggestion, and we live and thrive."

Carthoris eyed the food before him. It seemed real enough. He lifted a morsel to his lips. There was substance indeed. And flavor as well. Yes, even his palate was deceived.

Jav watched him, smiling, as he ate.

"Is it not entirely satisfying?" he asked.

"I must admit that it is," replied Carthoris. "But tell me, how does Tario live, and the other etherealists who maintain that food is unnecessary?"

Jav scratched his head.

"That is a question we often discuss," he replied. "It is the strongest evidence we have of the non-existence of the etherealists; but who may know other than Komal?"

"Who is Komal?" asked Carthoris. "I heard your jeddak speak of him."

Jav bent low toward the ear of the Heliumite, looking fearfully about before he spoke.

"Komal is the essence," he whispered. "Even the etherealists admit that mind itself must have substance in order to transmit to imaginings the appearance of substance. For if there really was no such thing as substance it could not be suggested—what never has been cannot be imagined. Do you follow me?"

"I am groping," replied Carthoris dryly.

"So the essence must be substance," continued Jav. "Komal is the essence of the All, as it were. He is maintained by substance.

He eats. He eats the real. To be explicit, he eats the realists. That is Tario's work.

"He says that inasmuch as we maintain that we alone are real we should, to be consistent, admit that we alone are proper food for Komal. Sometimes, as today, we find other food for him. He is very fond of Torquasians."

"And Komal is a man?" asked Carthoris.

"He is All, I told you," replied Jav. "I know not how to explain him in words that you will understand. He is the beginning and the end. All life emanates from Komal, since the substance which feeds the brain with imaginings radiates from the body of Komal.

"Should Komal cease to eat, all life upon Barsoom would cease to be. He cannot die, but he might cease to eat, and, thus, to radiate."

"And he feeds upon the men and women of your belief?" cried Carthoris.

"Women!" exclaimed Jav. "There are no women in Lothar. The last of the Lotharian females perished ages since, upon that cruel and terrible journey across the muddy plains that fringed the half-dried seas, when the green hordes scourged us across the world to this our last hiding place—our impregnable fortress of Lothar.

"Scarce twenty thousand men of all the countless millions of our race lived to reach Lothar. Among us were no women and no children. All these had perished by the way.

"As time went on, we, too, were dying and the race fast approaching extinction, when the Great Truth was revealed to us, that mind is all. Many more died before we perfected our powers, but at last we were able to defy death when we fully understood that death was merely a state of mind.

"Then came the creation of mind-people, or rather the materialization of imaginings. We first put these to practical use when the Torquasians discovered our retreat, and fortunate for us it was that it required ages of search upon their part before they found the single tiny entrance to the valley of Lothar.

"That day we threw our first bowmen against them. The intention was purely to frighten them away by the vast numbers of bowmen which we could muster upon our walls. All Lothar bristled with the bows and arrows of our ethereal host.

"But the Torquasians did not frighten. They are lower than the beasts—they know no fear. They rushed upon our walls, and standing upon the shoulders of others they built human approaches to the wall tops, and were on the very point of surging in upon us and overwhelming us.

"Not an arrow had been discharged by our bowmen—we did but cause them to run to and fro along the wall top, screaming taunts and threats at the enemy.

"Presently I thought to attempt the thing—*the great thing*. I centered all my mighty intellect upon the bowmen of my own creation—each of us produces and directs as many bowmen as his mentality and imagination is capable of.

"I caused them to fit arrows to their bows for the first time. I made them take aim at the hearts of the green men. I made the green men see all this, and then I made them see the arrows fly, and I made them think that the points pierced their hearts.

"It was all that was necessary. By hundreds they toppled from our walls, and when my fellows saw what I had done they were quick to follow my example, so that presently the hordes of Torquas had retreated beyond the range of our arrows.

"We might have killed them at any distance, but one rule of war we have maintained from the first—the rule of realism. We do nothing, or rather we cause our bowmen to do nothing within sight of the enemy that is beyond the understanding of the foe. Otherwise they might guess the truth, and that would be the end of us.

"But after the Torquasians had retreated beyond bowshot, they turned upon us with their terrible rifles, and by constant popping at us made life miserable within our walls.

"So then I bethought the scheme to hurl our bowmen through the gates upon them. You have seen this day how well it works. For ages they have come down upon us at intervals, but always with the same results."

"And all this is due to your intellect, Jav?" asked Carthoris. "I should think that you would be high in the councils of your people."

"I am," replied Jav, proudly. "I am next to Tario."

"But why, then, your cringing manner of approaching the throne?"

"Tario demands it. He is jealous of me. He only awaits the slightest excuse to feed me to Komal. He fears that I may someday usurp his power."

Carthoris suddenly sprang from the table.

"Jav!" he exclaimed. "I am a beast! Here I have been eating my fill, while the Princess of Ptarth may perchance be still without food. Let us return and find some means of furnishing her with nourishment."

The Lotharian shook his head.

"Tario would not permit it," he said. "He will, doubtless, make an etherealist of her."

"But I must go to her," insisted Carthoris. "You say that there are no women in Lothar. Then she must be among men, and if this be so I intend to be near where I may defend her if the need arises."

"Tario will have his way," insisted Jav. "He sent you away and you may not return until he sends for you."

"Then I shall go without waiting to be sent for."

"Do not forget the bowmen," cautioned Jav.

"I do not forget them," replied Carthoris, but he did not tell Jav that he remembered something else that the Lotharian had let drop—something that was but a conjecture, possibly, and yet one well worth pinning a forlorn hope to, should necessity arise.

Carthoris started to leave the room. Jav stepped before him, barring his way.

"I have learned to like you, red man," he said; "but do not forget that Tario is still my jeddak, and that Tario has commanded that you remain here."

Carthoris was about to reply, when there came faintly to the ears of both a woman's cry for help.

With a sweep of his arm the Prince of Helium brushed the Lotharian aside, and with drawn sword sprang into the corridor without.

VIII

THE HALL OF DOOM

s Thuvia of Ptarth saw Carthoris depart from the presence of Tario, leaving her alone with the man, a sudden qualm of terror seized her.

There was an air of mystery pervading the stately chamber. Its furnishings and appointments bespoke wealth and culture, and carried the suggestion that the room was often the scene of royal functions which filled it to its capacity.

And yet nowhere about her, in antechamber or corridor, was there sign of any other being than herself and the recumbent figure of Tario, the jeddak, who watched her through half-closed eyes from the gorgeous trappings of his regal couch.

For a time after the departure of Jav and Carthoris the man eyed her intently. Then he spoke.

"Come nearer," he said, and, as she approached: "Whose creature are you? Who has dared materialize his imaginings of woman? It is contrary to the customs and the royal edicts of Lothar. Tell me, woman, from whose brain have you sprung? Jav's? No, do not deny it. I know that it could be no other than that envious realist. He seeks to tempt me. He would see me fall beneath the spell of your charms, and then he, your master, would direct my destiny and—my end. I see it all! I see it all!"

The blood of indignation and anger had been rising to Thuvia's face. Her chin was up, a haughty curve upon her perfect lips.

"I know naught," she cried, "of what you are prating! I am Thuvia, Princess of Ptarth. I am no man's 'creature.' Never before today did I lay eyes upon him you call Jav, nor upon your ridiculous city, of which even the greatest nations of Barsoom have never dreamed.

"My charms are not for you, nor such as you. They are not for sale or barter, even though the price were a real throne. And as for using them to win your worse than futile power—" She ended her sentence with a shrug of her shapely shoulders, and a little scornful laugh.

When she had finished Tario was sitting upon the edge of his couch, his feet upon the floor. He was leaning forward with eyes no longer half closed, but wide with a startled expression in them.

He did not seem to note the *lese majeste* of her words and manner. There was evidently something more startling and compelling about her speech than that.

Slowly he came to his feet.

"By the fangs of Komal!" he muttered. "But you are *real!* A *real* woman! No dream! No vain and foolish figment of the mind!"

He took a step toward her, with hands outstretched.

"Come!" he whispered. "Come, woman! For countless ages have I dreamed that someday you would come. And now that you are here I can scarce believe the testimony of my eyes. Even now, knowing that you are real, I still half dread that you may be a lie."

Thuvia shrank back. She thought the man mad. Her hand stole to the jeweled hilt of her dagger. The man saw the move, and stopped. A cunning expression entered his eyes. Then they became at once dreamy and penetrating as they fairly bored into the girl's brain.

Thuvia suddenly felt a change coming over her. What the cause of it she did not guess; but somehow the man before her began to assume a new relationship within her heart.

No longer was he a strange and mysterious enemy, but an old and trusted friend. Her hand slipped from the dagger's hilt. Tario came closer. He spoke gentle, friendly words, and she answered him in a voice that seemed hers and yet another's.

He was beside her now. His hand was up her shoulder. His eyes were down-bent toward hers. She looked up into his face. His gaze seemed to bore straight through her to some hidden spring of sentiment within her.

Her lips parted in sudden awe and wonder at the strange revealment of her inner self that was being laid bare before her consciousness. She had known Tario forever. He was more than friend to her. She moved a little closer to him. In one swift flood of light she knew the truth. She loved Tario, Jeddak of Lothar! She had always loved him.

The man, seeing the success of his strategy, could not restrain a faint smile of satisfaction. Whether there was something in the expression of his face, or whether from Carthoris of Helium in a far chamber of the palace came a more powerful suggestion, who may say? But something there was that suddenly dispelled the strange, hypnotic influence of the man.

As though a mask had been torn from her eyes, Thuvia suddenly saw Tario as she had formerly seen him, and, accustomed as she was to the strange manifestations of highly developed mentality which are common upon Barsoom, she quickly guessed enough of the truth to know that she was in grave danger.

Quickly she took a step backward, tearing herself from his grasp. But the momentary contact had aroused within Tario all the long-buried passions of his loveless existence.

With a muffled cry he sprang upon her, throwing his arms about her and attempting to drag her lips to his.

"Woman!" he cried. "Lovely woman! Tario would make you queen of Lothar. Listen to me! Listen to the love of the last jeddaks of Barsoom."

Thuvia struggled to free herself from his embrace.

"Stop, creature!" she cried. "Stop! I do not love you. Stop, or I shall scream for help!"

Tario laughed in her face.

"'Scream for help,'" he mimicked. "And who within the halls of Lothar is there who might come in answer to your call? Who would dare enter the presence of Tario, unsummoned?"

"There is one," she replied, "who would come, and, coming, dare to cut you down upon your own throne, if he thought that you had offered affront to Thuvia of Ptarth!"

"Who, Jav?" asked Tario.

"Not Jav, nor any other soft-skinned Lotharian," she replied; "but a real man, a real warrior—Carthoris of Helium!"

Again the man laughed at her.

"You forget the bowmen," he reminded her. "What could your red warrior accomplish against my fearless legions?"

Again he caught her roughly to him, dragging her towards his couch.

"If you will not be my queen," he said, "you shall be my slave."

"Neither!" cried the girl.

As she spoke the single word there was a quick move of her right hand; Tario, releasing her, staggered back, both hands pressed to his side. At the same instant the room filled with bowmen, and then the jeddak of Lothar sank senseless to the marble floor.

At the instant that he lost consciousness the bowmen were about to release their arrows into Thuvia's heart. Involuntarily she gave a single cry for help, though she knew that not even Carthoris of Helium could save her now.

Then she closed her eyes and waited for the end. No slender shafts pierced her tender side. She raised her lids to see what stayed the hand of her executioners.

The room was empty save for herself and the still form of the jeddak of Lothar lying at her feet, a little pool of crimson staining the white marble of the floor beside him. Tario was unconscious.

Thuvia was amazed. Where were the bowmen? Why had they not loosed their shafts? What could it all mean?

An instant before the room had been mysteriously filled with armed men, evidently called to protect their jeddak; yet now, with the evidence of her deed plain before them, they had vanished as mysteriously as they had come, leaving her alone with the body of their ruler, into whose side she had slipped her long, keen blade.

The girl glanced apprehensively about, first for signs of the return of the bowmen, and then for some means of escape.

The wall behind the dais was pierced by two small doorways, hidden by heavy hangings. Thuvia was running quickly towards one of these when she heard the clank of a warrior's metal at the end of the apartment behind her.

Ah, if she had but an instant more of time she could have reached that screening arras and, perchance, have found some avenue of escape behind it; but now it was too late—she had been discovered!

With a feeling that was akin to apathy she turned to meet her fate, and there, before her, running swiftly across the broad chamber to her side, was Carthoris, his naked long-sword gleaming in his hand.

For days she had doubted his intentions of the Heliumite. She had thought him a party to her abduction. Since Fate had thrown them together she had scarce favored him with more than the most per-functory replies to his remarks, unless at such times as the weird and uncanny happenings at Lothar had surprised her out of her reserve.

She knew that Carthoris of Helium would fight for her; but whether to save her for himself or another, she was in doubt.

He knew that she was promised to Kulan Tith, Jeddak of Kaol, but if he had been instrumental in her abduction, his motives could not be prompted by loyalty to his friend, or regard for her honor.

And yet, as she saw him coming across the marble floor of the audience chamber of Tario of Lothar, his fine eyes filled with apprehension for her safety, his splendid figure personifying all that is finest in the fighting men of martial Mars, she could not believe that any faintest trace of perfidy lurked beneath so glorious an exterior.

Never, she thought, in all her life had the sight of any man been so welcome to her. It was with difficulty that she refrained from rushing forward to meet him.

She knew that he loved her; but, in time, she recalled that she was promised to Kulan Tith. Not even might she trust herself to show too great gratitude to the Heliumite, lest he misunderstand.

Carthoris was by her side now. His quick glance had taken in the scene within the room—the still figure of the jeddak sprawled upon the floor—the girl hastening toward a shrouded exit.

"Did he harm you, Thuvia?" he asked.

She held up her crimsoned blade that he might see it.

"No," she said, "he did not harm me."

A grim smile lighted Carthoris' face.

"Praised be our first ancestor!" he murmured. "And now let us see if we may not make good our escape from this accursed city before the Lotharians discover that their jeddak is no more."

With the firm authority that sat so well upon him in whose veins flowed the blood of John Carter of Virginia and Dejah Thoris of Helium, he grasped her hand and, turning back across the hall, strode toward the great doorway through which Jav had brought them into the presence of the jeddak earlier in the day.

They had almost reached the threshold when a figure sprang into the apartment through another entrance. It was Jav. He, too, took in the scene within at a glance.

Carthoris turned to face him, his sword ready in his hand, and his great body shielding the slender figure of the girl.

"Come, Jav of Lothar!" he cried. "Let us face the issue at once, for only one of us may leave this chamber alive with Thuvia of Ptarth." Then, seeing that the man wore no sword, he exclaimed: "Bring on your bowmen, then, or come with us as my prisoner until we have safely passed the outer portals of thy ghostly city."

"You have killed Tario!" exclaimed Jav, ignoring the other's challenge. "You have killed Tario! I see his blood upon the floor— real blood—real death. Tario was, after all, as real as I. Yet he was an etherealist. He would not materialize his sustenance. Can it be that they are right? Well, we, too, are right. And all these ages we have been quarreling—each saying that the other was wrong!

"However, he is dead now. Of that I am glad. Now shall Jav come into his own. Now shall Jav be Jeddak of Lothar!"

As he finished, Tario opened his eyes and then quickly sat up.

"Traitor! Assassin!" he screamed, and then: "Kadar! Kadar!" which is the Barsoomian for guard.

Jav went sickly white. He fell upon his belly, wriggling toward Tario.

"Oh, my Jeddak, my Jeddak!" he whimpered. "Jav had no hand in this. Jav, your faithful Jav, but just this instant entered the apartment to find you lying prone upon the floor and these two strangers about to leave. How it happened I know not. Believe me, most glorious Jeddak!"

"Cease, knave!" cried Tario. "I heard your words: 'However, he is dead now. Of that I am glad. Now shall Jav come into his own. Now shall Jav be Jeddak of Lothar.'

"At last, traitor, I have found you out. Your own words have condemned you as surely as the acts of these red creatures have sealed their fates—unless—" He paused. "Unless the woman—"

But he got no further. Carthoris guessed what he would have said, and before the words could be uttered he had sprung forward and struck the man across the mouth with his open palm.

Tario frothed in rage and mortification.

"And should you again affront the Princess of Ptarth," warned the Heliumite, "I shall forget that you wear no sword—not forever may I control my itching sword hand."

Tario shrank back toward the little doorways behind the dais. He was trying to speak, but so hideously were the muscles of his face working that he could utter no word for several minutes. At last he managed to articulate intelligibly.

"Die!" he shrieked. "Die!" and then he turned toward the exit at his back.

Jav leaped forward, screaming in terror.

"Have pity, Tario! Have pity! Remember the long ages that I have served you faithfully. Remember all that I have done for Lothar. Do not condemn me now to the death hideous. Save me! Save me!"

But Tario only laughed a mocking laugh and continued to back toward the hangings that hid the little doorway.

Jav turned toward Carthoris.

"Stop him!" he screamed. "Stop him! If you love life, let him not leave this room," and as he spoke he leaped in pursuit of his jeddak.

Carthoris followed Jav's example, but the "last of the jeddaks of Barsoom" was too quick for them. By the time they reached the arras behind which he had disappeared, they found a heavy stone door blocking their further progress.

Jav sank to the floor in a spasm of terror.

"Come, man!" cried Carthoris. "We are not dead yet. Let us hasten to the avenues and make an attempt to leave the city. We are still alive, and while we live we may yet endeavor to direct our own destinies. Of what avail, to sink spineless to the floor? Come, be a man!"

Jav but shook his head.

"Did you not hear him call the guards?" he moaned. "Ah, if we could have but intercepted him! Then there might have been hope;

but, alas, he was too quick for us."

"Well, well," exclaimed Carthoris impatiently. "What if he did call the guards? There will be time enough to worry about that after they come—at present I see no indication that they have any idea of overexerting themselves to obey their jeddak's summons."

Jav shook his head mournfully.

"You do not understand," he said. "The guards have already come—and gone. They have done their work and we are lost. Look to the various exits."

Carthoris and Thuvia turned their eyes in the direction of the several doorways which pierced the walls of the great chamber. Each was tightly closed by huge stone doors.

"Well?" asked Carthoris.

"We are to die the death," whispered Jav faintly.

Further than that he would not say. He just sat upon the edge of the jeddak's couch and waited.

Carthoris moved to Thuvia's side, and, standing there with naked sword, he let his brave eyes roam ceaselessly about the great chamber, that no foe might spring upon them unseen.

For what seemed hours no sound broke the silence of their living tomb. No sign gave their executioners of the time or manner of their death. The suspense was terrible. Even Carthoris of Helium began to feel the terrible strain upon his nerves. If he could but know how and whence the hand of death was to strike, he could meet it unafraid, but to suffer longer the hideous tension of this blighting ignorance of the plans of their assassins was telling upon him grievously.

Thuvia of Ptarth drew quite close to him. She felt safer with the feel of his arm against hers, and with the contact of her the man took a new grip upon himself. With his old-time smile he turned toward her.

"It would seem that they are trying to frighten us to death," he said, laughing; "and, shame be upon me that I should confess it, I think they were close to accomplishing their designs upon me."

She was about to make some reply when a fearful shriek broke from the lips of the Lotharian.

"The end is coming!" he cried. "The end is coming! The floor! The floor! Oh, Komal, be merciful!"

Thuvia and Carthoris did not need to look at the floor to be aware of the strange movement that was taking place.

Slowly the marble flagging was sinking in all directions toward the center. At first the movement, being gradual, was scarce noticeable; but presently the angle of the floor became such that one might stand easily only by bending one knee considerably.

Jav was shrieking still, and clawing at the royal couch that had already commenced to slide toward the center of the room, where both Thuvia and Carthoris suddenly noted a small orifice which grew in diameter as the floor assumed more closely a funnel-like contour.

Now it became more and more difficult to cling to the dizzy inclination of the smooth and polished marble.

Carthoris tried to support Thuvia, but himself commenced to slide and slip toward the ever-enlarging aperture.

Better to cling to the smooth stone he kicked off his sandals of zitidar hide and with his bare feet braced himself against the sickening tilt, at the same time throwing his arms supportingly about the girl.

In her terror her own hands clasped about the man's neck. Her cheek was close to his. Death, unseen and of unknown form, seemed close upon them, and because unseen and unknowable infinitely more terrifying.

"Courage, my princess," he whispered.

She looked up into his face to see smiling lips above hers and brave eyes, untouched by terror, drinking deeply of her own.

Then the floor sagged and tilted more swiftly. There was a sudden slipping rush as they were precipitated toward the aperture.

Jav's screams rose weird and horrible in their ears, and then the three found themselves piled upon the royal couch of Tario, which had stuck within the aperture at the base of the marble funnel.

For a moment they breathed more freely, but presently they discovered that the aperture was continuing to enlarge. The couch slipped downward. Jav shrieked again. There was a sickening sensation as they felt all let go beneath them, as they fell through darkness to an unknown death.

IX

THE BATTLE IN THE PLAIN

he distance from the bottom of the funnel to the floor of the chamber beneath it could not have been great, for all three of the victims of Tario's wrath alighted unscathed.

Carthoris, still clasping Thuvia tightly to his breast, came to the ground catlike, upon his feet, breaking the shock for the girl. Scarce had his feet touched the rough stone flagging of this new chamber than his sword flashed out ready for instant use. But though the room was lighted, there was no sign of enemy about.

Carthoris looked toward Jav. The man was pasty white with fear.

"What is to be our fate?" asked the Heliumite. "Tell me, man! Shake off your terror long enough to tell me, so I may be prepared to sell my life and that of the Princess of Ptarth as dearly as possible."

"Komal!" whispered Jav. "We are to be devoured by Komal!"

"Your deity?" asked Carthoris.

The Lotharian nodded his head. Then he pointed toward a low doorway at one end of the chamber.

"From thence will he come upon us. Lay aside your puny sword, fool. It will but enrage him the more and make our sufferings the worse."

Carthoris smiled, gripping his long-sword the more firmly.

Presently Jav gave a horrified moan, at the same time pointing toward the door.

"He has come," he whimpered.

Carthoris and Thuvia looked in the direction the Lotharian had indicated, expecting to see some strange and fearful creature in human form; but to their astonishment they saw the broad head and greatmaned shoulders of a huge banth, the largest that either ever had seen.

Slowly and with dignity the mighty beast advanced into the room. Jav had fallen to the floor, and was wriggling his body in the same servile manner that he had adopted toward Tario. He spoke to the fierce beast as he would have spoken to a human being, pleading with it for mercy.

Carthoris stepped between Thuvia and the banth, his sword ready to contest the beast's victory over them. Thuvia turned toward Jav.

"Is this Komal, your god?" she asked.

Jav nodded affirmatively. The girl smiled, and then, brushing past Carthoris, she stepped swiftly toward the growling carnivore.

In low, firm tones she spoke to it as she had spoken to the banths of the Golden Cliffs and the scavengers before the walls of Lothar.

The beast ceased its growling. With lowered head and cat-like purr, it came slinking to the girl's feet. Thuvia turned toward Carthoris.

"It is but a banth," she said. "We have nothing to fear from it."

Carthoris smiled.

"I did not fear it," he replied, "for I, too, believed it to be only a banth, and I have my long-sword."

Jav sat up and gazed at the spectacle before him—the slender girl weaving her fingers in the tawny mane of the huge creature that he had thought divine, while Komal rubbed his hideous snout against her side.

"So this is your god!" laughed Thuvia.

Jav looked bewildered. He scarce knew whether he dare chance offending Komal or not, for so strong is the power of superstition that even though we know that we have been reverencing a sham, yet still we hesitate to admit the validity of our newfound convictions.

"Yes," he said, "this is Komal. For ages the enemies of Tario have been hurled to this pit to fill his maw, for Komal must be fed."

"Is there any way out of this chamber to the avenues of the city?" asked Carthoris.

Jav shrugged.

"I do not know," he replied. "Never have I been here before, nor ever have I cared to do so."

"Come," suggested Thuvia, "let us explore. There must be a way out."

Together the three approached the doorway through which Komal had entered the apartment that was to have witnessed their deaths. Beyond was a low-roofed lair, with a small door at the far end.

This, to their delight, opened to the lifting of an ordinary latch, letting them into a circular arena, surrounded by tiers of seats.

"Here is where Komal is fed in public," explained Jav. "Had Tario dared it would have been here that our fates had been sealed; but he feared too much thy keen blade, red man, and so he hurled us all downward to the pit. I did not know how closely connected were the two chambers. Now we may easily reach the avenues and the city gates. Only the bowmen may dispute the right of way, and, knowing their secret, I doubt that they have power to harm us."

Another door led to a flight of steps that rose from the arena level upward through the seats to an exit at the back of the hall. Beyond this was a straight, broad corridor, running directly through the palace to the gardens at the side.

No one appeared to question them as they advanced, mighty Komal pacing by the girl's side.

"Where are the people of the palace—the jeddak's retinue?" asked Carthoris. "Even in the city streets as we came through I scarce saw sign of a human being, yet all about are evidences of a mighty population."

Jav sighed.

"Poor Lothar," he said. "It is indeed a city of ghosts. There are scarce a thousand of us left, who once were numbered in the millions. Our great city is peopled by the creatures of our own imaginings. For our own needs we do not take the trouble to materialize these peoples of our brain, yet they are apparent to us.

"Even now I see great throngs lining the avenue, hastening to and fro in the round of their duties. I see women and children laughing on the balconies—these we are forbidden to materialize; but yet I see them—they are here.... But why not?" he mused. "No longer need I fear Tario—he has done his worst, and failed. Why not indeed?

"Stay, friends," he continued. "Would you see Lothar in all her glory?"

Carthoris and Thuvia nodded their assent, more out of courtesy than because they fully grasped the import of his mutterings.

Jav gazed at them penetratingly for an instant, then, with a wave of his hand, cried: "Look!"

The sight that met them was awe-inspiring. Where before there had been naught but deserted pavements and scarlet swards, yawning windows and tenantless doors, now swarmed a countless multitude of happy, laughing people.

"It is the past," said Jav in a low voice. "They do not see us—they but live the old dead past of ancient Lothar—the dead and crumbled Lothar of antiquity, which stood upon the shore of Throxus, mightiest of the five oceans.

"See those fine, upstanding men swinging along the broad avenue? See the young girls and the women smile upon them? See the men greet them with love and respect? Those be seafarers coming up from their ships which lie at the quays at the city's edge.

"Brave men, they—ah, but the glory of Lothar has faded! See their weapons. They alone bore arms, for they crossed the five seas to strange places where dangers were. With their passing passed the martial spirit of the Lotharians, leaving, as the ages rolled by, a race of spineless cowards.

"We hated war, and so we trained not our youth in warlike ways. Thus followed our undoing, for when the seas dried and the green hordes encroached upon us we could do naught but flee. But we remembered the seafaring bowmen of the days of our glory—it is the memory of these which we hurl upon our enemies."

As Jav ceased speaking, the picture faded, and once more, the three took up their way toward the distant gates, along deserted avenues.

Twice they sighted Lotharians of flesh and blood. At sight of them and the huge banth which they must have recognized as Komal, the citizens turned and fled.

"They will carry word of our flight to Tario," cried Jav, "and soon he will send his bowmen after us. Let us hope that our theory is correct, and that their shafts are powerless against minds cognizant of their unreality. Otherwise we are doomed.

"Explain, red man, to the woman the truths that I have explained to you, that she may meet the arrows with a stronger countersuggestion of immunity."

Carthoris did as Jav bid him; but they came to the great gates without sign of pursuit developing. Here Jav set in motion the mechanism that rolled the huge, wheellike gate aside, and a moment later the three, accompanied by the banth, stepped out into the plain before Lothar.

Scarce had they covered a hundred yards when the sound of many men shouting arose behind them. As they turned they saw a company of bowmen debouching upon the plain from the gate through which they had but just passed.

Upon the wall above the gate were a number of Lotharians, among whom Jav recognized Tario. The jeddak stood glaring at them, evidently concentrating all the forces of his trained mind upon them. That he was making a supreme effort to render his imaginary creatures deadly was apparent.

Jav turned white, and commenced to tremble. At the crucial moment he appeared to lose the courage of his conviction. The great banth turned back toward the advancing bowmen and growled. Carthoris placed himself between Thuvia and the enemy and, facing them, awaited the outcome of their charge.

Suddenly an inspiration came to Carthoris.

"Hurl your own bowmen against Tario's!" he cried to Jav. "Let us see a materialized battle between two mentalities."

The suggestion seemed to hearten the Lotharian, and in another moment the three stood behind solid ranks of huge bowmen who hurled taunts and menaces at the advancing company emerging from the walled city.

Jav was a new man the moment his battalions stood between him and Tario. One could almost have sworn the man believed these creatures of his strange hypnotic power to be real flesh and blood.

With hoarse battle cries they charged the bowmen of Tario. Barbed shafts flew thick and fast. Men fell, and the ground was red with gore.

Carthoris and Thuvia had difficulty in reconciling the reality of it all with their knowledge of the truth. They saw utan after utan march from the gate in perfect step to reinforce the outnumbered company which Tario had first sent forth to arrest them.

They saw Jav's forces grow correspondingly until all about them rolled a sea of fighting, cursing warriors, and the dead lay in heaps about the field.

Jav and Tario seemed to have forgotten all else beside the

struggling bowmen that surged to and fro, filling the broad field between the forest and the city.

The wood loomed close behind Thuvia and Carthoris. The latter cast a glance toward Jav.

"Come!" he whispered to the girl. "Let them fight out their empty battle—neither, evidently, has power to harm the other. They are like two controversialists hurling words at one another. While they are engaged we may as well be devoting our energies to an attempt to find the passage through the cliffs to the plain beyond."

As he spoke, Jav, turning from the battle for an instant, caught his words. He saw the girl move to accompany the Heliumite. A cunning look leaped to the Lotharian's eyes.

The thing that lay beyond that look had been deep in his heart since first he had laid eyes upon Thuvia of Ptarth. He had not recognized it, however, until now that she seemed about to pass out of his existence.

He centered his mind upon the Heliumite and the girl for an instant.

Carthoris saw Thuvia of Ptarth step forward with outstretched hand. He was surprised at this sudden softening toward him, and it was with a full heart that he let his fingers close upon hers, as together they turned away from forgotten Lothar, into the woods, and bent their steps toward the distant mountains.

As the Lotharian had turned toward them, Thuvia had been surprised to hear Carthoris suddenly voice a new plan.

"Remain here with Jav," she had heard him say, "while I go to search for the passage through the cliffs."

She had dropped back in surprise and disappointment, for she knew that there was no reason why she should not have accompanied him. Certainly she should have been safer with him than left here alone with the Lotharian.

And Jav watched the two and smiled his cunning smile.

When Carthoris had disappeared within the wood, Thuvia seated herself apathetically upon the scarlet sward to watch the seemingly interminable struggles of the bowmen.

The long afternoon dragged its weary way toward darkness, and still the imaginary legions charged and retreated. The sun was about to set when Tario commenced to withdraw his troops slowly toward the city.

His plan for cessation of hostilities through the night evidently met with Jav's entire approval, for he caused his forces to form themselves in orderly utans and march just within the edge of the wood, where they were soon busily engaged in preparing their evening meal, and spreading down their sleeping silks and furs for the night.

Thuvia could scarce repress a smile as she noted the scrupulous care with which Jav's imaginary men attended to each tiny detail of deportment as truly as if they had been real flesh and blood.

Sentries were posted between the camp and the city. Officers clanked hither and thither issuing commands and seeing to it that they were properly carried out.

Thuvia turned toward Jav.

"Why is it," she asked, "that you observe such careful nicety in the regulation of your creatures when Tario knows quite as well as you that they are but figments of your brain? Why not permit them simply to dissolve into thin air until you again require their futile service?"

"You do not understand them," replied Jav. "While they exist they are real. I do but call them into being now, and in a way direct their general actions. But thereafter, until I dissolve them, they are as actual as you or I. Their officers command them, under my guidance. I am the general—that is all. And the psychological effect upon the enemy is far greater than were I to treat them merely as substanceless vagaries.

"Then, too," continued the Lotharian, "there is always the hope, which with us is little short of belief, that someday these materializations will merge into the real—that they will remain, some of them, after we have dissolved their fellows, and that thus we shall have discovered a means for perpetuating our dying race.

"Some there are who claim already to have accomplished the thing. It is generally supposed that the etherealists have quite a few among their number who are permanent materializations. It is even said that such is Tario, but that cannot be, for he existed before we had discovered the full possibilities of suggestion.

"There are others among us who insist that none of us is real. That we could not have existed all these ages without material food and water had we ourselves been material. Although I am a realist, I rather incline toward this belief myself.

"It seems well and sensibly based upon the belief that our ancient forbears developed before their extinction such wondrous mentalities that some of the stronger minds among them lived after the death of their bodies—that we are but the deathless minds of individuals long dead.

"It would appear possible, and yet in so far as I am concerned I have all the attributes of corporeal existence. I eat, I sleep"—he paused, casting a meaning look upon the girl—"I love!"

Thuvia could not mistake the palpable meaning of his words and expression. She turned away with a little shrug of disgust that was not lost upon the Lotharian.

He came close to her and seized her arm.

"Why not Jav?" he cried. "Who more honorable than the second of the world's most ancient race? Your Heliumite? He has gone. He has deserted you to your fate to save himself. Come, be Jav's!"

Thuvia of Ptarth rose to her full height, her lifted shoulder turned toward the man, her haughty chin upraised, a scornful twist to her lips.

"You lie!" she said quietly, "the Heliumite knows less of disloyalty than he knows of fear, and of fear he is as ignorant as the unhatched young."

"Then where is he?" taunted the Lotharian. "I tell you he has fled the valley. He has left you to your fate. But Jav will see that it is a pleasant one. Tomorrow we shall return into Lothar at the head of my victorious army, and I shall be jeddak and you shall be my consort. Come!" And he attempted to crush her to his breast.

The girl struggled to free herself, striking at the man with her metal armlets. Yet still he drew her toward him, until both were suddenly startled by a hideous growl that rumbled from the dark wood close behind them.

X

Kar Komak, the Bowman

s Carthoris moved through the forest toward the distant cliffs with Thuvia's hand still tight pressed in his, he wondered a little at the girl's continued silence, yet the contact of her cool palm against his was so pleasant that he feared to break the spell of her newfound reliance in him by speaking.

Onward through the dim wood they passed until the shadows of the quick coming Martian night commenced to close down upon them. Then it was that Carthoris turned to speak to the girl at his side.

They must plan together for the future. It was his idea to pass through the cliffs at once if they could locate the passage, and he was quite positive that they were now close to it; but he wanted her assent to the proposition.

As his eyes rested upon her, he was struck by her strangely ethereal appearance. She seemed suddenly to have dissolved into the tenuous substance of a dream, and as he continued to gaze upon her, she faded slowly from his sight.

For an instant he was dumbfounded, and then the whole truth flashed suddenly upon him. Jav had caused him to believe that Thuvia was accompanying him through the wood while, as a matter of fact, he had detained the girl for himself!

Carthoris was horrified. He cursed himself for his stupidity, and yet he knew that the fiendish power which the Lotharian had invoked to confuse him might have deceived any.

Scarce had he realized the truth than he had started to retrace his steps toward Lothar, but now he moved at a trot, the Earthly thews that he had inherited from his father carrying him swiftly over the soft carpet of fallen leaves and rank grass.

Thuria's brilliant light flooded the plain before the walled city of Lothar as Carthoris broke from the wood opposite the great gate that had given the fugitives egress from the city earlier in the day.

At first he saw no indication that there was another than himself anywhere about. The plain was deserted. No myriad bowmen camped now beneath the overhanging verdure of the giant trees. No gory heaps of tortured dead defaced the beauty of the scarlet sward. All was silence. All was peace.

The Heliumite, scarce pausing at the forest's verge, pushed on across the plain toward the city, when presently he descried a huddled form in the grass at his feet.

It was the body of a man, lying prone. Carthoris turned the figure over upon its back. It was Jav, but torn and mangled almost beyond recognition.

The prince bent low to note if any spark of life remained, and as he did so the lids raised and dull, suffering eyes looked up into his.

"The Princess of Ptarth!" cried Carthoris. "Where is she? Answer me, man, or I complete the work that another has so well begun."

"Komal," muttered Jav. "He sprang upon me . . . and would have devoured me but for the girl. Then they went away together into the wood—the girl and the great banth . . . her fingers twined in his tawny mane."

"Which way went they?" asked Carthoris.

"There," replied Jav faintly, "toward the passage through the cliffs."

The Prince of Helium waited to hear no more, but springing to his feet, raced back again into the forest.

It was dawn when he reached the mouth of the dark tunnel that would lead him to the other world beyond this valley of ghostly memories and strange hypnotic influences and menaces.

Within the long, dark passages he met with no accident or obstacle, coming at last into the light of day beyond the mountains, and no great distance from the southern verge of the domains of the Torquasians, not more than one hundred and fifty haad at the most.

From the boundary of Torquas to the city of Aaanthor is a distance of some two hundred haads, so that the Heliumite had before him a journey of more than one hundred and fifty Earth miles between him and Aaanthor.

He could at best but hazard a chance guess that toward Aaanthor Thuvia would take her flight. There lay the nearest water, and there might be expected someday a rescuing party from her father's empire; for Carthoris knew Thuvan Dihn well enough to know that he would leave no stone unturned until he had tracked down the truth as to his daughter's abduction, and learned all that there might be to learn of her whereabouts.

He realized, of course, that the trick which had laid suspicion upon him would greatly delay the discovery of the truth, but little did he guess to what vast proportions had the results of the villainy of Astok of Dusar already grown.

Even as he emerged from the mouth of the passage to look across the foothills in the direction of Aaanthor, a Ptarth battle fleet was winging its majestic way slowly toward the twin cities of Helium, while from far distant Kaol raced another mighty armada to join forces with its ally.

He did not know that in the face of the circumstantial evidence against him even his own people had commenced to entertain suspicions that he might have stolen the Ptarthian princess.

He did not know of the lengths to which the Dusarians had gone to disrupt the friendship and alliance which existed between the three great powers of the eastern hemisphere—Helium, Ptarth and Kaol.

How Dusarian emissaries had found employment in important posts in the foreign offices of the three great nations, and how, through these men, messages from one jeddak to another were altered and garbled until the patience and pride of the three rulers and former friends could no longer endure the humiliations and insults contained in these falsified papers—not any of this he knew.

Nor did he know how even to the last John Carter, Warlord of Mars, had refused to permit the jeddak of Helium to declare war against either Ptarth or Kaol, because of his implicit belief in his son, and that eventually all would be satisfactorily explained.

And now two great fleets were moving upon Helium, while the Dusarian spies at the court of Tardos Mors saw to it that the twin cities remained in ignorance of their danger.

War had been declared by Thuvan Dihn, but the messenger who had been dispatched with the proclamation had been a Dusarian who had seen to it that no word of warning reached the twin cities of the approach of a hostile fleet.

For several days diplomatic relations had been severed between Helium and her two most powerful neighbors, and with the departure of the ministers had come a total cessation of wireless communication between the disputants, as is usual upon Barsoom.

But of all this Carthoris was ignorant. All that interested him at present was the finding of Thuvia of Ptarth. Her trail beside that of the huge banth had been well marked to the tunnel, and was once more visible leading southward into the foothills.

As he followed rapidly downward toward the dead sea-bottom, where he knew he must lose the spoor in the resilient ochre vegetation, he was suddenly surprised to see a naked man approaching him from the northeast.

As the fellow drew closer, Carthoris halted to await his coming. He knew that the man was unarmed, and that he was apparently a Lotharian, for his skin was white and his hair auburn.

He approached the Heliumite without sign of fear, and when quite close called out the cheery Barsoomian "kaor" of greeting.

"Who are you?" asked Carthoris.

"I am Kar Komak, odwar of the bowmen," replied the other. "A strange thing has happened to me. For ages Tario has been bringing me into existence as he needed the services of the army of his mind. Of all the bowmen it has been Kar Komak who has been oftenest materialized.

"For a long time Tario has been concentrating his mind upon my permanent materialization. It has been an obsession with him that someday this thing could be accomplished and the future of Lothar assured. He asserted that matter was nonexistent except in the imagination of man—that all was mental, and so he believed that by persisting in his suggestion he could eventually make of me a permanent suggestion in the minds of all creatures.

"Yesterday he succeeded, but at such a time! It must have come all unknown to him, as it came to me without my knowledge, as, with my horde of yelling bowmen, I pursued the fleeing Torquasians back to their ochre plains.

"As darkness settled and the time came for us to fade once more into thin air, I suddenly found myself alone upon the edge of the great plain which lies yonder at the foot of the low hills.

"My men were gone back to the nothingness from which they had sprung, but I remained—naked and unarmed.

"At first I could not understand, but at last came a realization of what had occurred. Tario's long suggestions had at last prevailed, and Kar Komak had become a reality in the world of men; but my harness and my weapons had faded away with my fellows, leaving me naked and unarmed in a hostile country far from Lothar."

"You wish to return to Lothar?" asked Carthoris.

"No!" replied Kar Komak quickly. "I have no love for Tario.

102

Being a creature of his mind, I know him too well. He is cruel and tyrannical—a master I have no desire to serve. Now that he has succeeded in accomplishing my permanent materialization, he will be unbearable, and he will go on until he has filled Lothar with his creatures. I wonder if he has succeeded as well with the maid of Lothar."

"I thought there were no women there," said Carthoris.

"In a hidden apartment in the palace of Tario," replied Kar Komak, "the jeddak has maintained the suggestion of a beautiful girl, hoping that someday she would become permanent. I have seen her there. She is wonderful! But for her sake I hope that Tario succeeds not so well with her as he has with me.

"Now, red man, I have told you of myself—what of you?"

Carthoris liked the face and manner of the bowman. There had been no sign of doubt or fear in his expression as he had approached the heavily-armed Heliumite, and he had spoken directly and to the point.

So the Prince of Helium told the bowman of Lothar who he was and what adventure had brought him to this far country.

"Good!" exclaimed the other, when he had done. "Kar Komak will accompany you. Together we shall find the Princess of Ptarth and with you Kar Komak will return to the world of men—such a world as he knew in the long-gone past when the ships of mighty Lothar ploughed angry Throxus, and the roaring surf beat against the barrier of these parched and dreary hills."

"What mean you?" asked Carthoris. "Had you really a former actual existence?"

"Most assuredly," replied Kar Komak. "In my day I commanded the fleets of Lothar—mightiest of all the fleets that sailed the five salt seas.

"Wherever men lived upon Barsoom there was the name of Kar Komak known and respected. Peaceful were the land races in those distant days—only the seafarers were warriors; but now has the glory of the past faded, nor did I think until I met you that there remained upon Barsoom a single person of our own mould who lived and loved and fought as did the ancient seafarers of my time.

"Ah, but it will seem good to see men once again—real men! Never had I much respect for the landsmen of my day. They remained in their walled cities wasting their time in play, depending for their protection entirely upon the sea race. And the poor creatures who remain, the Tarios and Javs of Lothar, are even worse than their ancient forbears."

Carthoris was a trifle skeptical as to the wisdom of permitting the stranger to attach himself to him. There was always the chance that he was but the essence of some hypnotic treachery which Tario or Jav was attempting to exert upon the Heliumite; and yet, so sincere had been the manner and the words of the bowman, so much the fighting man did he seem, but Carthoris could not find it in his heart to doubt him.

The outcome of the matter was that he gave the naked odwar leave to accompany him, and together they set out upon the spoor of Thuvia and Komal.

Down to the ochre sea-bottom the trail led. There it disappeared, as Carthoris had known that it would; but where it entered the plain its direction had been toward Aaanthor and so toward Aaanthor the two turned their faces.

It was a long and tedious journey, fraught with many dangers. The bowman could not travel at the pace set by Carthoris, whose muscles carried him with great rapidity over the face of the small planet, the force of gravity of which exerts so much less retarding power than that of the Earth. Fifty miles a day is a fair average for a Barsoomian, but the son of John Carter might easily have covered a hundred or more miles had he cared to desert his newfound comrade.

All the way they were in constant danger of discovery by roving bands of Torquasians, and especially was this true before they reached the boundary of Torquas.

Good fortune was with them, however, and although they sighted two detachments of the savage green men, they were not themselves seen.

And so they came, upon the morning of the third day, within sight of the glistening domes of distant Aaanthor. Throughout the journey Carthoris had ever strained his eyes ahead in search of Thuvia and the great banth; but not till now had he seen aught to give him hope.

This morning, far ahead, halfway between themselves and Aaanthor, the men saw two tiny figures moving toward the city. For a moment they watched them intently. Then Carthoris, convinced, leaped forward at a rapid run, Kar Komak following as swiftly as he could.

The Heliumite shouted to attract the girl's attention, and presently he was rewarded by seeing her turn and stand looking toward him. At her side the great banth stood with up-pricked ears, watching the approaching man.

Not yet could Thuvia of Ptarth have recognized Carthoris, though that it was he she must have been convinced, for she waited there for him without sign of fear.

Presently he saw her point toward the northwest, beyond him. Without slackening his pace, he turned his eyes in the direction she indicated.

Racing silently over the thick vegetation, not half a mile behind, came a score of fierce green warriors, charging him upon their mighty thoats.

To their right was Kar Komak, naked and unarmed, yet running valiantly toward Carthoris and shouting warning as though he, too, had but just discovered the silent, menacing company that moved so swiftly forward with couched spears and ready long-swords.

Carthoris shouted to the Lotharian, warning him back, for he knew that he could but uselessly sacrifice his life by placing himself, all unarmed, in the path of the cruel and relentless savages.

But Kar Komak never hesitated. With shouts of encouragement to his new friend, he hurried onward toward the Prince of Helium. The red man's heart leaped in response to this exhibition of courage and self-sacrifice. He regretted now that he had not thought to give Kar Komak one of his swords; but it was too late to attempt it, for should he wait for the Lotharian to overtake him or return to meet him, the Torquasians would reach Thuvia of Ptarth before he could do so.

Even as it was, it would be nip and tuck as to who came first to her side.

Again he turned his face in her direction, and now, from Aaanthor way, he saw a new force hastening toward them—two medium-sized war craft—and even at the distance they still were from him he discerned the device of Dusar upon their bows.

Now, indeed, seemed little hope for Thuvia of Ptarth. With savage warriors of the hordes of Torquas charging toward her from one direction, and no less implacable enemies, in the form of the creatures of Astok, Prince of Dusar, bearing down upon her from another, while only a banth, a red warrior, and an unarmed bowman were near to defend her, her plight was quite hopeless and her cause already lost ere ever it was contested.

As Thuvia saw Carthoris approaching, she felt again that unaccountable sensation of entire relief from responsibility and fear that she had experienced upon a former occasion. Nor could she account for it while her mind still tried to convince her heart that the Prince of Helium had been instrumental in her abduction from her father's court. She only knew that she was glad when he was by her side, and that with him there all things seemed possible—even such impossible things as escape from her present predicament.

Now had he stopped, panting, before her. A brave smile of encouragement lit his face.

"Courage, my princess," he whispered.

To the girl's memory flashed the occasion upon which he had used those same words—in the throne-room of Tario of Lothar as they had commenced to slip down the sinking marble floor toward an unknown fate.

Then she had not chidden him for the use of that familiar salutation, nor did she chide him now, though she was promised to another. She wondered at herself—flushing at her own turpitude; for upon Barsoom it is a shameful thing for a woman to listen to those two words from another than her husband or her betrothed.

Carthoris saw her flush of mortification, and in an instant regretted his words. There was but a moment before the green warriors would be upon them.

"Forgive me!" said the man in a low voice. "Let my great love be my excuse—that, and the belief that I have but a moment more of life," and with the words he turned to meet the foremost of the green warriors.

The fellow was charging with couched spear, but Carthoris leaped to one side, and as the great thoat and its rider hurtled harmlessly past him he swung his long-sword in a mighty cut that clove the green carcass in twain.

At the same moment Kar Komak leaped with bare hands clawing at the leg of another of the huge riders; the balance of the horde raced in to close quarters, dismounting the better to wield their favorite long-swords; the Dusarian fliers touched the soft carpet of the ochre-clad sea-bottom, disgorging fifty fighting men from their bowels; and into the swirling sea of cutting, slashing swords sprang Komal, the great banth.

XI

GREEN MEN AND WHITE APES

Torquasian sword smote a glancing blow across the forehead of Carthoris. He had a fleeting vision of soft arms about his neck, and warm lips close to his before he lost consciousness.

How long he lay there senseless he could not guess; but when he opened his eyes again he was alone, except for the bodies of the dead green men and Dusarians, and the carcass of a great banth that lay half across his own.

Thuvia was gone, nor was the body of Kar Komak among the dead.

Weak from loss of blood, Carthoris made his way slowly toward Aaanthor, reaching its outskirts at dark.

He wanted water more than any other thing, and so he kept on up a broad avenue toward the great central plaza, where he knew the precious fluid was to be found in a half-ruined building opposite the great palace of the ancient jeddak, who once had ruled this mighty city.

Disheartened and discouraged by the strange sequence of events that seemed fore-ordained to thwart his every attempt to serve the Princess of Ptarth, he paid little or no attention to his surroundings, moving through the deserted city as though no great white apes lurked in the black shadows of the mystery-haunted piles that flanked the broad avenues and the great plaza.

But if Carthoris was careless of his surroundings, not so other eyes that watched his entrance into the plaza, and followed his slow footsteps toward the marble pile that housed the tiny, half-choked spring whose water one might gain only by scratching a deep hole in the red sand that covered it.

And as the Heliumite entered the small building a dozen mighty, grotesque figures emerged from the doorway of the palace to speed noiselessly across the plaza toward him.

For half an hour Carthoris remained in the building, digging for water and gaining the few much-needed drops which were the fruits of his labor. Then he rose and slowly left the structure. Scarce had he stepped beyond the threshold than twelve Torquasian warriors leaped upon him.

No time then to draw long-sword; but swift from his harness flew his long, slim dagger, and as he went down beneath them more than a single green heart ceased beating at the bite of that keen point.

Then they overpowered him and took his weapons away; but only nine of the twelve warriors who had crossed the plaza returned with their prize.

They dragged their prisoner roughly to the palace pits, where in utter darkness they chained him with rusty links to the solid masonry of the wall.

"Tomorrow Thar Ban will speak with you," they said. "Now he sleeps. But great will be his pleasure when he learns who has wandered amongst us—and great will be the pleasure of Hortan Gur when Thar Ban drags before him the mad fool who dared prick the great jeddak with his sword."

Then they left him to the silence and the darkness.

For what seemed hours Carthoris squatted upon the stone floor of his prison, his back against the wall in which was sunk the heavy eye-bolt that secured the chain which held him.

Then, from out of the mysterious blackness before him, there came to his ears the sound of naked feet moving stealthily upon stone—approaching nearer and nearer to where he lay, unarmed and defenseless.

Minutes passed—minutes that seemed hours—during which time periods of sepulchral silence would be followed by a repetition of the uncanny scraping of naked feet slinking warily upon him.

At last he heard a sudden rush of unshod soles across the empty blackness, and at a little distance a scuffling sound, heavy breathing, and once what he thought the muttered imprecation of a man battling against great odds. Then the clanging of a chain, and a noise as of the snapping back against stone of a broken link.

Again came silence. But for a moment only. Now he heard once more the soft feet approaching him. He thought that he discerned wicked eyes gleaming fearfully at him through the darkness. He knew that he could hear the heavy breathing of powerful lungs.

Then came the rush of many feet toward him, and the *things* were upon him.

Hands terminating in manlike fingers clutched at his throat and arms and legs. Hairy bodies strained and struggled against his own smooth hide as he battled in grim silence against these horrid foemen in the darkness of the pits of ancient Aaanthor.

Thewed like some giant god was Carthoris of Helium, yet in the clutches of these unseen creatures of the pit's Stygian night he was helpless as a frail woman.

Yet he battled on, striking futile blows against great, hispid breasts he could not see; feeling thick, squat throats beneath his fingers; the drool of saliva upon his cheek, and hot, foul breath in his nostrils.

Fangs, too, mighty fangs, he knew were close, and why they did not sink into his flesh he could not guess.

At last he became aware of the mighty surging of a number of his antagonists back and forth upon the great chain that held him, and presently came the same sound that he had heard at a little distance

110

from him a short time before he had been attacked—his chain had parted and the broken end snapped back against the stone wall.

Now he was seized upon either side and dragged at a rapid pace through the dark corridors—toward what fate he could not even guess.

At first he had thought his foes might be of the tribe of Torquas, but their hairy bodies belied that belief. Now he was at last quite sure of their identity, though why they had not killed and devoured him at once he could not imagine.

After half an hour or more of rapid racing through the underground passages that are a distinguishing feature of all Barsoomian cities, modern as well as ancient, his captors suddenly emerged into the moonlight of a courtyard, far from the central plaza.

Immediately Carthoris saw that he was in the power of a tribe of the great white apes of Barsoom. All that had caused him doubt before as to the identity of his attackers was the hairiness of their breasts, for the white apes are entirely hairless except for a great shock bristling from their heads.

Now he saw the cause of that which had deceived him—across the chest of each of them were strips of hairy hide, usually of banth, in imitation of the harness of the green warriors who so often camped at their deserted city.

Carthoris had read of the existence of tribes of apes that seemed to be progressing slowly toward higher standards of intelligence. Into the hands of such, he realized, he had fallen; but—what were their intentions toward him?

As he glanced about the courtyard, he saw fully fifty of the hideous beasts, squatting on their haunches, and at a little distance from him another human being, closely guarded.

As his eyes met those of his fellow-captive a smile lit the other's face, and: "Kaor, red man!" burst from his lips. It was Kar Komak, the bowman.

"Kaor!" cried Carthoris, in response. "How came you here, and what befell the princess?"

"Red men like yourself descended in mighty ships that sailed the air, even as the great ships of my distant day sailed the five seas," replied Kar Komak. "They fought with the green men of Torquas. They slew Komal, god of Lothar. I thought they were your friends, and I was glad when finally those of them who survived the battle carried the red girl to one of the ships and sailed away with her into the safety of the high air.

"Then the green men seized me, and carried me to a great, empty city, where they chained me to a wall in a black pit. Afterward came these and dragged me hither. And what of you, red man?"

Carthoris related all that had befallen him, and as the two men talked the great apes squatted about them watching them intently.

"What are we to do now?" asked the bowman.

"Our case looks rather hopeless," replied Carthoris ruefully. "These creatures are born man-eaters. Why they have not already devoured us I cannot imagine—there!" he whispered. "See? The end is coming."

Kar Komak looked in the direction Carthoris indicated to see a huge ape advancing with a mighty bludgeon.

"It is thus they like best to kill their prey," said Carthoris.

"Must we die without a struggle?" asked Kar Komak.

"Not I," replied Carthoris, "though I know how futile our best defense must be against these mighty brutes! Oh, for a long-sword!"

"Or a good bow," added Kar Komak, "and a utan of bowmen."

At the words Carthoris half sprang to his feet, only to be dragged roughly down by his guard.

"Kar Komak!" he cried. "Why cannot you do what Tario and Jav did? They had no bowmen other than those of their own creation. You must know the secret of their power. Call forth your own utan, Kar Komak!"

The Lotharian looked at Carthoris in wide-eyed astonishment as the full purport of the suggestion bore in upon his understanding.

"Why not?" he murmured.

The savage ape bearing the mighty bludgeon was slinking toward Carthoris. The Heliumite's fingers were working as he kept his eyes upon his executioner. Kar Komak bent his gaze penetratingly upon the apes. The effort of his mind was evidenced in the sweat upon his contracted brows.

The creature that was to slay the red man was almost within arm's reach of his prey when Carthoris heard a hoarse shout from the opposite side of the courtyard. In common with the squatting apes and the demon with the club he turned in the direction of the sound, to see a company of sturdy bowmen rushing from the doorway of a nearby building.

With screams of rage the apes leaped to their feet to meet the charge. A volley of arrows met them halfway, sending a dozen rolling lifeless to the ground. Then the apes closed with their adversaries. All their attention was occupied by the attackers—even the guard had deserted the prisoners to join in the battle.

"Come!" whispered Kar Komak. "Now may we escape while their attention is diverted from us by my bowmen."

"And leave those brave fellows leaderless?" cried Carthoris, whose loyal nature revolted at the merest suggestion of such a thing.

Kar Komak laughed.

"You forget," he said, "that they are but thin air—figments of my brain. They will vanish, unscathed, when we have no further need for them. Praised be your first ancestor, redman, that you thought of this chance in time! It would never have occurred to me to imagine that I might wield the same power that brought me into existence."

"You are right," said Carthoris. "Still, I hate to leave them, though there is naught else to do," and so the two turned from the courtyard, and making their way into one of the broad avenues, crept stealthily in the shadows of the building toward the great central plaza upon which were the buildings occupied by the green warriors when they visited the deserted city.

When they had come to the plaza's edge Carthoris halted.

"Wait here," he whispered. "I go to fetch thoats, since on foot we may never hope to escape the clutches of these green fiends."

To reach the courtyard where the thoats were kept it was necessary for Carthoris to pass through one of the buildings which surrounded the square. Which were occupied and which not he could not even guess, so he was compelled to take considerable chances to gain the enclosure in which he could hear the restless beasts squealing and quarreling among themselves.

Chance carried him through a dark doorway into a large chamber in which lay a score or more green warriors wrapped in their sleeping silks and furs. Scarce had Carthoris passed through the short hallway that connected the door of the building and the great room beyond it than he became aware of the presence of something or someone in the hallway through which he had but just passed.

He heard a man yawn, and then, behind him, he saw the figure of a sentry rise from where the fellow had been dozing, and stretching himself resume his wakeful watchfulness.

Carthoris realized that he must have passed within a foot of the warrior, doubtless rousing him from his slumber. To retreat now would be impossible. Yet to cross through that roomful of sleeping warriors seemed almost equally beyond the pale of possibility.

Carthoris shrugged his broad shoulders and chose the lesser evil. Warily he entered the room. At his right, against the wall, leaned several swords and rifles and spears—extra weapons which the warriors had stacked here ready to their hands should there be a night alarm calling them suddenly from slumber. Beside each sleeper lay his weapon—these were never far from their owners from childhood to death.

The sight of the swords made the young man's palm itch. He stepped quickly to them, selecting two short-swords—one for Kar Komak, the other for himself; also some trappings for his naked comrade.

Then he started directly across the center of the apartment among the sleeping Torquasians.

Not a man of them moved until Carthoris had completed more than half of the short though dangerous journey. Then a fellow directly in his path turned restlessly upon his sleeping silks and furs.

The Heliumite paused above him, one of the short-swords in readiness should the warrior awaken. For what seemed an eternity to the young prince the green man continued to move uneasily upon his couch, then, as though actuated by springs, he leaped to his feet and faced the red man.

Instantly Carthoris struck, but not before a savage grunt escaped the other's lips. In an instant the room was in turmoil. Warriors leaped to their feet, grasping their weapons as they rose, and shouting to one another for an explanation of the disturbance.

To Carthoris all within the room was plainly visible in the dim light reflected from without, for the further moon stood directly at zenith; but to the eyes of the newly-awakened green men objects as yet had not taken on familiar forms—they but saw vaguely the figures of warriors moving about their apartment.

Now one stumbled against the corpse of him whom Carthoris had slain. The fellow stooped and his hand came in contact with the cleft skull. He saw about him the giant figures of other green men, and so he jumped to the only conclusion that was open to him.

"The Thurds!" he cried. "The Thurds are upon us! Rise, warriors of Torquas, and drive home your swords within the hearts of Torquas' ancient enemies!"

Instantly the green men began to fall upon one another with naked swords. Their savage lust of battle was aroused. To fight, to kill, to die with cold steel buried in their vitals! Ah, that to them was Nirvana.

Carthoris was quick to guess their error and take advantage of it. He knew that in the pleasure of killing they might fight on long after they had discovered their mistake, unless their attention was distracted by sight of the real cause of the altercation, and so he lost no time in continuing across the room to the doorway upon the opposite side, which opened into the inner court, where the savage thoats were squealing and fighting among themselves.

Once here he had no easy task before him. To catch and mount one of these habitually rageful and intractable beasts was no child's play under the best of conditions; but now, when silence and time were such important considerations, it might well have seemed quite hopeless to a less resourceful and optimistic man than the son of the great warlord.

From his father he had learned much concerning the traits of these mighty beasts, and from Tars Tarkas, also, when he had visited that great green jeddak among his horde at Thark. So now he centered upon the work in hand all that he had ever learned about them from others and from his own experience, for he, too, had ridden and handled them many times.

The temper of the thoats of Torquas appeared even shorter than their vicious cousins among the Tharks and Warhoons, and for a time it seemed unlikely that he should escape a savage charge on the part of a couple of old bulls that circled, squealing, about him; but at last he managed to get close enough to one of them to touch the beast. With the feel of his hand upon the sleek hide the creature quieted, and in answer to the telepathic command of the red man sank to its knees.

In a moment Carthoris was upon its back, guiding it toward the great gate that leads from the courtyard through a large building at one end into an avenue beyond.

The other bull, still squealing and enraged, followed after his fellow. There was no bridle upon either, for these strange creatures are controlled entirely by suggestion—when they are controlled at all.

Even in the hands of the giant green men bridle reins would be hopelessly futile against the mad savagery and mastodonic strength of the thoat, and so they are guided by that strange telepathic power with which the men of Mars have learned to communicate in a crude way with the lower orders of their planet.

With difficulty Carthoris urged the two beasts to the gate, where, leaning down, he raised the latch. Then the thoat that he was riding placed his great shoulder to the skeel-wood planking, pushed through, and a moment later the man and the two beasts were swinging silently down the avenue to the edge of the plaza, where Kar Komak hid.

Here Carthoris found considerable difficulty in subduing the second thoat, and as Kar Komak had never before ridden one of the beasts, it seemed a most hopeless job; but at last the bowman managed to scramble to the sleek back, and again the two beasts fled softly down the moss-grown avenues toward the open sea-bottom beyond the city.

All that night and the following day and the second night they rode toward the northeast. No indication of pursuit developed, and at dawn of the second day Carthoris saw in the distance the waving ribbon of great trees that marked one of the long Barsoomian waterways.

Immediately they abandoned their thoats and approached the cultivated district on foot. Carthoris also discarded the metal from his harness, or such of it as might serve to identify him as a Heliumite, or of royal blood, for he did not know to what nation belonged this waterway, and upon Mars it is always well to assume every man and nation your enemy until you have learned the contrary.

It was mid-forenoon when the two at last entered one of the roads that cut through the cultivated districts at regular intervals, joining the arid wastes on either side with the great, white, central highway that follows through the center from end to end of the far-reaching, threadlike farm lands.

The high wall surrounding the fields served as a protection against surprise by raiding green hordes, as well as keeping the savage banths and other carnivora from the domestic animals and the human beings upon the farms.

Carthoris stopped before the first gate he came to, pounding for admission. The young man who answered his summons greeted the two hospitably, though he looked with considerable wonder upon the white skin and auburn hair of the bowman.

After he had listened for a moment to a partial narration of their escape from the Torquasians, he invited them within, took them to his house and bade the servants there prepare food for them.

As they waited in the low-ceiled, pleasant living room of the farmhouse until the meal should be ready, Carthoris drew his host into conversation that he might learn his nationality, and thus the nation under whose dominion lay the waterway where circumstance had placed him.

"I am Hal Vas," said the young man, "son of Vas Kor, of Dusar, a noble in the retinue of Astok, Prince of Dusar. At present I am Dwar of the Road for this district."

Carthoris was very glad that he had not disclosed his identity, for though he had no idea of anything that had transpired since he had left Helium, or that Astok was at the bottom of all his misfortunes, he well knew that the Dusarian had no love for him, and that he could hope for no assistance within the dominions of Dusar.

"And who are you?" asked Hal Vas. "By your appearance I take you for a fighting man, but I see no insignia upon your harness. Can it be that you are a panthan?"

Now, these wandering soldiers of fortune are common upon Barsoom, where most men love to fight. They sell their services wherever war exists, and in the occasional brief intervals when there is no organized warfare between the red nations, they join one of the numerous expeditions that are constantly being dispatched against the green men in protection of the waterways that traverse the wilder portions of the globe.

When their service is over they discard the metal of the nation they have been serving until they shall have found a new master. In the intervals they wear no insignia, their war-worn harness and grim weapons being sufficient to attest their calling.

The suggestion was a happy one, and Carthoris embraced the chance it afforded to account satisfactorily for himself. There was, however, a single drawback. In times of war such panthans as happened to be within the domain of a belligerent nation were compelled to don the insignia of that nation and fight with her warriors.

As far as Carthoris knew Dusar was not at war with any other nation, but there was never any telling when one red nation would be flying at the throat of a neighbor, even though the great and powerful alliance at the head of which was his father, John Carter, had managed to maintain a long peace upon the greater portion of Barsoom.

A pleasant smile lighted Hal Vas' face as Carthoris admitted his vocation.

"It is well," exclaimed the young man, "that you chanced to come hither, for here you will find the means of obtaining service in short order. My father, Vas Kor, is even now with me, having come hither to recruit a force for the new war against Helium."

XII

TO SAVE DUSAR

huvia of Ptarth, battling for more than life against
the lust of Jav, cast a quick glance over her shoulder toward the forest from which had rumbled the
fierce growl. Jav looked, too.

What they saw filled each with apprehension.
It was Komal, the banth-god, rushing wide-jawed upon them!

Which had he chosen for his prey? Or was it to be both?

They had not long to wait, for though the Lotharian attempted to
hold the girl between himself and the terrible fangs, the great beast
found him at last.

Then, shrieking, he attempted to fly toward Lothar, after pushing Thuvia bodily into the face of the man-eater. But his flight was of
short duration. In a moment Komal was upon him, rending his throat
and chest with demoniacal fury.

The girl reached their side a moment later, but it was with difficulty that she tore the mad beast from its prey. Still growling and
casting hungry glances back upon Jav, the banth at last permitted
itself to be led away into the wood.

With her giant protector by her side Thuvia set forth to find
the passage through the cliffs, that she might attempt the seemingly
impossible feat of reaching far-distant Ptarth across the more than
seventeen thousand haads of savage Barsoom.

She could not believe that Carthoris had deliberately deserted
her, and so she kept a constant watch for him; but as she bore too far

to the north in her search for the tunnel she passed the Heliumite as he was returning to Lothar in search of her.

Thuvia of Ptarth was having difficulty in determining the exact status of the Prince of Helium in her heart. She could not admit even to herself that she loved him, and yet she had permitted him to apply to her that term of endearment and possession to which a Barsoomian maid should turn deaf ears when voiced by other lips than those of her husband or fiancé my princess.

Kulan Tith, Jeddak of Kaol, to whom she was affianced, commanded her respect and admiration. Had it been that she had surrendered to her father's wishes because of pique that the handsome Heliumite had not taken advantage of his visits to her father's court to push the suit for her hand that she had been quite sure he had contemplated since that distant day the two had sat together upon the carved seat within the gorgeous Garden of the Jeddaks that graced the inner courtyard of the palace of Salensus Oll at Kadabra?

Did she love Kulan Tith? Bravely she tried to believe that she did; but all the while her eyes wandered through the coming darkness for the figure of a clean-limbed fighting man—black-haired and grey-eyed. Black was the hair of Kulan Tith; but his eyes were brown.

It was almost dark when she found the entrance to the tunnel. Safely she passed through to the hills beyond, and here, under the bright light of Mars' two moons, she halted to plan her future action.

Should she wait here in the hope that Carthoris would return in search of her? Or should she continue her way northeast toward Ptarth? Where, first, would Carthoris have gone after leaving the valley of Lothar?

Her parched throat and dry tongue gave her the answer— toward Aaanthor and water. Well, she, too, would go first to Aaanthor, where she might find more than the water she needed.

With Komal by her side she felt little fear, for he would protect her from all other savage beasts. Even the great white apes would flee the mighty banth in terror. Men only need she fear, but she must take this and many other chances before she could hope to reach her father's court again.

When at last Carthoris found her, only to be struck down by the long-sword of a green man, Thuvia prayed that the same fate might overtake her.

The sight of the red warriors leaping from their fliers had, for a moment, filled her with renewed hope—hope that Carthoris of Helium might be only stunned and that they would rescue him; but when she saw the Dusarian metal upon their harness, and that they sought only to escape with her alone from the charging Torquasians, she gave up.

Komal, too, was dead—dead across the body of the Heliumite. She was, indeed, alone now. There was none to protect her.

The Dusarian warriors dragged her to the deck of the nearest flier. All about them the green warriors surged in an attempt to wrest her from the red.

At last those who had not died in the conflict gained the decks of the two craft. The engines throbbed and purred—the propellers whirred. Quickly the swift boats shot heavenward.

Thuvia of Ptarth glanced about her. A man stood near, smiling down into her face. With a gasp of recognition she looked full into his eyes, and then with a little moan of terror and understanding she buried her face in her hands and sank to the polished skeelwood deck. It was Astok, Prince of Dusar, who bent above her.

Swift were the fliers of Astok of Dusar, and great the need for reaching his father's court as quickly as possible, for the fleets of war of Helium and Ptarth and Kaol were scattered far and wide above Barsoom. Nor would it go well with Astok or Dusar should anyone of them discover Thuvia of Ptarth a prisoner upon his own vessel.

Aaanthor lies in fifty south latitude, and forty east of Horz, the deserted seat of ancient Barsoomian culture and learning, while

Dusar lies fifteen degrees north of the equator and twenty degrees east from Horz.

Great though the distance is, the fliers covered it without a stop. Long before they had reached their destination Thuvia of Ptarth had learned several things that cleared up the doubts that had assailed her mind for many days. Scarce had they risen above Aaanthor than she recognized one of the crew as a member of the crew of that other flier that had borne her from her father's gardens to Aaanthor. The presence of Astok upon the craft settled the whole question. She had been stolen by emissaries of the Dusarian prince—Carthoris of Helium had had nothing to do with it.

Nor did Astok deny the charge when she accused him. He only smiled and pleaded his love for her.

"I would sooner mate with a white ape!" she cried, when he would have urged his suit.

Astok glowered sullenly upon her.

"You shall mate with me, Thuvia of Ptarth," he growled, "or, by your first ancestor, you shall have your preference—and mate with a white ape."

The girl made no reply, nor could he draw her into conversation during the balance of the journey.

As a matter of fact Astok was a trifle awed by the proportions of the conflict which his abduction of the Ptarthian princess had induced, nor was he over comfortable with the weight of responsibility which the possession of such a prisoner entailed.

His one thought was to get her to Dusar, and there let his father assume the responsibility. In the meantime he would be as careful as possible to do nothing to affront her, lest they all might be captured and he have to account for his treatment of the girl to one of the great jeddaks whose interest centered in her.

And so at last they came to Dusar, where Astok hid his prisoner in a secret room high in the east tower of his own palace. He had sworn his men to silence in the matter of the identity of the girl, for until he had seen his father, Nutus, Jeddak of Dusar, he dared not let anyone know whom he had brought with him from the south.

But when he appeared in the great audience chamber before the cruel-lipped man who was his sire, he found his courage oozing, and he dared not speak of the princess hid within his palace. It occurred to him to test his father's sentiments upon the subject, and so he told a tale of capturing one who claimed to know the whereabouts of Thuvia of Ptarth.

"And if you command it, Sire," he said, "I will go and capture her—fetching her here to Dusar."

Nutus frowned and shook his head.

"You have done enough already to set Ptarth and Kaol and Helium all three upon us at once should they learn your part in the theft of the Ptarth princess. That you succeeded in shifting the guilt upon the Prince of Helium was fortunate, and a masterly move of strategy; but were the girl to know the truth and ever return to her father's court, all Dusar would have to pay the penalty, and to have her here a prisoner amongst us would be an admission of guilt from the consequences of which naught could save us. It would cost me my throne, Astok, and that I have no mind to lose.

"If we had her here——" the elder man suddenly commenced to muse, repeating the phrase again and again. "If we had her here, Astok," he exclaimed fiercely. "Ah, if we but had her here and none knew that she was here! Can you not guess, man? The guilt of Dusar might be forever buried with her bones," he concluded in a low, savage whisper.

Astok, Prince of Dusar, shuddered.

Weak he was; yes, and wicked, too; but the suggestion that his father's words implied turned him cold with horror.

Cruel to their enemies are the men of Mars; but the word "enemies" is commonly interpreted to mean men only. Assassination runs riot in the great Barsoomian cities; yet to murder a woman is a crime so unthinkable that even the most hardened of the paid assassins would shrink from you in horror should you suggest such a thing to him.

Nutus was apparently oblivious to his son's all-too-patent terror at his suggestion. Presently he continued:

"You say that you know where the girl lies hid, since she was stolen from your people at Aaanthor. Should she be found by anyone of the three powers, her unsupported story would be sufficient to turn them all against us.

"There is but one way, Astok," cried the older man. "You must return at once to her hiding place and fetch her hither in all secrecy. And, look you here! Return not to Dusar without her, upon pain of death!"

Astok, Prince of Dusar, well knew his royal father's temper. He knew that in the tyrant's heart there pulsed no single throb of love for any creature.

Astok's mother had been a slave woman. Nutus had never loved her. He had never loved another. In youth he had tried to find a bride at the courts of several of his powerful neighbors, but their women would have none of him.

After a dozen daughters of his own nobility had sought self-destruction rather than wed him he had given up. And then it had been that he had legally wed one of his slaves that he might have a son to stand among the jeds when Nutus died and a new jeddak was chosen.

Slowly Astok withdrew from the presence of his father. With white face and shaking limbs he made his way to his own palace. As he crossed the courtyard his glance chanced to wander to the great east tower looming high against the azure of the sky.

At sight of it beads of sweat broke out upon his brow.

Issus! No other hand than his could be trusted to do the horrid thing. With his own fingers he must crush the life from that perfect throat, or plunge the silent blade into the red, red heart.

Her heart! The heart that he had hoped would brim with love for him!

But had it done so? He recalled the haughty contempt with which his protestations of love had been received. He went cold and then hot to the memory of it. His compunctions cooled as the self-satisfaction of a near revenge crowded out the finer instincts that had for a moment asserted themselves—the good that he had inherited from the slave woman was once again submerged in the bad blood that had come down to him from his royal sire; as, in the end, it always was.

A cold smile supplanted the terror that had dilated his eyes. He turned his steps toward the tower. He would see her before he set out upon the journey that was to blind his father to the fact that the girl was already in Dusar.

Quietly he passed in through the secret way, ascending a spiral runway to the apartment in which the Princess of Ptarth was immured.

As he entered the room he saw the girl leaning upon the sill of the east casement, gazing out across the roof tops of Dusar toward distant Ptarth. He hated Ptarth. The thought of it filled him with rage. Why not finish her now and have it done with?

At the sound of his step she turned quickly toward him. Ah, how beautiful she was! His sudden determination faded beneath the glorious light of her wondrous beauty. He would wait until he had returned from his little journey of deception—maybe there might be some other way then. Some other hand to strike the blow—with that face, with those eyes before him, he could never do it. Of that he was positive. He had always gloried in the cruelty of his nature, but, Issus! he was not that cruel. No, another must be found—one whom he could trust.

He was still looking at her as she stood there before him meeting his gaze steadily and unafraid. He felt the hot passion of his love mounting higher and higher.

Why not sue once more? If she would relent, all might yet be well. Even if his father could not be persuaded, they could fly to Ptarth, laying all the blame of the knavery and intrigue that had thrown four great nations into war, upon the shoulders of Nutus. And who was there that would doubt the justice of the charge?

"Thuvia," he said, "I come once again, for the last time, to lay my heart at your feet. Ptarth and Kaol and Dusar are battling with Helium because of you. Wed me, Thuvia, and all may yet be as it should be."

The girl shook her head.

"Wait!" he commanded, before she could speak. "Know the truth before you speak words that may seal, not only your own fate, but that of the thousands of warriors who battle because of you.

"Refuse to wed me willingly, and Dusar would be laid waste should ever the truth be known to Ptarth and Kaol and Helium. They would raze our cities, leaving not one stone upon another. They would scatter our peoples across the face of Barsoom from the frozen north to the frozen south, hunting them down and slaying them, until this great nation remained only as a hated memory in the minds of men.

"But while they are exterminating the Dusarians, countless thousands of their own warriors must perish—and all because of the stubbornness of a single woman who would not wed the prince who loves her.

"Refuse, Thuvia of Ptarth, and there remains but a single alternative—no man must ever know your fate. Only a handful of loyal servitors besides my royal father and myself know that you were stolen from the gardens of Thuvan Dihn by Astok, Prince of Dusar, or that today you be imprisoned in my palace.

"Refuse, Thuvia of Ptarth, and you must die to save Dusar—there is no other way. Nutus, the jeddak, has so decreed. I have spoken."

For a long moment the girl let her level gaze rest full upon the face of Astok of Dusar. Then she spoke, and though the words were few, the unimpassioned tone carried unfathomable depths of cold contempt.

"Better all that you have threatened," she said, "than you."

Then she turned her back upon him and went to stand once more before the east window, gazing with sad eyes toward distant Ptarth.

Astok wheeled and left the room, returning after a short interval of time with food and drink.

"Here," he said, "is sustenance until I return again. The next to enter this apartment will be your executioner. Commend yourself to your ancestors, Thuvia of Ptarth, for within a few days you shall be with them."

Then he was gone.

Half an hour later he was interviewing an officer high in the navy of Dusar.

"Whither went Vas Kor?" he asked. "He is not at his palace."

"South, to the great waterway that skirts Torquas," replied the other. "His son, Hal Vas, is Dwar of the Road there, and thither has Vas Kor gone to enlist recruits among the workers on the farms."

"Good," said Astok, and a half-hour more found him rising above Dusar in his swiftest flier.

XIII

TURJUN, THE PANTHAN

he face of carthoris of Helium gave no token of the
emotions that convulsed him inwardly as he heard
from the lips of Hal Vas that Helium was at war
with Dusar, and that fate had thrown him into the
service of the enemy.

That he might utilize this opportunity to the good of Helium
scarce sufficed to outweigh the chagrin he felt that he was not fighting
in the open at the head of his own loyal troops.

To escape the Dusarians might prove an easy matter; and then
again it might not. Should they suspect his loyalty (and the loyalty of
an impressed panthan was always open to suspicion), he might not
find an opportunity to elude their vigilance until after the termina-
tion of the war, which might occur within days, or, again, only after
long and weary years of bloodshed.

He recalled that history recorded wars in which actual military
operations had been carried on without cessation for five or six hundred years, and even now there were nations upon Barsoom with
which Helium had made no peace within the history of man.

The outlook was not cheering. He could not guess that within a
few hours he would be blessing the fate that had thrown him into the
service of Dusar.

"Ah!" exclaimed Hal Vas. "Here is my father now. Kaor! Vas Kor.
Here is one you will be glad to meet—a doughty panthan—" He
hesitated.

"Turjun," interjected Carthoris, seizing upon the first appellation that occurred to him.

As he spoke his eyes crossed quickly to the tall warrior who was entering the room. Where before had he seen that giant figure, that taciturn countenance, and the livid sword-cut from temple to mouth?

"Vas Kor," repeated Carthoris mentally. "Vas Kor!" Where had he seen the man before?

And then the noble spoke, and like a flash it all came back to Carthoris—the forward servant upon the landing-stage at Ptarth that time that he had been explaining the intricacies of his new compass to Thuvan Dihn; the lone slave that had guarded his own hangar that night he had left upon his ill-fated journey for Ptarth—the journey that had brought him so mysteriously to far Aaanthor.

"Vas Kor," he repeated aloud, "blessed be your ancestors for this meeting," nor did the Dusarian guess the wealth of meaning that lay beneath that hackneyed phrase with which a Barsoomian acknowledges an introduction.

"And blessed be yours, Turjun," replied Vas Kor.

Now came the introduction of Kar Komak to Vas Kor, and as Carthoris went through the little ceremony there came to him the only explanation he might make to account for the white skin and auburn hair of the bowman; for he feared that the truth might not be believed and thus suspicion be cast upon them both from the beginning.

"Kar Komak," he explained, "is, as you can see, a thern. He has wandered far from his icebound southern temples in search of adventure. I came upon him in the pits of Aaanthor; but though I have known him so short a time, I can vouch for his bravery and loyalty."

Since the destruction of the fabric of their false religion by John Carter, the majority of the therns had gladly accepted the new order of things, so that it was now no longer uncommon to see them mingling with the multitudes of red men in any of the great cities of the outer world, so Vas Kor neither felt nor expressed any great astonishment.

All during the interview Carthoris watched, catlike, for some indication that Vas Kor recognized in the battered panthan the erstwhile gorgeous Prince of Helium; but the sleepless nights, the long days of marching and fighting, the wounds and the dried blood had evidently sufficed to obliterate the last remnant of his likeness to his former self; and then Vas Kor had seen him but twice in all his life. Little wonder that he did not know him.

During the evening Vas Kor announced that on the morrow they should depart north toward Dusar, picking up recruits at various stations along the way.

In a great field behind the house a flier lay—a fair-sized cruiser-transport that would accommodate many men, yet swift and well armed also. Here Carthoris slept, and Kar Komak, too, with the other recruits, under guard of the regular Dusarian warriors that manned the craft.

Toward midnight Vas Kor returned to the vessel from his son's house, repairing at once to his cabin. Carthoris, with one of the Dusarians, was on watch. It was with difficulty that the Heliumite repressed a cold smile as the noble passed within a foot of him—within a foot of the long, slim, Heliumitic blade that swung in his harness.

How easy it would have been! How easy to avenge the cowardly trick that had been played upon him—to avenge Helium and Ptarth and Thuvia!

But his hand moved not toward the dagger's hilt, for first Vas Kor must serve a better purpose—he might know where Thuvia of Ptarth lay hidden now, if it had truly been Dusarians that had spirited her away during the fight before Aaanthor.

And then, too, there was the instigator of the entire foul plot.

He must pay the penalty; and who better than Vas Kor could lead the Prince of Helium to Astok of Dusar?

Faintly out of the night there came to Carthoris ears the purring of a distant motor. He scanned the heavens.

Yes, there it was far in the north, dimly outlined against the dark void of space that stretched illimitably beyond it, the faint suggestion of a flier passing, unlighted, through the Barsoomian night.

Carthoris, knowing not whether the craft might be friend or foe of Dusar, gave no sign that he had seen, but turned his eyes in another direction, leaving the matter to the Dusarian who stood watch with him.

Presently the fellow discovered the oncoming craft, and sounded the low alarm which brought the balance of the watch and an officer from their sleeping silks and furs upon the deck near by.

The cruiser-transport lay without lights, and, resting as she was upon the ground, must have been entirely invisible to the oncoming flier, which all presently recognized as a small craft.

It soon became evident that the stranger intended making a landing, for she was now spiraling slowly above them, dropping lower and lower in each graceful curve.

"It is the Thuria," whispered one of the Dusarian warriors. "I would know her in the blackness of the pits among ten thousand other craft."

"Right you are!" exclaimed Vas Kor, who had come on deck. And then he hailed:

"Kaor, Thuria!"

"Kaor!" came presently from above after a brief silence. Then: "What ship?"

"Cruiser-transport Kalksus, Vas Kor of Dusar."

"Good!" came from above. "Is there safe landing alongside?"

"Yes, close in to starboard. Wait, we will show our lights," and a moment later the smaller craft settled close beside the Kalksus, and the lights of the latter were immediately extinguished once more.

Several figures could be seen slipping over the side of the Thuria and advancing toward the Kalksus. Ever suspicious, the Dusarians stood ready to receive the visitors as friends or foes as closer inspection might prove them. Carthoris stood quite near the rail, ready to take sides with the newcomers should chance have it that they were Heliumites playing a bold stroke of strategy upon this lone Dusarian ship. He had led like parties himself, and knew that such a contingency was quite possible.

But the face of the first man to cross the rail undeceived him with a shock that was not at all unpleasurable—it was the face of Astok, Prince of Dusar.

Scarce noticing the others upon the deck of the Kalksus, Astok strode forward to accept Vas Kor's greeting, then he summoned the noble below. The warriors and officers returned to their sleeping silks and furs, and once more the deck was deserted except for the Dusarian warrior and Turjun, the panthan, who stood guard.

The latter walked quietly to and fro. The former leaned across the rail, wishing for the hour that would bring him relief. He did not see his companion approach the lights of the cabin of Vas Kor. He did not see him stoop with ear close pressed to a tiny ventilator.

"May the white apes take us all," cried Astok ruefully, "if we are not in as ugly a snarl as you have ever seen! Nutus thinks that we have her in hiding far away from Dusar. He has bidden me bring her here."

He paused. No man should have heard from his lips the thing he was trying to tell. It should have been forever the secret of Nutus and Astok, for upon it rested the safety of a throne. With that knowledge any man could wrest from the Jeddak of Dusar whatever he listed.

But Astok was afraid, and he wanted from this older man the suggestion of an alternative. He went on.

"I am to kill her," he whispered, looking fearfully around. "Nutus merely wishes to see the body that he may know his commands have been executed. I am now supposed to be gone to the spot where we have her hidden that I may fetch her in secrecy to Dusar. None is to know that she has ever been in the keeping of a Dusarian. I do not need to tell you what would befall Dusar should Ptarth and Helium and Kaol ever learn the truth."

The jaws of the listener at the ventilator clicked together with a vicious snap. Before he had but guessed at the identity of the subject of this conversation. Now he knew. And they were to kill her! His muscular fingers clenched until the nails bit into the palms.

"And you wish me to go with you while you fetch her to Dusar," Vas Kor was saying. "Where is she?"

Astok bent close and whispered into the other's ear. The suggestion of a smile crossed the cruel features of Vas Kor. He realized the power that lay within his grasp. He should be a jed at least.

"And how may I help you, my Prince?" asked the older man suavely.

"I cannot kill her," said Astok. "Issus! I cannot do it! When she turns those eyes upon me my heart becomes water."

Vas Kor's eyes narrowed.

"And you wish——" He paused, the interrogation unfinished, yet complete.

Astok nodded.

"*You* do not love her," he said.

"But I love my life—though I am only a lesser noble," he concluded meaningly.

"You shall be a greater noble—a noble of the first rank!" exclaimed Astok.

"I would be a jed," said Vas Kor bluntly.

Astok hesitated.

"A jed must die before there can be another jed," he pleaded.

"Jeds have died before," snapped Vas Kor. "It would doubtless be not difficult for you to find a jed you do not love, Astok—there are many who do not love you."

Already Vas Kor was commencing to presume upon his power over the young prince. Astok was quick to note and appreciate the subtle change in his lieutenant. A cunning scheme entered his weak and wicked brain.

"As you say, Vas Kor!" he exclaimed. "You shall be a jed when the thing is done," and then, to himself: "Nor will it then be difficult for me to find a jed I do not love."

"When shall we return to Dusar?" asked the noble.

"At once," replied Astok. "Let us get under way now—there is naught to keep you here?"

"I had intended sailing on the morrow, picking up such recruits as the various Dwars of the Roads might have collected for me, as we returned to Dusar."

"Let the recruits wait," said Astok. "Or, better still, come you to Dusar upon the Thuria, leaving the Kalksus to follow and pick up the recruits."

"Yes," acquiesced Vas Kor; "that is the better plan. Come; I am ready," and he rose to accompany Astok to the latter's flier.

The listener at the ventilator came to his feet slowly, like an old man. His face was drawn and pinched and very white beneath the light copper of his skin. She was to die! And he helpless to avert the tragedy. He did not even know where she was imprisoned.

The two men were ascending from the cabin to the deck. Turjun, the panthan, crept close to the companionway, his sinuous fingers closing tightly upon the hilt of his dagger. Could he dispatch them both before he was overpowered? He smiled. He could slay an entire utan of her enemies in his present state of mind.

They were almost abreast of him now. Astok was speaking.

"Bring a couple of your men along, Vas Kor," he said. "We are short-handed upon the Thuria, so quickly did we depart."

The panthan's fingers dropped from the dagger's hilt. His quick mind had grasped here a chance for succoring Thuvia of Ptarth. He might be chosen as one to accompany the assassins, and once he had learned where the captive lay he could dispatch Astok and Vas Kor as well as now. To kill them before he knew where Thuvia was hid was simply to leave her to death at the hands of others; for sooner or later Nutus would learn her whereabouts, and Nutus, Jeddak of Dusar, could not afford to let her live.

Turjun put himself in the path of Vas Kor that he might not be overlooked. The noble aroused the men sleeping upon the deck, but always before him the strange panthan whom he had recruited that same day found means for keeping himself to the fore.

Vas Kor turned to his lieutenant, giving instruction for the bringing of the Kalksus to Dusar, and the gathering up of the recruits; then he signed to two warriors who stood close behind the padwar.

"You two accompany us to the Thuria," he said, "and put yourselves at the disposal of her dwar."

It was dark upon the deck of the Kalksus, so Vas Kor had not a good look at the faces of the two he chose; but that was of no moment, for they were but common warriors to assist with the ordinary duties upon a flier, and to fight if need be.

One of the two was Kar Komak, the bowman. The other was not Carthoris.

The Heliumite was mad with disappointment. He snatched his dagger from his harness; but already Astok had left the deck of the Kalksus, and he knew that before he could overtake him, should he dispatch Vas Kor, he would be killed by the Dusarian warriors, who now were thick upon the deck. With either one of the two alive Thuvia was in as great danger as though both lived— it must be both!

As Vas Kor descended to the ground Carthoris boldly followed him, nor did any attempt to halt him, thinking, doubtless, that he was one of the party.

After him came Kar Komak and the Dusarian warrior who had been detailed to duty upon the Thuria. Carthoris walked close to the left side of the latter. Now they came to the dense shadow under the side of the Thuria. It was very dark there, so that they had to grope for the ladder.

Kar Komak preceded the Dusarian. The latter reached upward for the swinging rounds, and as he did so steel fingers closed upon his windpipe and a steel blade pierced the very center of his heart.

Turjun, the panthan, was the last to clamber over the rail of the Thuria, drawing the rope ladder in after him.

A moment later the flier was rising rapidly, headed for the north.

At the rail Kar Komak turned to speak to the warrior who had been detailed to accompany him. His eyes went wide as they rested upon the face of the young man whom he had met beside the granite cliffs that guard mysterious Lothar. How had he come in place of the Dusarian?

A quick sign, and Kar Komak turned once more to find the Thuria's dwar that he might report himself for duty. Behind him followed the panthan.

Carthoris blessed the chance that had caused Vas Kor to choose the bowman of all others, for had it been another Dusarian there would have been questions to answer as to the whereabouts of the warrior who lay so quietly in the field beyond the residence of Hal Vas, Dwar of the Southern Road; and Carthoris had no answer to that question other than his sword point, which alone was scarce adequate to convince the entire crew of the Thuria.

The journey to Dusar seemed interminable to the impatient Carthoris, though as a matter of fact it was quickly accomplished. Sometime before they reached their destination they met and spoke with another Dusarian war flier. From it they learned that a great battle was soon to be fought southeast of Dusar.

The combined navies of Dusar, Ptarth and Kaol had been

intercepted in their advance toward Helium by the mighty Helium-itic navy—the most formidable upon Barsoom, not alone in numbers and armament, but in the training and courage of its officers and warriors, and the zitidaric proportions of many of its monster battleships.

Not for many a day had there been the promise of such a battle. Four jeddaks were in direct command of their own fleets—Kulan Tith of Kaol, Thuvan Dihn of Ptarth, and Nutus of Dusar upon one side; while upon the other was Tardos Mors, Jeddak of Helium. With the latter was John Carter, Warlord of Mars.

From the far north another force was moving south across the barrier cliffs—the new navy of Talu, Jeddak of Okar, coming in response to the call from the warlord. Upon the decks of the sullen ships of war black-bearded yellow men looked over eagerly toward the south. Gorgeous were they in their splendid cloaks of orluk and apt. Fierce, formidable fighters from the hothouse cities of the frozen north.

And from the distant south, from the sea of Omean and the cliffs of gold, from the temples of the therns and the garden of Issus, other thousands sailed into the north at the call of the great man they all had learned to respect, and, respecting, love. Pacing the flagship of this mighty fleet, second only to the navy of Helium, was the ebon godar, Jeddak of the First Born, his heart beating strong in anticipation of the coming moment when he should hurl his savage crews and the weight of his mighty ships upon the enemies of the warlord.

But would these allies reach the theater of war in time to be of avail to Helium? Or, would Helium need them?

Carthoris, with the other members of the crew of the Thuria, heard the gossip and the rumors. None knew of the two fleets, the one from the south and the other from the north, that were coming to support the ships of Helium, and all of Dusar were convinced that nothing now could save the ancient power of Helium from being wiped forever from the upper air of Barsoom.

Carthoris, too, loyal son of Helium that he was, felt that even his beloved navy might not be able to cope successfully with the combined forces of three great powers.

Now the Thuria touched the landing-stage above the palace of Astok. Hurriedly the prince and Vas Kor disembarked and entered the drop that would carry them to the lower levels of the palace.

Close beside it was another drop that was utilized by common warriors. Carthoris touched Kar Komak upon the arm.

"Come!" he whispered. "You are my only friend among a nation of enemies. Will you stand by me?"

"To the death," replied Kar Komak.

The two approached the drop. A slave operated it.

"Where are your passes?" he asked.

Carthoris fumbled in his pocket pouch as though in search of them, at the same time entering the cage. Kar Komak followed him, closing the door. The slave did not start the cage downward. Every second counted. They must reach the lower level as soon as possible after Astok and Vas Kor if they would know whither the two went.

Carthoris turned suddenly upon the slave, hurling him to the opposite side of the cage.

"Bind and gag him, Kar Komak!" he cried.

Then he grasped the control lever, and as the cage shot downward at sickening speed, the bowman grappled with the slave. Carthoris could not leave the control to assist his companion, for should they touch the lowest level at the speed at which they were going, all would be dashed to instant death.

Below him he could now see the top of Astok's cage in the parallel shaft, and he reduced the speed of his to that of the other. The slave commenced to scream.

"Silence him!" cried Carthoris.

A moment later a limp form crumpled to the floor of the cage.

"He is silenced," said Kar Komak.

Carthoris brought the cage to a sudden stop at one of the higher levels of the palace. Opening the door, he grasped the still form of the slave and pushed it out upon the floor. Then he banged the gate and resumed the downward drop.

Once more he sighted the top of the cage that held Astok and Vas Kor. An instant later it had stopped, and as he brought his car to a halt, he saw the two men disappear through one of the exits of the corridor beyond.

XIV

KULAN TITH'S SACRIFICE

he morning of the second day of her incarceration in the east tower of the palace of Astok, Prince of Dusar, found Thuvia of Ptarth waiting in dull apathy the coming of the assassin.

She had exhausted every possibility of escape, going over and over again the door and the windows, the floor and the walls.

The solid ersite slabs she could not even scratch; the tough Barsoomian glass of the windows would have shattered to nothing less than a heavy sledge in the hands of a strong man. The door and the lock were impregnable. There was no escape. And they had stripped her of her weapons so that she could not even anticipate the hour of her doom, thus robbing them of the satisfaction of witnessing her last moments.

When would they come? Would Astok do the deed with his own hands? She doubted that he had the courage for it. At heart he was a coward—she had known it since first she had heard him brag as, a visitor at the court of her father, he had sought to impress her with his valor.

She could not help but compare him with another. And with whom would an affiancéd bride compare an unsuccessful suitor? With her betrothed? And did Thuvia of Ptarth now measure Astok of Dusar by the standards of Kulan Tith, Jeddak of Kaol?

She was about to die; her thoughts were her own to do with

as she pleased; yet furthest from them was Kulan Tith. Instead the figure of the tall and comely Heliumite filled her mind, crowding therefrom all other images.

She dreamed of his noble face, the quiet dignity of his bearing, the smile that lit his eyes as he conversed with his friends, and the smile that touched his lips as he fought with his enemies—the fighting smile of his Virginian sire.

And Thuvia of Ptarth, true daughter of Barsoom, found her breath quickening and heart leaping to the memory of this other smile—the smile that she would never see again. With a little half-sob the girl sank to the pile of silks and furs that were tumbled in confusion beneath the east windows, burying her face in her arms.

In the corridor outside her prison-room two men had paused in heated argument.

"I tell you again, Astok," one was saying, "that I shall not do this thing unless you be present in the room."

There was little of the respect due royalty in the tone of the speaker's voice. The other, noting it, flushed.

"Do not impose too far upon my friendship for you, Vas Kor," he snapped. "There is a limit to my patience."

"There is no question of royal prerogative here," returned Vas Kor. "You ask me to become an assassin in your stead, and against your jeddak's strict injunctions. You are in no position, Astok, to dictate to me; but rather should you be glad to accede to my reasonable request that you be present, thus sharing the guilt with me. Why should I bear it all?"

The younger man scowled, but he advanced toward the locked door, and as it swung in upon its hinges, he entered the room beyond at the side of Vas Kor.

Across the chamber the girl, hearing them enter, rose to her feet and faced them. Under the soft copper of her skin she blanched just a trifle; but her eyes were brave and level, and the haughty tilt of her firm little chin was eloquent of loathing and contempt.

"You still prefer death?" asked Astok.

"To YOU, yes," replied the girl coldly.

The Prince of Dusar turned to Vas Kor and nodded. The noble drew his short-sword and crossed the room toward Thuvia.

"Kneel!" he commanded.

"I prefer to die standing," she replied.

"As you will," said Vas Kor, feeling the point of his blade with his left thumb. "In the name of Nutus, Jeddak of Dusar!" he cried, and ran quickly toward her.

"In the name of Carthoris, Prince of Helium!" came in low tones from the doorway.

Vas Kor turned to see the panthan he had recruited at his son's house leaping across the floor toward him. The fellow brushed past Astok with an: "After him, you—calot!"

Vas Kor wheeled to meet the charging man.

"What means this treason?" he cried.

Astok, with bared sword, leaped to Vas Kor's assistance. The panthan's sword clashed against that of the noble, and in the first encounter Vas Kor knew that he faced a master swordsman.

Before he half realized the stranger's purpose he found the man between himself and Thuvia of Ptarth, at bay facing the two swords of the Dusarians. But he fought not like a man at bay. Ever was he the aggressor, and though always he kept his flashing blade between the girl and her enemies, yet he managed to force them hither and thither about the room, calling to the girl to follow close behind him.

Until it was too late neither Vas Kor nor Astok dreamed of that which lay in the panthan's mind; but at last as the fellow stood with his back toward the door, both understood—they were penned in their own prison, and now the intruder could slay them at his will, for Thuvia of Ptarth was bolting the door at the man's direction, first taking the key from the opposite side, where Astok had left it when they had entered.

Astok, as was his way, finding that the enemy did not fall immediately before their swords, was leaving the brunt of the fighting to Vas Kor, and now as his eyes appraised the panthan carefully they presently went wider and wider, for slowly he had come to recognize the features of the Prince of Helium.

The Heliumite was pressing close upon Vas Kor. The noble was bleeding from a dozen wounds. Astok saw that he could not for long withstand the cunning craft of that terrible sword hand.

"Courage, Vas Kor!" he whispered in the other's ear. "I have a plan. Hold him but a moment longer and all will be well," but the balance of the sentence, "with Astok, Prince of Dusar," he did not voice aloud.

Vas Kor, dreaming no treachery, nodded his head, and for a moment succeeded in holding Carthoris at bay. Then the Heliumite and the girl saw the Dusarian prince run swiftly to the opposite side of the chamber, touch something in the wall that sent a great panel swinging inward, and disappear into the black vault beyond.

It was done so quickly that by no possibility could they have intercepted him. Carthoris, fearful lest Vas Kor might similarly elude him, or Astok return immediately with reinforcements, sprang viciously in upon his antagonist, and a moment later the headless body of the Dusarian noble rolled upon the ersite floor.

"Come!" cried Carthoris. "There is no time to be lost. Astok will be back in a moment with enough warriors to overpower me."

But Astok had no such plan in mind, for such a move would have meant the spreading of the fact among the palace gossips that the Ptarthian princess was a prisoner in the east tower. Quickly would the word have come to his father, and no amount of falsifying could have explained away the facts that the jeddak's investigation would have brought to light.

Instead Astok was racing madly through a long corridor to reach the door of the tower-room before Carthoris and Thuvia left the apartment. He had seen the girl remove the key and place it in her pocket-pouch, and he knew that a dagger point driven into the key-hole from the opposite side would imprison them in the secret chamber till eight dead worlds circled a cold, dead sun.

As fast as he could run Astok entered the main corridor that led to the tower chamber. Would he reach the door in time? What if the Heliumite should have already emerged and he should run upon him in the passageway? Astok felt a cold chill run up his spine. He had no stomach to face that uncanny blade.

He was almost at the door. Around the next turn of the corridor it stood. No, they had not left the apartment. Evidently Vas Kor was still holding the Heliumite!

Astok could scarce repress a grin at the clever manner in which he had outwitted the noble and disposed of him at the same time. And then he rounded the turn and came face to face with an auburn-haired, white giant.

The fellow did not wait to ask the reason for his coming; instead he leaped upon him with a long-sword, so that Astok had to parry a dozen vicious cuts before he could disengage himself and flee back down the runway.

A moment later Carthoris and Thuvia entered the corridor from the secret chamber.

"Well, Kar Komak?" asked the Heliumite.

"It is fortunate that you left me here, red man," said the bow-man. "I but just now intercepted one who seemed overanxious to reach this door—it was he whom they call Astok, Prince of Dusar."

Carthoris smiled.

"Where is he now?" he asked.

"He escaped my blade, and ran down this corridor," replied Kar Komak.

"We must lose no time, then!" exclaimed Carthoris. "He will have the guard upon us yet!"

Together the three hastened along the winding passages through which Carthoris and Kar Komak had tracked the Dusarians by the marks of the latter's sandals in the thin dust that overspread the floors of these seldom-used passageways.

They had come to the chamber at the entrances to the lifts before they met with opposition. Here they found a handful of guardsmen, and an officer, who, seeing that they were strangers, questioned their presence in the palace of Astok.

Once more Carthoris and Kar Komak had recourse to their blades, and before they had won their way to one of the lifts the noise of the conflict must have aroused the entire palace, for they heard men shouting, and as they passed the many levels on their quick passage to the landing-stage they saw armed men running hither and thither in search of the cause of the commotion.

Beside the stage lay the Thuria, with three warriors on guard. Again the Heliumite and the Lotharian fought shoulder to shoulder, but the battle was soon over, for the Prince of Helium alone would have been a match for any three that Dusar could produce.

Scarce had the Thuria risen from the ways ere a hundred or more fighting men leaped to view upon the landing-stage. At their head was Astok of Dusar, and as he saw the two he had thought so safely in his power slipping from his grasp, he danced with rage and chagrin, shaking his fists and hurling abuse and vile insults at them.

With her bow inclined upward at a dizzy angle, the Thuria shot meteorlike into the sky. From a dozen points swift patrol boats darted after her, for the scene upon the landing-stage above the palace of the Prince of Dusar had not gone unnoticed.

A dozen times shots grazed the Thuria's side, and as Carthoris could not leave the control levers, Thuvia of Ptarth turned the muzzles of the craft's rapid-fire guns upon the enemy as she clung to the steep and slippery surface of the deck.

It was a noble race and a noble fight. One against a score now, for other Dusarian craft had joined in the pursuit; but Astok, Prince of Dusar, had built well when he built the Thuria. None in the navy of his sire possessed a swifter flier; no other craft so well armored or so well armed.

One by one the pursuers were distanced, and as the last of them fell out of range behind, Carthoris dropped the Thuria's nose to a horizontal plane, as with lever drawn to the last notch, she tore through the thin air of dying Mars toward the east and Ptarth.

Thirteen and a half thousand haads away lay Ptarth—a stiff thirty-hour journey for the swiftest of fliers, and between Dusar and Ptarth might lie half the navy of Dusar, for in this direction was the reported seat of the great naval battle that even now might be in progress.

Could Carthoris have known precisely where the great fleets of the contending nations lay, he would have hastened to them without delay, for in the return of Thuvia to her sire lay the greatest hope of peace.

Half the distance they covered without sighting a single warship, and then Kar Komak called Carthoris attention to a distant craft that rested upon the ochre vegetation of the great dead sea-bottom, above which the Thuria was speeding.

About the vessel many figures could be seen swarming. With the aid of powerful glasses, the Heliumite saw that they were green warriors, and that they were repeatedly charging down upon the crew of the stranded airship. The nationality of the latter he could not make out at so great a distance.

It was not necessary to change the course of the Thuria to permit of passing directly above the scene of battle, but Carthoris dropped his craft a few hundred feet that he might have a better and closer view.

If the ship was of a friendly power, he could do no less than stop and direct his guns upon her enemies, though with the precious freight he carried he scarcely felt justified in landing, for he could offer but two swords in reinforcement—scarce enough to warrant jeopardizing the safety of the Princess of Ptarth.

As they came close above the stricken ship, they could see that it would be but a question of minutes before the green horde would swarm across the armored bulwarks to glut the ferocity of their bloodlust upon the defenders.

"It would be futile to descend," said Carthoris to Thuvia. "The craft may even be of Dusar—she shows no insignia. All that we may do is fire upon the hordesmen"; and as he spoke he stepped to one of the guns and deflected its muzzle toward the green warriors at the ship's side.

At the first shot from the Thuria those upon the vessel below evidently discovered her for the first time. Immediately a device fluttered from the bow of the warship on the ground. Thuvia of Ptarth caught her breath quickly, glancing at Carthoris.

The device was that of Kulan Tith, Jeddak of Kaol—the man to whom the Princess of Ptarth was betrothed!

How easy for the Heliumite to pass on, leaving his rival to the fate that could not for long be averted! No man could accuse him of cowardice or treachery, for Kulan Tith was in arms against Helium, and, further, upon the Thuria were not enough swords to delay even temporarily the outcome that already was a foregone conclusion in the minds of the watchers.

What would Carthoris, Prince of Helium, do?

Scarce had the device broken to the faint breeze ere the bow of the Thuria dropped at a sharp angle toward the ground.

"Can you navigate her?" asked Carthoris of Thuvia.

The girl nodded.

"I am going to try to take the survivors aboard," he continued.

"It will need both Kar Komak and myself to man the guns while the Kaolians take to the boarding tackle. Keep her bow depressed against the rifle fire. She can bear it better in her forward armor, and at the same time the propellers will be protected."

He hurried to the cabin as Thuvia took the control. A moment later the boarding tackle dropped from the keel of the Thuria, and from a dozen points along either side stout, knotted leathern lines trailed downward. At the same time a signal broke from her bow:

"Prepare to board us."

A shout arose from the deck of the Kaolian warship. Carthoris, who by this time had returned from the cabin, smiled sadly. He was about to snatch from the jaws of death the man who stood between himself and the woman he loved.

"Take the port bow gun, Kar Komak," he called to the bowman, and himself stepped to the gun upon the starboard bow.

They could now feel the sharp shock of the explosions of the green warriors vomited their hail of death and destruction at the sides of the staunch Thuria.

It was a forlorn hope at best. At any moment the repulsive ray tanks might be pierced. The men upon the Kaolian ship were battling with renewed hope. In the bow stood Kulan Tith, a brave figure fighting beside his brave warriors, beating back the ferocious green men.

The Thuria came low above the other craft. The Kaolians were forming under their officers in readiness to board, and then a sudden fierce fusillade from the rifles of the green warriors vomited their hail of death and destruction into the side of the brave flier.

Like a wounded bird she dived suddenly Marsward careening drunkenly. Thuvia turned the bow upward in an effort to avert the imminent tragedy, but she succeeded only in lessening the shock of the flier's impact as she struck the ground beside the Kaolian ship.

When the green men saw only two warriors and a woman upon the deck of the Thuria, a savage shout of triumph arose from their ranks, while an answering groan broke from the lips of the Kaolians.

The former now turned their attention upon the new arrival, for they saw her defenders could soon be overcome and that from her deck they could command the deck of the better-manned ship.

As they charged a shout of warning came from Kulan Tith, upon the bridge of his own ship, and with it an appreciation of the valor of the act that had put the smaller vessel in these sore straits.

"Who is it," he cried, "that offers his life in the service of Kulan Tith? Never was wrought a nobler deed of self-sacrifice upon Barsoom!"

The green horde was scrambling over the Thuria's side as there broke from the bow the device of Carthoris, Prince of Helium, in reply to the query of the jeddak of Kaol. None upon the smaller flier had opportunity to note the effect of this announcement upon the Kaolians, for their attention was claimed slowly now by that which was transpiring upon their own deck.

Kar Komak stood behind the gun he had been operating, staring with wide eyes at the onrushing hideous green warriors. Carthoris, seeing him thus, felt a pang of regret that, after all, this man that he had thought so valorous should prove, in the hour of need, as spineless as Jav or Tario.

"Kar Komak—the man!" he shouted. "Grip yourself! Remember the days of the glory of the seafarers of Lothar. Fight! Fight, man! Fight as never man fought before. All that remains to us is to die fighting."

Kar Komak turned toward the Heliumite, a grim smile upon his lips.

"Why should we fight," he asked. "Against such fearful odds? There is another way—a better way. Look!" He pointed toward the companionway that led below deck.

The green men, a handful of them, had already reached the Thuria's deck, as Carthoris glanced in the direction the Lotharian had indicated. The sight that met his eyes set his heart to thumping in joy and relief—Thuvia of Ptarth might yet be saved? For from below there poured a stream of giant bowmen, grim and terrible. Not the bowmen of Tario or Jav, but the bowmen of an odwar of bowmen—savage fighting men, eager for the fray.

The green warriors paused in momentary surprise and consternation, but only for a moment. Then with horrid war-cries they leaped forward to meet these strange, new foemen.

A volley of arrows stopped them in their tracks. In a moment the only green warriors upon the deck of the Thuria were dead warriors, and the bowmen of Kar Komak were leaping over the vessel's sides to charge the hordesmen upon the ground.

Utan after utan tumbled from the bowels of the Thuria to launch themselves upon the unfortunate green men. Kulan Tith and his Kaolians stood wide-eyed and speechless with amazement as they saw thousands of these strange, fierce warriors emerge from the companionway of the small craft that could not comfortably have accommodated more than fifty.

At last the green men could withstand the onslaught of overwhelming numbers no longer. Slowly, at first, they fell back across the ochre plain. The bowmen pursued them. Kar Komak, standing upon the deck of the Thuria, trembled with excitement.

At the top of his lungs he voiced the savage war-cry of his forgotten day. He roared encouragement and commands at his battling utans, and then, as they charged further and further from the Thuria, he could no longer withstand the lure of battle.

Leaping over the ship's side to the ground, he joined the last of his bowmen as they raced off over the dead sea-bottom in pursuit of the fleeing green horde.

Beyond a low promontory of what once had been an island the

green men were disappearing toward the west. Close upon their heels raced the fleet bowmen of a bygone day, and forging steadily ahead among them Carthoris and Thuvia could see the mighty figure of Kar Komak, brandishing aloft the Torquasian short-sword with which he was armed, as he urged his creatures after the retreating enemy.

As the last of them disappeared behind the promontory, Carthoris turned toward Thuvia of Ptarth.

"They have taught me a lesson, these vanishing bowmen of Lothar," he said. "When they have served their purpose they remain not to embarrass their masters by their presence. Kulan Tith and his warriors are here to protect you. My acts have constituted the proof of my honesty of purpose. Goodbye," and he knelt at her feet, raising a bit of her harness to his lips.

The girl reached out a hand and laid it upon the thick black hair of the head bent before her. Softly she asked:

"Where are you going, Carthoris?"

"With Kar Komak, the bowman," he replied. "There will be fighting and forgetfulness."

The girl put her hands before her eyes, as though to shut out some mighty temptation from her sight.

"May my ancestors have mercy upon me," she cried, "if I say the thing I have no right to say; but I cannot see you cast your life away, Carthoris, Prince of Helium! Stay, my chieftain. Stay—I love you!"

A cough behind them brought both about, and there they saw standing, not two paces from them Kulan Tith, Jeddak of Kaol.

For a long moment none spoke. Then Kulan Tith cleared his throat.

"I could not help hearing all that passed," he said. "I am no fool, to be blind to the love that lies between you. Nor am I blind to the lofty honor that has caused you, Carthoris, to risk your life and hers to save mine, though you thought that that very act would rob you of the chance to keep her for your own.

"Nor can I fail to appreciate the virtue that has kept your lips sealed against words of love for this Heliumite, Thuvia, for I know that I have but just heard the first declaration of your passion for him. I do not condemn you. Rather should I have condemned you had you entered a loveless marriage with me.

"Take back your liberty, Thuvia of Ptarth," he cried, "and bestow it where your heart already lies enchained, and when the golden collars are clasped about your necks you will see that Kulan Tith's is the first sword to be raised in declaration of eternal friendship for the new Princess of Helium and her royal mate!"

The

CHESSMEN *of*
MARS

CONTENTS

Prelude

John Carter Comes to Earth

hea had just beaten me at chess, as usual, and, also as usual, I had gleaned what questionable satisfaction I might by twitting him with this indication of failing mentality by calling his attention to the nth time to that theory, propounded by certain scientists, which is based upon the assertion that phenomenal chess players are always found to be from the ranks of children under twelve, adults over seventy-two or the mentally defective—a theory that is lightly ignored upon those rare occasions that I win. Shea had gone to bed and I should have followed suit, for we are always in the saddle here before sunrise; but instead I sat there before the chess table in the library, idly blowing smoke at the dishonored head of my defeated king.

While thus profitably employed I heard the east door of the living-room open and someone enter. I thought it was Shea returning to speak with me on some matter of tomorrow's work; but when I raised my eyes to the doorway that connects the two rooms I saw framed there the figure of a bronzed giant, his otherwise naked body trapped with a jewel-encrusted harness from which there hung at one side an ornate short-sword and at the other a pistol of strange pattern. The black hair, the steel-gray eyes, brave and smiling, the noble features—I recognized them at once, and leaping to my feet I advanced with outstretched hand.

"John Carter!" I cried. "You?"

"None other, my son," he replied, taking my hand in one of his and placing the other upon my shoulder.

"And what are you doing here?" I asked. "It has been long years since you revisited Earth, and never before in the trappings of Mars. Lord! but it is good to see you—and not a day older in appearance than when you trotted me on your knee in my babyhood. How do you explain it, John Carter, Warlord of Mars, or do you try to explain it?"

"Why attempt to explain the inexplicable?" he replied. "As I have told you before, I am a very old man. I do not know how old I am. I recall no childhood; but recollect only having been always as you see me now and as you saw me first when you were five years old. You, yourself, have aged, though not as much as most men in a corresponding number of years, which may be accounted for by the fact that the same blood runs in our veins; but I have not aged at all. I have discussed the question with a noted Martian scientist, a friend of mine; but his theories are still only theories. However, I am content with the fact—I never age, and I love life and the vigor of youth.

"And now as to your natural question as to what brings me to Earth again and in this, to earthly eyes, strange habiliment. We may thank Kar Komak, the bowman of Lothar. It was he who gave me the idea upon which I have been experimenting until at last I have achieved success. As you know I have long possessed the power to cross the void in spirit, but never before have I been able to impart to inanimate things a similar power. Now, however, you see me for the first time precisely as my Martian fellows see me—you see the very short-sword that has tasted the blood of many a savage foeman; the harness with the devices of Helium and the insignia of my rank; the pistol that was presented to me by Tars Tarkas, Jeddak of Thark.

"Aside from seeing you, which is my principal reason for being here, and satisfying myself that I can transport inanimate things from Mars to Earth, and therefore animate things if I so desire, I have no purpose. Earth is not for me. My every interest is upon Barsoom—my

162

wife, my children, my work; all are there. I will spend a quiet evening with you and then back to the world I love even better than I love life."

As he spoke he dropped into the chair upon the opposite side of the chess table.

"You spoke of children," I said. "Have you more than Carthoris?"

"A daughter," he replied, "only a little younger than Carthoris, and, barring one, the fairest thing that ever breathed the thin air of dying Mars. Only Dejah Thoris, her mother, could be more beautiful than Tara of Helium."

For a moment he fingered the chessmen idly. "We have a game on Mars similar to chess," he said, "very similar."

"And there is a race there that plays it grimly with men and naked swords. We call the game jetan. It is played on a board like yours, except that there are a hundred squares and we use twenty pieces on each side. I never see it played without thinking of Tara of Helium and what befell her among the chessmen of Barsoom. Would you like to hear her story?"

I said that I would and so he told it to me, and now I shall try to re-tell it for you as nearly in the words of The Warlord of Mars as I can recall them, but in the third person. If there be inconsistencies and errors, let the blame fall not upon John Carter, but rather upon my faulty memory, where it belongs. It is a strange tale and utterly Barsoomian.

I

TARA IN A TANTRUM

ara of Helium rose from the pile of silks and soft furs upon which she had been reclining, stretched her lithe body languidly, and crossed toward the center of the room, where, above a large table, a bronze disc depended from the low ceiling. Her carriage was that of health and physical perfection—the effortless harmony of faultless coordination. A scarf of silken gossamer crossing over one shoulder was wrapped about her body; her black hair was piled high upon her head. With a wooden stick she tapped upon the bronze disc, lightly, and presently the summons was answered by a slave girl, who entered, smiling, to be greeted similarly by her mistress.

"Are my father's guests arriving?" asked the princess.

"Yes, Tara of Helium, they come," replied the slave. "I have seen Kantos Kan, Overlord of the Navy, and Prince Soran of Ptarth, and Djor Kantos, son of Kantos Kan," she shot a roguish glance at her mistress as she mentioned Djor Kantos' name, "and—oh, there were others, many have come."

"The bath, then, Uthia," said her mistress. "And why, Uthia," she added, "do you look thus and smile when you mention the name of Djor Kantos?"

The slave girl laughed gaily. "It is so plain to all that he worships you," she replied.

"It is not plain to me," said Tara of Helium. "He is the friend of my brother, Carthoris, and so he is here much; but not to see me. It is his friendship for Carthoris that brings him thus often to the palace of my father."

"But Carthoris is hunting in the north with Talu, Jeddak of Okar," Uthia reminded her.

"My bath, Uthia!" cried Tara of Helium. "That tongue of yours will bring you to some misadventure yet."

"The bath is ready, Tara of Helium," the girl responded, her eyes still twinkling with merriment, for she well knew that in the heart of her mistress was no anger that could displace the love of the princess for her slave. Preceding the daughter of The Warlord she opened the door of an adjoining room where lay the bath—a gleaming pool of scented water in a marble basin. Golden stanchions supported a chain of gold encircling it and leading down into the water on either side of marble steps. A glass dome let in the sun-light, which flooded the interior, glancing from the polished white of the marble walls and the procession of bathers and fishes, which, in conventional design, were inlaid with gold in a broad band that circled the room.

Tara of Helium removed the scarf from about her and handed it to the slave. Slowly she descended the steps to the water, the temperature of which she tested with a symmetrical foot, undeformed by tight shoes and high heels—a lovely foot, as God intended that feet should be and seldom are. Finding the water to her liking, the girl swam leisurely to and fro about the pool. With the silken ease of the seal she swam, now at the surface, now below, her smooth muscles rolling softly beneath her clear skin—a wordless song of health and happiness and grace. Presently she emerged and gave herself into the hands of the slave girl, who rubbed the body of her mistress with a sweet smelling semi-liquid substance contained in a golden urn, until the glowing skin was covered with a foamy lather, then a quick plunge into the pool, a drying with soft towels, and the bath was over. Typical of the life of the princess was the simple elegance of her bath—no retinue of useless slaves, no pomp, no idle waste of precious moments. In another half hour her hair was dried and built into the strange, but becoming, coiffure of her station; her leathern trappings, encrusted with gold and jewels, had been adjusted to her figure and she was ready to mingle with the guests that had been bidden to the midday function at the palace of The Warlord.

As she left her apartments to make her way to the gardens where the guests were congregating, two warriors, the insignia of the House of the Prince of Helium upon their harness, followed a few paces behind her, grim reminders that the assassin's blade may never be ignored upon Barsoom, where, in a measure, it counterbalances the great natural span of human life, which is estimated at not less than a thousand years.

As they neared the entrance to the garden another woman, similarly guarded, approached them from another quarter of the great palace. As she neared them Tara of Helium turned toward her with a smile and a happy greeting, while her guards knelt with bowed heads in willing and voluntary adoration of the beloved of Helium. Thus always, solely at the command of their own hearts, did the warriors of Helium greet Dejah Thoris, whose deathless beauty had more than once brought them to bloody warfare with other nations of Barsoom. So great was the love of the people of Helium for the mate of John Carter it amounted practically to worship, as though she were indeed the goddess that she looked.

The mother and daughter exhanged the gentle, Barsoomian, "kaor" of greeting and kissed. Then together they entered the gardens where the guests were. A huge warrior drew his short-sword and struck his metal shield with the flat of it, the brazen sound ringing out above the laughter and the speech.

"The Princess comes!" he cried. "Dejah Thoris! The Princess comes! Tara of Helium!" Thus always is royalty announced. The guests arose; the two women inclined their heads; the guards fell back upon either side of the entrance-way; a number of nobles advanced to pay their respects; the laughing and the talking were resumed and Dejah Thoris and her daughter moved simply and naturally among their guests, no suggestion of differing rank apparent in the bearing of any who were there, though there was more than a single Jeddak and many common warriors whose only title lay in brave deeds, or noble patriotism. Thus it is upon Mars where men are judged upon their own merits rather than upon those of their grandsires, even though pride of lineage be great.

Tara of Helium let her slow gaze wander among the throng of guests until presently it halted upon one she sought. Was the faint shadow of a frown that crossed her brow an indication of displeasure at the sight that met her eyes, or did the brilliant rays of the noonday sun distress her? Who may say! She had been reared to believe that one day she should wed Djor Kantos, son of her father's best friend. It had been the dearest wish of Kantos Kan and The Warlord that this should be, and Tara of Helium had accepted it as a matter of all but accomplished fact. Djor Kantos had seemed to accept the matter in the same way.

They had spoken of it casually as something that would, as a matter of course, take place in the indefinite future, as, for instance, his promotion in the navy, in which he was now a padwar; or the set functions of the court of her grandfather, Tardos Mors, Jeddak of Helium; or Death. They had never spoken of love and that had puzzled Tara of Helium upon the rare occasions she gave it thought, for she knew that people who were to wed were usually much occupied with the matter of love and she had all of a woman's curiosity—she wondered what love was like. She was very fond of Djor Kantos and she knew that he was very fond of her. They liked to be together, for they liked the same things and the same people and the same books and their dancing was a joy, not only to themselves but to those who watched them. She could not imagine wanting to marry anyone other than Djor Kantos.

So perhaps it was only the sun that made her brows contract just the tiniest bit at the same instant that she discovered Djor Kantos sitting in earnest conversation with Olvia Marthis, daughter of the Jed of Hastor. It was Djor Kantos' duty immediately to pay his respects to Dejah Thoris and Tara of Helium; but he did not do so and presently the daughter of The Warlord frowned indeed. She looked long at Olvia Marthis, and though she had seen her many times before and knew her well, she looked at her today through new eyes that saw, apparently for the first time, that the girl from Hastor was noticeably beautiful even among those other beautiful women of Helium. Tara of Helium was disturbed. She attempted to analyze her emotions; but found it difficult. Olvia Marthis was her friend—she was very fond of her and she felt no anger toward her. Was she angry with Djor Kantos? No, she finally decided that she was not. It was merely surprise, then, that she felt—surprise that Djor Kantos could be more interested in another than in herself. She was about to cross the garden and join them when she heard her father's voice directly behind her.

"Tara of Helium!" he called, and she turned to see him approaching with a strange warrior whose harness and metal bore devices with which she was unfamiliar. Even among the gorgeous trappings of the men of Helium and the visitors from distant empires those of the stranger were remarkable for their barbaric splendor. The leather of his harness was completely hidden beneath ornaments of platinum thickly set with brilliant diamonds, as were the scabbards of his swords and the ornate holster that held his long, Martian pistol. Moving through the sunlit garden at the side of the great Warlord, the scintillant rays of his countless gems enveloping him as in an aureole of light imparted to his noble figure a suggestion of godliness.

"Tara of Helium, I bring you Gahan, Jed of Gathol," said John

Carter, after the simple Barsoomian custom of presentation.

"Kaor! Gahan, Jed of Gathol," returned Tara of Helium.

"My sword is at your feet, Tara of Helium," said the young chieftain.

The Warlord left them and the two seated themselves upon an ersite bench beneath a spreading sorapus tree.

"Far Gathol," mused the girl. "Ever in my mind has it been connected with mystery and romance and the half-forgotten lore of the ancients. I cannot think of Gathol as existing today, possibly because I have never before seen a Gatholian."

"And perhaps too because of the great distance that separates Helium and Gathol, as well as the comparative insignificance of my little free city, which might easily be lost in one corner of mighty Helium," added Gahan. "But what we lack in power we make up in pride," he continued, laughing. "We believe ours the oldest inhabited city upon Barsoom. It is one of the few that has retained its freedom, and this despite the fact that its ancient diamond mines are the richest known and, unlike practically all the other fields, are today apparently as inexhaustible as ever."

"Tell me of Gathol," urged the girl. "The very thought fills me with interest," nor was it likely that the handsome face of the young jed detracted anything from the glamour of far Gathol.

Nor did Gahan seem displeased with the excuse for further monopolizing the society of his fair companion. His eyes seemed chained to her exquisite features, from which they moved no further than to a rounded breast, part hid beneath its jeweled covering, a naked shoulder or the symmetry of a perfect arm, resplendent in bracelets of barbaric magnificence.

"Your ancient history has doubtless told you that Gathol was built upon an island in Throxeus, mightiest of the five oceans of old Barsoom. As the ocean receded Gathol crept down the sides of the mountain, the summit of which was the island upon which she had been built, until today she covers the slopes from summit to base, while the bowels of the great hill are honeycombed with the galleries of her mines. Entirely surrounding us is a great salt marsh, which protects us from invasion by land, while the rugged and ofttimes vertical topography of our mountain renders the landing of hostile airships a precarious undertaking."

"That, and your brave warriors?" suggested the girl.

Gahan smiled. "We do not speak of that except to enemies," he said, "and then with tongues of steel rather than of flesh."

"But what practice in the art of war has a people which nature has thus protected from attack?" asked Tara of Helium, who had liked the young jed's answer to her previous question, but yet in whose mind persisted a vague conviction of the possible effeminacy of her companion, induced, doubtless, by the magnificence of his trappings and weapons which carried a suggestion of splendid show rather than grim utility.

"Our natural barriers, while they have doubtless saved us from defeat on countless occasions, have not by any means rendered us immune from attack," he explained, "for so great is the wealth of Gathol's diamond treasury that there yet may be found those who will risk almost certain defeat in an effort to loot our unconquered city; so thus we find occasional practice in the exercise of arms; but there is more to Gathol than the mountain city. My country extends from Polodona (Equator) north ten karads and from the tenth karad west of Horz to the twentieth west, including thus a million square haads, the greater proportion of which is fine grazing land where run our great herds of thoats and zitidars.

"Surrounded as we are by predatory enemies our herdsmen must indeed be warriors or we should have no herds, and you may be assured they get plenty of fighting. Then there is our constant need of workers in the mines. The Gatholians consider themselves a race of warriors and as such prefer not to labor in the mines. The law is, however, that each male Gatholian shall give an hour a day in labor to the government. That is practically the only tax that is levied upon them. They prefer however, to furnish a substitute to perform this labor, and as our own people will not hire out for labor in the mines it has been necessary to obtain slaves, and I do not need to tell you that slaves are not won without fighting. We sell these slaves in the public market, the proceeds going, half and half, to the government and the warriors who bring them in. The purchasers are credited with the amount of labor performed by their particular slaves. At the end of a year a good slave will have performed the labor tax of his master for six years, and if slaves are plentiful he is freed and permitted to return to his own people."

"You fight in platinum and diamonds?" asked Tara, indicating his gorgeous trappings with a quizzical smile.

Gahan laughed. "We are a vain people," he admitted, good-naturedly, "and it is possible that we place too much value on personal appearances. We vie with one another in the splendor of our accouterments when trapped for the observance of the lighter duties of life, though when we take the field our leather is the plainest I ever have seen worn by fighting men of Barsoom. We pride ourselves, too, upon our physical beauty, and especially upon the beauty of our women. May I dare to say, Tara of Helium, that I am hoping for the day when you will visit Gathol that my people may see one who is really beautiful?"

"The women of Helium are taught to frown with displeasure upon the tongue of the flatterer," rejoined the girl, but Gahan, Jed of Gathol, observed that she smiled as she said it.

A bugle sounded, clear and sweet, above the laughter and the talk. "The Dance of Barsoom!" exclaimed the young warrior. "I claim you for it, Tara of Helium."

The girl glanced in the direction of the bench where she had last seen Djor Kantos. He was not in sight. She inclined her head in assent to the claim of the Gatholian. Slaves were passing among the guests, distributing small musical instruments of a single string. Upon each instrument were characters which indicated the pitch and length of its tone. The instruments were of skeel, the string of gut, and were shaped to fit the left forearm of the dancer, to which it was strapped. There was also a ring wound with gut which was worn between the first and second joints of the index finger of the right hand and which, when passed over the string of the instrument, elicited the single note required of the dancer.

The guests had risen and were slowly making their way toward the expanse of scarlet sward at the south end of the gardens where the dance was to be held, when Djor Kantos came hurriedly toward Tara of Helium. "I claim——" he exclaimed as he neared her; but she interrupted him with a gesture.

"You are too late, Djor Kantos," she cried in mock anger. "No laggard may claim Tara of Helium; but haste now lest thou lose also Olvia Marthis, whom I have never seen wait long to be claimed for this or any other dance."

"I have already lost her," admitted Djor Kantos ruefully.

"And you mean to say that you came for Tara of Helium only after having lost Olvia Marthis?" demanded the girl, still simulating displeasure.

"Oh, Tara of Helium, you know better than that," insisted the young man. "Was it not natural that I should assume that you would expect me, who alone has claimed you for the Dance of Barsoom for at least twelve times past?"

"And sit and play with my thumbs until you saw fit to come for me?" she questioned. "Ah, no, Djor Kantos; Tara of Helium is for no laggard," and she threw him a sweet smile and passed on toward the assembling dancers with Gahan, Jed of far Gathol.

The Dance of Barsoom bears a relation similar to the more formal dancing functions of Mars that The Grand March does to ours, though it is infinitely more intricate and more beautiful. Before a Martian youth of either sex may attend an important social function where there is dancing, he must have become proficient in at least three dances—The Dance of Barsoom, his national dance, and the dance of his city. In these three dances the dancers furnish their own music, which never varies; nor do the steps or figures vary, having been handed down from time immemorial. All Barsoomian dances are stately and beautiful, but The Dance of Barsoom is a wondrous epic of motion and harmony— there is no grotesque posturing, no vulgar or suggestive movements. It has been described as the inter-pretation of the highest ideals of a world that aspired to grace and beauty and chastity in woman, and strength and dignity and loyalty in man.

Today, John Carter, Warlord of Mars, with Dejah Thoris, his mate, led in the dancing, and if there was another couple that vied with them in possession of the silent admiration of the guests it was the resplendent Jed of Gathol and his beautiful partner. In the ever-changing figures of the dance the man found himself now with the girl's hand in his and again with an arm about the lithe body that the jeweled harness but inadequately covered, and the girl, though she had danced a thousand dances in the past, realized for the first time the personal contact of a man's arm against her naked flesh. It troubled her that she should notice it, and she looked up questioningly and almost with displeasure at the man as though it was his fault. Their eyes met and she saw in his that which she had never seen in the eyes of Djor Kantos. It was at the very end of the dance and they both stopped suddenly with the music and stood there looking straight into each other's eyes. It was Gahan of Gathol who spoke first.

"Tara of Helium, I love you!" he said.

The girl drew herself to her full height. "The Jed of Gathol for-gets himself," she exclaimed haughtily.

"The Jed of Gathol would forget everything but you, Tara of

Helium," he replied. Fiercely he pressed the soft hand that he still retained from the last position of the dance. "I love you, Tara of Helium," he repeated. "Why should your ears refuse to hear what your eyes but just now did not refuse to see—and answer?"

"What meanest thou?" she cried. "Are the men of Gathol such boors, then?"

"They are neither boors nor fools," he replied, quietly. "They know when they love a woman—and when she loves them."

Tara of Helium stamped her little foot in anger. "Go!" she said, "before it is necessary to acquaint my father with the dishonor of his guest."

She turned and walked away. "Wait!" cried the man. "Just another word."

"Of apology?" she asked.

"Of prophecy," he said.

"I do not care to hear it," replied Tara of Helium, and left him standing there. She was strangely unstrung and shortly thereafter returned to her own quarter of the palace, where she stood for a long time by a window looking out beyond the scarlet tower of Greater Helium toward the northwest.

Presently she turned angrily away. "I hate him!" she exclaimed aloud.

"Whom?" inquired the privileged Uthia.

Tara of Helium stamped her foot. "That ill-mannered boor, the Jed of Gathol," she replied.

Uthia raised her slim brows.

At the stamping of the little foot, a great beast rose from the corner of the room and crossed to Tara of Helium where it stood looking up into her face. She placed her hand upon the ugly head. "Dear old Woola," she said; "no love could be deeper than yours, yet it never offends. Would that men might pattern themselves after you!"

II

At the Gale's Mercy

ara of Helium did not return to her father's
guests, but awaited in her own apartments the
word from Djor Kantos which she knew must
come, begging her to return to the gardens.
She would then refuse, haughtily. But no appeal
came from Djor Kantos. At first Tara of Helium was angry, then she
was hurt, and always she was puzzled. She could not understand.
Occasionally she thought of the Jed of Gathol and then she would
stamp her foot, for she was very angry indeed with Gahan. The
presumption of the man! He had insinuated that he read love for
him in her eyes. Never had she been so insulted and humiliated.
Never had she so thoroughly hated a man. Suddenly she turned
toward Uthia.

"My flying leather!" she commanded.

"But the guests!" exclaimed the slave girl. "Your father, The
Warlord, will expect you to return."

"He will be disappointed," snapped Tara of Helium.

The slave hesitated. "He does not approve of your flying alone,"
she reminded her mistress.

The young princess sprang to her feet and seized the unhappy
slave by the shoulders, shaking her. "You are becoming unbearable,
Uthia," she cried. "Soon there will be no alternative than to send you
to the public slave-market. Then possibly you will find a master to
your liking."

Tears came to the soft eyes of the slave girl. "It is because I love you, my princess," she said softly. Tara of Helium melted. She took the slave in her arms and kissed her.

"I have the disposition of a thoat, Uthia," she said. "Forgive me! I love you and there is nothing that I would not do for you and nothing would I do to harm you. Again, as I have so often in the past, I offer you your freedom."

"I do not wish my freedom if it will separate me from you, Tara of Helium," replied Uthia. "I am happy here with you—I think that I should die without you."

Again the girls kissed. "And you will not fly alone, then?" questioned the slave.

Tara of Helium laughed and pinched her companion. "You persistent little pest," she cried. "Of course I shall fly—does not Tara of Helium always do that which pleases her?"

Uthia shook her head sorrowfully. "Alas! she does," she admitted. "Iron is the Warlord of Barsoom to the influences of all but two. In the hands of Dejah Thoris and Tara of Helium he is as potters' clay."

"Then run and fetch my flying leather like the sweet slave you are," directed the mistress.

Far out across the ochre sea-bottoms beyond the twin cities of Helium raced the swift flier of Tara of Helium. Thrilling to the speed and the buoyancy and the obedience of the little craft the girl drove toward the northwest. Why she should choose that direction she did not pause to consider. Perhaps because in that direction lay the least known areas of Barsoom, and, ergo, Romance, Mystery, and Adventure. In that direction also lay far Gathol; but to that fact she gave no conscious thought.

She did, however, think occasionally of the jed of that distant kingdom, but the reaction to these thoughts was scarcely pleasurable. They still brought a flush of shame to her cheeks and a surge of angry blood to her heart. She was very angry with the Jed of Gathol, and though she should never see him again she was quite sure that hate of him would remain fresh in her memory forever. Mostly her thoughts revolved about another—Djor Kantos. And when she thought of him she thought also of Olvia Marthis of Hastor. Tara of Helium thought that she was jealous of the fair Olvia and it made her very angry to think that. She was angry with Djor Kantos and herself, but she was not angry at all with Olvia Marthis, whom she loved, and so of course she was not jealous really. The trouble was, that Tara of Helium had failed for once to have her own way. Djor Kantos had not come running like a willing slave when she had expected him, and, ah, here was the nub of the whole thing! Gahan, Jed of Gathol, a stranger, had been a witness to her humiliation. He had seen her unclaimed at the beginning of a great function and he had had to come to her rescue to save her, as he doubtless thought, from the inglorious fate of a wallflower. At the recurring thought, Tara of Helium could feel her whole body burning with scarlet shame and then she went suddenly white and cold with rage; whereupon she turned her flier about so abruptly that she was all but torn from her lashings upon the flat, narrow deck. She reached home just before dark. The guests had departed. Quiet had descended upon the palace. An hour later she joined her father and mother at the evening meal.

"You deserted us, Tara of Helium," said John Carter. "It is not what the guests of John Carter should expect."

"They did not come to see me," replied Tara of Helium. "I did not ask them."

"They were no less your guests," replied her father.

The girl rose, and came and stood beside him and put her arms about his neck.

"My proper old Virginian," she cried, rumpling his shock of black hair.

"In Virginia you would be turned over your father's knee and spanked," said the man, smiling.

She crept into his lap and kissed him. "You do not love me any more," she announced. "No one loves me," but she could not compose her features into a pout because bubbling laughter insisted upon breaking through.

"The trouble is there are too many who love you," he said. "And now there is another."

"Indeed!" she cried. "What do you mean?"

"Gahan of Gathol has asked permission to woo you."

The girl sat up very straight and tilted her chin in the air. "I would not wed with a walking diamond-mine," she said. "I will not have him."

"I told him as much," replied her father, "and that you were as good as betrothed to another. He was very courteous about it; but at the same time he gave me to understand that he was accustomed to getting what he wanted and that he wanted you very much. I suppose it will mean another war. Your mother's beauty kept Helium at war for many years, and—well, Tara of Helium, if I were a young man I should doubtless be willing to set all Barsoom afire to win you, as I still would to keep your divine mother," and he smiled across the sorapus table and its golden service at the undimmed beauty of Mars' most beautiful woman.

"Our little girl should not yet be troubled with such matters," said Dejah Thoris. "Remember, John Carter, that you are not dealing with an Earth child, whose span of life would be more than half completed before a daughter of Barsoom reached actual maturity."

"But do not the daughters of Barsoom sometimes marry as early as twenty?" he insisted.

"Yes, but they will still be desirable in the eyes of men after forty generations of Earth folk have returned to dust—there is no hurry, at least, upon Barsoom. We do not fade and decay here as you tell me those of your planet do, though you, yourself, belie your own words. When the time seems proper Tara of Helium shall wed with Djor Kantos, and until then let us give the matter no further thought."

"No," said the girl, "the subject irks me, and I shall not marry Djor Kantos, or another—I do not intend to wed."

Her father and mother looked at her and smiled. "When Gahan of Gathol returns he may carry you off," said the former.

"He has gone?" asked the girl.

"His flier departs for Gathol in the morning," John Carter replied.

"I have seen the last of him then," remarked Tara of Helium with a sigh of relief.

"He says not," returned John Carter.

The girl dismissed the subject with a shrug and the conversation passed to other topics. A letter had arrived from Thuvia of Ptarth, who was visiting at her father's court while Carthoris, her mate, hunted in Okar. Word had been received that the Tharks and Warhoons were again at war, or rather that there had been an engagement, for war was their habitual state. In the memory of man there had been no peace between these two savage green hordes—only a single temporary truce. Two new battleships had been launched at Hastor. A little band of holy therns was attempting to revive the ancient and discredited religion of Issus, who they claimed still lived in spirit and had communicated with them. There were rumors of war from Dusar. A scientist claimed to have discovered human life on the further moon. A madman had attempted to destroy the atmosphere plant. Seven people had been assassinated in Greater Helium during the last ten zodes (the equivalent of an Earth day).

Following the meal Dejah Thoris and The Warlord played at jetan, the Barsoomian game of chess, which is played upon a board of a hundred alternate black and orange squares. One player has twenty black pieces, the other, twenty orange pieces. A brief description of the game may interest those Earth readers who care for chess, and will not be lost upon those who pursue this narrative to its conclusion, since before they are done they will find that a knowledge of jetan will add to the interest and the thrills that are in store for them.

The men are placed upon the board as in chess upon the first two rows next the players. In order from left to right on the line of squares nearest the players, the jetan pieces are Warrior, Padwar, Dwar, Flier, Chief, Princess, Flier, Dwar, Padwar, Warrior. In the next line all are Panthans except the end pieces, which are called Thoats, and represent mounted warriors.

The Panthans, which are represented as warriors with one feather, may move one space in any direction except backward; the Thoats, mounted warriors with three feathers, may move one straight and one diagonal, and may jump intervening pieces; Warriors, foot soldiers with two feathers, straight in any direction, or diagonally, two spaces; Padwars, lieutenants wearing two feathers, two diagonal in any direction, or combination; Dwars, captains wearing three feathers, three spaces straight in any direction, or combination; Fliers, represented by a propellor with three blades, three spaces in any direction, or combination, diagonally, and may jump intervening pieces; the Chief, indicated by a diadem with ten jewels, three spaces in any direction, straight, or diagonal; Princess, diadem with a single jewel, same as Chief, and can jump intervening pieces.

The game is won when a player places any of his pieces on the same square with his opponent's Princess, or when a Chief takes a Chief. It is drawn when a Chief is taken by any opposing piece other than the opposing Chief; or when both sides have been reduced to three pieces, or less, of equal value, and the game is not terminated in the following ten moves, five apiece. This is but a general outline of the game, briefly stated.

It was this game that Dejah Thoris and John Carter were playing when Tara of Helium bid them good night, retiring to her own quarters and her sleeping silks and furs. "Until morning, my beloved," she called back to them as she passed from the apartment, nor little did she guess, nor her parents, that this might indeed be the last time that they would ever set eyes upon her.

The morning broke dull and gray. Ominous clouds billowed restlessly and low. Beneath them torn fragments scudded toward the northwest. From her window Tara of Helium looked out upon this unusual scene. Dense clouds seldom overcast the Barsoomian sky. At this hour of the day it was her custom to ride one of those small thoats that are the saddle animals of the red Martians, but the sight of the billowing clouds lured her to a new adventure. Uthia still slept and the girl did not disturb her. Instead, she dressed quietly and went to the hangar upon the roof of the palace directly above her quarters where her own swift flier was housed. She had never driven through the clouds. It was an adventure that always she had longed to experience. The wind was strong and it was with difficulty that she maneuvered the craft from the hangar without accident, but once away it raced swiftly out above the twin cities. The buffeting winds caught and tossed it, and the girl laughed aloud in sheer joy of the resultant thrills. She handled the little ship like a veteran, though few veterans would have faced the menace of such a storm in so light a craft. Swiftly she rose toward the clouds, racing with the scudding streamers of the storm-swept fragments, and a moment later she was swallowed by the dense masses billowing above. Here was a new world, a world of chaos unpeopled except for herself; but it was a cold, damp, lonely world and she found it depressing after the novelty of it had been dissipated, by an overpowering sense of the magnitude of the forces surging about her. Suddenly she felt very lonely and very cold and very little. Hurriedly, therefore, she rose until presently her craft broke through into the glorious sunlight that transformed the upper surface of the somber element into rolling masses of burnished silver. Here it was still cold, but without the dampness of the clouds, and

in the eye of the brilliant sun her spirits rose with the mounting needle of her altimeter. Gazing at the clouds, now far beneath, the girl
experienced the sensation of hanging stationary in mid-heaven; but
the whirring of her propellor, the wind beating upon her, the high
figures that rose and fell beneath the glass of her speedometer, these
told her that her speed was terrific. It was then that she determined
to turn back.

The first attempt she made above the clouds, but it was unsuccessful. To her surprise she discovered that she could not even turn against
the high wind, which rocked and buffeted the frail craft. Then she
dropped swiftly to the dark and wind-swept zone between the hurtling clouds and the gloomy surface of the shadowed ground. Here she
tried again to force the nose of the flier back toward Helium, but the
tempest seized the frail thing and hurled it remorselessly about, rolling it over and over and tossing it as it were a cork in a cataract. At last
the girl succeeded in righting the flier, perilously close to the ground.
Never before had she been so close to death, yet she was not terrified.
Her coolness had saved her, that and the strength of the deck lashings
that held her. Traveling with the storm she was safe, but where was it
bearing her? She pictured the apprehension of her father and mother
when she failed to appear at the morning meal. They would find her
flier missing and they would guess that somewhere in the path of
the storm it lay a wrecked and tangled mass upon her dead body, and
then brave men would go out in search of her, risking their lives;
and that lives would be lost in the search, she knew, for she realized now that never in her life-time had such a tempest raged
upon Barsoom.

She must turn back! She must reach Helium before her mad
lust for thrills had cost the sacrifice of a single courageous life! She
determined that greater safety and likelihood of success lay above
the clouds, and once again she rose through the chilling, wind-
tossed vapor. Her speed again was terrific, for the wind seemed to

have increased rather than to have lessened. She sought gradually to check the swift flight of her craft, but though she finally succeeded in reversing her motor the wind but carried her on as it would. Then it was that Tara of Helium lost her temper. Had her world not always bowed in acquiescence to her every wish? What were these elements that they dared to thwart her? She would demonstrate to them that the daughter of The Warlord was not to be denied! They would learn that Tara of Helium might not be ruled even by the forces of nature!

And so she drove her motor forward again and then with her firm, white teeth set in grim determination she drove the steering lever far down to port with the intention of forcing the nose of her craft straight into the teeth of the wind, and the wind seized the frail thing and toppled it over upon its back, and twisted and turned it and hurled it over and over; the propellor raced for an instant in an air pocket and then the tempest seized it again and twisted it from its shaft, leaving the girl helpless upon an unmanageable atom that rose and fell, and rolled and tumbled—the sport of the elements she had defied. Tara of Helium's first sensation was one of surprise—that she had failed to have her own way. Then she commenced to feel concern—not for her own safety but for the anxiety of her parents and the dangers that the inevitable searchers must face. She reproached herself for the thoughtless selfishness that had jeopardized the peace and safety of others. She realized her own grave danger, too; but she was still unterrified, as befitted the daughter of Dejah Thoris and John Carter. She knew that her buoyancy tanks might keep her afloat indefinitely, but she had neither food nor water, and she was being borne toward the least-known area of Barsoom. Perhaps it would be better to land immediately and await the coming of the searchers, rather than to allow herself to be carried still further from Helium, thus greatly reducing the chances of early discovery; but when she dropped toward the ground she discovered that the violence of the wind rendered an attempt to land tantamount to destruction and she rose again, rapidly.

Carried along a few hundred feet above the ground she was better able to appreciate the Titanic proportions of the storm than when she had flown in the comparative serenity of the zone above the clouds, for now she could distinctly see the effect of the wind upon the surface of Barsoom. The air was filled with dust and flying bits of vegetation and when the storm carried her across an irrigated area of farm land she saw great trees and stone walls and buildings lifted high in the air and scattered broadcast over the devastated country; and then she was carried swiftly on to other sights that forced in upon her consciousness a rapidly growing conviction that after all Tara of Helium was a very small and insignificant and helpless person. It was quite a shock to her self-pride while it lasted, and toward evening she was ready to believe that it was going to last forever. There had been no abatement in the ferocity of the tempest, nor was there indication of any. She could only guess at the distance she had been carried for she could not believe in the correctness of the high figures that had been piled upon the record of her odometer. They seemed unbelievable and yet, had she known it, they were quite true—in twelve hours she had flown and been carried by the storm full seven thousand haads. Just before dark she was carried over one of the deserted cities of ancient Mars. It was Torquas, but she did not know it. Had she, she might readily have been forgiven for abandoning the last vestige of hope, for to the people of Helium Torquas seems as remote as do the South Sea Islands to us. And still the tempest, its fury unabated, bore her on.

All that night she hurtled through the dark beneath the clouds, or rose to race through the moonlit void beneath the glory of Barsoom's two satellites. She was cold and hungry and altogether miserable, but her brave little spirit refused to admit that her plight was hopeless even though reason proclaimed the truth. Her reply to reason, sometime spoken aloud in sudden defiance, recalled the Spartan stubbornness of her sire in the face of certain annihilation: "I still live!"

That morning there had been an early visitor at the palace of The Warlord. It was Gahan, Jed of Gathol. He had arrived shortly after the absence of Tara of Helium had been noted, and in the excitement he had remained unannounced until John Carter had happened upon him in the great reception corridor of the palace as The Warlord was hurrying out to arrange for the dispatch of ships in search of his daughter.

Gahan read the concern upon the face of The Warlord. "Forgive me if I intrude, John Carter," he said. "I but came to ask the indulgence of another day since it would be fool-hardy to attempt to navigate a ship in such a storm."

"Remain, Gahan, a welcome guest until you choose to leave us," replied The Warlord; "but you must forgive any seeming inattention upon the part of Helium until my daughter is restored to us."

"You daughter! Restored! What do you mean?" exclaimed the Gatholian. "I do not understand."

"She is gone, together with her light flier. That is all we know. We can only assume that she decided to fly before the morning meal and was caught in the clutches of the tempest. You will pardon me, Gahan, if I leave you abruptly—I am arranging to send ships in search of her;" but Gahan, Jed of Gathol, was already speeding in the direction of the palace gate. There he leaped upon a waiting thoat and followed by two warriors in the metal of Gathol, he dashed through the avenues of Helium toward the palace that had been set aside for his entertainment.

III

THE HEADLESS HUMANS

bove the roof of the palace that housed the Jed of Gathol and his entourage, the cruiser *Vanator* tore at her stout moorings. The groaning tackle bespoke the mad fury of the gale, while the worried faces of those members of the crew whose duties demanded their presence on the straining craft gave corroborative evidence of the gravity of the situation. Only stout lashings prevented these men from being swept from the deck, while those upon the roof below were constantly compelled to cling to rails and stanchions to save themselves from being carried away by each new burst of meteoric fury. Upon the prow of the *Vanator* was painted the device of Gathol, but no pennants were displayed in the upper works since the storm had carried away several in rapid succession, just as it seemed to the watching men that it must carry away the ship itself. They could not believe that any tackle could withstand for long this Titanic force. To each of the twelve lashings clung a brawny warrior with drawn short-sword. Had but a single mooring given to the power of the tempest eleven short-swords would have cut the others; since, partially moored, the ship was doomed, while free in the tempest it stood at least some slight chance for life.

"By the blood of Issus, I believe they will hold!" screamed one warrior to another.

"And if they do not hold may the spirits of our ancestors reward the brave warriors upon the *Vanator*," replied another of those upon the roof of the palace, "for it will not be long from the moment her cables part before her crew dons the leather of the dead; but yet, Tanus, I believe they will hold. Give thanks at least that we did not sail before the tempest fell, since now each of us has a chance to live."

"Yes," replied Tanus, "I should hate to be abroad today upon the stoutest ship that sails the Barsoomian sky."

It was then that Gahan the Jed appeared upon the roof. With him were the balance of his own party and a dozen warriors of Helium. The young chief turned to his followers.

"I sail at once upon the *Vanator*," he said, "in search of Tara of Helium who is thought to have been carried away upon a one-man flier by the storm. I do not need to explain to you the slender chances the *Vanator* has to withstand the fury of the tempest, nor will I order you to your deaths. Let those who wish remain behind without dishonor. The others will follow me," and he leaped for the rope ladder that lashed wildly in the gale.

The first man to follow him was Tanus and when the last reached the deck of the cruiser there remained upon the palace roof only the twelve warriors of Helium, who, with naked swords, had taken the posts of the Gatholians at the moorings.

Not a single warrior who had remained aboard the *Vanator* would leave her now.

"I expected no less," said Gahan, as with the help of those already on the deck he and the others found secure lashings. The commander of the *Vanator* shook his head. He loved his trim craft, the pride of her class in the little navy of Gathol. It was of her he thought—not of himself. He saw her lying torn and twisted upon the ochre vegetation of some distant sea-bottom, to be presently overrun and looted by some savage, green horde. He looked at Gahan.

"Are you ready, San Tothis?" asked the Jed.

"All is ready."

"Then cut away!"

Word was passed across the deck and over the side to the Heliumetic warriors below that at the third gun they were to cut away. Twelve keen swords must strike simultaneously and with equal power, and each must sever completely and instantly three strands of heavy cable that no loose end fouling a block bring immediate disaster upon the *Vanator*.

Boom! The voice of the signal gun rolled down through the screaming wind to the twelve warriors upon the roof. *Boom!* Twelve swords were raised above twelve brawny shoulders. *Boom!* Twelve keen edges severed twelve complaining moorings, clean and as one.

The *Vanator,* her propellors whirling, shot forward with the storm. The tempest struck her in the stern as with a mailed fist and stood the great ship upon her nose, and then it caught her and spun her as a child's top spins; and upon the palace roof the twelve men looked on in silent helplessness and prayed for the souls of the brave warriors who were going to their death. And others saw, from Helium's lofty landing stages and from a thousand hangars upon a thousand roofs; but only for an instant did the preparations stop that would send other brave men into the frightful maelstrom of that apparently hopeless search, for such is the courage of the warriors of Barsoom.

But the *Vanator* did not fall to the ground, within sight of the city at least, though as long as the watchers could see her never for an instant did she rest upon an even keel. Sometimes she lay upon one side or the other, or again she hurtled along keel up, or rolled over and over, or stood upon her nose or her tail at the caprice of the great force that carried her along. And the watchers saw that this great ship was merely being blown away with the other bits of debris great and small that filled the sky. Never in the memory of man or the annals of recorded history had such a storm raged across the face of Barsoom.

And in another instant was the *Vanator* forgotten as the lofty, scarlet tower that had marked Lesser Helium for ages crashed to ground, carrying death and demolition upon the city beneath. Panic reigned.

A fire broke out in the ruins. The city's every force seemed crippled, and it was then that The Warlord ordered the men that were about to set forth in search of Tara of Helium to devote their energies to the salvation of the city, for he too had witnessed the start of the *Vanator* and realized the futility of wasting men who were needed sorely if Lesser Helium was to be saved from utter destruction.

Shortly after noon of the second day the storm commenced to abate, and before the sun went down, the little craft upon which Tara of Helium had hovered between life and death these many hours drifted slowly before a gentle breeze above a landscape of rolling hills that once had been lofty mountains upon a Martian continent. The girl was exhausted from loss of sleep, from lack of food and drink, and from the nervous reaction consequent to the terrifying experiences through which she had passed. In the near distance, just topping an intervening hill, she caught a momentary glimpse of what appeared to be a dome-capped tower. Quickly she dropped the flier until the hill shut it off from the view of the possible occupants of the structure she had seen. The tower meant to her the habitation of man, suggesting the presence of water and, perhaps, of food. If the tower was the deserted relic of a bygone age she would scarcely find food there, but there was still a chance that there might be water. If it was inhabited, then must her approach be cautious, for only enemies might be expected to abide in so far distant a land. Tara of Helium knew that she must be far from the twin cities of her grandfather's empire, but had she guessed within even a thousand haads of the reality, she had been stunned by realization of the utter hopelessness of her state.

Keeping the craft low, for the buoyancy tanks were still intact, the girl skimmed the ground until the gently-moving wind had carried her to the side of the last hill that intervened between her and the structure she had thought a man-built tower. Here she brought the flier to the ground among some stunted trees, and dragging it beneath one where it might be somewhat hidden from craft passing above, she made it fast and set forth to reconnoiter. Like most women of her class she was armed only with a single slender blade, so that in such an emergency as now confronted her she must depend almost solely upon her cleverness in remaining undiscovered by enemies. With utmost caution she crept warily toward the crest of the hill, taking advantage of every natural screen that the landscape afforded to conceal her approach from possible observers ahead, while momentarily she cast quick glances rearward lest she be taken by surprise from that quarter.

She came at last to the summit, where, from the concealment of a low bush, she could see what lay beyond. Beneath her spread a beautiful valley surrounded by low hills. Dotting it were numerous circular towers, dome-capped, and surrounding each tower was a stone wall enclosing several acres of ground. The valley appeared to be in a high state of cultivation. Upon the opposite side of the hill and just beneath her was a tower and enclosure. It was the roof of the former that had first attracted her attention. In all respects it seemed identical in construction with those further out in the valley—a high, plastered wall of massive construction surrounding a similarly constructed tower, upon whose gray surface was painted in vivid colors a strange device. The towers were about forty sofads in diameter, approximately forty earth-feet, and sixty in height to the base of the dome. To an Earth man they would have immediately suggested the silos in which dairy farmers store ensilage for their herds; but closer scrutiny, revealing an occasional embrasured opening together with the strange construction of the domes, would have altered such a conclusion. Tara of Helium saw that the domes seemed to be faced with innumerable prisms of glass, those that were exposed to the declining sun scintillating so gorgeously as to remind her suddenly of the magnificent trappings of Gahan of Gathol. As she thought of the man she shook her head angrily, and moved cautiously forward a foot or two that she might get a less obstructed view of the nearer tower and its enclosure.

As Tara of Helium looked down into the enclosure surrounding the nearest tower, her brows contracted momentarily in frowning surprise, and then her eyes went wide in an expression of incredulity tinged with horror, for what she saw was a score or two of human bodies—naked and headless. For a long moment she watched, breathless; unable to believe the evidence of her own eyes—that these gruesome things moved and had life! She saw them crawling about on hands and knees over and across one another, searching about with their fingers. And she saw some of them at troughs, for which the others seemed to be searching, and those at the troughs were taking something from these receptacles and apparently putting it in a hole where their necks should have been. They were not far beneath her—she could see them distinctly and she saw that there were the bodies of both men and women, and that they were beautifully proportioned, and that their skin was similar to hers, but of a slightly lighter red. At first she had thought that she was looking upon a shambles and that the bodies, but recently decapitated, were moving under the impulse of muscular reaction; but presently she realized that this was their normal condition. The horror of them fascinated her, so that she could scarce take her eyes from them. It was evident from their groping hands that they were eyeless, and their sluggish movements suggested a rudimentary nervous system and a correspondingly minute brain. The girl wondered how they subsisted for she could not, even by the wildest stretch of imagination, picture these imperfect creatures as intelligent tillers of the soil. Yet that the soil of the valley was tilled was evident and that these things had food was equally so. But who tilled the soil? Who kept and fed these unhappy things, and for what purpose? It was an enigma beyond her powers of deduction.

The sight of food aroused again a consciousness of her own gnawing hunger and the thirst that parched her throat. She could see both food and water within the enclosure; but would she dare enter even should she find means of ingress? She doubted it, since the very thought of possible contact with these gruesome creatures sent a shudder through her frame.

Then her eyes wandered again out across the valley until presently they picked out what appeared to be a tiny stream winding its way through the center of the farm lands—a strange sight upon Barsoom. Ah, if it were but water! Then might she hope with a real hope, for the fields would give her sustenance which she could gain by night, while by day she hid among the surrounding hills, and sometime, yes, sometime she knew, the searchers would come, for John Carter, Warlord of Barsoom, would never cease to search for his daughter until every square haad of the planet had been combed again and again. She knew him and she knew the warriors of Helium and so she knew that could she but manage to escape harm until they came, they would indeed come at last.

She would have to wait until dark before she dare venture into the valley, and in the meantime she thought it well to search out a place of safety nearby where she might be reasonably safe from savage beasts. It was possible that the district was free from carnivora, but one might never be sure in a strange land. As she was about to withdraw behind the brow of the hill her attention was again attracted to the enclosure below. Two figures had emerged from the tower. Their beautiful bodies seemed identical with those of the headless creatures among which they moved, but the newcomers were not headless. Upon their shoulders were heads that seemed human, yet which the girl intuitively sensed were not human. They were just a trifle too far away for her to see them distinctly in the waning light of the dying day, but she knew that they were too large, they were out of proportion to the perfectly proportioned bodies, and they were oblate in form. She could see that the men wore some manner of harness to which were slung the customary long-sword and short-sword of the Barsoomian warrior, and that about their short necks were massive leather collars cut to fit closely over the shoulders and snugly to the lower part of the head. Their features were scarce discernible, but there was a suggestion of grotesqueness about them that carried to her a feeling of revulsion.

The two carried a long rope to which were fastened, at intervals of about two sofads, what she later guessed were light manacles, for she saw the warriors passing among the poor creatures in the enclosure and about the right wrist of each they fastened one of the manacles. When all had been thus fastened to the rope one of the warriors commenced to pull and tug at the loose end as though attempting to drag the headless company toward the tower, while the other went among them with a long, light whip with which he flicked them upon the naked skin. Slowly, dully, the creatures rose to their feet and between the tugging of the warrior in front and the lashing of him behind the hopeless band was finally herded within the tower. Tara of Helium shuddered as she turned away. What manner of creatures were these?

Suddenly it was night. The Barsoomian day had ended, and then the brief period of twilight that renders the transition from daylight to darkness almost as abrupt as the switching off of an electric light, and Tara of Helium had found no sanctuary. But perhaps there were no beasts to fear, or rather to avoid—Tara of Helium liked not the word fear. She would have been glad, however, had there been a cabin, even a very tiny cabin, upon her small flier; but there was no cabin. The interior of the hull was completely taken up by the buoyancy tanks. Ah, she had it! How stupid of her not to have thought of it before! She could moor the craft to the tree beneath which it rested and let it rise the length of the rope. Lashed to the deck rings she would then be safe from any roaming beast of prey that chanced along. In the morning she could drop to the ground again before the craft was discovered.

As Tara of Helium crept over the brow of the hill down toward the valley, her presence was hidden by the darkness of the night from the sight of any chance observer who might be loitering by a window in the nearby tower. Cluros, the farther moon, was just rising above the horizon to commence his leisurely journey through the heavens. Eight zodes later he would set—a trifle over nineteen and a half Earth hours—and during that time Thuria, his vivacious mate, would have circled the planet twice and be more than halfway around on her third trip. She had but just set. It would be more than three and a half hours before she shot above the opposite horizon to hurtle, swift and low, across the face of the dying planet. During this temporary absence of the mad moon Tara of Helium hoped to find both food and water, and gain again the safety of her flier's deck.

She groped her way through the darkness, giving the tower and its enclosure as wide a berth as possible. Sometimes she stumbled, for in the long shadows cast by the rising Cluros objects were grotesquely distorted though the light from the moon was still not sufficient to be of much assistance to her. Nor, as a matter of fact, did she want light. She could find the stream in the dark, by the simple expedient of going down hill until she walked into it and she had seen that bearing trees and many crops grew throughout the valley, so that she would pass food in plenty ere she reached the stream. If the moon showed her the way more clearly and thus saved her from an occasional fall, he would, too, show her more clearly to the strange denizens of the towers, and that, of course, must not be. Could she have waited until the following night conditions would have been better, since Cluros would not appear in the heavens at all and so, during Thuria's absence, utter darkness would reign; but the pangs of thirst and the gnawing of hunger could be endured no longer with food and drink both in sight, and so she had decided to risk discovery rather than suffer longer.

Safely past the nearest tower, she moved as rapidly as she felt consistent with safety, choosing her way wherever possible so that she might take advantage of the shadows of the trees that grew at intervals and at the same time discover those which bore fruit. In this latter she met with almost immediate success, for the very third tree beneath which she halted was heavy with ripe fruit. Never, thought Tara of Helium, had aught so delicious impinged upon her palate, and yet it was naught else than the almost tasteless usa, which is considered to be palatable only after having been cooked and highly spiced. It grows easily with little irrigation and the trees bear abundantly. The fruit, which ranks high in food value, is one of the staple foods of the less well-to-do, and because of its cheapness and nutritive value forms one of the principal rations of both armies and navies upon Barsoom, a use which has won for it a Martian *sobriquet* which, freely translated into English, would be, The Fighting Potato. The girl was wise enough to eat but sparingly, but she filled her pocket-pouch with the fruit before she continued upon her way.

Two towers she passed before she came at last to the stream, and here again was she temperate, drinking but little and that very slowly, contenting herself with rinsing her mouth frequently and bathing her face, her hands, and her feet; and even though the night was cold, as Martian nights are, the sensation of refreshment more than compensated for the physical discomfort of the low temperature. Replacing her sandals she sought among the growing track near the stream for whatever edible berries or tubers might be planted there, and found a couple of varieties that could be eaten raw. With these she replaced some of the usa in her pocket-pouch, not only to insure a variety but because she found them more palatable. Occasionally she returned to the stream to drink, but each time moderately. Always were her eyes and ears alert for the first signs of danger, but she had neither seen nor heard aught to disturb her. And presently the time approached when she felt she must return to her flier lest she be caught in the revealing light of low swinging Thuria. She dreaded leaving the water for she knew that she must become very thirsty before she could hope to come again to the stream. If she only had some little receptacle in which to carry water, even a small amount would tide her over until the following night; but she had nothing and so she must content herself as best she could with the juices of the fruit and tubers she had gathered.

After a last drink at the stream, the longest and deepest she had allowed herself, she rose to retrace her steps toward the hills; but even as she did so she became suddenly tense with apprehension. What was that? She could have sworn that she saw something move in the shadows beneath a tree not far away. For a long minute the girl did not move—she scarce breathed. Her eyes remained fixed upon the dense shadows below the tree, her ears strained through the silence of the night. A low moaning came down from the hills where her flier was hidden. She knew it well—the weird note of the hunting banth. And the great carnivore lay directly in her path. But he was not so close as this other thing, hiding there in the shadows just a little way off. What was it? It was the strain of uncertainty that weighed heaviest upon her. Had she known the nature of the creature lurking there half its meanace would have vanished. She cast quickly about her in search of some haven of refuge should the thing prove dangerous.

Again arose the moaning from the hills, but this time closer. Almost immediately it was answered from the opposite side of the valley, behind her, and then from the distance to the right of her, and twice upon her left. Her eyes had found a tree, quite near. Slowly, and without taking her eyes from the shadows of that other tree, she moved toward the overhanging branches that might afford her sanctuary in the event of need, and at her first move a low growl rose from the spot she had been watching and she heard the sudden moving of a big body. Simultaneously the creature shot into the moonlight in full charge upon her, its tail erect, its tiny ears laid flat, its great mouth with its multiple rows of sharp and powerful fangs already yawning for its prey, its ten legs carrying it forward in great leaps, and now from the beast's throat issued the frightful roar with which it seeks to paralyze its prey. It was a banth—the great, maned lion of Barsoom. Tara of Helium saw it coming and leaped for the tree toward which she had been moving, and the banth realized her intention and redoubled his speed. As his hideous roar awakened the echoes in the hills, so too it awakened echoes in the valley; but these echoes came from the living throats of others of his kind, until it seemed to the girl that Fate had thrown her into the midst of a countless multitude of these savage beasts.

Almost incredibly swift is the speed of a charging banth, and fortunate it was that the girl had not been caught farther in the open. As it was, her margin of safety was next to negligible, for as she swung nimbly to the lower branches the creature in pursuit of her crashed among the foliage almost upon her as it sprang upward to seize her. It was only a combination of good fortune and agility that saved her. A stout branch deflected the raking talons of the carnivore, but so close was the call that a giant forearm brushed her flesh in the instant before she scrambled to the higher branches.

Baffled, the banth gave vent to his rage and disappointment in a series of frightful roars that caused the very ground to tremble, and to these were added the roarings and the growlings and the moanings of his fellows as they approached from every direction, in the hope of wresting from him whatever of his kill they could take by craft or prowess. And now he turned snarling upon them as they circled the tree, while the girl, huddled in a crotch above them, looked down upon the gaunt, yellow monsters padding on noiseless feet in a restless circle about her. She wondered now at the strange freak of fate that had permitted her to come down this far into the valley by night unharmed, but even more she wondered how she was to return to the hills. She knew that she would not dare venture it by night and she guessed, too, that by day she might be confronted by even graver perils. To depend upon this valley for sustenance she now saw to be beyond the pale of possibility because of the banths that would keep her from food and water by night, while the dwellers in the towers would doubtless make it equally impossible for her to forage by day. There was but one solution of her difficulty and that was to return to her flier and pray that the wind would waft her to some less terrorful land; but when might she return to the flier? The banths gave little evidence of relinquishing hope of her, and even if they wandered out of sight would she dare risk the attempt? She doubted it.

Hopeless indeed seemed her situation—hopeless it was.

IV

CAPTURED

s Thuria, swift racer of the night, shot again into the sky the scene changed. As by magic a new aspect fell athwart the face of Nature. It was as though in the instant one had been transported from one planet to another. It was the age-old miracle of the Martian nights that is always new, even to Martians—two moons resplendent in the heavens, where one had been but now; conflicting, fast-changing shadows that altered the very hills themselves; far Cluros, stately, majestic, almost stationary, shedding his steady light upon the world below; Thuria, a great and glorious orb, swinging swift across the vaulted dome of the blue-black night, so low that she seemed to graze the hills, a gorgeous spectacle that held the girl now beneath the spell of its enchantment as it always had and always would.

"Ah, Thuria, mad queen of heaven!" murmured Tara of Helium. "The hills pass in stately procession, their bosoms rising and falling; the trees move in restless circles; the little grasses describe their little arcs; and all is movement, restless, mysterious movement without sound, while Thuria passes." The girl sighed and let her gaze fall again to the stern realities beneath. There was no mystery in the huge banths. He who had discovered her squatted there looking hungrily up at her. Most of the others had wandered away in search of other prey, but a few remained hoping yet to bury their fangs in that soft body.

The night wore on. Again Thuria left the heavens to her lord and master, hurrying on to keep her tryst with the Sun in other skies. But a single banth waited impatiently beneath the tree which harbored Tara of Helium. The others had left, but their roars, and growls, and moans thundered or rumbled, or floated back to her from near and far. What prey found they in this little valley? There must be something that they were accustomed to find here that they should be drawn in so great numbers. The girl wondered what it could be.

How long the night! Numb, cold, and exhausted, Tara of Helium clung to the tree in growing desperation, for once she had dozed and almost fallen. Hope was low in her brave little heart. How much more could she endure? She asked herself the question and then, with a brave shake of her head, she squared her shoulders. "I still live!" she said aloud.

The banth looked up and growled.

Came Thuria again and after awhile the great Sun—a flaming lover, pursuing his heart's desire. And Cluros, the cold husband, continued his serene way, as placid as before his house had been violated by this hot Lothario. And now the Sun and both Moons rode together in the sky, lending their far mysteries to make weird the Martian dawn. Tara of Helium looked out across the fair valley that spread upon all sides of her. It was rich and beautiful, but even as she looked upon it she shuddered, for to her mind came a picture of the headless things that the towers and the walls hid. Those by day and the banths by night! Ah, was it any wonder that she shuddered?

With the coming of the Sun the great Barsoomian lion rose to his feet. He turned angry eyes upon the girl above him, voiced a single ominous growl, and slunk away toward the hills. The girl watched him, and she saw that he gave the towers as wide a berth as possible and that he never took his eyes from one of them while he was passing it. Evidently the inmates had taught these savage creatures to respect them. Presently he passed from sight in a narrow defile, nor in any direction that she could see was there another. Momentarily at least the landscape was deserted. The girl wondered if she dared to attempt to regain the hills and her flier. She dreaded the coming of the workmen to the fields as she was sure they would come. She shrank from again seeing the headless bodies, and found herself wondering if these things would come out into the fields and work. She looked toward the nearest tower. There was no sign of life there. The valley lay quiet now and deserted. She lowered herself stiffly to the ground. Her muscles were cramped and every move brought a twinge of pain. Pausing a moment to drink again at the stream she felt refreshed and then turned without more delay toward the hills. To cover the distance as quickly as possible seemed the only plan to pursue. The trees no longer offered concealment and so she did not go out of her way to be near them. The hills seemed very far away. She had not thought, the night before, that she had traveled so far. Really it had not been far, but now, with the three towers to pass in broad daylight, the distance seemed great indeed.

The second tower lay almost directly in her path. To make a detour would not lessen the chance of detection, it would only lengthen the period of her danger, and so she laid her course straight for the hill where her flier was, regardless of the tower. As she passed the first enclosure she thought that she heard the sound of movement within, but the gate did not open and she breathed more easily when it lay behind her. She came then to the second enclosure, the outer wall of which she must circle, as it lay across her route. As she passed close along it she distinctly heard not only movement within, but voices. In the world-language of Barsoom she heard a man issuing instructions—so many were to pick usa, so many were to irrigate this field, so many to cultivate that, and so on, as a foreman lay out the day's work for his crew.

Tara of Helium had just reached the gate in the outer wall. Without warning it swung open toward her. She saw that for a moment it would hide her from those within and in that moment she turned and ran, keeping close to the wall, until, passing out of sight beyond the curve of the structure, she came to the opposite side of the enclosure. Here, panting from her exertion and from the excitement of her narrow escape, she threw herself among some tall weeds that grew close to the foot of the wall. There she lay trembling for sometime, not even daring to raise her head and look about. Never before had Tara of Helium felt the paralyzing effects of terror. She was shocked and angry at herself, that she, daughter of John Carter, Warlord of Barsoom, should exhibit fear. Not even the fact that there had been none there to witness it lessened her shame and anger, and the worst of it was she knew that under similar circumstances she would again be equally as craven. It was not the fear of death—she knew that. No, it was the thought of those headless bodies and that she might see them and that they might even touch her—lay hands upon her— seize her. She shuddered and trembled at the thought.

After a while she gained sufficient command of herself to raise her head and look about. To her horror she discovered that everywhere she looked she saw people working in the fields or preparing to do so. Workmen were coming from other towers. Little bands were passing to this field and that. There were even some already at work within thirty ads of her—about a hundred yards. There were ten, perhaps, in the party nearest her, both men and women, and all were beautiful of form and grotesque of face. So meager were their trappings that they were practically naked; a fact that was in no way remarkable among the tillers of the fields of Mars. Each wore the peculiar, high leather collar that completely hid the neck, and each wore sufficient other leather to support a single sword and a pocket-pouch. The leather was very old and worn, showing long, hard service, and was absolutely plain with the exception of a single device upon the left shoulder. The heads, however, were covered with ornaments of precious metals and jewels, so that little more than eyes, nose, and mouth were discernible. These were hideously inhuman and yet grotesquely human at the same time. The eyes were far apart and protruding, the nose scarce more than two small, parallel slits set vertically above a round hole that was the mouth. The heads were peculiarly repulsive—so much so that it seemed unbelievable to the girl that they formed an integral part of the beautiful bodies below them.

So fascinated was Tara of Helium that she could scarce take her eyes from the strange creatures—a fact that was to prove her undoing, for in order that she might see them she was forced to expose a part of her own head and presently, to her consternation, she saw that one of the creatures had stopped his work and was staring directly at her. She did not dare move, for it was still possible that the thing had not seen her, or at least was only suspicious that some creature lay hid among the weeds. If she could allay this suspicion by remaining motionless the creature might believe that he had been mistaken and return to his work; but, alas, such was not to be the case. She saw the thing call the attention of others to her and almost immediately four or five of them started to move in her direction.

It was impossible now to escape discovery. Her only hope lay in flight. If she could elude them and reach the hills and the flier ahead of them she might escape, and that could be accomplished in but one way—flight, immediate and swift. Leaping to her feet she darted along the base of the wall which she must skirt to the opposite side, beyond which lay the hill that was her goal. Her act was greeted by strange whistling sounds from the things behind her, and casting a glance over her shoulder she saw them all in rapid pursuit.

There were also shrill commands that she halt, but to these she paid no attention. Before she had half circled the enclosure she discovered that her chances for successful escape were great, since it was evident to her that her pursuers were not so fleet as she. High indeed then were her hopes as she came in sight of the hill, but they were soon dashed by what lay before her, for there, in the fields that lay between, were fully a hundred creatures similar to those behind her and all were on the alert, evidently warned by the whistling of their fellows. Instructions and commands were shouted to and fro, with the result that those before her spread roughly into a great half circle to intercept her, and when she turned to the right, hoping to elude the net, she saw others coming from fields beyond, and to the left the same was true. But Tara of Helium would not admit defeat. Without once pausing she turned directly toward the center of the advancing semi-circle, beyond which lay her single chance of escape, and as she ran she drew her long, slim dagger. Like her valiant sire, if die she must, she would die fighting. There were gaps in the thin line confronting her and toward the widest of one of these she directed her course. The things on either side of the opening guessed her intent for they closed in to place themselves in her path. This widened the openings on either side of them and as the girl appeared almost to rush into their arms she turned suddenly at right angles, ran swiftly in the new direction for a few yards, and then dashed quickly toward the hill again. Now only a single warrior, with a wide gap on either side of him, barred her clear way to freedom, though all the others were speeding as rapidly as they could to intercept her. If she could pass this one without too much delay she could escape, of that she was certain. Her every hope hinged on this. The creature before her realized it, too, for he moved cautiously, though swiftly, to intercept her, as a Rugby fullback might maneuver in the realization that he alone stood between the opposing team and a touchdown.

At first Tara of Helium had hoped that she might dodge him, for she could not but guess that she was not only more fleet but infinitely more agile than these strange creatures; but soon there came to her the realization that in the time consumed in an attempt to elude his grasp his nearer fellows would be upon her and escape then impossible, so she chose instead to charge straight for him, and when he guessed her decision he stood, half crouching and with outstretched arms, awaiting her. In one hand was his sword, but a voice arose, crying in tones of authority. "Take her alive! Do not harm her!" Instantly the fellow returned his sword to its scabbard and then Tara of Helium was upon him. Straight for that beautiful body she sprang and in the instant that the arms closed to seize her her sharp blade drove deep into the naked chest. The impact hurled them both to the ground and as Tara of Helium sprang to her feet again she saw, to her horror, that the loathsome head had rolled from the body and was now crawling away from her on six short, spider-like legs. The body struggled spasmodically and lay still. As brief as had been the delay caused by the encounter, it still had been of sufficient duration to undo her, for even as she rose two more of the things fell upon her and instantly thereafter she was surrounded. Her blade sank once more into naked flesh and once more a head rolled free and crawled away. Then they overpowered her and in another moment she was surrounded by fully a hundred of the creatures, all seeking to lay hands upon her. At first she thought that they wished to tear her to pieces in revenge for her having slain two of their fellows, but presently she realized that they were prompted more by curiosity than by any sinister motive.

"Come!" said one of her captors, both of whom had retained a hold upon her. As he spoke he tried to lead her away with him toward the nearest tower.

"She belongs to me," cried the other. "Did not I capture her? She will come with me to the tower of Moak."

"Never!" insisted the first. "She is Luud's. To Luud I will take her, and whosoever interferes may feel the keenness of my sword— in the head!" He almost shouted the last three words.

"Come! Enough of this," cried one who spoke with some show of authority. "She was captured in Luud's fields—she will go to Luud."

"She was discovered in Moak's fields, at the very foot of the tower of Moak," insisted he who had claimed her for Moak.

"You have heard the Nolach speak," cried the Luud. "It shall be as he says."

"Not while this Moak holds a sword," replied the other. "Rather will I cut her in twain and take my half to Moak than to relinquish her all to Luud," and he drew his sword, or rather he laid his hand upon its hilt in a threatening gesture; but before ever he could draw it the Luud had whipped his out and with a fearful blow cut deep into the head of his adversary. Instantly the big, round head collapsed, almost as a punctured balloon collapses, as a grayish, semi-fluid matter spurted from it. The protruding eyes, apparently lidless, merely stared, the sphincter-like muscle of the mouth opened and closed, and then the head toppled from the body to the ground. The body stood dully for a moment and then slowly started to wander aimlessly about until one of the others seized it by the arm.

One of the two heads crawling about on the ground now approached. "This rykor belongs to Moak," it said. "I am a Moak. I will take it," and without further discussion it commenced to crawl up the front of the headless body, using its six short, spider-like legs and two stout chelae which grew just in front of its legs and strongly resembled those of an Earthly lobster, except that they were both of the same size. The body in the meantime stood in passive indifference, its arms hanging idly at its sides. The head climbed to the shoulders and settled itself inside the leather collar that now hid its chelae and legs. Almost immediately the body gave evidence of intelligent animation. It raised its hands and adjusted the collar more comfortably, it took the head between its palms and settled it in place and when it moved around it did not wander aimlessly, but instead its steps were firm and to some purpose.

The girl watched all these things in growing wonder, and presently, no other of the Moaks seeming inclined to dispute the right of the Luud to her, she was led off by her captor toward the nearest tower. Several accompanied them, including one who carried the loose head under his arm. The head that was being carried conversed with the head upon the shoulders of the thing that carried it. Tara of Helium shivered. It was horrible! All that she had seen of these frightful creatures was horrible. And to be a prisoner, wholly in their power. Shadow of her first ancestor! What had she done to deserve so cruel a fate?

At the wall enclosing the tower they paused while one opened the gate and then they passed within the enclosure, which, to the girl's horror, she found filled with headless bodies. The creature who carried the bodiless head now set its burden upon the ground and the latter immediately crawled toward one of the bodies that was lying near by. Some wandered stupidly to and fro, but this one lay still. It was a female. The head crawled to it and made its way to the shoulders where it settled itself. At once the body sprang lightly erect. Another of those who had accompanied them from the fields approached with the harness and collar that had been taken from the dead body that the head had formerly topped. The new body now appropriated these and the hands deftly adjusted them. The creature was now as good as before Tara of Helium had struck down its former body with her slim blade. But there was a difference. Before it had been male—now it was female. That, however, seemed to make no difference to the head. In fact, Tara of Helium had noticed during the scramble and the fight about her that sex differences seemed of little moment to her captors. Males and females had taken equal part in her pursuit, both were identically harnessed and both carried swords, and she had seen as many females as males draw their weapons at the moment that a quarrel between the two factions seemed imminent.

The girl was given but brief opportunity for further observation of the pitiful creatures in the enclosure as her captor, after having directed the others to return to the fields, led her toward the tower, which they entered, passing into an apartment about ten feet wide and twenty long, in one end of which was a stairway leading to an upper level and in the other an opening to a similar stairway leading downward. The chamber, though on a level with the ground, was brilliantly lighted by windows in its inner wall, the light coming from a circular court in the center of the tower. The walls of this court appeared to be faced with what resembled glazed, white tile and the whole interior of it was flooded with dazzling light, a fact which immediately explained to the girl the purpose of the glass prisms of which the domes were constructed. The stairways themselves were sufficient to cause remark, since in nearly all Barsoomian architecture inclined runways are utilized for purposes of communication between different levels, and especially is this true of the more ancient forms and of those of remote districts where fewer changes have come to alter the customs of antiquity.

Down the stairway her captor led Tara of Helium. Down and down through chambers still lighted from the brilliant well. Occasionally they passed others going in the opposite direction and these always stopped to examine the girl and ask questions of her captor.

"I know nothing but that she was found in the fields and that I caught her after a fight in which she slew two rykors and in which I slew a Moak, and that I take her to Luud, to whom, of course, she belongs. If Luud wishes to question her that is for Luud to do—not for me." Thus always he answered the curious.

Presently they reached a room from which a circular tunnel led away from the tower, and into this the creature conducted her. The tunnel was some seven feet in diameter and flattened on the bottom to form a walk. For a hundred feet from the tower it was lined with the same tile-like material of the light well and amply illuminated by reflected light from that source. Beyond it was faced with stone of various shapes and sizes, neatly cut and fitted together—a very fine mosaic without a pattern. There were branches, too, and other tunnels which crossed this, and occasionally openings not more than a foot in diameter; these latter being usually close to the floor.

Above each of these smaller openings was painted a different device, while upon the walls of the larger tunnels at all intersections and points of convergence hieroglyphics appeared. These the girl could not read though she guessed that they were the names of the tunnels, or notices indicating the points to which they led. She tried to study some of them out, but there was not a character that was familiar to her, which seemed strange, since, while the written languages of the various nations of Barsoom differ, it still is true that they have many characters and words in common.

She had tried to converse with her guard but he had not seemed inclined to talk with her and she had finally desisted. She could not but note that he had offered her no indignities, nor had he been either unnecessarily rough or in any way cruel. The fact that she had slain two of the bodies with her dagger had apparently aroused no animosity or desire for revenge in the minds of the strange heads that surmounted the bodies—even those whose bodies had been killed. She did not try to understand it, since she could not approach the peculiar relationship between the heads and the bodies of these creatures from the basis of any past knowledge or experience of her own. So far their treatment of her seemed to augur naught that might arouse her fears. Perhaps, after all, she had been fortunate to fall into the hands of these strange people, who might not only protect her from harm, but even aid her in returning to Helium. That they were repulsive and uncanny she could not forget, but if they meant her no harm she could, at least, overlook their repulsiveness. Renewed hope aroused within her a spirit of greater cheerfulness, and it was almost blithely now that she moved at the side of her weird companion. She even caught herself humming a gay little rune that was then popular in Helium. The creature at her side turned its expressionless eyes upon her.

"What is that noise that you are making?" it asked.

"I was but humming an air," she replied.

"'Humming an air,'" he repeated. "I do not know what you mean; but do it again, I like it."

This time she sang the words, while her companion listened intently. His face gave no indication of what was passing in that strange head. It was as devoid of expression as that of a spider. It reminded her of a spider. When she had finished he turned toward her again.

"That was different," he said. "I liked that better, even, than the other. How do you do it?"

"Why," she said, "it is singing. Do you not know what song is?"

"No," he replied. "Tell me how you do it."

"It is difficult to explain," she told him. "since any explanation of it presupposes some knowledge of melody and of music, while your very question indicates that you have no knowledge of either."

"No," he said, "I do not know what you are talking about; but tell me how you do it."

"It is merely the melodious modulations of my voice," she explained. "Listen!" and again she sang.

"I do not understand," he insisted; "but I like it. Could you teach me to do it?"

"I do not know, but I shall be glad to try."

"We will see what Luud does with you," he said. "If he does not want you I will keep you and you shall teach me to make sounds like that."

At his request she sang again as they continued their way along the winding tunnel, which was now lighted by occasional bulbs which appeared to be similar to the radium bulbs with which she was familiar and which were common to all the nations of Barsoom, insofar as she knew, having been perfected at so remote a period that their very origin was lost in antiquity. They consist, usually, of a hemispherical bowl of heavy glass in which is packed a compound containing what, according to John Carter, must be radium. The bowl is then cemented into a metal plate with a heavily insulated back and the whole affair set in the masonry of wall or ceiling as desired, where it gives off light of greater or less intensity, according to the composition of the filling material, for an almost incalculable period of time.

As they proceeded they met a greater number of the inhabitants of this underground world, and the girl noted that among many of these the metal and harness were more ornate than had been those of the workers in the fields above. The heads and bodies, however, were similar, even identical, she thought. No one offered her harm and she was now experiencing a feeling of relief almost akin to happiness, when her guide turned suddenly into an opening on the right side of the tunnel and she found herself in a large, well lighted chamber.

V

THE PERFECT BRAIN

he song that had been upon her lips as she entered died there—frozen by the sight of horror that met her eyes. In the center of the chamber a headless body lay upon the floor—a body that had been partially devoured—while over and upon it crawled a half a dozen heads upon their short, spider legs, and they tore at the flesh of the woman with their chelae and carried the bits to their awful mouths. They were eating human flesh—eating it raw!

Tara of Helium gasped in horror and turning away covered her eyes with her palms.

"Come!" said her captor. "What is the matter?"

"They are eating the flesh of the woman," she whispered in tones of horror.

"Why not?" he inquired. "Did you suppose that we kept the rykor for labor alone? Ah, no. They are delicious when kept and fattened. Fortunate, too, are those that are bred for food, since they are never called upon to do aught but eat."

"It is hideous!" she cried.

He looked at her steadily for a moment, but whether in surprise, in anger, or in pity his expressionless face did not reveal. Then he led her on across the room past the frightful thing, from which she turned away her eyes. Lying about the floor near the walls were half a dozen headless bodies in harness. These she guessed had been abandoned temporarily by the feasting heads until they again required their services. In the walls of this room there were many of the small, round openings she had noticed in various parts of the tunnels, the purpose of which she could not guess.

They passed through another corridor and then into a second chamber, larger than the first and more brilliantly illuminated. Within were several of the creatures with heads and bodies assembled, while many headless bodies lay about near the walls. Here her captor halted and spoke to one of the occupants of the chamber.

"I seek Luud," he said. "I bring to Luud a creature that I captured in the fields above."

The others crowded about to examine Tara of Helium. One of them whistled, whereupon the girl learned something of the smaller openings in the walls, for almost immediately there crawled from them, like giant spiders, a score or more of the hideous heads. Each sought one of the recumbent bodies and fastened itself in place. Immediately the bodies reacted to the intelligent direction of the heads. They arose, the hands adjusted the leather collars and put the balance of the harness in order, then the creatures crossed the room to where Tara of Helium stood. She noted that their leather was more highly ornamented than that worn by any of the others she had previously seen, and so she guessed that these must be higher in authority than the others. Nor was she mistaken. The demeanor of her captor indicated it. He addressed them as one who holds intercourse with superiors.

Several of those who examined her felt her flesh, pinching it gently between thumb and forefinger, a familiarity that the girl resented. She struck down their hands. "Do not touch me!" she cried, imperiously, for was she not a princess of Helium? The expression on those terrible faces did not change. She could not tell whether they were angry or amused, whether her action had filled them with respect for her, or contempt. Only one of them spoke immediately.

"She will have to be fattened more," he said.

The girl's eyes went wide with horror. She turned upon her captor. "Do these frightful creatures intend to devour me?" she cried.

"That is for Luud to say," he replied, and then he leaned closer so that his mouth was near her ear. "That noise you made which you called song pleased me," he whispered, "and I will repay you by warning you not to antagonize these kaldanes. They are very powerful. Luud listens to them. Do not call them frightful. They are very handsome. Look at their wonderful trappings, their gold, their jewels."

"Thank you," she said. "You called them kaldanes—what does that mean?"

"We are all kaldanes," he replied.

"You, too?" and she pointed at him, her slim finger directed toward his chest.

"No, not this," he explained, touching his body; "this is a rykor; but this," and he touched his head, "is a kaldane. It is the brain, the intellect, the power that directs all things. The rykor," he indicated his body, "is nothing. It is not so much even as the jewels upon our harness; no, not so much as the harness itself. It carries us about. It is true that we would find difficulty getting along without it; but it has less value than harness or jewels because it is less difficult to reproduce." He turned again to the other kaldanes. "Will you notify Luud that I am here?" he asked.

"Sept has already gone to Luud. He will tell him," replied one. "Where did you find this rykor with the strange kaldane that cannot detach itself?"

The girl's captor narrated once more the story of her capture. He stated facts just as they had occurred, without embellishment, his voice as expressionless as his face, and his story was received in the same manner that it was delivered. The creatures seemed totally lacking in emotion, or, at least, the capacity to express it. It was

214

impossible to judge what impression the story made upon them, or even if they heard it. Their protruding eyes simply stared and occasionally the muscles of their mouths opened and closed. Familiarity did not lessen the horror the girl felt for them. The more she saw of them the more repulsive they seemed. Often her body was shaken by convulsive shudders as she looked at the kaldanes, but when her eyes wandered to the beautiful bodies and she could for a moment expunge the heads from her consciousness the effect was soothing and refreshing, though when the bodies lay, headless, upon the floor they were quite as shocking as the heads mounted on bodies. But by far the most gruesome and uncanny sight of all was that of the heads crawling about upon their spider legs. If one of these should approach and touch her Tara of Helium was positive that she should scream, while should one attempt to crawl up her person— ugh! the very idea induced a feeling of faintness.

Sept returned to the chamber. "Luud will see you and the captive. Come!" he said, and turned toward a door opposite that through which Tara of Helium had entered the chamber. "What is your name?" His question was directed to the girl's captor.

"I am Ghek, third foreman of the fields of Luud," he answered.

"And hers?"

"I do not know."

"It makes no difference. Come!"

The patrician brows of Tara of Helium went high. It made no difference, indeed! She, a princess of Helium; only daughter of The Warlord of Barsoom!

"Wait!" she cried. "It makes much difference who I am. If you are conducting me into the presence of your jed you may announce The Princess Tara of Helium, daughter of John Carter, The Warlord of Barsoom."

"Hold your peace!" commanded Sept. "Speak when you are spoken to. Come with me!"

The anger of Tara of Helium all but choked her. "Come," admonished Ghek, and took her by the arm, and Tara of Helium came. She was naught but a prisoner. Her rank and titles meant nothing to these inhuman monsters. They led her through a short, S-shaped passageway into a chamber entirely lined with the white, tile-like material with which the interior of the light wall was faced. Close to the base of the walls were numerous smaller apertures, circular in shape, but larger than those of similar aspect that she had noted elsewhere. The majority of these apertures were sealed. Directly opposite the entrance was one framed in gold, and above it a peculiar device was inlaid in the same precious metal.

Sept and Ghek halted just within the room, the girl between them, and all three stood silently facing the opening in the opposite wall. On the floor beside the aperture lay a headless male body of almost heroic proportions, and on either side of this stood a heavily armed warrior, with drawn sword. For perhaps five minutes the three waited and then something appeared in the opening. It was a pair of large chelae and immediately thereafter there crawled forth a hideous kaldane of enormous proportions. He was half again as large as any that Tara of Helium had yet seen and his whole aspect infinitely more terrible. The skin of the others was a bluish gray—this one was of a little bluer tinge and the eyes were ringed with bands of white and scarlet, as was its mouth.

From each nostril a band of white and one of scarlet extended outward horizontally the width of the face.

No one spoke or moved. The creature crawled to the prostrate body and affixed itself to the neck. Then the two rose as one and approached the girl. He looked at her and then he spoke to her captor.

"You are the third foreman of the fields of Luud?" he asked.

"Yes, Luud; I am called Ghek."

"Tell me what you know of this," and he nodded toward Tara of Helium.

Ghek did as he was bid and then Luud addressed the girl.

"What were you doing within the borders of Bantoom?" he asked.

"I was blown hither in a great storm that injured my flier and carried me I knew not where. I came down into the valley at night for food and drink. The banths came and drove me to the safety of a tree, and then your people caught me as I was trying to leave the valley. I do not know why they took me. I was doing no harm. All I ask is that you let me go my way in peace."

"None who enters Bantoom ever leaves," replied Luud.

"But my people are not at war with yours. I am a princess of Helium; my great-grandfather is a jeddak; my grandfather a jed; and my father is Warlord of all Barsoom. You have no right to keep me and I demand that you liberate me at once."

"None who enters Bantoom ever leaves," repeated the creature without expression. "I know nothing of the lesser creatures of Barsoom, of whom you speak. There is but one high race—the race of Bantoomians. All Nature exists to serve them. You shall do your share, but not yet—you are too skinny. We shall have to put some fat upon it, Sept. I tire of rykor. Perhaps this will have a different flavor. The banths are too rank and it is seldom that any other creature enters the valley. And you, Ghek; you shall be rewarded. I shall promote you from the fields to the burrows. Hereafter you shall remain underground as every Bantoomian longs to. No more shall you be forced to endure the hated sun, or look upon the hideous sky, or the hateful growing things that defile the surface. For the present you shall look after this thing that you have brought me, seeing that it sleeps and eats—and does nothing else. You understand me, Ghek; nothing else!"

"I understand, Luud," replied the other.

"Take it away!" commanded the creature.

Ghek turned and led Tara of Helium from the apartment. The

girl was horrified by contemplation of the fate that awaited her—a fate from which it seemed, there was no escape. It was only too evident that these creatures possessed no gentle or chivalric sentiments to which she could appeal, and that she might escape from the labyrinthine mazes of their underground burrows appeared impossible.

Outside the audience chamber Sept overtook them and conversed with Ghek for a brief period, then her keeper led her through a confusing web of winding tunnels until they came to a small apartment.

"We are to remain here for a while. It may be that Luud will send for you again. If he does you will probably not be fattened—he will use you for another purpose." It was fortunate for the girl's peace of mind that she did not realize what he meant. "Sing for me," said Ghek, presently.

Tara of Helium did not feel at all like singing, but she sang, nevertheless, for there was always the hope that she might escape if given the opportuniy and if she could win the friendship of one of the creatures, her chances would be increased proportionately. All during the ordeal, for such it was to the overwrought girl, Ghek stood with his eyes fixed upon her.

"It is wonderful," he said, when she had finished; "but I did not tell Luud—you noticed that I did not tell Luud about it. Had he known, he would have had you sing to him and that would have resulted in your being kept with him that he might hear you sing whenever he wished; but now I can have you all the time."

"How do you know he would like my singing?" she asked.

"He would have to," replied Ghek. "If I like a thing he has to like it, for are we not identical—all of us?"

"The people of my race do not all like the same things," said the girl.

"How strange!" commented Ghek. "All kaldanes like the same things and dislike the same things. If I discover something new and like it I know that all kaldanes will like it. That is how I know that Luud would like your singing. You see we are all exactly alike."

"But you do not look like Luud," said the girl.

"Luud is king. He is larger and more gorgeously marked; but otherwise he and I are identical, and why not? Did not Luud produce the egg from which I hatched?"

"What?" queried the girl; "I do not understand you."

"Yes," explained Ghek, "all of us are from Luud's eggs, just as all the swarm of Moak are from Moak's eggs."

"Oh!" exclaimed Tara of Helium understandingly; "you mean that Luud has many wives and that you are the offspring of one of them."

"No, not that at all," replied Ghek. "Luud has no wife. He lays the eggs himself. You do not understand."

Tara of Helium admitted that she did not.

"I will try to explain, then," said Ghek, "if you will promise to sing to me later."

"I promise," she said.

"We are not like the rykors," he began. "They are creatures of a low order, like yourself and the banths and such things. We have no sex—not one of us except our king, who is bi-sexual. He produces many eggs from which we, the workers and the warriors, are hatched; and one in every thousand eggs is another king egg, from which a king is hatched. Did you notice the sealed openings in the room where you saw Luud? Sealed in each of those is another king. If one of them escaped he would fall upon Luud and try to kill him and if he succeeded we should have a new king; but there would be no difference. His name would be Luud and all would go on as before, for are we not all alike? Luud has lived a long time and has produced many kings, so he lets only a few live that there may be a successor to him when he dies. The others he kills."

"Why does he keep more than one?" queried the girl.

"Sometimes accidents occur," replied Ghek, "and all the kings that a swarm has saved are killed. When this happens the swarm comes and obtains another king from a neighboring swarm."

"Are all of you the children of Luud?" she asked.

"All but a few, who are from the eggs of the preceding king, as was Luud; but Luud has lived a long time and not many of the others are left."

"You live a long time, or short?" Tara asked.

"A very long time."

"And the rykors, too; they live a long time?"

"No; the rykors live for ten years, perhaps," he said, "if they remain strong and useful. When they can no longer be of service to us, either through age or sickness, we leave them in the fields and the banths come at night and get them."

"How horrible!" she exclaimed.

"Horrible?" he repeated. "I see nothing horrible about that.

"The rykors are but brainless flesh. They neither see, nor feel, nor hear. They can scarce move but for us. If we did not bring them food they would starve to death. They are less deserving of thought than our leather. All that they can do for themselves is to take food from a trough and put it in their mouths, but with us—look at them!" and he proudly exhibited the noble figure that he surmounted, palpitant with life and energy and feeling.

"How do you do it?" asked Tara of Helium. "I do not understand it at all."

"I will show you," he said, and lay down upon the floor. Then he detached himself from the body, which lay as a thing dead. On his spider legs he walked toward the girl. "Now look," he admonished her. "Do you see this thing?" and he extended what appeared to be a bundle of tentacles from the posterior part of his head. "There is an aperture just back of the rykor's mouth and directly over the upper end of his spinal column. Into this aperture I insert my tentacles and seize the spinal cord. Immediately I control every muscle of the rykor's body—it becomes my own, just as you direct the movement of the muscles of your body. I feel what the rykor would feel if he had a head and brain. If he is hurt, I would suffer if I remained connected with him; but the instant one of them is injured or becomes sick we desert it for another. As we would suffer the pains of their physical injuries, similarly do we enjoy the physical pleasures of the rykors. When your body becomes fatigued you are comparatively useless; it is sick, you are sick; if it is killed, you die. You are the slave of a mass of stupid flesh and bone and blood. There is nothing more wonderful about your carcass than there is about the carcass of a banth. It is only your brain that makes you superior to the banth, but your brain is bound by the limitations of your body. Not so, ours. With us brain is everything. Ninety per centum of our volume is brain. We have only the simplest of vital organs and they are very small for they do not have to assist in the support of a complicated system of nerves, muscles, flesh and bone. We have no lungs, for we do not require air. Far below the levels to which we can take the rykors is a vast network of burrows where the real life of the kaldane is lived. There the air-breathing rykor would perish as you would perish. There we have stored vast quantities of food in hermetically sealed chambers. It will last forever. Far beneath the surface is water that will flow for countless ages after the surface water is exhausted. We are preparing for the time we know must come—the time when the last vestige of the Barsoomian atmosphere is spent—when the waters and the food are gone. For this purpose were we created, that there might not perish from the planet Nature's divinest creation— the perfect brain."

"But what purpose can you serve when that time comes?" asked the girl.

"You do not understand," he said. "It is too big for you to grasp, but I will try to explain it. Barsoom, the moons, the sun, the stars, were created for a single purpose. From the beginning of time Nature has labored arduously toward the consummation of this purpose. At the very beginning things existed with life, but with no brain. Gradually rudimentary nervous systems and minute brains evolved. Evolution proceeded. The brains became larger and more powerful. In us you see the highest development; but there are those of us who believe that there is yet another step—that sometime in the far future our race shall develop into the super-thing—just brain. The incubus of legs and chelae and vital organs will be removed. The future kaldane will be nothing but a great brain. Deaf, dumb, and blind it will lie sealed in its buried vault far beneath the surface of Barsoom—just a great, wonderful, beautiful brain with nothing to distract it from eternal thought."

"You mean it will just lie there and think?" cried Tara of Helium.

"Just that!" he exclaimed. "Could aught be more wonderful?"

"Yes," replied the girl, "I can think of a number of things that would be infinitely more wonderful."

VI

In the Toils of Horror

hat the creature had told her gave Tara of Helium food for thought. She had been taught that every created thing fulfilled some useful purpose, and she tried conscientiously to discover just what was the rightful place of the kaldane in the universal scheme of things. She knew that it must have its place but what that place was it was beyond her to conceive. She had to give it up. They recalled to her mind a little group of people in Helium who had forsworn the pleasures of life in the pursuit of knowledge. They were rather patronizing in their relations with those whom they thought not so intellectual. They considered themselves quite superior. She smiled at recollection of a remark her father had once made concerning them, to the effect that if one of them ever dropped his egotism and broke it it would take a week to fumigate Helium. Her father liked normal people—people who knew too little and people who knew too much were equally a bore. Tara of Helium was like her father in this respect and like him, too, she was both sane and normal.

Outside of her personal danger there was much in this strange world that interested her. The rykors aroused her keenest pity, and vast conjecture. How and from what form had they evolved? She asked Ghek.

"Sing to me again and I will tell you," he said. "If Luud would let me have you, you should never die. I should keep you always to sing to me."

The girl marvelled at the effect her voice had upon the creature. Somewhere in that enormous brain there was a chord that was touched by melody. It was the sole link between herself and the brain when detached from the rykor. When it dominated the rykor it might have other human instincts; but these she dreaded even to think of. After she had sung she waited for Ghek to speak. For a long time he was silent, just looking at her through those awful eyes.

"I wonder," he said presently, "if it might not be pleasant to be of your race. Do you all sing?"

"Nearly all, a little," she said; "but we do many other interesting and enjoyable things. We dance and play and work and love and sometimes we fight, for we are a race of warriors."

"Love!" said the kaldane. "I think I know what you mean; but we, fortunately, are above sentiment—when we are detached. But when we dominate the rykor—ah, that is different, and when I hear you sing and look at your beautiful body I know what you mean by love. I could love you."

The girl shrank from him. "You promised to tell me the origin of the rykor," she reminded him.

"Ages ago," he commenced, "our bodies were larger and our heads smaller. Our legs were very weak and we could not travel fast or far. There was a stupid creature that went upon four legs. It lived in a hole in the ground, to which it brought its food, so we ran our burrows into this hole and ate the food it brought; but it did not bring enough for all—for itself and all the kaldanes that lived upon it, so we had also to go abroad and get food. This was hard work for our weak legs. Then it was that we commenced to ride upon the backs of these primitive rykors. It took many ages, undoubtedly, but at last came the time when the kaldane had found means to guide the rykor, until presently the latter depended entirely upon the superior brain of his master to guide him to food. The brain of the rykor grew smaller as time went on. His ears went and his eyes, for he no longer had use for them—the kaldane saw and heard for him. By similar steps the rykor came to go upon its hind feet that the kaldane might be able to see farther. As the brain shrank, so did the head. The mouth was the only feature of the head that was used and so the mouth alone remains. Members of the red race fell into the hands of our ancestors from time to time. They saw the beauties and the advantages of the form that nature had given the red race over that which the rykor was developing into. By intelligent crossing the present rykor was achieved. He is really solely the product of the super-intelligence of the kaldane—he is our body, to do with as we see fit, just as you do what you see fit with your body, only we have the advantage of possessing an unlimited supply of bodies. Do you not wish that you were a kaldane?"

For how long they kept her in the subterranean chamber Tara of Helium did not know. It seemed a very long time. She ate and slept and watched the interminable lines of creatures that passed the entrance to her prison. There was a laden line passing from above carrying food, food, food. In the other line they returned empty handed. When she saw them she knew that it was daylight above. When they did not pass she knew it was night, and that the banths were about devouring the rykors that had been abandoned in the fields the previous day. She commenced to grow pale and thin. She did not like the food they gave her—it was not suited to her kind— nor would she have eaten overmuch palatable food, for the fear of becoming fat. The idea of plumpness had a new significance here—a horrible significance.

Ghek noted that she was growing thin and white. He spoke to her about it and she told him that she could not thrive thus beneath the ground—that she must have fresh air and sunshine, or she would wither and die. Evidently he carried her words to Luud, since it was not long after that he told her that the king had ordered that she be confined in the tower and to the tower she was taken. She had hoped against hope that this very thing might result from her conversation with Ghek. Even to see the sun again was something, but now there sprang to her breast a hope that she had not dared to nurse before, while she lay in the terrible labyrinth from which she knew she could never have found her way to the outer world; but now there was some slight reason to hope. At least she could see the hills and if she could see them might there not come also the opportunity to reach them? If she could have but ten minutes—just ten little minutes! The flier was still there—she knew that it must be. Just ten minutes and she would be free—free forever from this frightful place; but the days wore on and she was never alone, not even for half of ten minutes. Many times she planned her escape. Had it not been for the banths it had been easy of accomplishment by night. Ghek always detached his body then and sank into what seemed a semi-comatose condition. It could not be said that he slept, or at least it did not appear like sleep, since his lidless eyes were unchanged; but he lay quietly in a corner. Tara of Helium enacted a thousand times in her mind the scene of her escape. She would rush to the side of the rykor and seize the sword that hung in its harness. Before Ghek knew what she purposed, she would have this and then before he could give an alarm she would drive the blade through his hideous head. It would take but a moment to reach the enclosure. The rykors could not stop her, for they had no brains to tell them that she was escaping. She had watched from her window the opening and closing of the gate that led from the enclosure out into the fields and she knew how the great latch operated. She would pass through and make a quick dash for the hill. It was so near that they could not overtake her. It was so easy! Or it would have been but for the banths! The banths at night and the workers in the fields by day.

Confined to the tower and without proper exercise or food, the girl failed to show the improvement that her captors desired. Ghek questioned her in an effort to learn why it was that she did not grow round and plump; that she did not even look as well as when they had captured her. His concern was prompted by repeated inquiries on the part of Luud and finally resulted in suggesting to Tara of Helium a plan whereby she might find a new opportunity of escape.

"I am accustomed to walking in the fresh air and the sunlight," she told Ghek. "I cannot become as I was before if I am to be always shut away in this one chamber, breathing poor air and getting no proper exercise. Permit me to go out in the fields everyday and walk about while the sun is shining. Then, I am sure, I shall become nice and fat."

"You would run away," he said.

"But how could I if you were always with me?" she asked. "And even if I wished to run away where could I go? I do not know even the direction of Helium. It must be very far. The very first night the banths would get me, would they not?"

"They would," said Ghek. "I will ask Luud about it."

The following day he told her that Luud had said that she was to be taken into the fields. He would try that for a time and see if she improved.

"If you do not grow fatter he will send for you anyway," said Ghek; "but he will not use you for food."

Tara of Helium shuddered.

That day and for many days thereafter she was taken from the tower, through the enclosure and out into the fields. Always was she alert for an opportunity to escape; but Ghek was always close by her side. It was not so much his presence that deterred her from making the attempt as the number of workers that were always between her and the hills where the flier lay. She could easily have eluded Ghek, but there were too many of the others. And then, one day, Ghek told her as he accompanied her into the open that this would be the last time.

"Tonight you go to Luud," he said. "I am sorry as I shall not hear you sing again."

"Tonight!" She scarce breathed the word, yet it was vibrant with horror.

She glanced quickly toward the hills. They were so dose! Yet between were the inevitable workers—perhaps a score of them.

"Let us walk over there?" she said, indicating them. "I should like to see what they are doing."

"It is too far," said Ghek. "I hate the sun. It is much pleasanter here where I can stand beneath the shade of this tree."

"All right," she agreed; "then you stay here and I will walk over. It will take me but a minute."

"No," he answered. "I will go with you. You want to escape; but you are not going to."

"I cannot escape," she said.

"I know it," agreed Ghek; "but you might try. I do not wish you to try. Possibly it will be better if we return to the tower at once. It would go hard with me should you escape."

Tara of Helium saw her last chance fading into oblivion. There would never be another after today. She cast about for some pretext to lure him even a little nearer to the hills.

"It is very little that I ask," she said. "Tonight you will want me to sing to you. It will be the last time, if you do not let me go and see what those kaldanes are doing I shall never sing to you again."

Ghek hesitated. "I will hold you by the arm all the time, then," he said.

"Why, of course, if you wish," she assented. "Come!"

The two moved toward the workers and the hills. The little party was digging tubers from the ground. She had noted this and that nearly always they were stooped low over their work, the hideous eyes bent upon the upturned soil. She led Ghek quite close to them, pretending that she wished to see exactly how they did the work, and all the time he held her tightly by her left wrist.

"It is very interesting," she said, with a sigh, and then, suddenly; "Look, Ghek!" and pointed quickly back in the direction of the tower. The kaldane, still holding her turned half away from her to look in the direction she had indicated and simultaneously, with the quickness of a banth, she struck him with her right fist, backed by every ounce of strength she possessed—struck the back of the pulpy head just above the collar. The blow was sufficient to accomplish her design, dislodging the kaldane from its rykor and tumbling it to the ground. Instantly the grasp upon her wrist relaxed as the body, no longer controlled by the brain of Ghek, stumbled aimlessly about for an instant before it sank to its knees and then rolled over on its back; but Tara of Helium waited not to note the full results of her act. The instant the fingers loosened upon her wrist she broke away and dashed toward the hills. Simultaneously a warning whistle broke from Ghek's lips and in instant response the workers leaped to their feet, one almost in the girl's path. She dodged the outstretched arms and was away again toward the hills and freedom, when her foot caught in one of the hoe-like instruments with which the soil had been upturned and which had been left, half imbedded in the ground. For an instant she ran on, stumbling, in a mad effort to regain her equilibrium, but the upturned furrows caught her feet—again she stumbled and this time went down, and as she scrambled to rise again a heavy body fell upon her and seized her arms. A moment later she was surrounded and dragged to her feet and as she looked around she saw Ghek crawling to his prostrate rykor. A moment later he advanced to her side.

The hideous face, incapable of registering emotion, gave no clue to what was passing in the enormous brain. Was he nursing thoughts of anger, of hate, of revenge? Tara of Helium could not guess, nor did she care. The worst had happened. She had tried to escape and she had failed. There would never be another opportunity.

"Come!" said Ghek. "We will return to the tower." The deadly monotone of his voice was unbroken. It was worse than anger, for it revealed nothing of his intentions. It but increased her horror of these great brains that were beyond the possibility of human emotions.

And so she was dragged back to her prison in the tower and Ghek took up his vigil again, squatting by the doorway, but now he carried a naked sword in his hand and did not quit his rykor, only to change to another that be had brought to him when the first gave indications of weariness. The girl sat looking at him. He had not been unkind to her, but she felt no sense of gratitude, nor, on the other hand, any sense of hatred. The brains, incapable themselves of any of the finer sentiments, awoke none in her. She could not feel gratitude, or affection, or hatred of them. There was only the same unceasing sense of horror in their presence. She had heard great scientists discuss the future of the red race and she recalled that some had maintained that eventually the brain would entirely dominate the man. There would be no more instinctive acts or emotions, nothing would be done on impulse; but on the contrary reason would direct our every act. The propounder of the theory regretted that he might never enjoy the blessings of such a state, which, he argued, would result in the ideal life for mankind.

Tara of Helium wished with all her heart that this learned scientist might be here to experience to the full the practical results of the fulfillment of his prophecy. Between the purely physical rykor and the purely mental kaldane there was little choice; but in the happy medium of normal, and imperfect man, as she knew him, lay the most desirable state of existence. It would have been a splendid object lesson, she thought, to all those idealists who seek mass perfection in any phase of human endeavor, since here they might discover the truth that absolute perfection is as little to be desired as is its antithesis.

Gloomy were the thoughts that filled the mind of Tara of Helium as she awaited the summons from Luud—the summons that could mean for her but one thing; death. She guessed why he had sent for her and she knew that she must find the means for self-destruction before the night was over; but still she clung to hope and to life. She would not give up until there was no other way. She startled Ghek once by exclaiming aloud, almost fiercely: "I still live!"

"What do you mean?" asked the kaldane.

"I mean just what I say," she replied. "I still live and while I live I may still find a way. Dead, there is no hope."

"Find a way to what?" he asked.

"To life and liberty and mine own people," she responded.

"None who enters Bantoom ever leaves," he droned.

She did not reply and after a time he spoke again. "Sing to me," he said.

It was while she was singing that four warriors came to take her to Luud. They told Ghek that he was to remain where he was.

"Why?" asked Ghek.

"You have displeased Luud," replied one of the warriors.

"How?" demanded Ghek.

"You have demonstrated a lack of uncontaminated reasoning power. You have permitted sentiment to influence you, thus demonstrating that you are a defective. You know the fate of defectives."

"I know the fate of defectives, but I am no defective," insisted Ghek.

"You permitted the strange noises which issue from her throat to please and soothe you, knowing well that their origin and purpose had nothing whatever to do with logic or the powers of reason. This in itself constitutes an unimpeachable indictment of weakness, Then, influenced doubtless by an illogical feeling of sentiment, you permitted her to walk abroad in the fields to a place where she was able to make an almost successful attmept to escape. Your own reasoning power, were it not defective, would convince you that you are unfit.

The natural, and reasonable, consequence is destruction. Therefore you will be destroyed in such a way that the example will be beneficial to all other kaldanes of the swarm of Luud. In the meantime you will remain where you are."

"You are right," said Ghek. "I will remain here until Luud sees fit to destroy me in the most reasonable manner."

Tara of Helium shot a look of amazement at him as they led her from the chamber. Over her shoulder she called back to him: "Remember, Ghek, you still live!" Then they led her along the interminable tunnels to where Luud awaited her.

When she was conducted into his presence he was squatting in a corner of the chamber upon his six spidery legs. Near the opposite wall lay his rykor, its beautiful form trapped in gorgeous harness—a dead thing without a guiding kaldane. Luud dismissed the warriors who had accompanied the prisoner. Then he sat with his terrible eyes fixed upon her and without speaking for sometime. Tara of Helium could but wait. What was to come she could only guess. When it came would be sufficiently the time to meet it. There was no neccessity for anticipating the end. Presently Luud spoke.

"You think to escape," he said, in the deadly, expressionless monotone of his kind—the only possible result of orally expressing reason uninfluenced by sentiment. "You will not escape. You are merely the embodiment of two imperfect things—an imperfect brain and an imperfect body. The two cannot exist together in perfection. There you see a perfect body." He pointed toward the rykor. "It has no brain. Here," and he raised one of his chelae to his head, "is the perfect brain. It needs no body to function perfectly and properly as a brain. You would pit your feeble intellect against mine! Even now you are planning to slay me. If you are thwarted in that you expect to slay yourself. You will learn the power of mind over matter. I am the mind. You are the matter. What brain you have is too weak and ill-developed to deserve the name of brain. You have permitted it to be weakened by impulsive acts dictated by sentiment. It has no value. It has practically no control over your existence. You will not kill me. You will not kill yourself. When I am through with you you shall be killed if it seems the logical thing to do. You have no conception of the possibilities for power which lie in a perfectly developed brain. Look at that rykor. He has no brain. He can move but slightly of his own volition. An inherent mechanical instinct that we have permitted to remain in him allows him to carry food to his mouth; but he could not find food for himself. We have to place it within his reach and always in the same place. Should we put food at his feet and leave him alone he would starve to death. But now watch what a real brain may accomplish."

He turned his eyes upon the rykor and squatted there glaring at the insensate thing. Presently, to the girl's horror, the headless body moved. It rose slowly to its feet and crossed the room to Luud; it stooped and took the hideous head in its hands; it raised the head and set it on its shoulders.

"What chance have you against such power?" asked Luud. "As I did with the rykor so can I do with you."

Tara of Helium made no reply. Evidently no vocal reply was necessary.

"You doubt my ability!" stated Luud, which was precisely the fact, though the girl had only thought it—she had not said it.

Luud crossed the room and lay down. Then he detached himself from the body and crawled across the floor until he stood directly in front of the circular opening through which she had seen him emerge the day that she had first been brought to his presence. He stopped there and fastened his terrible eyes upon her. He did not speak, but his eyes seemed to be boring straight to the center of her brain. She felt an almost irresistible force urging her toward the kaldane. She fought to resist it; she tried to turn away her eyes, but she could not. They were held as in horrid fascination upon the glittering, lidless orbs of the great brain that faced her. Slowly, every step a painful struggle of resistance, she moved toward the horrific monster. She tried to cry aloud in an effort to awaken her numbing faculties, but no sound passed her lips. If those eyes would but turn away, just for an instant, she felt that she might regain the power to control her steps; but the eyes never left hers. They seemed but to burn deeper and deeper, gathering up every vestige of control of her entire nervous system.

As she approached the thing it backed slowly away upon its spider legs. She noticed that its chelae waved slowly to and fro before it as it backed, backed, backed, through the round aperture in the wall. Must she follow it there, too? What new and nameless horror lay concealed in that hidden chamber? No! she would not do it. Yet before she reached the wall she found herself down and crawling upon her hands and knees straight toward the hole from which the two eyes still clung to hers. At the very threshold of the opening she made a last, heroic stand, battling against the force that drew her on; but in the end she succumbed. With a gasp that ended in a sob Tara of Helium passed through the aperture into the chamber beyond.

The opening was but barely large enough to admit her. Upon the opposite side she found herself in a small chamber. Before her squatted Luud. Against the opposite wall lay a large and beautiful male rykor. He was without harness or other trappings.

"You see now," said Luud, "the futility of revolt."

The words seemed to release her momentarily from the spell. Quickly she turned away her eyes.

"Look at me!" commanded Luud.

Tara of Helium kept her eyes averted. She felt a new strength, or at least a diminution of the creature's power over her. Had she stumbled upon the secret of its uncanny domination over her will? She dared not hope. With eyes averted she turned toward the aperture through which those baleful eyes had drawn her. Again Luud commanded her to stop, but the voice alone lacked all authority to influence her. It was not like the eyes. She heard the creature whistle and knew that it was summoning assistance, but because she did not dare look toward it she did not see it turn and concentrate its gaze upon the great, headless body lying by the further wall.

The girl was still slightly under the spell of the creature's influence—she had not regained full and independent domination of her powers. She moved as one in the throes of some hideous nightmare—slowly, painfully, as though each limb was hampered by a great weight, or as she were dragging her body through a viscous fluid. The aperture was close, ah, so close, yet, struggle as she would, she seemed to be making no appreciable progress toward it.

Behind her, urged on by the malevolent power of the great brain, the headless body crawled upon all-fours toward her. At last she had reached the aperture. Something seemed to tell her that once beyond it the domination of the kaldane would be broken. She was almost through into the adjoining chamber when she felt a heavy hand close upon her ankle. The rykor had reached forth and seized her, and though she struggled the thing dragged her back into the room with Luud. It held her tight and drew her close, and then, to her horror, it commenced to caress her.

"You see now," she heard Luud's dull voice, "the futility of revolt—and its punishment."

Tara of Helium fought to defend herself, but pitifully weak were her muscles against this brainless incarnation of brute power. Yet she fought, fought on in the face of hopeless odds for the honor of the proud name she bore—fought alone, she whom the fighting men of a mighty empire, the flower of Martian chivalry, would gladly have lain down their lives to save.

VII

A REPELLENT SIGHT

he cruiser *Vanator* careened through the tempest. That she had not been dashed to the ground, or twisted by the force of the elements into tangled wreckage, was due entirely to the caprice of Nature. For all the duration of the storm she rode, a helpless derelict, upon those storm-tossed waves of wind. But for all the dangers and vicissitudes they underwent, she and her crew might have borne charmed lives up to within an hour of the abating of the hurricane. It was then that the catastrophe occurred a catastrophe indeed to the crew of the *Vanator* and the kingdom of Gathol.

The men had been without food or drink since leaving Helium, and they had been hurled about and buffeted in their lashings until all were worn to exhaustion. There was a brief lull in the storm during which one of the crew attempted to reach his quarters, after releasing the lashings which had held him to the precarious safety of the deck. The act in itself was a direct violation of orders and, in the eyes of the other members of the crew, the effect, which came with startling suddenness, took the form of a swift and terrible retribution. Scarce had the man released the safety snaps ere a swift arm of the storm-monster encircled the ship, rolling it over and over, with the result that the foolhardy warrior went overboard at the first turn.

Unloosed from their lashing by the constant turning and twisting of the ship and the force of the wind, the boarding and landing tackle had been trailing beneath the keel, a tangled mass of cordage and leather. Upon the occasions that the *Vanator* rolled completely over, these things would be wrapped around her until another revolution in the opposite direction, or the wind itself, carried them once again clear of the deck to trail, whipping in the storm, beneath the hurtling ship.

Into this fell the body of the warrior, and as a drowning man clutches at a straw so the fellow clutched at the tangled cordage that caught him and arrested his fall. With the strength of desperation he clung to the cordage, seeking frantically to entangle his legs and body in it. With each jerk of the ship his hand holds were all but torn loose, and though he knew that eventually they would be and that he must be dashed to the ground beneath, yet he fought with the madness that is born of hopelessness for the pitiful second which but prolonged his agony.

It was upon this sight then that Gahan of Gathol looked, over the edge of the careening deck of the *Vanator,* as he sought to learn the fate of his warrior. Lashed to the gunwale close at hand a single landing leather that had not fouled the tangled mass beneath whipped free from the ship's side, the hook snapping at its outer end. The Jed of Gathol grasped the situation in a single glance. Below him one of his people looked into the eyes of Death. To the jed's hand lay the means for succor.

There was no instant's hesitation. Casting off his deck lashings, he seized the landing leather and slipped over the ship's side. Swinging like a bob upon a mad pendulum he swung far out and back again, turning and twisting three thousand feet above the surface of Barsoom, and then, at last, the thing he had hoped for occurred. He was carried within reach of the cordage where the warrior still clung, though with rapidly diminishing strength. Catching one leg on a loop of the tangled strands Gahan pulled himself close enough to seize another quite near to the fellow. Clinging precariously to this new hold the jed slowly drew in the landing leather, down which he had clambered until he could grasp the hook at its end. This he fastened to a ring in the warrior's harness, just before the man's weakened fingers slipped from their hold upon the cordage.

Temporarily, at least, he had saved the life of his subject, and now he turned his attention toward insuring his own safety. Inextricably entangled in the mess to which he was clinging were numerous other landing hooks such as he had attached to the warrior's harness, and with one of these he sought to secure himself until the storm should abate sufficiently to permit him to climb to the deck, but even as he reached for one that swung near him the ship was caught in a renewed burst of the storm's fury, the thrashing cordage whipped and snapped to the lunging of the great craft and one of the heavy metal hooks, lashing through the air, struck the Jed of Gathol fair between the eyes.

Momentarily stunned, Gahan's fingers slipped from their hold upon the cordage and the man shot downward through the thin air of dying Mars toward the ground three thousand feet beneath, while upon the deck of the rolling *Vanator* his faithful warriors clung to their lashings all unconscious of the fate of their beloved leader; nor was it until more than an hour later, after the storm had materially subsided, that they realized he was lost, or knew the self-sacrificing heroism of the act that had sealed his doom. The *Vanator* now rested upon an even keel as she was carried along by a strong, though steady, wind. The warriors had cast off their deck lashings and the officers were taking account of losses and damage when a weak cry was heard from oversides, attracting their attention to the man hanging in the cordage beneath the keel. Strongs arms hoisted him to the deck and then it was that the crew of the *Vanator* learned of the heroism of their jed and his end. How far they had traveled since his loss they could only vaguely guess, nor could they return in search of him in the disabled condition of the ship. It was a saddened company that drifted onward through the air toward whatever destination Fate was to choose for them.

And Gahan, Jed of Gathol—what of him? Plummet-like he fell for a thousand feet and then the storm seized him in its giant clutch and bore him far aloft again. As a bit of paper borne upon a gale he was tossed about in mid-air, the sport and plaything of the wind. Over and over it turned him and upward and downward it carried him, but after each new sally of the element he was brought nearer to the ground. The freaks of cyclonic storms are the rule of cyclonic storms, demolish giant trees, and in the same gust they transport frail infants for miles and deposit them unharmed in their wake.

And so it was with Gahan of Gathol. Expecting momentarily to be dashed to destruction he presently found himself deposited gently upon the soft, ochre moss of a dead sea-bottom, bodily no worse off for his harrowing adventure than in the possession of a slight swelling upon his forehead where the metal hook had struck him. Scarcely able to believe that Fate had dealt thus gently with him, the jed arose slowly, as though more than half convinced that he should discover crushed and splintered bones that would not support his weight. But he was intact. He looked about him in a vain effort at orientation. The air was filled with flying dust and debris. The Sun was obliterated. His vision was confined to a radius of a few hundred yards of ochre moss and dust-filled air. Five hundred yards away in any direction there might have arisen the walls of a great city and he not known it. It was useless to move from where he was until the air cleared, since he could not know in what direction he was moving, and so he stretched himself upon the moss and waited, pondering the fate of his warriors and his ship, but giving little thought to his own precarious situation.

Lashed to his harness were his swords, his pistols, and a dagger, and in his pocket-pouch a small quantity of the concentrated rations that form a part of the equipment of the fighting men of Barsoom.

These things together with trained muscles, high courage, and an undaunted spirit sufficed him for whatever misadventures might lie between him and Gathol, which lay in what direction he knew not, nor at what distance.

The wind was falling rapidly and with it the dust that obscured the landscape. That the storm was over he was convinced, but he chafed at the inactivity the low visibility put upon him, nor did conditions better materially before night fell, so that he was forced to await the new day at the very spot at which the tempest had deposited him. Without his sleeping silks and furs he spent a far from comfortable night, and it was with feelings of unmixed relief that he saw the sudden dawn burst upon him. The air was now clear and in the light of the new day he saw an undulating plain stretching in all directions about him, while to the northwest there were barely discernible the outlines of low hills. Toward the southeast of Gathol was such a country, and as Gahan surmised the direction and the velocity of the storm to have carried him somewhere in the vicinity of the country he thought he recognized, he assumed that Gathol lay behind the hills he now saw, whereas, in reality, it lay far to the northeast.

It was two days before Gahan had crossed the plain and reached the summit of the hills from which he hoped to see his own country, only to meet at last with disappointment. Before him stretched another plain, of even greater proportions than that he had but just crossed, and beyond this other hills. In one material respect this plain differed from that behind him in that it was dotted with occasional isolated hills. Convinced, however, that Gathol lay somewhere in the direction of his search he descended into the valley and bent his steps toward the northwest.

For weeks Gahan of Gathol crossed valleys and hills in search of some familiar landmark that might point his way toward his native land, but the summit of each succeeding ridge revealed but another unfamiliar view. He saw few animals and no men, until he finally came to the belief that he had fallen upon that fabled area of ancient Barsoom which lay under the curse of her olden gods—the once rich and fertile country whose people in their pride and arrogance had denied the deities, and whose punishment had been extermination.

And then, one day, he scaled low hills and looked into an inhabited valley—a valley of trees and cultivated fields and plots of ground enclosed by stone walls surrounding strange towers. He saw people working in the fields, but he did not rash down to greet them. First he must know more of them and whether they might be assumed to be friends or enemies. Hidden by concealing shrubbery he crawled to a vantage point upon a hill that projected further into the valley, and here he lay upon his belly watching the workers closest to him. They were still quite a distance from him and he could not be quite sure of them, but there was something verging upon the unnatural about them. Their heads seemed out of proportion to their bodies—too large.

For a long time he lay watching them and ever more forcibly it was borne in upon his consciousness that they were not as he, and that it would be rash to trust himself among them. Presently he saw a couple appear from the nearest enclosure and slowly approach those who were working nearest to the hill where he lay in hiding. Immediately he was aware that one of these differed from all the others. Even at the greater distance he noted that the head was smaller and as they approached, he was confident that the harness of one of them was not as the harness of its companion or of that of any of those who tilled the fields.

The two stopped often, apparently in argument, as though one would proceed in the direction that they were going while the other demurred. But each time the smaller won reluctant consent from the other, and so they came closer and closer to the last line of workers toiling between the enclosure from which they had come and the hill where Gahan of Gathol lay watching, and then suddenly the smaller figure struck its companion full in the face. Gahan, horrified, saw the latter's head topple from its body, saw the body stagger and fall to the ground. The man half rose from his concealment the better to view the happening in the valley below. The creature that had felled its companion was dashing madly in the direction of the hill upon which he was hidden, it dodged one of the workers that sought to seize it. Gahan hoped that it would gain its liberty, why he did not know other than at closer range it had every appearance of being a creature of his own race. Then he saw it stumble and go down and instantly its pursuers were upon it. Then it was that Gahan's eyes chanced to return to the figure of the creature the fugitive had felled.

What horror was this that he was witnessing? Or were his eyes playing some ghastly joke upon him? No, impossible though it was— it was true—the head was moving slowly to the fallen body. It placed itself upon the shoulders, the body rose, and the creature, seemingly as good as new, ran quickly to where its fellows were dragging the hapless captive to its feet.

The watcher saw the creature take its prisoner by the arm and lead it back to the enclosure, and even across the distance that separated them from him he could note dejection and utter hopelessness in the bearing of the prisoner, and, too, he was half convinced that it was a woman, perhaps a red Martian of his own race. Could he be sure that this was true he must make some effort to rescue her even though the customs of his strange world required it only in case she was of his own country; but he was not sure; she might not be a red Martian at all, or, if she were, it was as possible that she sprang from an enemy people as not. His first duty was to return to his own people with as little personal risk as possible, and though the thought of adventure stirred his blood he put the temptation aside with a sigh and turned away from the peaceful and beautiful valley that he longed to enter, for it was his intention to skirt its eastern edge and continue his search for Gathol beyond.

As Gahan of Gathol turned his steps along the southern slopes of the hills that bound Bantoom upon the south and east, his attention was attracted toward a small cluster of trees a short distance to his right. The low sun was casting long shadows. It would soon be night. The trees were off the path that he had chosen and he had little mind to be diverted from his way; but as he looked again he hesitated. There was something there besides boles of trees, and underbrush. There were suggestions of familiar lines of the handicraft of man. Gahan stopped and strained his eyes in the direction of the thing that had arrested his attention. No, he must be mistaken—the branches of the trees and a low bush had taken on an unnatural semblance in the horizontal rays of the setting sun. He turned and continued upon his way; but as he cast another side glance in the direction of the object of his interest, the sun's rays were shot back into his eyes from a glistening point of radiance among the trees.

Gahan shook his head and walked quickly toward the mystery, determined now to solve it. The shining object still lured him on and when he had come closer to it his eyes went wide in surprise, for the thing they saw was naught else than the jewel-encrusted emblem upon the prow of a small flier. Gahan, his hand upon his short-sword, moved silently forward, but as he neared the craft he saw that he had naught to fear, for it was deserted. Then he turned his attention toward the emblem. As its significance was flashed to his understanding his face paled and his heart went cold—it was the insignia of the house of The Warlord of Barsoom. Instantly he saw the dejected figure of the captive being led back to her prison in the valley just beyond the hills. Tara of Helium! And he had been so near to deserting her to her fate. The cold sweat stood in beads upon his brow.

A hasty examination of the deserted craft unfolded to the young jed the whole tragic story. The same tempest that had proved his undoing had borne Tara of Helium to this distant country. Here, doubtless, she had landed in hope of obtaining food and water since, without a propeller, she could not hope to reach her native city, or any other friendly port, other than by the merest caprice of Fate. The flier seemed intact except for the missing propeller and the fact that it had been carefully moored in the shelter of the clump of trees indicated that the girl had expected to return to it, while the dust and leaves upon its deck spoke of the long days, and even weeks, since she had landed. Mute yet eloquent proofs, these things, that Tara of Helium was a prisoner, and that she was the very prisoner whose bold dash for liberty he had so recently witnessed he now had not the slightest doubt.

The question now revolved solely about her rescue. He knew to which tower she had been taken—that much and no more. Of the number, the kind, or the disposition of her captors he renew nothing; nor did he care—for Tara of Helium he would face a hostile world alone. Rapidly he considered several plans for succoring her; but the one that appealed most strongly to him was that which offered the greatest chance of escape for the girl should he be successful in reaching her. His decision reached he turned his attention quickly toward the flier. Casting off its lashings he dragged it out from beneath the trees, and, mounting to the deck tested out the various controls. The motor started at a touch and purred sweetly, the buoyancy tanks were well stocked, and the ship answered perfectly to the controls which regulated her altitude. There was nothing needed but a propellor to make her fit for the long voyage to Helium. Gahan shrugged impatiently—there must not be a propellor within a thousand haads. But what mattered it? The craft even without a propellor would still answer the purpose his plan required of it—provided the captors of Tara of Helium were a people without ships, and he had seen nothing to suggest that they had ships. The architecture of their towers and enclosures assured him that they had not.

The sudden Barsoomian night had fallen. Cluros rode majestically the high heavens. The rumbling roar of a banth reverberated among the hills. Gahan of Gathol let the ship rise a few feet from the ground, then, seizing a bow rope, he dropped over the side. To tow the little craft was now a thing of ease, and as Gahan moved rapidly toward the brow of the hill above Bantoom the flier floated behind him as lightly as a swan upon a quiet lake. Now down the hill toward the tower dimly visible in the moonlight the Gatholian turned his steps. Closer behind him sounded the roar of the hunting banth. He wondered if the beast sought him or was following some other spoor. He could not be delayed now by any hungry beast of prey, for what might that very instant be befalling Tara of Helium he could not guess; and so he hastened his steps. But closer and closer came the horrid screams of the great carnivore, and now he heard the swift fall of padded feet upon the hillside behind him. He glanced back just in time to see the beast break into a rapid charge. His hand leaped to the hilt of his long-sword, but he did not draw, for in the same instant he saw the futility of armed resistance, since behind the first banth came a herd of at least a dozen others. There was but a single alternative to a futile stand and that he grasped in the instant that he saw the over-whelming numbers of his antagonists.

Springing lightly from the ground he swarmed up the rope toward the bow of the flier. His weight drew the craft slightly lower and at the very instant that the man drew himself to the deck at the bow of the vessel, the leading banth sprang for the stern. Gahan leaped to his feet and rushed toward the great beast in the hope of dislodging it before it had succeeded in clambering aboard. At the same instant he saw that others of the banths were racing toward them with the quite evident intention of following their leader to the ship's deck. Should they reach it in any numbers he would be lost. There was but a single hope. Leaping for the altitude control Gahan pulled it wide. Simultaneously three banths leaped for the deck. The craft rose swiftly. Gahan felt the impact of a body against the keel, followed by the soft thuds of the great bodies as they struck the ground beneath.

His act had not been an instant too soon. And now the leader had gained the deck and stood at the stern with glaring eyes and snarling jaws. Gahan drew his sword. The beast, possibly disconcerted by the novelty of its position, did not charge. Instead it crept slowly toward its intended prey. The craft was rising and Gahan placed a foot upon the control and stopped the ascent. He did not wish to chance rising to some higher air current that would bear him away. Already the craft was moving slowly toward the tower, carried thither by the impetus of the banth's heavy body leaping upon it from astern.

The man watched the slow approach of the monster, the slavering jowls, the malignant expression of the devilish face. The creature, finding the deck stable, appeared to be gaining confidence, and then the man leaped suddenly to one side of the deck and the tiny flier heeled as suddenly in response. The banth slipped and clutched frantically at the deck. Gahan leaped in with his naked sword; the great beast caught itself and reared upon its hind legs to reach forth and seize this presumptuous mortal that dared question its right to the flesh it craved; and then the man sprang to the opposite side of the deck. The banth toppled sideways at the same instant that it attempted to spring; a raking talon passed close to Gahan's head at the moment that his sword lunged through the savage heart, and as the warrior wrenched his blade from the carcass it slipped silently over the side of the ship.

A glance below showed that the vessel was drifting in the direction of the tower to which Gahan had seen the prisoner led. In another moment or two it would be directly over it. The man sprang to the control and let the craft drop quickly toward the ground where followed the banths, still hot for their prey. To land outside the enclosure spelled certain death, while inside he could see many forms huddled upon the ground as in sleep. The ship floated now but a few feet above the wall of the enclosure. There was nothing for it but to risk all on a bold bid for fortune, or drift helplessly past without hope of returning through the banth-infested valley, from many points of which he could now hear the roars and growls of these fierce Barsoomian lions.

Slipping over the side Gahan descended by the trailing anchor-rope until his feet touched the top of the wall, where he had no difficulty in arresting the slow drifting of the ship. Then he drew up the anchor and lowered it inside the enclosure. Still there was no movement upon the part of the sleepers beneath—they lay as dead men. Dull lights shone from openings in the tower; but there was no sign of guard or waking inmate. Clinging to the rope Gahan lowered himself within the enclosure, where he had his first close view of the creatures lying there in what he had thought sleep. With a half smothered exclamation of horror the man drew back from the headless bodies of the rykors. At first he thought them the corpses of decapitated humans like himself, which was quite bad enough; but when he saw them move and realized that they were endowed with life, his horror and disgust became even greater.

Here then was the explanation of the thing he had witnessed that afternoon, when Tara of Helium had struck the back to its body. And to think that the pearl of Helium was in the power of such hideous things as these. Again the man shuddered, but he hastened to make fast the flier, clamber again to its deck and lower it to the floor of the enclosure. Then he strode toward a door in the base of the tower, stepping lightly over the recumbent forms of the unconscious rykors, and crossing the threshold disappeared within.

VIII

CLOSE WORK

hek, in his happier days third foreman of the fields of Luud, sat nursing his anger and his humiliation. Recently something had awakened within him the existence of which he had never before even dreamed. Had the influence of the strange captive woman aught to do with this unrest and dissatisfaction? He did not know. He missed the soothing influence of the noise she called singing. Could it be that there were other things more desirable than cold logic and undefiled brain power? Was well balanced imperfection more to be sought after then, than the high development of a single characteristic? He thought of the great, ultimate brain toward which all kaldanes were striving. It would be deaf, and dumb, and blind. A thousand beautiful strangers might sing and dance about it, but it could derive no pleasure from the singing or the dancing since it would possess no perceptive faculties. Already had the kaldanes shut themselves off from most of the gratifications of the senses. Ghek wondered if much was to be gained by denying themselves still further, and with the thought came a question as to the whole fabric of their theory. After all perhaps the girl was right; what purpose could a great brain serve sealed in the bowels of the earth?

And he, Ghek, was to die for this theory. Luud had decreed it. The injustice of it overwhelmed him with rage. But he was helpless. There was no escape. Beyond the enclosure the banths awaited him;

within, his own kind, equally as merciless and ferocious. Among them there was no such thing as love, or loyalty, or friendship— they were just brains. He might kill Luud; but what would that profit him? Another king would be loosed from his sealed chamber and Ghek would be killed. He did not know it but he would not even have the poor satisfaction of satisfied revenge, since he was not capable of feeling so abstruse a sentiment.

Ghek, mounted upon his rykor, paced the floor of the tower chamber in which he had been ordered to remain. Ordinarily he would have accepted the sentence of Luud with perfect equanimity, since it was but the logical result of reason; but now it seemed different. The stranger woman had bewitched him. Life appeared a pleasant thing—there were great possibilities in it. The dream of the ultimate brain had receded into a tenuous haze far in the background of his thoughts.

At that moment there appeared in the doorway of the chamber a red warrior with naked sword. He was a male counterpart of the prisoner whose sweet voice had undermined the cold, calculating reason of the kaldane.

"Silence!" admonished the newcomer, his straight brows gathered in an ominous frown and the point of his long-sword playing menacingly before the eyes of the kaldane. "I seek the woman, Tara of Helium. Where is she? If you value your life speak quickly and speak the truth."

If he valued his life! It was a truth that Ghek had but just learned. He thought quickly. After all, a great brain is not without its uses. Perhaps here lay escape from the sentence of Luud.

"You are of her kind?" he asked. "You come to rescue her?"

"Yes."

"Listen, then. I have befriended her, and because of this I am to die. If I help you to liberate her, will you take me with you?"

Gahan of Gathol eyed the weird creature from crown to

foot—the perfect body, the grotesque head, the expressionless face. Among such as these had the beautiful daughter of Helium been held captive for days and weeks.

"If she lives and is unharmed," he said, "I will take you with us."

"When they took her from me she was alive and unharmed," replied Ghek. "I cannot say what has befallen her since. Luud sent for her."

"Who is Luud? Where is he? Lead me to him." Gahan spoke quickly in tones vibrant with authority.

"Come, then," said Ghek, leading the way from the apartment and down a stairway toward the underground burrows of the kaldanes. "Luud is my king. I will take you to his chambers."

"Hasten!" urged Gahan.

"Sheathe your sword," warned Ghek, "so that should we pass others of my kind I may say to them that you are a new prisoner with some likelihood of winning their belief."

Gahan did as he was bid, but warning the kaldane that his hand was ever ready at his dagger's hilt.

"You need have no fear of treachery," said Ghek "My only hope of life lies in you."

"And if you fail me," Gahan admonished him, "I can promise you as sure a death as even your king might guarantee you."

Ghek made no reply, but moved rapidly through the winding subterranean corridors until Gahan began to realize how truly was he in the hands of this strange monster. If the fellow should prove false it would profit Gahan nothing to slay him, since without his guidance the red man might never hope to retrace his way to the tower and freedom.

Twice they met and were accosted by other kaldanes; but in both instances Ghek's simple statement that he was taking a new prisoner to Luud appeared to allay all suspicion, and then at last they came to the antechamber of the king.

"Here, now, red man, thou must fight, if ever," whispered Ghek. "Enter there!" and he pointed to a doorway before them.

"And you?" asked Gahan, still fearful of treachery.

"My rykor is powerful," replied the kaldane. "I shall accompany you and fight at your side. As well die thus as in torture later at the will of Luud. Come!"

But Gahan had already crossed the room and entered the chamber beyond. Upon the opposite side of the room was a circular opening guarded by two warriors. Beyond this opening he could see two figures straggling upon the floor, and the fleeting glimpse he had of one of the faces suddenly endowed him with the strength of ten warriors and the ferocity of a wounded banth. It was Tara of Helium, fighting for her honor or her life.

The warriors, startled by the unexpected appearance of a red man, stood for a moment in dumb amazement, and in that moment Gahan of Gathol was upon them, and one was down, a sword-thrust through its heart.

"Strike at the heads," whispered the voice of Ghek in Gahan's ear. The latter saw the head of the fallen warrior crawl quickly within the aperture leading to the chamber where he had seen Tara of Helium in the clutches of a headless body. Then the sword of Ghek struck the kaldane of the remaining warrior from its rykor and Gahan ran his sword through the repulsive head.

Instantly the red warrior leaped for the aperture, while close behind him came Ghek.

"Look not upon the eyes of Luud," warned the kaldane, "or you are lost."

Within the chamber Gahan saw Tara of Helium in the clutches of a mighty body, while close to the wall upon the opposite side of the apartment crouched the hideous, spider-like Luud. Instantly the king realized the menace to himself and sought to fasten his eyes upon the eyes of Gahan, and in doing so he was forced to relax his concentration upon the rykor in whose embraces Tara straggled, so that almost immediately the girl found herself able to tear away from the awful, headless thing.

As she rose quickly to her feet she saw for the first time the cause of the interruption of Luud's plans. A red warrior! Her heart leaped in rejoicing and thanksgiving. What miracle of fate had sent him to her? She did not recognize him, though, this travel-worn warrior in the plain harness which showed no single jewel. How could she have guessed him the same as the scintillant creature of platinum and diamonds that she had seen for a brief hour under such different circumstances at the court of her august sire?

Luud saw Ghek following the strange warrior into the chamber. "Strike him down, Ghek!" commanded the king. "Strike down the stranger and your life shall be yours."

Gahan glanced at the hideous face of the king.

"Seek not his eyes," screamed Tara in warning; but it was too late. Already the horrid hypnotic gaze of the king kaldane had seized upon the eyes of Gahan. The red warrior hesitated in his stride. His sword point drooped slowly toward the floor. Tara glanced toward Ghek. She saw the creature glaring with his expressionless eyes upon the broad back of the stranger. She saw the hand of the creature's rykor creeping stealthily toward the hilt of its dagger.

And then Tara of Helium raised her eyes aloft and poured forth the notes of Mars' most beautiful melody, The Song of Love.

Ghek drew his dagger from its sheath. His eyes turned toward the singing girl. Luud's glance wavered from the eyes of the man to the face of Tara, and the instant that the latter's song distracted his attention from his victim, Gahan of Gathol shook himself and as with a supreme effort of will forced his eyes to the wall above Luud's hideous head. Ghek raised his dagger above his right shoulder, took a single quick step forward, and struck. The girl's song ended in a stifled scream as she leaped forward with the evident intention of frustrating the kaldane's purpose; but she was too late, and well it was, for an instant later she realized the purpose of Ghek's act as she saw the dagger fly from his hand, pass Gahan's shoulder, and sink full to the guard in the soft face of Luud.

"Come!" cried the assassin, "we have no time to lose," and started for the aperture through which they had entered the chamber; but in his stride he paused as his glance was arrested by the form of the mighty rykor lying prone upon the floor—a king's rykor; the most beautiful, the most powerful, that the breeders of Bantoom could produce. Ghek realized that in his escape he could take with him but a single rykor, and there was none in Bantoom that could give him better service than this giant lying here. Quickly he transferred himself to the shoulders of the great, inert hulk. Instantly the latter was transformed to a sentient creature, filled with pulsing life and alert energy.

"Now," said the kaldane, "we are ready. Let whoso would revert to nothingness impede me." Even as he spoke he stooped and crawled into the chamber beyond, while Gahan, taking Tara by the arm, motioned her to follow. The girl looked him full in the eyes for the first time. "The Gods of my people have been kind," she said; "you came just in time. To the thanks of Tara of Helium shall be added those of The Warlord of Barsoom and his people. Thy reward shall surpass thy greatest desires."

Gahan of Gathol saw that she did not recognize him, and quickly he checked the warm greeting that had been upon his lips.

"Be thou Tara of Helium or another," he replied, "is immaterial, to serve thus a red woman of Barsoom is in itself sufficient reward."

As they spoke the girl was making her way through the aperture after Ghek, and presently all three had quitted the apartments of Luud and were moving rapidly along the winding corridors toward the tower. Ghek repeatedly urged them to greater speed, but the red men of Barsoom were never keen for retreat, and so the two that followed him moved all too slowly for the kaldane.

"There are none to impede our progress," urged Gahan, "so why tax the strength of the Princess by needless haste?"

"I fear not so much opposition ahead, for there are none there who know the thing that has been done in Luud's chambers this night; but the kaldane of one of the warriors who stood guard before Luud's apartment escaped, and you may count it a truth that he lost no time in seeking aid. That it did not come before we left is due solely to the rapidity with which events transpired in the king'sroom. Long before we reach the tower they will be upon us from behind, and that they will come in numbers far superior to ours and with great and powerful rykors I well know."

Nor was Ghek's prophecy long in fulfilment. Presently the sounds of pursuit became audible in the distant clanking of accouterments and the whistling call to arms of the kaldanes.

"The tower is but a short distance now," cried Ghek. "Make haste while yet you may, and if we can barricade it until the sun rises we may yet escape."

"We shall need no barricades for we shall not linger in the tower," replied Gahan, moving more rapidly as he realized from the volume of sound behind them the great number of their pursuers.

"But we may not go further than the tower tonight," insisted Ghek. "Beyond the tower await the banths and certain death."

Gahan smiled. "Fear not the banths," he assured them. "Can we but reach the enclosure a little ahead of our pursuers we have naught to fear from any evil power within this accursed valley."

Ghek made no reply, nor did his expressionless face denote either belief or skepticism. The girl looked into the face of the man questioningly. She did not understand.

"Your flier," he said. "It is moored before the tower."

Her face lighted with pleasure and relief. "You found it!" she exclaimed. "What fortune!"

"It was fortune indeed," he replied. "Since it not only told that you were a prisoner here; but it saved me from the banths as I was crossing the valley from the hills to this tower into which I saw them take you this afternoon after your brave attempt at escape."

"How did you know it was I?" she asked, her puzzled brows scanning his face as though she sought to recall from past memories some scene in which he figured.

"Who is there but knows of the loss of the Princess Tara of Helium?" he replied. "And when I saw the device upon your flier I knew at once, though I had not known when I saw you among them in the fields a short time earlier. Too great was the distance for me to make certain whether the captive was man or woman. Had chance not divulged the hiding place of your flier I had gone my way, Tara of Helium. I shudder to think how close was the chance at that. But for the momentary shining of the sun upon the emblazoned device on the prow of your craft, I had passed on unknowing."

The girl shuddered. "The Gods sent you," she whispered reverently.

"The Gods sent me, Tara of Helium," he replied.

"But I do not recognize you," she said. "I have tried to recall you, but I have failed. Your name, what may it be?"

"It is not strange that so great a princess should not recall the face of every roving panthan of Barsoom," he replied with a smile.

"But your name?" insisted the girt.

"Call me Turan," replied the man, for it had come to him that if Tara of Helium recognized him as the man whose impetuous avowal of love had angered her that day in the gardens of The Warlord, her situation might be rendered infinitely less bearable than were she to believe him a total stranger. Then, too, as a simple panthanhe might win a greater degree of her confidence by his loyalty and faithfulness and a place in her esteem that seemed to have been closed to the resplendent Jed of Gathol.

They had reached the tower now, and as they entered it from the subterranean corridor a backward glance revealed the van of their pursuers—hideous kaldanes mounted upon swift and powerful rykors. As rapidly as might be the three ascended the stairways leading to the ground level, but after them, even more rapidly, came the minions of Luud. Ghek led the way, grasping one of Tara's hands the more easily to guide and assist her, while Gahan of Gathol followed a few paces in their rear, his bared sword ready for the assault that all realized must come upon them now before ever they reached the enclosure and the flier.

"Let Ghek drop behind to your side," said Tara, "and fight with you."

"There is but room for a single blade in these narrow corridors," replied the Gatholian. "Hasten on with Ghek and win to the deck of the flier. Have your hand upon the control, and if I come far enough ahead of these to reach the dangling cable you can rise at my word and I can clamber to the deck at my leisure; but if one of them emerges first into the enclosure you will know that I shall never come, and you will rise quickly and trust to the Gods of our ancestors to give you a fair breeze in the direction of a more hospitable people."

Tara of Helium shook her head. "We will not desert you, panthan," she said.

Gahan, ignoring her reply, spoke above her head to Ghek. "Take her to the craft moored within the enclosure," he commanded. "It is our only hope. Alone, I may win to its deck; but have I to wait upon you two at the last moment the chances are that none of us will escape. Do as I bid." His tone was haughty and arrogant—the tone of a man who has commanded other men from birth, and whose will has been law. Tara of Helium was both angered and vexed. She was not accustomed to being either commanded or ignored, but with all her royal pride she was no fool, and she knew the man was right, that he was risking his life to save hers, so she hastened on with Ghek as she was bid, and after the first flush of anger she smiled, for the realization came to her that this fellow was but a rough untutored warrior, skilled not in the finer usages of cultured courts. His heart was right, though; a brave and loyal heart, and gladly she forgave him the offense of his tone and manner. But what a tone! Recollection of it gave her sudden pause. Panthans were rough and ready men. Often they rose to positions of high command, so it was not the note of authority in the fellow's voice that seemed remarkable; but something else—a quality that was indefinable, yet as distinct as it was familiar. She had heard it before when the voice of her great-grandsire, Tardos Mors, Jeddak of Helium, had risen in command; and in the voice of her grandfather, Mors Kajak, the jed; and in the ringing tones of her illustrious sire, John Carter, Warlord of Barsoom, when he addressed his warriors.

But now she had no time to speculate upon so trivial a thing, for behind her came the sudden clash of arms and she knew that Turan, the panthan, had crossed swords with the first of their pursuers. As she glanced back he was still visible beyond a turn in the stairway, so that she could see the quick swordplay that ensued. Daughter of a world's greatest swordsman, she knew well the finest points of the art. She saw the clumsy attack of the kaldane and the quick, sure return of the panthan. As she looked down from above upon his almost naked body, trapped only in the simplest of unadorned harness, and saw the play of the lithe muscles beneath the red-bronze skin, and witnessed the quick and delicate play of his sword point, to her sense of obligation was added a spontaneous admission of admiration that was but the natural tribute of a woman to skill and bravery and, perchance, some trifle to manly symmetry and strength.

Three times the panthan's blade changed its position—once to fend a savage cut; once to feint; and once to thrust. And as he withdrew it from the last position the kaldane rolled lifeless from its stumbling rykor and Turan sprang quickly down the steps to engage the next behind, and then Ghek had drawn Tara upward and a turn in the stairway shut the battling panthan from her view; but still she heard the ring of steel on steel, the clank of accouterments and the shrill whistling of the kaldanes. Her heart moved her to turn back to the side of her brave defender; but her judgment told her that she could serve him best by being ready at the control of the flier at the moment he reached the enclosure.

IX

Adrift Over Strange Regions

resently Ghek pushed aside a door that opened from the stairway, and before them Tara saw the moonlight flooding the walled court where the headless rykors lay beside their feeding-troughs. She saw the perfect bodies, muscled as the best of her father's fighting men, and the females whose figures would have been the envy of many of Helium's most beautiful women. Ah, if she could but endow these with the power to act! Then indeed might the safety of the panthan be assured; but they were only poor lumps of clay, nor had she the power to quicken them to life. Ever must they lie thus until dominated by the cold, heartless brain of the kaldane. The girl sighed in pity even as she shuddered in disgust as she picked her way over and among the sprawled creatures toward the flier.

Quickly she and Ghek mounted to the deck after the latter had cast off the moorings. Tara tested the control, raising and lowering the ship a few feet within the walled space. It responded perfectly. Then she lowered it to the ground again and waited. From the open doorway came the sounds of conflict, now nearing them, now receding. The girl, having witnessed her champion's skill, had little fear of the outcome. Only a single antagonist could face him at a time upon the narrow stairway, he had the advantage of position and of the defensive, and he was a master of the sword while they were clumsy bunglers by comparison. Their sole advantage was in their numbers, unless they might find a way to come upon him from behind.

She paled at the thought. Could she have seen him she might have been further perturbed, for he took no advantage of many opportunities to win nearer the enclosure. He fought coolly, but with a savage persistence that bore little semblance to purely defensive action. Often he clambered over the body of a fallen foe to leap against the next behind, and once there lay five dead kaldanes behind him, so far had he pushed back his antagonists. They did not know it; these kaldanes that he fought, nor did the girl awaiting him upon the flier, but Gahan of Gathol was engaged in a more alluring sport than winning to freedom, for he was avenging the indignities that had been put upon the woman he loved; but presently he realized that he might be jeopardizing her safety uselessly, and so he struck down another before him and turning leaped quickly up the stairway, while the leading kaldanes slipped upon the brain-covered floor and stumbled in pursuit.

Gahan reached the enclosure twenty paces ahead of them and raced toward the flier. "Rise!" he shouted to the girl. "I will ascend the cable."

Slowly the small craft rose from the ground as Gahan leaped the inert bodies of the rykors lying in his path. The first of the pursuers sprang from the tower just as Gahan seized the trailing rope.

"Faster!" he shouted to the girl above, "or they will drag us down!" But the ship seemed scarcely to move, though in reality she was rising as rapidly as might have been expected of a one-man flier carrying a load of three. Gahan swung free above the top of the wall, but the end of the rope still dragged the ground as the kaldanes reached it. They were pouring in a steady stream from the tower into the enclosure. The leader seized the rope.

"Quick!" he cried. "Lay hold and we will drag them down."

It needed but the weight of a few to accomplish his design. The ship was stopped in its flight and then, to the horror of the girl, she felt it being dragged steadily downward. Gahan, too, realized the danger and the necessity for instant action. Clinging to the rope with his left hand, he had wound a leg about it, leaving his right hand free for his long-sword which he had not sheathed. A downward cut clove the soft head of a kaldane, and another severed the taut rope beneath the panthan's feet. The girl heard a sudden renewal of the shrill whistling of her foes, and at the same time she realized that the craft was rising again. Slowly it drifted upward, out of reach of the enemy, and a moment later she saw the figure of Turan clamber over the side. For the first time in many weeks her heart was filled with the joy of thanksgiving; but her first thought was of another.

"You are not wounded?" she asked.

"No, Tara of Helium," he replied. "They were scarce worth the effort of my blade, and never were they a menace to me because of their swords."

"They should have slain you easily," said Ghek. "So great and highly developed is the power of reason among us that they should have known before you struck just where, logically, you must seek to strike, and so they should have been able to parry your every thrust and easily find an opening to your heart."

"But they did not, Ghek," Gahan reminded him. "Their theory of development is wrong, for it does not tend toward a perfectly balanced whole. You have developed the brain and neglected the body and you can never do with the hands of another what you can do with your own hands. Mine are trained to the sword—every muscle responds instantly and accurately, and almost mechanically, to the need of the instant. I am scarcely objectively aware that I think when I fight, so quickly does my point take advantage of every opening, or spring to my defense if I am threatened that it is almost as though the cold steel had eyes and brains. You, with your kaldane brain and your rykor body, never could hope to achieve in the same degree of perfection those things that I can achieve. Development of the brain should not be the sum total of human endeavor. The richest and happiest peoples will be those who attain closest to well-balanced perfection of both mind and body, and even these must always be short of perfection. In absolute and general perfection lies stifling monotony and death. Nature must have contrasts; she must have shadows as well as high lights; sorrow with happiness; both wrong and right; and sin as well as virtue."

"Always have I been taught differently," replied Ghek; "but since I have known this woman and you, of another race, I have come to believe that there may be other standards fully as high and desirable as those of the kaldanes. At least I have had a glimpse of the thing you call happiness and I realize that it may be good even though I have no means of expressing it. I cannot laugh nor smile, and yet within me is a sense of contentment when this woman sings—a sense that seems to open before me wondrous vistas of beauty and unguessed pleasure that far transcend the cold joys of a perfectly functioning brain. I would that I had been born of thy race."

Caught by a gentle current of air the flier was drifting slowly toward the northeast across the valley of Bantoom. Below them lay the cultivated fields, and one after another they passed over the strange towers of Moak and Nolach and the other kings of the swarms that inhabited this weird and terrible land. Within each enclosure surrounding the towers grovelled the rykors, repellent, headless things, beautiful yet hideous.

"A lesson, those," remarked Gahan, indicating the rykors in an enclosure above which they were drifting at the time, "to that fortunately small minority of our race which worships the flesh and makes a god of appetite. You know them, Tara of Helium; they can tell you exactly what they had at the midday meal two weeks ago, and how the loin of the thoat should be prepared, and what drink should be served with the rump of the zitidar."

Tara of Helium laughed. "But not one of them could tell you the name of the man whose painting took the Jeddak's Award in The

Temple of Beauty this year," she said. "Like the rykors, their development has not been balanced."

"Fortunate indeed are those in which there is combined a little good and a little bad, a little knowledge of many things outside their own callings, a capacity for love and a capacity for hate, for such as these can look with tolerance upon all, unbiased by the egotism of him whose head is so heavy on one side that all his brains run to that point."

As Gahan ceased speaking Ghek made a little noise in his throat as one does who would attract attention. "You speak as one who has thought much upon many subjects. Is it, then, possible that you of the red race have pleasure in thought? Do you know aught of the joys of introspection? Do reason and logic form any part of your lives?"

"Most assuredly," replied Gahan, "but not to the extent of occupying all our time—at least not objectively. You, Ghek, are an example of the egotism of which I spoke. Because you and your kind devote your lives to the worship of mind, you believe that no other created beings think. And possibly we do not in the sense that you do, who think only of yourselves and your great brains. We think of many things that concern the welfare of a world. Had it not been for the red men of Barsoom even the kaldanes had perished from the planet, for while you may live without air the things upon which you depend for existence cannot, and there had been no air in sufficient quantities upon Barsoom these many ages had not a red man planned and built the great atmosphere plant which gave new life to a dying world.

"What have all the brains of all the kaldanes that have ever lived done to compare with that single idea of a single red man?"

Ghek was stumped. Being a kaldane he knew that brains spelled the sum total of universal achievement, but it had never occurred to him that they should be put to use in practical and profitable ways. He turned away and looked down upon the valley of his ancestors across which he was slowly drifting, into what unknown world? He should be a veritable god among the underlings, he knew; but somehow a doubt assailed him. It was evident that these two from that other world were ready to question his preeminence. Even through his great egotism was filtering a suspicion that they patronized him; perhaps even pitied him. Then he began to wonder what was to become of him. No longer would he have many rykors to do his bidding. Only this single one and when it died there could not be another. When it tired, Ghek must lie almost helpless while it rested. He wished that he had never seen this red woman. She had brought him only discontent and dishonor and now exile. Presently Tara of Helium commenced to hum a rune and Ghek, the kaldane, was content.

Gently they drifted beneath the hurtling moons above the mad shadows of a Martian night. The roaring of the banths came in diminishing volume to their ears as their craft passed on beyond the boundaries of Bantoom, leaving behind the terrors of that unhappy land. But to what were they being borne? The girl looked at the man sitting cross-legged upon the deck of the tiny flier, gazing off into the night ahead, apparently absorbed in thought.

"Where are we?" she asked. "Toward what are we drifting?"

Turan shrugged his broad shoulders. "The stars tell me that we are drifting toward the northeast," he replied, "but where we are, or what lies in our path I cannot even guess. A week since I could have sworn that I knew what lay behind each succeeding ridge that I approached; but now I admit in all humility that I have no conception of what lies a mile in any direction. Tara of Helium, I am lost, and that is all that I can tell you."

He was smiling and the girl smiled back at him. There was a slightly puzzled expression on her face—there was something tantalizingly familiar about that smile of his. She had met many a panthan—they came and went, following the fighting of a world—but she could not place this one.

"From what country are you, Turan?" she asked suddenly.

"Know you not, Tara of Helium," he countered, "that a panthan has no country? Today he fights beneath the banner of one master, tomorrow beneath that of another."

"But you must own allegiance to some country when you are not fighting," she insisted. "What banner, then, owns you now?"

He rose and stood before her, then, bowing low. "And I am acceptable," he said, "I serve beneath the banner of the daughter of The Warlord now—and forever."

She reached forth and touched his arm with a slim brown hand. "Your services are accepted," she said; "and if ever we reach Helium I promise that your reward shall be all that your heart could desire."

"I shall serve faithfully, hoping for that reward," he said; but Tara of Helium did not guess what was in his mind, thinking rather that he was mercenary. For how could the proud daughter of The Warlord guess that a simple panthan aspired to her hand and heart?

The dawn found them moving rapidly over an unfamiliar landscape. The wind had increased during the night and had borne them far from Bantoom. The country below them was rough and inhospitable. No water was visible and the surface of the ground was cut by deep gorges, while nowhere was any but the most meager vegetation discernible. They saw no life of any nature, nor was there any indication that the country could support life. For two days they drifted over this horrid wasteland. They were without food or water and suffered accordingly. Ghek had temporarily abandoned his rykor after enlisting Turan's assistance in lashing it safely to the deck. The less he used it the less would its vitality be spent. Already it was showing the effects of privation. Ghek crawled about the vessel like a great spider—over the side, down beneath the keel, and up over the opposite rail. He seemed equally at home one place as another. For his companions, however, the quarters were cramped, for the deck of a one-man flier is not intended for three.

Turan sought always ahead for signs of water. Water they must have, or that water-giving plant which makes life possible upon many of the seemingly arid areas of Mars; but there was neither the one nor the other for these two days and now the third night was upon them. The girl did not complain, but Turan knew that she must be suffering and his heart was heavy within him. Ghek suffered least of all, and he explained to them that his kind could exist for long periods without food or water. Turan almost cursed him as he saw the form of Tara of Helium slowly wasting away before his eyes, while the hideous kaldane seemed as full of vitality as ever.

"There are circumstances," remarked Ghek, "under which a gross and material body is less desirable than a highly developed brain."

Turan looked at him, but said nothing. Tara of Helium smiled faintly. "One cannot blame him," she said, "were we not a bit boastful in the pride of our superiority? When our stomachs were filled," she added.

"Perhaps there is something to be said for their system," Turan admitted. "If we could but lay aside our stomachs when they cried for food and water I have no doubt but that we should do so."

"I should never miss mine now," assented Tara; "it is mighty poor company."

A new day had dawned, revealing a less desolate country and renewing again the hope that had been low within them. Suddenly Turan leaned forward, pointing ahead.

"Look, Tara of Helium!" he cried. "A city! As I am Ga—as I am Turan the panthan, a city."

Far in the distance the domes and walls and slender towers of a city shone in the rising sun. Quickly the man seized the control and the ship dropped rapidly behind a low range of intervening hills, for well Turan knew that they must not be seen until they could discover whether friend or foe inhabited the strange city. Chances were that they were far from the abode of friends and so must the panthan move with the utmost caution; but there was a city and where a city was, was water, even though it were a deserted city, and food if it were inhabited.

To the red man food and water, even in the citadel of an enemy, meant food and drink for Tara of Helium. He would accept it from friends or he would take it from enemies. Just so long as it was there he would have it—and there was shown the egotism of the fighting man, though Turan did not see it, nor Tara who came from a long line of fighting men; but Ghek might have smiled had he known how.

Turan permitted the flier to drift closer behind the screening hills, and then when he could advance no farther without fear of discovery, he dropped the craft gently to ground in a little ravine, and leaping over the side made her fast to a stout tree. For several moments they discussed their plans—whether it would be best to wait where they were until darkness hid their movements and then approach the city in search of food and water, or approach it now, taking advantage of what cover they could, until they could glean something of the nature of its inhabitants.

It was Turan's plan which finally prevailed. They would approach as close as safety dictated in the hope of finding water outside the city; food, too, perhaps. If they did not they could at least reconnoiter the ground by daylight, and then when night came Turan could quickly come close to the city and in comparative safety prosecute his search for food and drink.

Following the ravine upward they finally topped the summit of the ridge, from which they had an excellent view of that part of the city which lay nearest them, though themselves hidden by the brush behind which they crouched. Ghek had resumed his rykor, which had suffered less than either Tara or Turan through their enforced fast.

The first glance at the city, now much closer than when they had first discovered it, revealed the fact that it was inhabited. Banners and pennons broke from many a staff. People were moving about the gate before them. The high white walls were paced by sentinels at far intervals. Upon the roofs of higher buildings the women could be seen airing the sleeping silks and furs. Turan watched it all in silence for sometime.

"I do not know them," he said at last. "I cannot guess what city this may be. But it is an ancient city. Its people have no fliers and no firearms. It must be old indeed."

"How do you know they have not these things?" asked the girl.

"There are no landing-stages upon the roofs—not one that can be seen from here; while were we looking similarly at Helium we would see hundreds. And they have no firearms because their defenses are all built to withstand the attack of spear and arrow, with spear and arrow. They are an ancient people."

"If they are ancient perhaps they are friendly," suggested the girl. "Did we not learn as children in the history of our planet that it was once peopled by a friendly, peace-loving race?"

"But I fear they are not as ancient as that," replied Turan, laughing. "It has been long ages since the men of Barsoom loved peace."

"My father loves peace," returned the girl.

"And yet he is always at war," said the man.

She laughed. "But he says he likes peace."

"We all like peace," he rejoined; "peace with honor; but our neighbors will not let us have it, and so we must fight."

"And to fight well men must like to fight," she added.

"And to like to fight they must know how to fight," he said, "for no man likes to do the thing that he does not know how to do well."

"Or that some other man can do better than he."

"And so always there will be wars and men will fight," he concluded, "for always the men with hot blood in their veins will practice the art of war."

"We have settled a great question," said the girl, smiling; "but our stomachs are still empty."

"Your panthan is neglecting his duty," replied Turan; "and how can he with the great reward always before his eyes!"

She did not guess in what literal a sense he spoke.

"I go forthwith," he continued, "to wrest food and drink from the ancients."

"No," she cried, laying a hand upon his arm, "not yet. They would slay you or make you prisoner. You are a brave panthan and a mighty one, but you cannot overcome a city single-handed."

She smiled up into his face and her hand still lay upon his arm. He felt the thrill of hot blood coursing through his veins. He could have seized her in his arms and crushed her to him. There was only Ghek the kaldane there, but there was something stronger within him that restrained his hand. Who may define it—that inherent chivalry that renders certain men the natural protectors of women?

From their vantage point they saw a body of armed warriors ride forth from the gate, and winding along a well-beaten road pass from sight about the foot of the hill from which they watched. The men were red, like themselves, and they rode the small saddle thoats of the red race. Their trappings were barbaric and magnificent, and in their head-dress were many feathers as had been the custom of ancients. They were armed with swords and long spears and they rode almost naked, their bodies being painted in ochre and blue and white. There were, perhaps, a score of them in the party and as they galloped away on their tireless mounts they presented a picture at once savage and beautiful.

"They have the appearance of splendid warriors," said Turan. "I have a great mind to walk boldly into their city and seek service."

Tara shook her head. "Wait," she admonished. "What would I do without you, and if you were captured how could you collect your reward?"

"I should escape," he said. "At any rate I shall try it," and he started to rise.

"You shall not," said the girl, her tone all authority.

The man looked at her quickly—questioningly.

"You have entered my service," she said, a trifle haughtily.

"You have entered my service for hire and you shall do as I bid you."

Turan sank down beside her again with a half smile upon his lips. "It is yours to command, Princess," he said.

The day passed. Ghek, tiring of the sunlight, had deserted his rykor and crawled down a hole he had discovered close by. Tara and Turan reclined beneath the scant shade of a small tree. They watched the people coming and going through the gate. The party of horsemen did not return. A small herd of zitidars was driven into the city during the day, and once a caravan of broad-wheeled carts drawn by these huge animals wound out of the distant horizon and came down to the city. It, too, passed from their sight within the gateway. Then darkness came and Tara of Helium bid her panthan search for food and drink; but she cautioned him against attempting to enter the city. Before he left her he bent and kissed her hand as a warrior may kiss the hand of his queen.

X

ENTRAPPED

uran the panthan approached the strange city under cover of the darkness. He entertained little hope of finding either food or water outside the wall, but he would try and then, if he failed, he would attempt to make his way into the city, for Tara of Helium must have sustenance and have it soon. He saw that the walls were poorly sentineled, but they were sufficiently high to render an attempt to scale them foredoomed to failure. Taking advantage of underbrush and trees, Turan managed to reach the base of the wall without detection. Silently he moved north past the gateway which was closed by a massive gate which effectively barred even the slightest glimpse within the city beyond. It was Turan's hope to find upon the north side of the city away from the hills a level plain where grew the crops of the inhabitants, and here too water from their irrigating system, but though he traveled far along that seemingly interminable wall he found no fields nor any water. He searched also for some means of ingress to the city, yet here, too, failure was his only reward, and now as he went keen eyes watched him from above and a silent stalker kept pace with him for a time upon the summit of the wall; but presently the shadower descended to the pavement within and hurrying swiftly raced ahead of the stranger without.

He came presently to a small gate beside which was a low building and before the doorway of the building a warrior standing guard. He spoke a few quick words to the warrior and then entered the building only to return almost immediately to the street, followed by fully forty warriors. Cautiously opening the gate the fellow peered carefully along the wall upon the outside in the direction from which he had come. Evidently satisfied, he issued a few words of instruction to those behind him, whereupon half the warriors returned to the interior of the building, while the other half followed the man stealthily through the gateway where they crouched low among the shrubbery in a half circle just north of the gateway which they had left open. Here they waited in utter silence, nor had they long to wait before Turan the panthan came cautiously along the base of the wall. To the very gate he came and when he found it and that it was open he paused for a moment, listening; then he approached and looked within. Assured that there was none within sight to apprehend him he stepped through the gateway into the city.

He found himself in a narrow street that paralleled the wall. Upon the opposite side rose buildings of an architecture unknown to him, yet strangely beautiful. While the buildings were packed closely together there seemed to be no two alike and their fronts were of all shapes and heights and of many hues. The skyline was broken by spire and dome and minaret and tall, slender towers, while the walls supported many a balcony and in the soft light of Cluros, the farther moon, now low in the west, he saw, to his surprise and consternation, the figures of people upon the balconies. Directly opposite him were two women and a man. They sat leaning upon the rail of the balcony looking, apparently, directly at him; but if they saw him they gave no sign.

Turan hesitated a moment in the face of almost certain discovery and then, assured that they must take him for one of their own people, he moved boldly into the avenue. Having no idea of the direction in which he might best hope to find what he sought, and not wishing to arouse suspicion by further hesitation, he turned to the left and stepped briskly along the pavement with the intention of placing himself as quickly as possible beyond the observation of those nocturnal watchers. He knew that the night must be far spent; and so he could not but wonder why people should sit upon their balconies when they should have been asleep among their silks and furs. At first he had thought them the late guests of some convivial host; but the windows behind them were shrouded in darkness and utter quiet prevailed, quite upsetting such a theory. And as he proceeded he passed many another group sitting silently upon other balconies. They paid no attention to him, seeming not even to note his passing. Some leaned with a single elbow upon the rail, their chins resting in their palms; others leaned upon both arms across the balcony, looking down into the street, while several that he saw held musical instruments in their hands, but their fingers moved not upon the strings.

And then Turan came to a point where the avenue turned to the right, to skirt a building that jutted from the inside of the city wall, and as he rounded the corner he came full upon two warriors standing upon either side of the entrance to a building upon his right. It was impossible for them not to be aware of his presence, yet neither moved, nor gave other evidence that they had seen him. He stood there waiting, his hand upon the hilt of his long-sword, but they neither challenged nor halted him. Could it be that these also thought him one of their own kind? Indeed upon no other grounds could he explain their inaction.

As Turan had passed through the gateway into the city and taken his unhindered way along the avenue, twenty warriors had entered the city and closed the gate behind them, and then one had taken to the wall and followed along its summit in the rear of Turan, and another had followed him along the avenue, while a third had crossed the street and entered one of the buildings upon the opposite side.

The balance of them, with the exception of a single sentinel beside the gate, had re-entered the building from which they had been summoned. They were well built, strapping, painted fellows, their naked figures covered now by gorgeous robes against the chill of night. As they spoke of the stranger they laughed at the ease with which they had tricked him, and were still laughing as they threw themselves upon their sleeping silks and furs to resume their broken slumber. It was evident that they constituted a guard detailed for the gate beside which they slept, and it was equally evident that the gates were guarded and the city watched much more carefully than Turan had believed. Chagrined indeed had been the Jed of Gathol had he dreamed that he was being so neatly tricked.

As Turan proceeded along the avenue he passed other sentries beside other doors but now he gave them small heed, since they neither challenged nor otherwise outwardly noted his passing; but while at nearly every turn of the erratic avenue he passed one or more of these silent sentinels he could not guess that he had passed one of them many times and that his every move was watched by silent, clever stalkers. Scarce had he passed a certain one of these rigid guardsmen before the fellow awoke to sudden life, bounded across the avenue, entered a narrow opening in the outer wall where he swiftly followed a corridor built within the wall itself until presently he emerged a little distance ahead of Turan, where he assumed the stiff and silent attitude of a soldier upon guard. Nor did Turan know that a second followed in the shadows of the buildings behind him, nor of the third who hastened ahead of him upon some urgent mission.

And so the panthan moved through the silent streets of the strange city in search of food and drink for the woman he loved. Men and women looked down upon him from shadowy balconies, but spoke not; and sentinels saw him pass and did not challenge. Presently from along the avenue before him came the familiar sound of clanking accouterments, the herald of marching warriors, and almost simultaneously he saw upon his right an open doorway dimly lighted from within. It was the only available place where he might seek to hide from the approaching company, and while he had passed several sentries unquestioned he could scarce hope to escape scrutiny and questioning from a patrol, as he naturally assumed this body of men to be.

Inside the doorway he discovered a passage turning abruptly to the right and almost immediately thereafter to the left. There was none in sight within and so he stepped cautiously around the second turn the more effectually to be hidden from the street. Before him stretched a long corridor, dimly lighted like the entrance. Waiting there he heard the party approach the building, he heard someone at the entrance to his hiding place, and then he heard the door past which he had come slam to. He laid his hand upon his sword, expecting momentarily to hear footsteps approaching along the corridor; but none came. He approached the turn and looked around it; the corridor was empty to the closed door. Whoever had closed it had remained upon the outside.

Turan waited, listening. He heard no sound. Then he advanced to the door and placed an ear against it. All was silence in the street beyond. A sudden draft must have closed the door, or perhaps it was the duty of the patrol to see to such things. It was immaterial. They had evidently passed on and now he would return to the street and continue upon his way. Somewhere there would be a public fountain where he could obtain water, and the chance of food lay in the strings of dried vegetables and meat which hung before the doorways of nearly every Barsoomian home of the poorer classes that he had ever seen. It was this district he was seeking, and it was for this reason his search had led him away from the main gate of the city which he knew would not be located in a poor district.

He attempted to open the door only to find that it resisted his every effort—it was locked upon the outside. Here indeed was a sorry contretemps. Turan the panthan scratched his head. "Fortune frowns upon me," he murmured; but beyond the door, Fate, in the form of a painted warrior, stood smiling. Neatly had he tricked the unwary stranger. The lighted doorway, the marching patrol—these had been planned and timed to a nicety by the third warrior who had sped ahead of Turan along another avenue, and the stranger had done precisely what the fellow had thought he would do—no wonder, then, that he smiled.

This exit barred to him Turan turned back into the corridor. He followed it cautiously and silently. Occasionally there was a door on one side or the other. These he tried only to find each securely locked. The corridor wound more erratically the farther he advanced. A locked door barred his way at its end, but a door upon his right opened and he stepped into a dimly-lighted chamber, about the walls of which were three other doors, each of which he tried in turn. Two were locked; the other opened upon a runway leading downward. It was spiral and he could see no farther than the first turn. A door in the corridor he had quitted opened after he had passed, and the third warrior stepped out and followed after him. A faint smile still lingered upon the fellow's grim lips.

Turan drew his short-sword and cautiously descended. At the bottom was a short corridor with a closed door at the end. He approached the single heavy panel and listened. No sound came to him from beyond the mysterious portal. Gently he tried the door, which swung easily toward him at his touch. Before him was a low-ceiled chamber with a dirt floor. Set in its walls were several other doors and all were closed. As Turan stepped cautiously within, the third warrior descended the spiral runway behind him. The panthan crossed the room quickly and tried a door. It was locked. He heard a muffled click behind him and turned about with ready sword. He was alone; but the door through which he had entered was closed—it was the click of its lock that he had heard.

With a bound he crossed the room and attempted to open it; but to no avail. No longer did he seek silence, for he knew now that the thing had gone beyond the sphere of chance. He threw his weight against the wooden panel; but the thick skeel of which it was constructed would have withstood a battering ram. From beyond came a low laugh.

Rapidly Turan examined each of the other doors. They were all locked. A glance about the chamber revealed a wooden table and a bench. Set in the walls were several heavy rings to which rusty chains were attached—all too significant of the purpose to which the room was dedicated. In the dirt floor near the wall were two or three holes resembling the mouths of burrows—doubtless the habitat of the giant Martian rat. He had observed this much when suddenly the dim light was extinguished, leaving him in darkness utter and complete. Turan, groping about, sought the table and the bench. Placing the latter against the wall he drew the table in front of him and sat down upon the bench, his long-sword gripped in readiness before him. At least they should fight before they took him.

For sometime he sat there waiting for he knew not what. No sound penetrated to his subterranean dungeon. He slowly revolved in his mind the incidents of the evening—the open, unguarded gate; the lighted doorway—the only one he had seen thus open and lighted along the avenue he had followed; the advance of the warriors at precisely the moment that he could find no other avenue of escape or concealment; the corridors and chambers that led past many locked doors to this underground prison leaving no other path for him to pursue.

"By my first ancestor!" he swore; "but it was simple and I a simpleton. They tricked me neatly and have taken me without exposing themselves to a scratch; but for what purpose?"

He wished that he might answer that question and then his thoughts turned to the girl waiting there on the hill beyond the city for him—and he would never come. He knew the ways of the more savage peoples of Barsoom. No, he would never come, now. He had disobeyed her. He smiled at the sweet recollection of those words of command that had fallen from her dear lips. He had disobeyed her and now he had lost the reward.

But what of her? What now would be her fate—starving before a hostile city with only an inhuman kaldane for company? Another thought—a horrid thought—obtruded itself upon him. She had told him of the hideous sights she had witnessed in the burrows of the kaldanes and he knew that they ate human flesh. Ghek was starving. Should he eat his rykor he would be helpless; but—there was sustenance there for them both, for the rykor and the kaldane. Turan cursed himself for a fool. Why had he left her? Far better to have remained and died with her, ready always to protect her, than to have left her at the mercy of the hideous Bantoomian.

Now Turan detected a heavy odor in the air. It oppressed him with a feeling of drowsiness. He would have risen to fight off the creeping lethargy, but his legs seemed weak, so that he sank again to the bench. Presently his sword slipped from his fingers and he sprawled forward upon the table his head resting upon his arms.

Tara of Helium, as the night wore on and Turan did not return, became more and more uneasy, and when dawn broke with no sign of him she guessed that he had failed. Something more than her own unhappy predicament brought a feeling of sorrow to her heart—of sorrow and loneliness. She realized now how she had come to depend upon this panthan not only for protection but for companionship as well. She missed him, and in missing him realized suddenly that he had meant more to her than a mere hired warrior. It was as though a friend had been taken from her—an old and valued friend. She rose from her place of concealment that she might have a better view of the city.

U-Dor, dwar of the 8th Utan of O-Tar, Jeddak of Manator, rode back in the early dawn toward Manator from a brief excursion to a neighboring village. As he was rounding the hills south of the city, his keen eyes were attracted by a slight movement among the shrubbery close to the summit of the nearest hill. He halted his vicious mount and watched more closely. He saw a figure rise facing away from him and peer down toward Manator beyond the hill.

"Come!" he signalled to his followers, and with a word to this thoat turned the beast at a rapid gallop up the hillside. In his wake swept his twenty savage warriors, the padded feet of their mounts soundless upon the soft turf. It was the rattle of sidearms and harness that brought Tara of Helium suddenly about, facing them. She saw a score of warriors with couched lances bearing down upon her.

She glanced at Ghek. What would the spiderman do in this emergency? She saw him crawl to his rykor and attach himself. Then he arose, the beautiful body once again animated and alert. She thought that the creature was preparing for flight. Well, it made little difference to her. Against such as were streaming up the hill toward them a single mediocre swordsman such as Ghek was worse than no defense at all.

"Hurry, Ghek!" she admonished him. "Back into the hills! You may find there a hiding-place;" but the creature only stepped between her and the oncoming riders, drawing his long-sword.

"It is useless, Ghek," she said, when she saw that he intended to defend her. "What can a single sword accomplish against such odds?"

"I can die but once," replied the kaldane. "You and your panthan saved me from Luud and I but do what your panthan would do were he here to protect you."

"It is brave, but it is useless," she replied. "Sheathe your sword. They may not intend us harm."

Ghek let the point of his weapon drop to the ground, but he did not sheathe it, and thus the two stood waiting as U-Dor the dwar stopped his thoat before them while his twenty warriors formed a rough circle about. For a long minute U-Dor sat his mount in silence, looking searchingly first at Tara of Helium and then at her hideous companion.

"What manner of creature are you?" he asked presently. "And what do you before the gates of Manator?"

"We are from far countries," replied the girl, "and we are lost and starving. We ask only food and rest and the privilege to go our way seeking our own homes."

U-Dor smiled a grim smile. "Manator and the hills which guard it alone know the age of Manator," he said; "yet in all the ages that have rolled by since Manator first was, there be no record in the annals of Manator of a stranger departing from Manator."

"But I am a princess," cried the girl haughtily, "and my country is not at war with yours. You must give me and my companions aid and assist us to return to our own land. It is the law of Barsoom."

"Manator knows only the laws of Manator," replied U-Dor; "but come. You shall go with us to the city, where you, being beautiful, need have no fear. I, myself, will protect you if O-Tar so decrees. And as for your companion—but hold! You said 'companions'— there are others of your party then?"

"You see what you see," replied Tara haughtily.

"Be that as it may," said U-Dor. "If there be more they shall not escape Manator; but as I was saying, if your companion fights well he too may live, for O-Tar is just, and just are the laws of Manator. Come!"

Ghek demurred.

"It is useless," said the girl, seeing that he would have stood his ground and fought them. "Let us go with them. Why pit your puny blade against their mighty ones when there should lie in your great brain the means to outwit them?" She spoke in a low whisper, rapidly.

"You are right, Tara of Helium," he replied and sheathed his sword.

And so they moved down the hillside toward the gates of Manator—Tara, Princess of Helium, and Ghek, the kaldane of Bantoom—and surrounding them rode the savage, painted warriors of U-Dor, dwar of the 8th Utan of O-Tar, Jeddak of Manator.

XI

THE CHOICE OF TARA

he dazzling sunlight of Barsoom clothed Manator
in an aureole of splendor as the girl and her
captors rode into the city through The Gate of
Enemies. Here the wall was some fifty feet thick,
and the sides of the passageway within the gate
were covered with parallel shelves of masonry from bottom to top.
Within these shelves, or long, horizontal niches, stood row upon row
of small figures, appearing like tiny, grotesque statuettes of men,
their long, black hair falling below their feet and sometimes trailing
to the shelf beneath. The figures were scarce a foot in height and but
for their diminutive proportions might have been the mummified
bodies of once living men. The girl noticed that as they passed, the
warriors saluted the figures with their spears after the manner of
Barsoomian fighting men in extending a military courtesy, and then
they rode on into the avenue beyond, which ran, wide and stately,
through the city toward the east.

On either side were great buildings wondrously wrought. Paintings of great beauty and antiquity covered many of the walls, their
colors softened and blended by the suns of ages. Upon the pavement
the life of the newly-awakened city was already afoot. Women in
brilliant trappings, befeathered warriors, their bodies daubed with
paint; artisans, armed but less gaily caparisoned, took their various
ways upon the duties of the day. A giant zitidar, magnificent in rich
harness, rumbled its broad-wheeled cart along the stone pavement

toward The Gate of Enemies. Life and color and beauty wrought together a picture that filled the eyes of Tara of Helium with wonder and with admiration, for here was a scene out of the dead past of dying Mars. Such had been the cities of the founders of her race before Throxeus, mightiest of oceans, had disappeared from the face of a world. And from balconies on either side men and women looked down in silence upon the scene below.

The people in the street looked at the two prisoners, especially at the hideous Ghek, and called out in question or comment to their guard; but the watchers upon the balconies spoke not, nor did one so much as turn a head to note their passing. There were many balconies on each building and not a one that did not hold its silent party of richly trapped men and women, with here and there a child or two, but even the children maintained the uniform silence and immobility of their elders. As they approached the center of the city the girl saw that even the roofs bore companies of these idle watchers, harnessed and bejeweled as for some gala-day of laughter and music, but no laughter broke from those silent lips, nor any music from the strings of the instruments that many of them held in jeweled fingers.

And now the avenue widened into an immense square, at the far end of which rose a stately edifice gleaming white in virgin marble among the gaily painted buildings surrounding it and its scarlet sward and gaily-flowering, green-foliaged shrubbery. Toward this U-Dor led his prisoners and their guard to the great arched entrance before which a line of fifty mounted warriors barred the way. When the commander of the guard recognized U-Dor the guardsmen fell back to either side leaving a broad avenue through which the party passed. Directly inside the entrance were inclined runways leading upward on either side. U-Dor turned to the left and led them upward to the second floor and down a long corridor. Here they passed other mounted men and in chambers upon either side they saw more. Occasionally there was another runway leading either up or down. A warrior, his steed at full gallop, dashed into sight from one of these and raced swiftly past them upon some errand.

Nowhere as yet had Tara of Helium seen a man afoot in this great building; but when at a turn, U-Dor led them to the third floor she caught glimpses of chambers in which many riderless thoats were penned and others adjoining where dismounted warriors lolled at ease or played games of skill or chance and many there were who played at jetan, and then the party passed into a long, wide hall of state, as magnificent an apartment as even a princess of mighty Helium ever had seen. The length of the room ran an arched ceiling ablaze with countless radium bulbs. The mighty spans extended from wall to wall leaving the vast floor unbroken by a single column. The arches were of white marble, apparently quarried in single, huge blocks from which each arch was cut complete. Between the arches, the ceiling was set solid about the radium bulbs with precious stones whose scintillant fire and color and beauty filled the whole apartment. The stones were carried down the walls in an irregular fringe for a few feet, where they appeared to hang like a beautiful and gorgeous drapery against the white marble of the wall. The marble ended some six or seven feet from the floor, the walls from that point down being wainscoted in solid gold. The floor itself was of marble richly inlaid with gold. In that single room was a vast treasure equal to the wealth of many a large city.

But what riveted the girl's attention even more than the fabulous treasure of decorations were the files of gorgeously harnessed warriors who sat their thoats in grim silence and immobility on either side of the central aisle, rank after rank of them to the farther walls, and as the party passed between them she could not note so much as the flicker of an eyelid, or the twitching of a thoat's ear.

"The Hall of Chiefs," whispered one of her guard, evidently noting her interest. There was a note of pride in the fellow's voice and something of hushed awe. Then they passed through a great doorway into the chamber beyond, a large, square room in which a dozen mounted warriors lolled in their saddles.

As U-Dor and his party entered the room, the warriors came quickly erect in their saddles and formed a line before another door upon the opposite side of the wall. The padwar commanding them saluted U-Dor who, with his party, had halted facing the guard.

"Send one to O-Tar announcing that U-Dor brings two prisoners worthy of the observation of the great jeddak," said U-Dor; "one because of her extreme beauty, the other because of his extreme ugliness."

"O-Tar sits in council with the lesser chiefs," replied the lieutenant; "but the words of U-Dor the dwar shall be carried to him," and he turned and gave instructions to one who sat his thoat behind him.

"What manner of creature is the male?" he asked of U-Dor. "It cannot be that both are of one race."

"They were together in the hills south of the city," explained U-Dor, "and they say that they are lost and starving."

"The woman is beautiful," said the padwar. "She will not long go begging in the city of Manator," and then they spoke of other matters—of the doings of the palace, of the expedition of U-Dor, until the messenger returned to say that O-Tar bade them bring the prisoners to him.

They passed then through a massive doorway, which, when opened, revealed the great council chamber of O-Tar, Jeddak of Manator, beyond. A central aisle led from the doorway the full length of the great hall, terminating at the steps of a marble dais upon which a man sat in a great throne-chair. Upon either side of the aisle were ranged rows of highly carved desks and chairs of skeel a hard wood of great beauty. Only a few of the desks were occupied—those in the front row, just below the rostrum.

At the entrance U-Dor dismounted with four of his followers who formed a guard about the two prisoners who were then conducted toward the foot of the throne, following a few paces behind U-Dor. As they halted at the foot of the marble steps, the proud gaze of Tara of Helium rested upon the enthroned figure of the man above her. He sat erect without stiffness—a commanding presence trapped in the barbaric splendor that the Barsoomian chieftain loves. He was a large man, the perfection of whose handsome face was marred only by the hauteur of his cold eyes and the suggestion of cruelty imparted by too thin lips. It needed no second glance to assure the least observing that here indeed was a ruler of men—a fighting jeddak whose people might worship but not love, and for whose slightest favor warriors would vie with one another to go forth and die. This was O-Tar, Jeddak of Manator, and as Tara of Helium saw him for the first time she could not but acknowledge a certain admiration for this savage chieftain who so virilely personified the ancient virtues of the God of War.

U-Dor and the jeddak interchanged the simple greetings of Barsoom, and then the former recounted the details of the discovery and capture of the prisoners. O-Tar scrutinized them both intently during U-Dor's narration of events, his expression revealing naught of what passed in the brain behind those inscrutable eyes. When the officer had finished the jeddak fastened his gaze upon Ghek.

"And you," he asked, "what manner of thing are you? From what country? Why are you in Manator?"

"I am a kaldane," replied Ghek; "the highest type of created creature upon the face of Barsoom; I am mind, you are matter. I come from Bantoom. I am here because we were lost and starving."

"And you!" O-Tar turned suddenly on Tara "You, too, are a kaldane?"

"I am a princess of Helium," replied the girl. "I was a prisoner in Bantoom. This kaldane and a warrior of my own race rescued me. The warrior left us to search for food and water. He has doubtless fallen into the hands of your people. I ask you to free him and give us food and drink and let us go upon our way. I am a granddaughter of a jeddak, the daughter of a jeddak of jeddaks, The Warlord of Barsoom. I ask only the treatment that my people would accord you or yours."

"Helium," repeated O-Tar. "I know naught of Helium, nor does the Jeddak of Helium rule Manator. I, O-Tar, am Jeddak of Manator. I alone rule. I protect my own. You have never seen a woman or a warrior of Manator captive in Helium! Why should I protect the people of another jeddak? It is his duty to protect them. If he cannot, he is weak, and his people must fall into the hands of the strong. I, O-Tar, am strong. I will keep you. That——" he pointed at Ghek— "can it fight?"

"It is brave," replied Tara of Helium, "but it has not the skill at arms which my people possess."

"There is none then to fight for you?" asked O-Tar. "We are a just people," he continued without waiting for a reply, "and had you one to fight for you he might win to freedom for himself and you as well."

"But U-Dor assured me that no stranger ever had departed from Manator," she answered.

O-Tar shrugged. "That does not disprove the justice of the laws of Manator," replied O-Tar, "but rather that the warriors of Manator are invincible. Had there come one who could defeat our warriors that one had won to liberty."

"And you fetch my warrior," cried Tara haughtily, "you shall see such swordplay as doubtless the crumbling walls of your decaying city never have witnessed, and if there be no trick in your offer we are already as good as free."

O-Tar smiled more broadly than before and U-Dor smiled, too, and the chiefs and warriors who looked on nudged one another and whispered, laughing. And Tara of Helium knew then that there was trickery in their justice; but though her situation seemed hopeless she did not cease to hope, for was she not the daughter of John Carter,

Warlord of Barsoom, whose famous challenge to Fate, "I still live!" remained the one irreducible defense against despair? At thought of her noble sire the patrician chin of Tara of Helium rose a shade higher. Ah! if he but knew where she was there were little to fear then. The hosts of Helium would batter at the gates of Manator, the great green warriors of John Carter's savage allies would swarm up from the dead sea bottoms lusting for pillage and for loot, the stately ships of her beloved navy would soar above the unprotected towers and minarets of the doomed city which only capitulation and heavy tribute could then save.

But John Carter did not know! There was only one other to whom she might hope to look—Turan the panthan; but where was he? She had seen his sword in play and she knew that it had been wielded by a master hand, and who should know swordplay better than Tara of Helium, who had learned it well under the constant tutorage of John Carter himself. Tricks she knew that discounted even far greater physical prowess than her own, and a method of attack that might have been at once the envy and despair of the cleverest of warriors. And so it was that her thoughts turned to Turan the panthan, though not alone because of the protection he might afford her. She had realized, since he had left her in search of food, that there had grown between them a certain comradeship that she now missed. There had been that about him which seemed to have bridged the gulf between their stations in life. With him she had failed to consider that he was a panthan or that she was a princess—they had been comrades. Suddenly she realized that she missed him for himself more than for his sword. She turned toward O-Tar.

"Where is Turan, my warrior?" she demanded.

"You shall not lack for warriors," replied the jeddak. "One of your beauty will find plenty ready to fight for her. Possibly it shall not be necessary to look farther than the jeddak of Manator. You please me, woman. What say you to such an honor?"

Through narrowed lids the Princess of Helium scrutinized the Jeddak of Manator, from feathered headdress to sandaled foot and back to feathered headdress.

"'Honor'!" she mimicked in tones of scorn. "I please thee, do I? Then know, swine, that thou pleaseth me not—that the daughter of John Carter is not for such as thou!"

A sudden, tense silence fell upon the assembled chiefs. Slowly the blood receded from the sinister face of O-Tar, Jeddak of Manator, leaving him a sickly purple in his wrath. His eyes narrowed to two thin slits, his lips were compressed to a bloodless line of malevolence. For a long moment there was no sound in the throne room of the palace at Manator. Then the jeddak turned toward U-Dor.

"Take her away," he said in a level voice that belied his appearance of rage. "Take her away, and at the next games let the prisoners and the common warriors play at Jetan for her."

"And this?" asked U-Dor, pointing at Ghek.

"To the pits until the next games," replied O-Tar.

"So this is your vaunted justice!" cried Tara of Helium; "that two strangers who have not wronged you shall be sentenced without trial? And one of them is a woman. The swine of Manator are as just as they are brave."

"Away with her!" shouted O-Tar, and at a sign from U-Dor the guards formed about the two prisoners and conducted them from the chamber.

Outside the palace, Ghek and Tara of Helium were separated. The girl was led through long avenues toward the center of the city and finally into a low building, topped by lofty towers of massive construction. Here she was turned over to a warrior who wore the insignia of a dwar, or captain.

"It is O-Tar's wish," explained U-Dor to this one, "that she be kept until the next games, when the prisoners and the common warriors shall play for her. Had she not the tongue of a thoat she had been a worthy stake for our noblest steel," and U-Dor sighed. "Perhaps even yet I may win a pardon for her. It were too bad to see such beauty fall to the lot of some common fellow. I would have honored her myself."

"If I am to be imprisoned, imprison me," said the girl. "I do not recall that I was sentenced to listen to the insults of every low-born boor who chanced to admire me."

"You see, A-Kor," cried U-Dor, "the tongue that she has. Even so and worse spoke she to O-Tar the jeddak."

"I see," replied A-Kor, whom Tara saw was with difficulty restraining a smile. "Come, then, with me, woman," he said, "and we shall find a safe place within The Towers of Jetan—but stay! what ails thee?"

The girl had staggered and would have fallen had not the man caught her in his arms. She seemed to gather herself then and bravely sought to stand erect without support. A-Kor glanced at U-Dor. "Knew you the woman was ill?" he asked.

"Possibly it is lack of food," replied the other. "She mentioned, I believe, that she and her companions had not eaten for several days."

"Brave are the warriors of O-Tar," sneered A-Kor; "lavish their hospitality. U-Dor, whose riches are uncounted, and the brave O-Tar, whose squealing thoats are stabled within marble halls and fed from troughs of gold, can spare no crust to feed a starving girl."

The black haired U-Dor scowled. "Thy tongue will yet pierce thy heart, son of a slave!" he cried. "Once too often mayst thus try the patience of the just O-Tar. Hereafter guard thy speech as well as thy towers."

"Think not to taunt me with my mother's state," said A-Kor. "'Tis the blood of the slave woman that fills my veins with pride, and my only shame is that I am also the son of thy jeddak."

"And O-Tar heard this?" queried U-Dor.

"O-Tar has already heard it from my own lips," replied A-Kor; "this, and more."

He turned upon his heel, a supporting arm still around the waist of Tara of Helium and thus he half led, half carried her into The Towers of Jetan, while U-Dor wheeled his thoat and galloped back in the direction of the palace.

Within the main entrance to The Tower of Jetan lolled a half-dozen warriors. To one of these spoke A-Kor, keeper of the towers. "Fetch Lan-O, the slave girl, and bid her bring food and drink to the upper level of the Thurian tower," then he lifted the half-fainting girl in his arms and bore her along the spiral, inclined runway that led upward within the tower.

Somewhere in the long ascent Tara lost consciousness. When it returned she found herself in a large, circular chamber, the stone walls of which were pierced by windows at regular intervals about the entire circumference of the room. She was lying upon a pile of sleeping silks and furs while there knelt above her a young woman who was forcing drops of some cooling beverage between her parched lips. Tara of Helium half rose upon an elbow and looked about. In the first moments of returning consciousness there were swept from the screen of recollection the happenings of many weeks. She thought that she awoke in the palace of The Warlord at Helium. Her brows knit as she scrutinized the strange face bending over her.

"Who are you?" she asked, and, "Where is Uthia?"

"I am Lan-O the slave girl," replied the other. "I know none by the name of Uthia."

Tara of Helium sat erect and looked about her. This rough stone was not the marble of her father's halls. "Where am I?" she asked.

"In The Thurian Tower," replied the girl, and then seeing that the other still did not understand she guessed the truth. "You are a prisoner in The Towers of Jetan in the city of Manator," she explained.

"You were brought to this chamber, weak and fainting, by A-Kor, Dwar of The Towers of Jetan, who sent me to you with food and drink, for kind is the heart of A-Kor."

"I remember, now," said Tara, slowly. "I remember; but where is Turan, my warrior? Did they speak of him?"

"I heard naught of another," replied Lan-O; "you alone were brought to the towers. In that you are fortunate, for there be no nobler man in Manator than A-Kor. It is his mother's blood that makes him so. She was a slave girl from Gathol."

"Gathol!" exclaimed Tara of Helium. "Lies Gathol close by Manator?"

"Not close, yet still the nearest country," replied Lan-O. "About twenty-two degreeseast, it lies."

"Gathol!" murmured Tara, "Far Gathol!"

"But you are not from Gathol," said the slave girl; "your harness is not of Gathol."

"I am from Helium," said Tara.

"It is far from Helium to Gathol;" said the slave girl, "but in our studies we learned much of the greatness of Helium, we of Gathol, so it seems not so far away."

"You, too, are from Gathol?" asked Tara.

"Many of us are from Gathol who are slaves in Manator," replied the girl. "It is to Gathol, nearest country, that the Manatorians look for slaves most often. They go in great numbers at intervals of three or seven years and haunt the roads that lead to Gathol, and thus they capture whole caravans leaving none to bear warning to Gathol of their fate. Nor do any ever escape from Manator to carry word of us back to Gahan our jed."

Tara of Helium ate slowly and in silence. The girl's words aroused memories of the last hours she had spent in her father's palace and the great midday function at which she had met Gahan of Gathol. Even now she flushed as she recalled his daring words.

Upon her reveries the door opened and a burly warrior appeared in the opening—a hulking fellow, with thick lips and an evil, leering face. The slave girl sprang to her feet, facing him.

"What does this mean, E-Med?" she cried, "was it not the will of A-Kor that this woman be not disturbed?"

"The will of A-Kor, indeed!" and the man sneered. "The will of A-Kor is without power in The Towers of Jetan, or elsewhere, for A-Kor lies now in the pits of O-Tar, and E-Med is dwar of the Towers."

Tara of Helium saw the face of the slave girl pale and the terror in her eyes.

XII

GHEK PLAYS A PRANK

hile Tara of Helium was being led to The Towers of Jetan, Ghek was escorted to the pits beneath the palace where he was imprisoned in a dimly-lighted chamber. Here he found a bench and a table standing upon the dirt floor near the wall, and set in the wall several rings from which depended short lengths of chain. At the base of the walls were several holes in the dirt floor. These, alone, of the several things he saw, interested him. Ghek sat down upon the bench and waited in silence, listening. Presently the lights were extinguished. If Ghek could have smiled he would have then, for Ghek could see as well in the dark as in the light—better, perhaps. He watched the dark openings of the holes in the floor and waited. Presently he detected a change in the air about him—it grew heavy with a strange odor, and once again might Ghek have smiled, could he have smiled.

Let them replace all the air in the chamber with their most deadly fumes; it would be all the same to Ghek, the kaldane, who, having no lungs, required no air. With the rykor it might be different. Deprived of air it would die; but if only a sufficient amount of the gas was introduced to stupefy an ordinary creature it would have no effect upon the rykor, who had no objective mind to overcome. So long as the excess of carbon dioxide in the blood was not sufficient to prevent heart action, the rykor would suffer only a diminution of vitality; but would still respond to the exciting agency of the kaldane's brain.

Ghek caused the rykor to assume a sitting position with its back against the wall where it might remain without direction from his brain. Then he released his contact with its spinal cord; but remained in position upon its shoulders, waiting and watching, for the kaldane's curiosity was aroused. He had not long to wait before the lights were flashed on arid one of the locked doors opened to admit a half-dozen warriors. They approached him rapidly and worked quickly. First they removed all his weapons and then, snapping a fetter about one of the rykor's ankles, secured him to the end of one of the chains hanging from the walls. Next they dragged the long table to a new position and there bolted it to the floor so that an end, instead of the middle, was directly before the prisoner. On the table before him they set food and water and upon the opposite end of the table they laid the key to the fetter. Then they unlocked and opened all the doors and departed.

When Turan the panthan regained consciousness it was to the realization of a sharp pain in one of his forearms. The effects of the gas departed as rapidly as they had overcome him so that as he opened his eyes he was in full possession of all his faculties. The lights were on again and in their glow there was revealed to the man the figure of a giant Martian rat crouching upon the table and gnawing upon his arm. Snatching his arm away he reached for his short-sword, while the rat, growling, sought to seize his arm again. It was then that Turan discovered that his weapons had been removed—short-sword, long-sword, dagger, and pistol. The rat charged him then and striking the creature away with his hand the man rose and backed off, searching for something with which to strike a harder blow. Again the rat charged and as Turan stepped quickly back to avoid the menacing jaws, something seemed to jerk suddenly upon his right ankle, and as he drew his left foot back to regain his equilibrium his heel caught upon a taut chain and he fell heavily backward to the floor just as the rat leaped upon his breast and sought his throat.

The Martian rat is a fierce and unlovely thing. It is many-legged and hairless, its hide resembling that of a newborn mouse in repulsiveness. In size and weight it is comparable to a large Airedale terrier. Its eyes are small and close-set, and almost hidden in deep, fleshy apertures. But its most ferocious and repulsive feature is its jaws, the entire bony structure of which protrudes several inches beyond the flesh, revealing five sharp, spadelike teeth in the upper jaw and the same number of similar teeth in the lower, the whole suggesting the appearance of a rotting face from which much of the flesh has sloughed away.

It was such a thing that leaped upon the breast of the panthan to tear at his jugular. Twice Turan struck it away as he sought to regain his feet, but both times it returned with increased ferocity to renew the attack. Its only weapons are its jaws since its broad, splay feet are armed with blunt talons. With its protruding jaws it excavates its winding burrows and with its broad feet it pushes the dirt behind it. To keep the jaws from his flesh then was Turan's only concern and this he succeeded in doing until chance gave him a hold upon the creature's throat. After that the end was but a matter of moments. Rising at last he flung the lifeless thing from him with a shudder of disgust.

Now he turned his attention to a hurried inventory of the new conditions which surrounded him since the moment of his incarceration. He realized vaguely what had happened. He had been anaesthetized and stripped of his weapons, and as he rose to his feet he saw that one ankle was fettered to a chain in the wall. He looked about the room. All the doors swung wide open! His captors would render his imprisonment the more cruel by leaving ever before him tempting glimpses of open aisles to the freedom he could not attain. Upon the end of the table and within easy reach was food and drink. This at least was attainable and at sight of it his starved stomach seemed almost to cry aloud for sustenance. It was with difficulty that he ate and drank in moderation.

As he devoured the food his eyes wandered about the confines of his prison until suddenly they seized upon a thing that lay on the table at the end farthest from him. It was a key. He raised his fettered ankle and examined the lock. There could be no doubt of it! The key that lay there on the table before him was the key to that very lock. A careless warrior had laid it there and departed, forgetting.

Hope surged high in the breast of Gahan of Gathol, of Turan the panthan. Furtively his eyes sought the open doorways. There was no one in sight. Ah, if he could but gain his freedom! He would find some way from this odious city back to her side and never again would he leave her until he had won safety for her or death for himself.

He rose and moved cautiously toward the opposite end of the table where lay the coveted key. The fettered ankle halted his first step, but he stretched at full length along the table, extending eager fingers toward the prize. They almost laid hold upon it—a little more and they would touch it. He strained and stretched, but still the thing lay just beyond his reach. He hurled himself forward until the iron fetter bit deep into his flesh, but all futilely. He sat back upon the bench then and glared at the open doors and the key, realizing now that they were part of a well-laid scheme of refined torture, none the less demoralizing because it inflicted no physical suffering.

For just a moment the man gave way to useless regret and foreboding, then he gathered himself together, his brows cleared, and he returned to his unfinished meal. At least they should not have the satisfaction of knowing how sorely they had hit him. As he ate it occurred to him that by dragging the table along the floor he could bring the key within his reach, but when he essayed to do so, he found that the table had been securely bolted to the floor during the period of his unconsciousness, Again Gahan smiled and shrugged and resumed his eating.

When the warriors had departed from the prison in which Ghek was confined, the kaldane crawled from the shoulders of the rykor to the table. Here he drank a little water and then directed the hands of the rykor to the balance of it and to the food, upon which the brainless thing fell with avidity. While it was thus engaged Ghek took his spider-like way along the table to the opposite end where lay the key to the fetter. Seizing it in a chela he leaped to the floor and scurried rapidly toward the mouth of one of the burrows against the wall, into which he disappeared. For long had the brain been contemplating these burrow entrances. They appealed to his kaldanean tastes, and further, they pointed a hiding place for the key and a lair for the only kind of food that the kaldane relished—flesh and blood.

Ghek had never seen an ulsio, since these great Martian rats had long ago disappeared from Bantoom, their flesh and blood having been greatly relished by the kaldanes; but Ghek had inherited, almost unimpaired, every memory of every ancestor, and so he knew that ulsio inhabited these lairs and that ulsio was good to eat, and he knew what ulsio looked like and what his habits were, though he had never seen him nor any picture of him. As we breed animals for the transmission of physical attributes, so the Kaldanes breed themselves for the transmission of attributes of the mind, including memory and the power of recollection, and thus have they raised what we term instinct, above the level of the threshold of the objective mind where it may be commanded and utilized by recollection. Doubtless in our own subjective minds lie many of the impressions and experiences of our forebears. These may impinge upon our consciousness in dreams only, or in vague, haunting suggestions that we have before experienced some transient phase of our present existence. Ah, if we had but the power to recall them! Before us would unfold the forgotten story of the lost eons that have preceded us. We might even walk with God in the garden of His stars while man was still but a budding idea within His mind.

Ghek descended into the burrow at a steep incline for some ten feet, when he found himself in an elaborate and delightful network of burrows! The kaldane was elated. This indeed was life! He moved rapidly and fearlessly and he went as straight to his goal as you could to the kitchen of your own home. This goal lay at a low level in a spheroidal cavity about the size of a large barrel. Here, in a nest of torn bits of silk and fur lay six baby ulsios.

When the mother returned there were but five babies and a great spider-like creature, which she immediately sprang to attack only to be met by powerful chelae which seized and held her so that she could not move. Slowly they dragged her throat toward a hideous mouth and in a little moment she was dead.

Ghek might have remained in the nest for a long time, since there was ample food for many days; but he did not do so. Instead he explored the burrows. He followed them into many subterranean chambers of the city of Manator, and upward through walls to rooms above the ground. He found many ingeniously devised traps, and he found poisoned food and other signs of the constant battle that the inhabitants of Manator waged against these repulsive creatures that dwelt beneath their homes and public buildings.

His exploration revealed not only the vast proportions of the network of runways that apparently traversed every portion of the city, but the great antiquity of the majority of them. Tons upon tons of dirt must have been removed, and for a long time he wondered where it had been deposited, until in following downward a tunnel of great size and length he sensed before him the thunderous rush of subterranean waters, and presently came to the bank of a great, underground river, tumbling onward, no doubt, the length of a world to the buried sea of Omean. Into this torrential sewer had unthinkable generations of ulsios pushed their few handsful of dirt in the excavating of their vast labyrinth.

For only a moment did Ghek tarry by the river, for his seemingly aimless wanderings were in reality prompted by a definite purpose, and this he pursued with vigor and singleness of design. He followed such runways as appeared to terminate in the pits or other chambers of the inhabitants of the city, and these he explored, usually from the safety of a burrow's mouth, until satisfied that what he sought was not there. He moved swiftly upon his spider legs and covered remarkable distances in short periods of time.

His search not being rewarded with immediate success, he decided to return to the pit where his rykor lay chained and look to its wants. As he approached the end of the burrow that terminated in the pit he slackened his pace, stopping just within the entrance of the runway that he might scan the interior of the chamber before entering it. As he did so he saw the figure of a warrior appear suddenly in an opposite doorway. The rykor sprawled upon the table, his hands groping blindly for more food. Ghek saw the warrior pause and gaze in sudden astonishment at the rykor; he saw the fellow's eyes go wide and an ashen hue replace the copper bronze of his cheek. He stepped back as though someone had struck him in the face. For an instant only he stood thus as in a paralysis of fear, then he uttered a smothered shriek and turned and fled. Again was it a catastrophe that Ghek, the kaldane, could not smile.

Quickly entering the room he crawled to the table top and affixed himself to the shoulders of his rykor, and there he waited; and who may say that Ghek, though he could not smile, possessed not a sense of humor? For a half-hour he sat there, and then there came to him the sound of men approaching along corridors of stone. He could hear their arms clank against the rocky walls and he knew that they came at a rapid pace; but just before they reached the entrance to his prison they paused and advanced more slowly. In the lead was an officer, and just behind him, wide-eyed and perhaps still a little ashen, the warrior who had so recently departed in haste. At the doorway they halted and the officer turned sternly upon the warrior. With upraised finger he pointed at Ghek.

"There sits the creature! Didst thou dare lie, then, to thy dwar?"

"I swear," cried the warrior, "that I spoke the truth. But a moment since the thing groveled, headless, upon this very table! And may my first ancestor strike me dead upon the spot if I speak other than a true word!"

The officer looked puzzled. The men of Mars seldom if ever lie. He scratched his head. Then he addressed Ghek. "How long have you been here?" he asked.

"Who knows better than those who placed me here and chained me to a wall?" he returned in reply.

"Saw you this warrior enter here a few minutes since?"

"I saw him," replied Ghek.

"And you sat there where you sit now?" continued the officer.

"Look thou to my chain and tell me then where else might I sit!" cried Ghek. "Art the people of thy city all fools?"

Three other warriors pressed behind the two in front, craning their necks to view the prisoner while they grinned at the discomfiture of their fellow. The officer scowled at Ghek.

"Thy tongue is as venomous as that of the she-banth O-Tar sent to The Towers of Jetan," he said.

"You speak of the young woman who was captured with me?" asked Ghek, his expressionless monotone and face revealing naught of the interest he felt.

"I speak of her," replied the dwar, and then turning to the warrior who had summoned him: "return to thy quarters and remain there until the next games. Perhaps by that time thy eyes may have learned not to deceive thee."

The fellow cast a venomous glance at Ghek and turned away. The officer shook his head. "I do not understand it," he muttered. "Always has U-Van been a true and dependable warrior. Could it be—?" he glanced piercingly at Ghek. "Thou hast a strange head that misfits thy body, fellow," he cried. "Our legends tell us of those ancient creatures that placed hallucinations upon the mind of their fellows. If thou be such then maybe U-Van suffered from thy forbidden powers. If thou be such O-Tar will know well how to deal with thee." He wheeled about and motioned his warriors to follow him.

"Wait!" cried Ghek. "Unless I am to be starved, send me food."

"You have had food," replied the warrior.

"Am I to be fed but once a day?" asked Ghek. "I require food oftener than that. Send me food."

"You shall have food," replied the officer. "None may say that the prisoners of Manator are ill-fed. Just are the laws of Manator," and he departed.

No sooner had the sounds of their passing died away in the distance than Ghek clambered from the shoulders of his rykor, and scurried to the burrow where he had hidden the key. Fetching it he unlocked the fetter from about the creature's ankle, locked it empty and carried the key farther down into the burrow. Then he returned to his place upon his brainless servitor. After a while he heard footsteps approaching, whereupon he rose and passed into another corridor from that down which he knew the warrior was coming. Here he waited out of sight, listening. He heard the man enter the chamber and halt. He heard a muttered exclamation, followed by the jangle of metal dishes as a salver was slammed upon a table; then rapidly retreating footsteps, which quickly died away in the distance.

Ghek lost no time in returning to the chamber, recovering the key, relocking the rykor to his chain. Then he replaced the key in the burrow and squatting on the table beside his headless body, directed its hands toward the food. While the rykor ate Ghek sat listening for the scraping sandals and clattering arms that he knew soon would come. Nor had he long to wait. Ghek scrambled to the shoulders of his rykor as he heard them coming. Again it was the officer who had been summoned by U-Van and with him were three warriors. The one directly behind him was evidently the same who had brought the food, for his eyes went wide when he saw Ghek sitting at the table and he looked very foolish as the dwar turned his stern glance upon him.

"It is even as I said," he cried. "He was not here when I brought his food."

"But he is here now," said the officer grimly, "and his fetter is locked about his ankle. Look! it has not been opened—but where is the key? It should be upon the table at the end opposite him. Where is the key, creature?" he shouted at Ghek.

"How should I, a prisoner, know better than my jailer the whereabouts of the key to my fetters?" he retorted.

"But it lay here," cried the officer, pointing to the other end of the table.

"Did you see it?" asked Ghek.

The officer hesitated. "No but it must have been there," he parried.

"Did you see the key lying there?" asked Ghek, pointing to another warrior.

The fellow shook his head negatively. "And you? and you?" continued the kaldane addressing the others.

They both admitted that they never had seen the key. "And if it had been there how could I have reached it?" he continued.

"No, he could not have reached it," admitted the officer; "but there shall be no more of this! I-Zav, you will remain here on guard with this prisoner until you are relieved."

I-Zav looked anything but happy as this intelligence was transmitted to him, and he eyed Ghek suspiciously as the dwar and the other warriors turned and left him to his unhappy lot.

XIII

A Desperate Deed

-Med crossed the tower chamber toward Tara of Helium and the slave girl, Lan-O. He seized the former roughly by a shoulder. "Stand!" he commanded. Tara struck his hand from her and rising, backed away.

"Lay not your hand upon the person of a princess of Helium, beast!" she warned.

E-Med laughed. "Think you that I play at jetan for you without first knowing something of the stake for which I play?" he demanded. "Come here!"

The girl drew herself to her full height, folding her arms across her breast, nor did E-Med note that the slim fingers of her right hand were inserted beneath the broad leather strap of her harness where it passed over her left shoulder.

"And O-Tar learns of this you shall rue it, E-Med," cried the slave girl; "there be no law in Manator that gives you this girl before you shall have won her fairly."

"What cares O-Tar for her fate?" replied E-Med. "Have I not heard? Did she not flout the great jeddak, heaping abuse upon him? By my first ancestor, I think O-Tar might make a jed of the man who subdued her," and again he advanced toward Tara.

"Wait!" said the girl in low, even tone. "Perhaps you know not what you do. Sacred to the people of Helium are the persons of the women of Helium. For the honor of the humblest of them would

the great jeddak himself unsheathe his sword. The greatest nations
of Barsoom have trembled to the thunders of war in defense of the
person of Dejah Thoris, my mother. We are but mortal and so may
die; but we may not be defiled. You may play at jetan for a princess
of Helium, but though you may win the match, never may you claim
the reward. If thou wouldst possess a dead body press me too far, but
know, man of Manator, that the blood of The Warlord flows not in
the veins of Tara of Helium for naught. I have spoken."

"I know naught of Helium and O-Tar is our warlord," replied
E-Med; "but I do know that I would examine more closely the prize
that I shall play for and win. I would test the lips of her who is to be
my slave after the next games; nor is it well, woman, to drive me too
far to anger." His eyes narrowed as he spoke, his visage taking on the
semblance of that of a snarling beast. "If you doubt the truth of my
words ask Lan-O, the slave girl."

"He speaks truly, O woman of Helium," interjected Lan-O. "Try
not the temper of E-Med, if you value your life."

But Tara of Helium made no reply. Already had she spoken. She
stood in silence now facing the burly warrior who approached her. He
came close and then quite suddenly he seized her and, bending, tried
to draw her lips to his.

Lan-O saw the woman from Helium half turn, and with a quick
movement jerk her right hand from where it had lain upon her breast.
She saw the hand shoot from beneath the arm of E-Med and rise
behind his shoulder and she saw in the hand a long, slim blade. The
lips of the warrior were drawing closer to those of the woman, but
they never touched them, for suddenly the man straightened, stiffly, a
shriek upon his lips, and then he crumpled like an empty fur and lay,
a shrunken heap, upon the floor. Tara of Helium stooped and wiped
her blade upon his harness.

Lan-O, wide-eyed, looked with horror upon the corpse. "For
this we shall both die," she cried.

"And who would live a slave in Manator?" asked Tara of Helium.

"I am not so brave as thou," said the slave girl, "and life is sweet and there is always hope."

"Life is sweet," agreed Tara of Helium, "but honor is sacred. But do not fear. When they come I shall tell them the truth—that you had no hand in this and no opportunity to prevent it."

For a moment the slave girl seemed to be thinking deeply. Suddenly her eyes lighted. "There is a way, perhaps," she said, "to turn suspicion from us. He has the key to this chamber upon him. Let us open the door and drag him out—maybe we shall find a place to hide him."

"Good!" exclaimed Tara of Helium, and the two immediately set about the matter Lan-O had suggested. Quickly they found the key and unlatched the door and then, between them, they half carried, half dragged, the corpse of E-Med from the room and down the stairway to the next level where Lan-O said there were vacant chambers. The first door they tried was unlatched, and through this the two bore their grisly burden into a small room lighted by a single window. The apartment bore evidence of having been utilized as a living-room rather than as a cell, being furnished with a degree of comfort and even luxury. The walls were paneled to a height of about seven feet from the floor, while the plaster above and the ceiling were decorated with faded paintings of a nother day.

As Tara's eyes ran quickly over the interior her attention was drawn to a section of paneling that seemed to be separated at one edge from the piece next adjoining it. Quickly she crossed to it, discovering that one vertical edge of an entire panel projected a half-inch beyond the others. There was a possible explanation which piqued her curiosity, and acting upon its suggestion she seized upon the projecting edge and pulled outward. Slowly the panel swung toward her, revealing a dark aperture in the wall behind.

"Look, Lan-O!" she cried. "See what I have found—a hole in which we may hide the thing upon the floor."

Lan-O joined her and together the two investigated the dark aperture, finding a small platform from which a narrow runway led downward into Stygian darkness. Thick dust covered the floor within the doorway, indicating that a great period of time had elapsed since human foot had trod it—a secret way, doubtless, unknown to living Manatorians. Here they dragged the corpse of E-Med, leaving it upon the platform, and as they left the dark and forbidden closet Lan-O would have slammed to the panel had not Tara prevented.

"Wait!" she said, and fell to examining the door frame and the stile.

"Hurry!" whispered the slave girl. "If they come we are lost."

"It may serve us well to know how to open this place again," replied Tara of Helium, and then suddenly she pressed a foot against a section of the carved base at the right of the open panel. "Ah!" she breathed, a note of satisfaction in her tone, and closed the panel until it fitted snugly in its place. "Come!" she said and turned toward the outer doorway of the chamber.

They reached their own cell without detection, and closing the door Tara locked it from the inside and placed the key in a secret pocket in her harness.

"Let them come," she said. "Let them question us! What could two poor prisoners know of the whereabouts of their noble jailer? I ask you, Lan-O, what could they?"

"Nothing," admitted Lan-O, smiling with her companion.

"Tell me of these men of Manator," said Tara presently. "Are they all like E-Med, or are some of them like A-Kor, who seemed a brave and chivalrous character?"

"They are not unlike the peoples of other countries," replied Lan-O. "There be among them both good and bad. They are brave warriors and mighty. Among themselves they are not without chivalry and honor, but in their dealings with strangers they know but one law—the law of might. The weak and unfortunate of other lands fill them with contempt and arouse all that is worst in their natures, which doubtless accounts for their treatment of us, their slaves."

"But why should they feel contempt for those who have suffered the misfortune of falling into their hands?" queried Tara.

"I do not know," said Lan-O; "A-Kor says that he believes that it is because their country has never been invaded by a victorious foe. In their stealthy raids never have they been defeated, because they have never waited to face a powerful force; and so they have come to believe themselves invincible, and the other peoples are held in contempt as inferior in valor and the practice of arms."

"Yet A-Kor is one of them," said Tara.

"He is a son of O-Tar, the jeddak," replied Lan-O; "but his mother was a high born Gatholian, captured and made slave by O-Tar, and A-Kor boasts that in his veins runs only the blood of his mother, and indeed is he different from the others. His chivalry is of a gentler form, though not even his worst enemy has dared question his courage, while his skill with the sword, and the spear, and the thoat is famous throughout the length and breadth of Manator."

"What think you they will do with him?" asked Tara of Helium.

"Sentence him to the games," replied Lan-O. "If O-Tar be not greatly angered he may be sentenced to but a single game, in which case he may come out alive; but if O-Tar wishes really to dispose of him he will be sentenced to the entire series, and no warrior has ever survived the full ten, or rather none who was under a sentence from O-Tar."

"What are the games? I do not understand," said Tara "I have heard them speak of playing at jetan, but surely no one can be killed at jetan. We play it often at home."

"But not as they play it in the arena at Manator," replied Lan-O.

"Come to the window," and together the two approached an aperture facing toward the east.

Below her Tara of Helium saw a great field entirely surrounded by the low building, and the lofty towers of which that in which she was imprisoned was but a unit. About the arena were tiers of seats; but the a thing that caught her attention was a gigantic jetan board laid out upon the floor of the arena in great squares of alternate orange and black.

"Here they play at jetan with living pieces. They play for great stakes and usually for a woman—some slave of exceptional beauty. O-Tar himself might have played for you had you not angered him, but now you will be played for in an open game by slaves and criminals, and you will belong to the side that wins—not to a single warrior, but to all who survive the game."

The eyes of Tara of Helium flashed, but she made no comment.

"Those who direct the play do not necessarily take part in it," continued the slave girl, "but sit in those two great thrones which you see at either end of the board and direct their pieces from square to square."

"But where lies the danger?" asked Tara of Helium. "If a piece be taken it is merely removed from the board—this is a rule of jetan as old almost as the civilization of Barsoom."

"But here in Manator, when they play in the great arena with living men, that rule is altered," explained Lan-O. "When a warrior is moved to a square occupied by an opposing piece, the two battle to the death for possession of the square and the one that is successful advantages by the move. Each is caparisoned to simulate the piece he represents and in addition he wears that which indicates whether he be slave, a warrior serving a sentence, or a volunteer. If serving a sentence the number of games he must play is also indicated, and thus the one directing the moves knows which pieces to risk and which to conserve, and further than this, a man's chances are affected by the position that is assigned him for the game. Those whom they wish to die are always Panthans in the game, for the Panthan has the least chance of surviving."

"Do those who direct the play ever actually take part in it?" asked Tara.

"Oh, yes," said Lan-O. "Often when two warriors, even of the highest class, hold a grievance against one another O-Tar compels them to settle it upon the arena. Then it is that they take active part and with drawn swords direct their own players from the position of Chief. They pick their own players, usually the best of their own warriors and slaves, if they be powerful men who possess such, or their friends may volunteer, or they may obtain prisoners from the pits. These are games indeed—the very best that are seen. Often the great chiefs themselves are slain."

"It is within this amphitheater that the justice of Manator is meted, then?" asked Tara.

"Very largely," replied Lan-O.

"How, then, through such justice, could a prisoner win his liberty?" continued the girl from Helium.

"If a man, and he survived ten games his liberty would be his," replied Lan-O.

"But none ever survives?" queried Tara. "And if a woman?"

"No stranger within the gates of Manator ever has survived ten games," replied the slave girl. "They are permitted to offer themselves into perpetual slavery if they prefer that to fighting at jetan. Of course they may be called upon, as any warrior, to take part in a game, but their chances then of surviving are increased, since they may never again have the chance of winning to liberty."

"But a woman," insisted Tara; "how may a woman win her freedom?"

Lan-O laughed. "Very simply," she cried derisively. "She has but to find a warrior who will fight through ten consecutive games for her and survive."

"'Just are the laws of Manator,'" quoted Tara, scornfully.

Then it was that they heard footsteps outside their cell and a moment later a key turned in the lock and the door opened. A warrior faced them.

"Hast seen E-Med the dwar?" he asked.

"Yes," replied Tara, "he was here sometime ago."

The man glanced quickly about the bare chamber and then searchingly first at Tara of Helium and then at the slave girl, Lan-O. The puzzled expression upon his face increased. He scratched his head. "It is strange," he said. "A score of men saw him ascend into this tower; and though there is but a single exit, and that well guarded, no man has seen him pass out."

Tara of Helium hid a yawn with the back of a shapely hand. "The Princess of Helium is hungry, fellow," she drawled; "tell your master that she would eat."

It was an hour later that food was brought, an officer and several warriors accompanying the bearer. The former examined the room carefully, but there was no sign that aught amiss had occurred there. The wound that had sent E-Med the dwar to his ancestors had not bled, fortunately for Tara of Helium.

"Woman," cried the officer, turning upon Tara, "you were the last to see E-Med the dwar. Answer me now and answer me truthfully. Did you see him leave this room?"

"I did," answered Tara of Helium.

"Where did he go from here?"

"How should I know? Think you that I can pass through a locked door of skeel?" the girl's tone was scornful.

"Of that we do not know," said the officer. "Strange things have happened in the cell of your companion in the pits of Manator. Perhaps you could pass through a locked door of skeel as easily as he performs seemingly more impossible feats."

"Whom do you mean," she cried; "Turan the panthan? He lives, then? Tell me, is he here in Manator unharmed?"

"I speak of that thing which calls itself Ghek the kaldane," replied the officer.

"But Turan! Tell me, padwar, have you heard aught of him?" Tara's tone was insistent and she leaned a little forward toward the officer, her lips slightly parted in expectancy.

Into the eyes of the slave girl, Lan-O, who was watching her, there crept a soft light of understanding; but the officer ignored Tara's question—what was the fate of another slave to him? "Men do not disappear into thin air," he growled, "and if E-Med be not found soon O-Tar himself may take a hand in this. I warn you, woman, if you be one of those horrid Corphals that by commanding the spirits of the wicked dead gains evil mastery over the living, as many now believe the thing called Ghek to be, that lest you return E-Med, O-Tar will have no mercy on you."

"What foolishness is this?" cried the girl. "I am a princess of Helium, as I have told you all a score of times. Even if the fabled Corphals existed, as none but the most ignorant now believes, the lore of the ancients tells us that they entered only into the bodies of wicked criminals of the lowest class. Man of Manator, thou art a fool, and thy jeddak and all his people," and she turned her royal back upon the padwar, and gazed through the window across the Field of Jetan and the roofs of Manator through the low hills and the rolling country and freedom.

"And you know so much of Corphals, then," he cried, "you know that while no common man dare harm them they may be slain by the hand of a jeddak with impunity!"

The girl did not reply, nor would she speak again, for all his threats and rage, for she knew now that none in all Manator dared harm her save O-Tar, the jeddak, and after a while the padwar left, taking his men with him. And after they had gone Tara stood for long looking out upon the city of Manator, and wondering what more of cruel wrongs Fate held in store for her. She was standing thus in silent meditation when there rose to her the strains of martial music from the city below—the deep, mellow tones of the long war trumpets of mounted troops, the clear, ringing notes of footsoldiers' music. The girl raised her head and looked about, listening, and Lan-O, standing at an opposite window, looking toward the west, motioned Tara to join her. Now they could see across roofs and avenues to The Gate of Enemies, through which troops were marching into the city.

"The Great Jed is coming," said Lan-O, "none other dares enter thus, with blaring trumpets, the city of Manator. It is U-Thor, Jed of Manatos, second city of Manator. They call him The Great Jed the length and breadth of Manator, and because the people love him, O-Tar hates him. They say, who know, that it would need but slight provocation to inflame the two to war. How such a war would end no one could guess; for the people of Manator worship the great O-Tar, though they do not love him. U-Thor they love, but he is not the jeddak," and Tara understood, as only a Martian may, how much that simple statement encompassed.

The loyalty of a Martian to his jeddak is almost an instinct, and second not even to the instinct of self-preservation at that. Nor is this strange in a race whose religion includes ancestor worship, and where families trace their origin back into remote ages and a jeddak sits upon the same throne that his direct progenitors have occupied for, perhaps, hundreds of thousands of years, and rules the descendants of the same people that his forebears ruled. Wicked jeddaks have been dethroned, but seldom are they replaced by other than members of the imperial house, even though the law gives to the jeds the right to select whom they please.

"U-Thor is a just man and good, then?" asked Tara of Helium.

"There be none nobler," replied Lan-O. "In Manatos none but wicked criminals who deserve death are forced to play at jetan, and

313

even then the play is fair and they have their chance for freedom. Volunteers may play, but the moves are not necessarily to the death—a wound, and even sometimes points in swordplay, deciding the issue. There they look upon jetan as a martial sport— here it is but butchery. And U-Thor is opposed to the ancient slave raids and to the policy that keeps Manator forever isolated from the other nations of Barsoom; but U-Thor is not jeddak and so there is no change."

The two girls watched the column moving up the broad avenue from The Gate of Enemies toward the palace of O-Tar. A gorgeous, barbaric procession of painted warriors in jewel-studded harness and waving feathers; vicious, squealing thoats caparisoned in rich trappings; far above their heads the long lances of their riders bore fluttering pennons; foot-soldiers swinging easily along the stone pavement, their sandals of zitidar hide giving forth no sound; and at the rear of each utan a train of painted chariots, drawn by mammoth zitidars, carrying the equipment of the company to which they were attached. Utan after utan entered through the great gate, and even when the head of the column reached the palace of O-Tar they were not all within the city.

"I have been here many years," said the girl, Lan-O; "but never have I seen even The Great Jed bring so many fighting men into the city of Manator."

Through half-closed eyes Tara of Helium watched the warriors marching up the broad avenue, trying to imagine them the fighting men of her beloved Helium coming to the rescue of their princess. That splendid figure upon the great thoat might be John Carter, himself, Warlord of Barsoom, and behind him utan after utan of the veterans of the empire, and then the girl opened her eyes again and saw the host of painted, befeathered barbarians, and sighed. But yet she watched, fascinated by the martial scene, and now she noted again the groups of silent figures upon the balconies. No waving silks; no cries of welcome; no showers of flowers and jewels such as would have marked the entry of such a splendid, friendly pageant into the twin cities of her birth.

"The people do not seem friendly to the warriors of Manatos," she remarked to Lan-O; "I have not seen a single welcoming sign from the people on the balconies."

The slave girl looked at her in surprise. "It cannot be that you do not know!" she exclaimed. "Why, they are—" but she got no further. The door swung open and an officer stood before them.

"The slave girl, Tara, is summoned to the presence of O-Tar, the jeddak!" he announced.

XIV

AT GHEK'S COMMAND

uran the panthan chafed in his chains. Time dragged; silence and monotony prolonged minutes into hours. Uncertainty of the fate of the woman he loved turned each hour into an eternity of hell. He listened impatiently for the sound of approaching footsteps that he might see and speak to some living creature and learn, perchance, some word of Tara of Helium. After torturing hours his ears were rewarded by the rattle of harness and arms. Men were coming! He waited breathlessly. Perhaps they were his executioners; but he would welcome them notwithstanding. He would question them. But if they knew naught of Tara he would not divulge the location of the hiding place in which he had left her.

Now they came—a half-dozen warriors and an officer, escorting an unarmed man; a prisoner, doubtless. Of this Turan was not left long in doubt, since they brought the newcomer and chained him to an adjoining ring. Immediately the panthan commenced to question the officer in charge of the guard.

"Tell me," he demanded, "why I have been made prisoner, and if other strangers were captured since I entered your city."

"What other prisoners?" asked the officer.

"A woman, and a man with a strange head," replied Turan.

"It is possible," said the officer; "but what were their names?"

"The woman was Tara, Princess of Helium, and the man was Ghek, a kaldane, of Bantoom."

"These were your friends?" asked the officer.

"Yes," replied Turan.

"It is what I would know," said the officer, and with a curt command to his men to follow him he turned and left the cell.

"Tell me of them!" cried Turan after him. "Tell me of Tara of Helium! Is she safe?" but the man did not answer and soon the sound of their departure died in the distance.

"Tara of Helium was safe, but a short time since," said the prisoner chained at Turan's side.

The panthan turned toward the speaker, seeing a large man, handsome of face and with a manner both stately and dignified. "You have seen her?" he asked. "They captured her then? She is in danger?"

"She is being held in The Towers of Jetan as a prize for the next games," replied the stranger.

"And who are you?" asked Turan. "And why are you here, a prisoner?"

"I am A-Kor the dwar, keeper of The Towers of Jetan," replied the other. "I am here because I dared speak the truth of O-Tar the jeddak, to one of his officers."

"And your punishment?" asked Turan.

"I do not know. O-Tar has not yet spoken. Doubtless the games— perhaps the full ten, for O-Tar does not love A-Kor, his son."

"You are the jeddak's son?" asked Turan.

"I am the son of O-Tar and of a slave, Haja of Gathol, who was a princess in her own land."

Turan looked searchingly at the speaker. A son of Haja of Gathol! A son of his mother's sister, this man, then, was his own cousin. Well did Gahan remember the mysterious disappearance of the Princess Haja and an entire utan of her personal troops. She had been upon a visit far from the city of Gathol and returning home had vanished with her whole escort from the sight of man. So this was the secret of the seeming mystery? Doubtless it explained many other similar disappearances that extended nearly as far back as the history of Gathol. Turan scrutinized his companion, discovering many evidences of resemblance to his mother's people. A-Kor might have been ten years younger than he, but such differences in age are scarce accounted among a people who seldom or never age outwardly after maturity and whose span of life may be a thousand years.

"And where lies Gathol?" asked Turan.

"Almost due east of Manator," replied A-Kor.

"And how far?"

"Some twenty-one degrees it is from the city of Manator to the city of Gathol," replied A-Kor; "but little more than ten degrees between the boundaries of the two countries. Between them, though, there lies a country of torn rocks and yawning chasms."

Well did Gahan know this country that bordered his upon the west—even the ships of the air avoided it because of the treacherous currents that rose from the deep chasms, and the almost total absence of safe landings. He knew now where Manator lay and for the first time in long weeks the way to his own Gathol, and here was a man, a fellow prisoner, in whose veins flowed the blood of his own ancestors—a man who knew Manator; its people, its customs and the country surrounding it—one who could aid him, with advice at least, to find a plan for the rescue of Tara of Helium and for escape. But would A-Kor—could he dare broach the subject? He could do no less than try.

"And O-Tar you think will sentence you to death?" he asked; "and why?"

"He would like to," replied A-Kor, "for the people chafe beneath his iron hand and their loyalty is but the loyalty of a people to the long line of illustrious jeddaks from which he has sprung. He is a jealous man and has found the means of disposing of most of those whose blood might entitle them to a claim upon the throne, and whose place in the affections of the people endowed them with any political significance. The fact that I was the son of a slave relegated me to a position of minor importance in the consideration of O-Tar, yet I am still the son of a jeddak and might sit upon the throne of Manator with as perfect congruity as O-Tar himself. Combined with this is the fact that of recent years the people, and especially many of the younger warriors, have evinced a growing affection for me, which I attribute to certain virtues of character and training derived from my mother, but which O-Tar assumes to be the result of an ambition upon my part to occupy the throne of Manator.

"And now, I am firmly convinced, he has seized upon my criticism of his treatment of the slave girl Tara as a pretext for ridding himself of me."

"But if you could escape and reach Gathol," suggested Turan.

"I have thought of that," mused A-Kor; "but how much better off would I be? In the eyes of the Gatholians I would be, not a Gatholian; but a stranger and doubtless they would accord me the same treatment that we of Manator accord strangers."

"Could you convince them that you are the son of the Princess Haja your welcome would be assured," said Turan; "while on the other hand you could purchase your freedom and citizenship with a brief period of labor in the diamond mines."

"How know you all these things?" asked A-Kor. "I thought you were from Helium."

"I am a panthan," replied Turan, "and I have served many countries, among them Gathol."

"It is what the slaves from Gathol have told me," said A-Kor, thoughtfully, "and my mother, before O-Tar sent her to live at Manatos. I think he must have feared her power and influence among the slaves from Gathol and their descendants, who number perhaps a million people throughout the land of Manator."

"Are these slaves organized?" asked Turan.

A-Kor looked straight into the eyes of the panthan for a long moment before he replied. "You are a man of honor," he said; "I read it in your face, and I am seldom mistaken in my estimate of a man; but——" and he leaned closer to the other——"even the walls have ears," he whispered, and Turan's question was answered.

It was later in the evening that warriors came and unlocked the fetter from Turan's ankle and led him away to appear before O-Tar, the jeddak. They conducted him toward the palace along narrow, winding streets and broad avenues; but always from the balconies there looked down upon them in endless ranks the silent people of the city. The palace itself was filled with life and activity. Mounted warriors galloped through the corridors and up and down the run-ways connecting adjacent floors. It seemed that no one walked within the palace other than a few slaves. Squealing, fighting tho-ats were stabled in magnificent halls while their riders, if not upon some duty of the palace, played at jetan with small figures carved from wood.

Turan noted the magnificence of the interior architecture of the palace, the lavish expenditure of precious jewels and metals, the gor-geous mural decorations which depicted almost exclusively martial scenes, and principally duels which seemed to be fought upon jetan boards of heroic size. The capitals of many of the columns supporting the ceilings of the corridors and chambers through which they passed were wrought into formal likenesses of jetan pieces—everywhere there seemed a suggestion of the game. Along the same path that Tara of Helium had been led Turan was conducted toward the throne room of O-Tar the jeddak, and when he entered the Hall of Chiefs his interest turned to wonder and admiration as he viewed the ranks of statuesque thoatmen decked in their gorgeous, martial panoply. Never, he thought, had he seen upon Barsoom more soldierly fig-ures or thoats so perfectly trained to perfection of immobility as these. Not a muscle quivered, not a tail lashed, and the riders were as motionless as their mounts—each warlike eye straight to the front, the great spears inclined at the same angle. It was a picture to fill the breast of a fighting man with awe and reverence. Nor did it fail in its effect upon Turan as they conducted him the length of the chamber, where he waited before great doors until he should be summoned into the presence of the ruler of Manator.

When Tara of Helium was ushered into the throne room of O-Tar she found the great hall filled with the chiefs and officers of O-Tar and U-Thor, the latter occupying the place of honor at the foot of the throne, as was his due. The girl was conducted to the foot of the aisle and halted before the jeddak, who looked down upon her from his high throne with scowling brows and fierce, cruel eyes.

"The laws of Manator are just," said O-Tar, addressing her; "thus is it that you have been summoned here again to be judged by the highest authority of Manator. Word has reached me that you are suspected of being a Corphal. What word have you to say in refutation of the charge?"

Tara of Helium could scarce restrain a sneer as she answered the ridiculous accusation of witchcraft. "So ancient is the culture of my people," she said, "that authentic history reveals no defense for that which we know existed only in the ignorant and superstitious minds of the most primitive peoples of the past. To those who are yet so untutored as to believe in the existence of Corphals, there can be no argument that will convince them of their error—only long ages of refinement and culture can accomplish their release from the bondage of ignorance. I have spoken."

"Yet you do not deny the accusation," said O-Tar.

"It is not worthy the dignity of a denial," she responded haughtily.

"And I were you, woman," said a deep voice at her side, "I should, nevertheless, deny it."

Tara of Helium turned to see the eyes of U-Thor, the great jed of Manatos, upon her. Brave eyes they were, but neither cold nor cruel.

O-Tar rapped impatiently upon the arm of his throne. "U-Thor forgets," he cried, "that O-Tar is the jeddak."

"U-Thor remembers," replied the jed of Manatos, "that the laws of Manator permit any who may be accused to have advice and counsel before their judge."

Tara of Helium saw that for some reason this man would have assisted her, and so she acted upon his advice.

"I deny the charge," she said, "I am no Corphal."

"Of that we shall learn," snapped O-Tar. "U-Dor, where are those who have knowledge of the powers of this woman?"

And U-Dor brought several who recounted the little that was known of the disappearance of E-Med, and others who told of the capture of Ghek and Tara, suggesting by deduction that having been found together they had sufficient in common to make it reasonably certain that one was as bad as the other, and that, therefore, it remained but to convict one of them of Corphalism to make certain the guilt of both. And then O-Tar called for Ghek, and immediately the hideous kaldane was dragged before him by warriors who could not conceal the fear in which they held this creature.

"And you!" said O-Tar in cold accusing tones. "Already have I been told enough of you to warrant me in passing through your heart the jeddak's steel—of how you stole the brains from the warrior U-Van so that he thought he saw your headless body still endowed with life; of how you caused another to believe that you had escaped, making him to see naught but an empty bench and a blank wall where you had been."

"Ah, O-Tar, but that is as nothing!" cried a young padwar who had come in command of the escort that brought Ghek. "The thing which he did to I-Zav, here, would prove his guilt alone."

"What did he to the warrior I-Zav?" demanded O-Tar. "Let I-Zav speak!"

The warrior I-Zav, a great fellow of bulging muscles and thick neck, advanced to the foot of the throne. He was pale and still trembling visibly as from a nervous shock.

"Let my first ancestor be my witness, O-Tar, that I speak the truth," he began. "I was left to guard this creature, who sat upon a bench, shackled to the wall. I stood by the open doorway at the opposite side of the chamber. He could not reach me, yet, O-Tar, may Iss engulf me if he did not drag me to him helpless as an unhatched egg. He dragged me to him, greatest of jeddaks, with his eyes! With his eyes he seized upon my eyes and dragged me to him and he made me lay my swords and dagger upon the table and back off into a corner, and still keeping his eyes upon my eyes his head quitted his body and crawling upon six short legs it descended to the floor and backed part way into the hole of an ulsio, but not so far that the eyes were not still upon me and then it returned with the key to its fetter and after resuming its place upon its own shoulders it unlocked the fetter and again dragged me across the room and made me to sit upon the bench where it had been and there it fastened the fetter about my ankle, and I could do naught for the power of its eyes and the fact that it wore my two swords and my dagger. And then the head disappeared down the hole of the ulsio with the key, and when it returned, it resumed its body and stood guard over me at the doorway until the padwar came to fetch it hither."

"It is enough!" said O-Tar, sternly. "Both shall receive the jeddak's steel," and rising from his throne he drew his long sword and descended the marble steps toward them, while two brawny warriors seized Tara by either arm and two seized Ghek, holding them facing the naked blade of the jeddak.

"Hold, just O-Tar!" cried U-Dor. "There be yet another to be judged. Let us confront him who calls himself Turan with these his fellows before they die."

"Good!" exclaimed O-Tar, pausing halfway down the steps. "Fetch Turan, the slave!"

When Turan had been brought into the chamber he was placed a little to Tara's left and a step nearer the throne. O-Tar eyed him menacingly.

"You are Turan," he asked, "friend and companion of these?"

The panthan was about to reply when Tara of Helium spoke. "I know not this fellow," she said. "Who dares say that he be a friend and companion of the Princess Tara of Helium?"

Turan and Ghek looked at her in surprise, but at Turan she did not look, and to Ghek she passed a quick glance of warning, as to say: "Hold thy peace."

The panthan tried not to fathom her purpose for the head is useless when the heart usurps its functions, and Turan knew only that the woman he loved had denied him, and though he tried not even to think it his foolish heart urged but a single explanation—that she refused to recognize him lest she be involved in his difficulties.

O-Tar looked first at one and then at another of them; but none of them spoke.

"Were they not captured together?" he asked of U-Dor.

"No," replied the dwar. "He who is called Turan was found seeking entrance to the city and was enticed to the pits. The following morning I discovered the other two upon the hill beyond The Gate of Enemies."

"But they are friends and companions," said a young padwar, "for this Turan inquired of me concerning these two, calling them by name and saying that they were his friends."

"It is enough," stated O-Tar, "all three shall die," and he took another step downward from the throne.

"For what shall we die?" asked Ghek. "Your people prate of the just laws of Manator, and yet you would slay three strangers without telling them of what crime they are accused."

"He is right," said a deep voice. It was the voice of U-Thor, the great jed of Manatos. O-Tar looked at him and scowled; but there came voices from other portions of the chamber seconding the demand for justice.

"Then know, though you shall die anyway," cried O-Tar, "that all three are convicted of Corphalism and that as only a jeddak may slay such as you in safety you are about to be honored with the steel of O-Tar."

"Fool!" cried Turan. "Know you not that in the veins of this woman flows the blood of ten thousand jeddaks—that greater than yours is her power in her own land? She is Tara, Princess of Helium, great-granddaughter of Tardos Mors, daughter of John Carter, Warlord of Barsoom. She cannot be a Corphal. Nor is this creature Ghek, nor am I. And you would know more, I can prove my right to be heard and to be believed if I may have word with the Princess Haja of Gathol, whose son is my fellow prisoner in the pits of O-Tar, his father."

At this U-Thor rose to his feet and faced O-Tar. "What means this?" he asked. "Speaks the man the truth? Is the son of Haja a prisoner in thy pits, O-Tar?"

"And what is it to the jed of Manatos who be the prisoners in the pits of his jeddak?" demanded O-Tar, angrily.

"It is this to the jed of Manatos," replied U-Thor in a voice so low as to be scarce more than a whisper and yet that was heard the whole length and breadth of the great throne room of O-Tar, Jeddak of Manator. "You gave me a slave woman, Haja, who had been a princess in Gathol, because you feared her influence among the slaves from Gathol. I have made of her a free woman, and I have married her and made her thus a princess of Manatos.

Her son is my son, O-Tar, and though thou be my jeddak, I say to you that for any harm that befalls A-Kor you shall answer to U-Thor of Manatos."

O-Tar looked long at U-Thor, but he made no reply. Then he turned again to Turan. "If one be a Corphal," he said, "then all of you be Corphals, and we know well from the things that this creature has done," he pointed at Ghek, "that he is a Corphal, for no mortal has such powers as he. And as you are all Corphals you must all die." He took another step downward, when Ghek spoke.

"These two have no such powers as I," he said. "They are but ordinary, brainless things such as yourself. I have done all the things that your poor, ignorant warriors have told you; but this only demonstrates that I am of a higher order than yourselves, as is indeed the fact. I am a kaldane, not a Corphal. There is nothing supernatural or mysterious about me, other than that to the ignorant all things which they cannot understand are mysterious. Easily might I have eluded your warriors and escaped your pits; but I remained in the hope that I might help these two foolish creatures who have not the brains to escape without help. They befriended me and saved my life. I owe them this debt. Do not slay them—they are harmless. Slay me if you will. I offer my life if it will appease your ignorant wrath. I cannot return to Bantoom and so I might as well die, for there is no pleasure in intercourse with the feeble intellects that cumber the face of the world outside the valley of Bantoom."

"Hideous egotist," said O-Tar, "prepare to die and assume not to dictate to O-Tar the jeddak. He has passed sentence and all three of you shall feel the jeddak's naked steel. I have spoken!"

He took another step downward and then a strange thing happened. He paused, his eyes fixed upon the eyes of Ghek. His sword slipped from nerveless fingers, and still he stood there swaying forward and back. A jed rose to rush to his side; but Ghek stopped him with a word.

"Wait!" he cried. "The life of your jeddak is in my hands. You believe me a Corphal and so you believe, too, that only the sword of a jeddak may slay me, therefore your blades are useless against me. Offer harm to anyone of us, or seek to approach your jeddak until I have spoken, and he shall sink lifeless to the marble. Release the two prisoners and let them come to my side—I would speak to them, privately. Quick! do as I say; I would as lief as not slay O-Tar. I but let him live that I may gain freedom for my friends—obstruct me and he dies."

The guards fell back, releasing Tara and Turan, who came close to Ghek's side.

"Do as I tell you and do it quickly," whispered the kaldane. "I cannot hold this fellow long, nor could I kill him thus. There are many minds working against mine and presently mine will tire and O-Tar will be himself again. You must make the best of your opportunity while you may. Behind the arras that you see hanging in the rear of the throne above you is a secret opening. From it a corridor leads to the pits of the palace, where there are storerooms containing food and drink. Few people go there. From these pits lead others to all parts of the city. Follow one that runs due west and it will bring you to The Gate of Enemies. The rest will then lie with you. I can do no more; hurry before my waning powers fail me—I am not as Luud, who was a king. He could have held this creature forever. Make haste! Go!"

XV

THE OLD MAN OF THE PITS

shall not desert you, Ghek," said Tara of Helium, simply.

"Go! Go!" whispered the kaldane. "You can do me no good. Go, or all I have done is for naught."

Tara shook her head. "I cannot," she said.

"They will slay her," said Ghek to Turan, and the panthan, torn between loyalty to this strange creature who had offered its life for him, and love of the woman, hesitated but a moment, then he swept Tara from her feet and lifting her in his arms leaped up the steps that led to the throne of Manator. Behind the throne he parted the arras and found the secret opening. Into this he bore the girl and down a long, narrow corridor and winding runways that led to lower levels until they came to the pits of the palace of O-Tar. Here was a labyrinth of passages and chambers presenting a thousand hiding-places.

As Turan bore Tara up the steps toward the throne a score of warriors rose as though to rush forward to intercept them. "Stay!" cried Ghek, "or your jeddak dies," and they halted in their tracks, waiting the will of this strange, uncanny creature.

Presently Ghek took his eyes from the eyes of O-Tar and the jeddak shook himself as one who would be rid of a bad dream and straightened up, half dazed still.

"Look," said Ghek, then, "I have given your jeddak his life, nor have I harmed one of those whom I might easily have slain when they were in my power. No harm have I or my friends done in the city of Manator. Why then should you persecute us? Give us our lives. Give us our liberty."

O-Tar, now in command of his faculties, stooped and regained his sword. In the room was silence as all waited to hear the jeddak's answer.

"Just are the laws of Manator," he said at last. "Perhaps, after all, there is truth in the words of the stranger. Return him then to the pits and pursue the others and capture them. Through the mercy of O-Tar they shall be permitted to win their freedom upon the Field of Jetan, in the coming games."

Still ashen was the face of the jeddak as Ghek was led away and his appearance was that of a man who had been snatched from the brink of eternity into which he has gazed, not with the composure of great courage, but with fear. There were those in the throne room who knew that the execution of the three prisoners had but been delayed and the responsibility placed upon the shoulders of others, and one of those who knew was U-Thor, the great jed of Manatos. His curling lip betokened his scorn of the jeddak who had chosen humiliation rather than death. He knew that O-Tar had lost more of prestige in those few moments than he could regain in a lifetime, for the Martians are jealous of the courage of their chiefs—there can be no evasions of stern duty, no temporizing with honor. That there were others in the room who shared U-Thor's belief was evidenced by the silence and the grim scowls.

O-Tar glanced quickly around. He must have sensed the hostility and guessed its cause, for he went suddenly angry, and as one who seeks by the vehemence of his words to establish the courage of his heart he roared forth what could be considered as naught other than a challenge.

"The will of O-Tar, the jeddak, is the law of Manator," he cried, "and the laws of Manator are just—they cannot err. U-Dor, dispatch those who will search the palace, the pits, and the city, and return the fugitives to their cells.

"And now for you, U-Thor of Manatos! Think you with impunity to threaten your jeddak—to question his right to punish traitors and instigators of treason? What am I to think of your own loyalty, who takes to wife a woman I have banished from my court because of her intrigues against the authority of her jeddak and her master? But O-Tar is just. Make your explanations and your peace, then, before it is too late."

"U-Thor has nothing to explain," replied the jed of Manatos; "nor is he at war with his jeddak; but he has the right that every jed and every warrior enjoys, of demanding justice at the hands of the jeddak for whomsoever he believes to be persecuted. With increasing rigor has the jeddak of Manator persecuted the slaves from Gathol since he took to himself the unwilling Princess Haja. If the slaves from Gathol have harbored thoughts of vengeance and escape 'tis no more than might be expected from a proud and courageous people Ever have I counselled greater fairness in our treatment of our slaves, many of whom, in their own lands, are people of great distinction and power; but always has O-Tar, the jeddak, flouted with arrogance my every suggestion. Though it has been through none of my seeking that the question has arisen now I am glad that it has, for the time was bound to come when the jeds of Manator would demand from O-Tar the respect and consideration that is their due from the man who holds his high office at their pleasure. Know, then, O-Tar, that you must free A-Kor, the dwar, forthwith or bring him to fair trial before the assembled jeds of Manator. I have spoken."

"You have spoken well and to the point, U-Thor," cried O-Tar, "for you have revealed to your jeddak and your fellow jeds the depth of the disloyalty that I have long suspected. A-Kor already has been tried and sentenced by the supreme tribunal of Manator—O-Tar, the jeddak; and you too shall receive justice from the same unfailing source. In the meantime you are under arrest. To the pits with him! To the pits with U-Thor the false jed!" He clapped his hands to summon the surrounding warriors to do his bidding. A score leaped forward to seize U-Thor. They were warriors of the palace, mostly; but two score leaped to defend U-Thor, and with ringing steel they fought at the foot of the steps to the throne of Manator where stood O-Tar, the jeddak, with drawn sword ready to take his part in the dispute.

At the clash of steel, palace guards rushed to the scene from other parts of the great building until those who would have defended U-Thor were outnumbered two to one, and then the jed of Manatos slowly withdrew with his forces, and fighting his way through the corridors and chambers of the palace came at last to the avenue. Here he was reinforced by the little army that had marched with him into Manator. Slowly they retreated toward The Gate of Enemies between the rows of silent people looking down upon them from the balconies and there, within the city walls, they made their stand.

In a dimly-lighted chamber beneath the palace of O-Tar the jeddak, Turan the panthan lowered Tara of Helium from his arms and faced her. "I am sorry, Princess," he said, "that I was forced to disobey your commands, or to abandon Ghek; but there was no other way. Could he have saved you I would have stayed in his place. Tell me that you forgive me."

"How could I do less?" she replied graciously. "But it seemed cowardly to abandon a friend."

"Had we been three fighting men it had been different," he said. "We could only have remained and died together, fighting; but you know, Tara of Helium, that we may not jeopardize a woman's safety even though we risk the loss of honor."

"I know that, Turan," she said; "but no one may say that

you have risked honor, who knows the honor and bravery that are yours."

He heard her with surprise for these were the first words that she had spoken to him that did not savor of the attitude of a princess to a panthan—though it was more in her tone than the actual words that he apprehended the difference. How at variance were they to her recent repudiation of him! He could not fathom her, and so he blurted out the question that had been in his mind since she had told O-Tar that she did not know him.

"Tara of Helium," he said, "your words are balm to the wound you gave me in the throne room of O-Tar. Tell me, Princess, why you denied me."

She turned her great, deep eyes up to his and in them was a little of reproach.

"You did not guess," she asked, "that it was my lips alone and not my heart that denied you? O-Tar had ordered that I die, more because I was a companion of Ghek than because of any evidence against me, and so I knew that if I acknowledged you as one of us, you would be slain, too."

"It was to save me, then?" he cried, his face suddenly lighting.

"It was to save my brave panthan," she said in a low voice.

"Tara of Helium," said the warrior, dropping to one knee, "your words are as food to my hungry heart," and he took her fingers in his and pressed them to his lips.

Gently she raised him to his feet. "You need not tell me, kneeling," she said, softly.

Her hand was still in his as he rose and they were very close, and the man was still flushed with the contact of her body since he had carried her from the throne room of O-Tar. He felt his heart pounding in his breast and the hot blood surging through his veins as he looked at her beautiful face, with its downcast eyes and the half-parted lips that he would have given a kingdom to possess, and then he swept her to him and as he crushed her against his breast his lips smothered hers with kisses.

But only for an instant. Like a tigress the girl turned upon him, striking him, and thrusting him away. She stepped back, her head high and her eyes flashing fire. "You would dare?" she cried. "You would dare thus defile a princess of Helium?"

His eyes met hers squarely and there was no shame and no remorse in them.

"Yes, I would dare," he said. "I would dare love Tara of Helium; but I would not dare defile her or any woman with kisses that were not prompted by love of her alone." He stepped closer to her and laid his hands upon her shoulders. "Look into my eyes, daughter of The Warlord," he said, "and tell me that you do not wish the love of Turan, the panthan."

"I do not wish your love," she cried, pulling away. "I hate you!" and then turning away she bent her head into the hollow of her arm, and wept.

The man took a step toward her as though to comfort her when he was arrested by the sound of a crackling laugh behind him. Wheeling about, he discovered a strange figure of a man standing in a doorway. It was one of those rarities occasionally to be seen upon Barsoom—an old man with the signs of age upon him. Bent and wrinkled, he had more the appearance of a mummy than a man.

"Love in the pits of O-Tar!" he cried, and again his thin laughter jarred upon the silence of the subterranean vaults. "A strange place to woo! A strange place to woo, indeed! When I was a young man we roamed in the gardens beneath giant pimalias and stole our kisses in the brief shadows of hurtling Thuria. We came not to the gloomy pits to speak of love; but times have changed and ways have changed, though I had never thought to live to see the time when the way of a man with a maid, or a maid with a man would change. Ah, but we kissed them then! And what if they objected, eh? What if they objected? Why, we kissed them more. Ey, ey, those were the days!" and he cackled again. "Ey, well do I recall the first of them I ever kissed, and I've kissed an army of them since; she was a fine girl, but she tried to slip a dagger into me while I was kissing her. Ey, ey, those were the days! But I kissed her. She's been dead over a thousand years now, but she was never kissed again like that while she lived, I'll swear, not since she's been dead, either. And then there was that other——" but Turan, seeing a thousand or more years of osculatory memoirs portending, interrupted.

"Tell me, ancient one," he said, "not of thy loves but of thyself. Who are you? What do you here in the pits of O-Tar?"

"I might ask you the same, young man," replied the other. "Few there are who visit the pits other than the dead, except my pupils—ey! That is it—you are new pupils! Good! But never before have they sent a woman to learn the great art from the greatest artist. But times have changed. Now, in my day the women did no work—they were just for kissing and loving. Ey, those were the women. I mind the one we captured in the south—ey! she was a devil, but how she could love. She had breasts of marble and a heart of fire. Why, she——"

"Yes, yes," interrupted Turan; "we are pupils, and we are anxious to get to work. Lead on and we will follow."

"Ey, yes! Ey, yes! Come! All is rush and hurry as though there were not another countless myriad of ages ahead. Ey, yes! as many as lie behind. Two thousand years have passed since I broke my shell and always rush, rush, rush, yet I cannot see that aught has been accomplished. Manator is the same today as it was then—except the girls. We had the girls then. There was one that I gained upon The Fields of Jetan. Ey, but you should have seen——"

"Lead on!" cried Turan. "After we are at work you shall tell us of her."

"Ey, yes," said the old fellow and shuffled off down a dimly lighted passage. "Follow me!"

"You are going with him?" asked Tara.

"Why not?" replied Turan. "We know not where we are, or the way from these pits; for I know not east from west; but he doubtless knows and if we are shrewd we may learn from him that which we would know. At least we cannot afford to arouse his suspicions"; and so they followed him—followed along winding corridors and through many chambers, until they came at last to a room in which there were several marble slabs raised upon pedestals some three feet above the floor and upon each slab lay a human corpse.

"Here we are," exclaimed the old man. "These are fresh and we shall have to get to work upon them soon. I am working now on one for The Gate of Enemies. He slew many of our warriors. Truly is he entitled to a place in The Gate. Come, you shall see him."

He led them to an adjoining apartment. Upon the floor were many fresh, human bones and upon a marble slab a mass of shapeless flesh.

"You will learn this later," announced the old man; "but it will not harm you to watch me now, for there are not many thus prepared, and it may be long before you will have the opportunity to see another prepared for The Gate of Enemies. First, you see, I remove all the bones, carefully that the skin may be damaged as little as possible. The skull is the most difficult, but it can be removed by a skilful artist. You see, I have made but a single opening. This I now sew up, and that done, the body is hung so," and he fastened a piece of rope to the hair of the corpse and swung the horrid thing to a ring in the ceiling. Directly below it was a circular manhole in the floor from which he removed the cover revealing a well partially filled with a reddish liquid. "Now we lower it into this, the formula for which you shall learn in due time. We fasten it thus to the bottom of the cover, which we now replace. In a year it will be ready; but it must be examined often in the meantime and the liquid kept above the level of its crown. It will be a very beautiful piece, this one, when it is ready.

"And you are fortunate again, for there is one to come out today." He crossed to the opposite side of the room and raised another cover, reached in and dragged a grotesque looking figure from the hole. It was a human body, shrunk by the action of the chemical in which it had been immersed, to a little figure scarce a foot high.

"Ey! is it not fine?" cried the little old man. "Tomorrow it will take its place in The Gate of Enemies." He dried it off with cloths and packed it away carefully in a basket. "Perhaps you would like to see some of my life work," he suggested, and without waiting for their assent led them to another apartment, a large chamber in which were forty or fifty people. All were sitting or standing quietly about the walls, with the exception of one huge warrior who bestrode a great thoat in the very center of the room, and all were motionless. Instantly there sprang to the minds of Tara and Turan the rows of silent people upon the balconies that lined the avenues of the city, and the noble array of mounted warriors in The Hall of Chiefs, and the same explanation came to both but neither dared voice the question that was in his mind, for fear of revealing by his ignorance the fact that they were strangers in Manator and therefore impostors in the guise of pupils.

"It is very wonderful," said Turan. "It must require great skill and patience and time."

"That it does," replied the old man, "though having done it so long I am quicker than most; but mine are the most natural. Why, I would defy the wife of that warrior to say that insofar as appearances are concerned he does not live," and he pointed at the man upon the thoat. "Many of them, of course, are brought here wasted or badly wounded and these I have to repair. That is where great skill is required, for everyone wants his dead to look as they did at their best in life; but you shall learn—to mount them and paint them and repair them and sometimes to make an ugly one look beautiful. And it will be a great comfort to be able to mount your own. Why, for fifteen hundred years no one has mounted my own dead but myself.

"I have many, my balconies are crowded with them; but I keep a great room for my wives. I have them all, as far back as the first one, and many is the evening I spend with them—quiet evenings and very pleasant. And then the pleasure of preparing them and making them even more beautiful than in life partially recompenses one for their loss. I take my time with them, looking for a new one while I am working on the old. When I am not sure about a new one I bring her to the chamber where my wives are, and compare her charms with theirs, and there is always a great satisfaction at such times in knowing that they will not object. I love harmony."

"Did you prepare all the warriors in The Hall of Chiefs?" asked Turan.

"Yes, I prepare them and repair them," replied the old man. "O-Tar will trust no other. Even now I have two in another room who were damaged in some way and brought down to me. O-Tar does not like to have them gone long, since it leaves two riderless thoats in the Hall; but I shall have them ready presently. He wants them all there in the event any momentous question arises upon which the living jeds cannot agree, or do not agree with O-Tar. Such questions he carries to the jeds in The Hall of Chiefs. There he shuts himself up alone with the great chiefs who have attained wisdom through death. It is an excellent plan and there is never any friction or misunderstandings. O-Tar has said that it is the finest deliberative body upon Barsoom—much more intelligent than that composed of the living jeds. But come, we must get to work; come into the next chamber and I will begin your instruction."

He led the way into the chamber in which lay the several

corpses upon their marble slabs, and going to a cabinet he donned a pair of huge spectacles and commenced to select various tools from little compartments. This done he turned again toward his two pupils.

"Now let me have a look at you," he said. "My eyes are not what they once were, and I need these powerful lenses for my work, or to see distinctly the features of those around me."

He turned his eyes upon the two before him. Turan held his breath for he knew that now the man must discover that they wore not the harness or insignia of Manator. He had wondered before why the old fellow had not noticed it, for he had not known that he was half blind. The other examined their faces, his eyes lingering long upon the beauty of Tara of Helium, and then they drifted to the harness of the two. Turan thought that he noted an appreciable start of surprise on the part of the taxidermist, but if the old man noticed anything his next words did not reveal it.

"Come with I-Gos," he said to Turan, "I have materials in the next room that I would have you fetch hither. Remain here, woman, we shall be gone but a moment."

He led the way to one of the numerous doors opening into the chamber and entered ahead of Turan. Just inside the door he stopped, and pointing to a bundle of silks and furs upon the opposite side of the room directed Turan to fetch them. The latter had crossed the room and was stooping to raise the bundle when he heard the click of a lock behind him. Wheeling instantly he saw that he was alone in the room and that the single door was closed. Running rapidly to it he strove to open it, only to find that he was a prisoner.

I-Gos, stepping out and locking the door behind him, turned toward Tara.

"Your leather betrayed you," he said, laughing his cackling laugh. "You sought to deceive old I-Gos, but you found that though his eyes are weak his brain is not. But it shall not go ill with you.

You are beautiful and I-Gos loves beautiful women. I might not have you elsewhere in Manator, but here there is none to deny old I-Gos. Few come to the pits of the dead—only those who bang the dead and they hasten away as fast as they can. No one will know that I-Gos has a beautiful woman locked with his dead. I shall ask you no questions and then I will not have to give you up, for I will not know to whom you belong, eh? And when you die I shall mount you beautifully and place you in the chamber with my other women. Will not that be fine, eh?" He had approached until he stood close beside the horrified girl. "Come!" he cried, seizing her by the wrist. "Come to I-Gos!"

XVI

ANOTHER CHANGE OF NAME

uran dashed himself against the door of his prison in a vain effort to break through the solid skeel to the side of Tara whom he knew to be in grave danger, but the heavy panels held and he succeeded only in bruising his shoulders and his arms. At last he desisted and set about searching his prison for some other means of escape. He found no other opening in the stone walls, but his search revealed a heterogeneous collection of odds and ends of arms and apparel, of harness and ornaments and insignia, and sleeping silks and furs in great quantities. There were swords and spears and several large, two-bladed battle-axes, the heads of which bore a striking resemblance to the propellor of a small flier. Seizing one of these he attacked the door once more with great fury. He expected to hear something from I-Gos at this ruthless destruction, but no sound came to him from beyond the door, which was, he thought, too thick for the human voice to penetrate; but he would have wagered much that I-Gos heard him. Bits of the hard wood splintered at each impact of the heavy axe, but it was slow work and heavy. Presently he was compelled to rest, and so it went for what seemed hours—working almost to the verge of exhaustion and then resting for a few minutes; but ever the hole grew larger though he could see nothing of the interior of the room beyond because of the hanging that I-Gos had drawn across it after he had locked Turan within.

At last, however, the panthan had hewn an opening through which his body could pass, and seizing a long-sword that he had brought close to the door for the purpose he crawled through into the next room. Flinging aside the arras he stood ready, sword in hand, to fight his way to the side of Tara of Helium—but she was not there. In the center of the room lay I-Gos, dead upon the floor; but Tara of Helium was nowhere to be seen.

Turan was nonplussed. It must have been her hand that had struck down the old man, yet she had made no effort to release Turan from his prison. And then he thought of those last words of hers: "I do not want your love! I hate you," and the truth dawned upon him—she had seized upon this first opportunity to escape him. With downcast heart Turan turned away. What should he do? There could be but one answer. While he lived and she lived he must still leave no stone unturned to effect her escape and safe return to the land of her people. But how? How was he even to find his way from this labyrinth? How was he to find her again? He walked to the nearest doorway. It chanced to be that which led into the room containing the mounted dead, awaiting transportation to balcony or grim room or whatever place was to receive them. His eyes travelled to the great, painted warrior on the thoat and as they ran over the splendid trappings and the serviceable arms a new light came into the pain-dulled eyes of the panthan. With a quick step he crossed to the side of the dead warrior and dragged him from his mount. With equal celerity he stripped him of his harness and his arms, and tearing off his own, donned the regalia of the dead man. Then he hastened back to the room in which he had been trapped, for there he had seen that which he needed to make his disguise complete. In a cabinet he found them—pots of paint that the old taxidermist had used to place the war-paint in its wide bands across the cold faces of dead warriors.

A few moments later Gahan of Gathol emerged from the room a warrior of Manator in every detail of harness, equipment, and ornamentation. He had removed from the leather of the dead man the insignia of his house and rank so that he might pass, with the least danger of arousing suspicion, as a common warrior.

To search for Tara of Helium in the vast, dim labyrinth of the pits of O-Tar seemed to the Gatholian a hopeless quest, foredoomed to failure. It would be wiser to seek the streets of Manator where he might hope to learn first if she had been recaptured and, if not, then he could return to the pits and pursue the hunt for her. To find egress from the maze he must perforce travel a considerable distance through the winding corridors and chambers, since he had no idea as to the location or direction of any exit. In fact, he could not have retraced his steps a hundred yards toward the point at which he and Tara had entered the gloomy caverns, and so he set out in the hope that he might find by accident either Tara of Helium or a way to the street level above.

For a time he passed room after room filled with the cunningly preserved dead of Manator, many of which were piled in tiers after the manner that firewood is corded, and as he moved through corridor and chamber he noticed hieroglyphics painted upon the walls above every opening and at each fork or crossing of corridors, until by observation he reached the conclusion that these indicated the designations of passageways, so that one who understood them might travel quickly and surely through the pits; but Turan did not understand them. Even could he have read the language of Manator they might not materially have aided one unfamiliar with the city; but he could not read them at all since, though there is but one spoken language upon Barsoom, there are as many different written languages as there are nations. One thing, however, soon became apparent to him—the hieroglyphic of a corridor remained the same until the corridor ended.

It was not long before Turan realized from the distance that he had traveled that the pits were part of a vast system undermining, possibly, the entire city. At least he was convinced that he had passed beyond the precincts of the palace. The corridors and chambers varied in appearance and architecture from time to time. All were lighted, though usually quite dimly, with radium bulbs. For a long time he saw no signs of life other than an occasional ulsio, then quite suddenly he came face to face with a warrior at one of the numerous crossings. The fellow looked at him, nodded, and passed on. Turan breathed a sigh of relief as he realized that his disguise was effective, but he was caught in the middle of it by a hail from the warrior who had stopped and turned toward him. The panthan was glad that a sword hung at his side, and glad too that they were buried in the dim recesses of the pits and that there would be but a single antagonist, for time was precious.

"Heard you any word of the other?" called the warrior to him.

"No," replied Turan, who had not the faintest idea to whom or what the fellow referred.

"He cannot escape," continued the warrior. "The woman ran directly into our arms, but she swore that she knew not where her companion might be found."

"They took her back to O-Tar?" asked Turan, for now he knew whom the other meant, and he would know more.

"They took her back to The Towers of Jetan," replied the warrior. "Tomorrow the games commence and doubtless she will be played for, though I doubt if any wants her, beautiful as she is. She fears not even O-Tar. By Cluros! but she would make a hard slave to subdue—a regular she-banth she is. Not for me," and he continued on his way shaking his head.

Turan hurried on searching for an avenue that led to the level of the streets above when suddenly he came to the open doorway of a small chamber in which sat a man who was chained to the wall.

Turan voiced a low exclamation of surprise and pleasure as he recognized that the man was A-Kor, and that he had stumbled by accident upon the very cell in which he had been imprisoned. A-Kor looked at him questioningly. It was evident that he did not recognize his fellow prisoner. Turan crossed to the table and leaning close to the other whispered to him.

"I am Turan the panthan," he said, "who was chained beside you."

A-Kor looked at him closely. "Your own mother would never know you!" he said; "but tell me, what has transpired since they took you away?"

Turan recounted his experiences in the throne room of O-Tar and in the pits beneath, "and now," he continued, "I must find these Towers of Jetan and see what may be done toward liberating the Princess of Helium."

A-Kor shook his head. "Long was I dwar of the Towers," he said, "and I can say to you, stranger, that you might as well attempt to reduce Manator, single handed, as to rescue a prisoner from The Towers of Jetan."

"But I must," replied Turan.

"Are you better than a good swordsman?" asked A-Kor presently.

"I am accounted so," replied Turan.

"Then there is a way—sst!" he was suddenly silent and pointing toward the base of the wall at the end of the room.

Turan looked in the direction the other's forefinger indicated, to see projecting from the mouth of an ulsio's burrow two large chelae and a pair of protruding eyes.

"Ghek!" he cried and immediately the hideous kaldane crawled out upon the floor and approached the table. A-Kor drew back with a half-stifled ejaculation of repulsion. "Do not fear," Turan reassured him. "It is my friend—he whom I told you held O-Tar while Tara and I escaped."

Ghek climbed to the table top and squatted between the two warriors. "You are safe in assuming," he said addressing A-Kor, "that Turan the panthan has no master in all Manator where the art of sword-play is concerned. I overheard your conversation—go on."

"You are his friend," continued A-Kor, "and so I may explain safely in your presence the only plan I know whereby he may hope to rescue the Princess of Helium. She is to be the stake of one of the games and it is O-Tar's desire that she be won by slaves and common warriors, since she repulsed him. Thus would he punish her. Not a single man, but all who survive upon the winning side are to possess her. With money, however, one may buy off the others before the game. That you could do, and if your side won and you survived she would become your slave."

"But how may a stranger and a hunted fugitive accomplish this?" asked Turan.

"No one will recognize you. You will go tomorrow to the keeper of the Towers and enlist in that game for which the girl is to be the stake, telling the keeper that you are from Manataj, the farthest city of Manator. If he questions you, you may say that you saw her when she was brought into the city after her capture. If you win her, you will find thoats stabled at my palace and you will carry from me a token that will place all that is mine at your disposal."

"But how can I buy off the others in the game without money?" asked Turan. "I have none—not even of my own country."

A-Kor opened his pocket-pouch and drew forth a packet of Manatorian money.

"Here is sufficient to buy them off twice over," he said, handing a portion of it to Turan.

"But why do you do this for a stranger?" asked the panthan.

"My mother was a captive princess here." replied A-Kor. "I but do for the Princess of Helium what my mother would have me do."

"Under the circumstances, then, Manatorian," replied Turan, "I cannot but accept your generosity on behalf of Tara of Helium and live in hope that someday I may do for you something in return."

"Now you must be gone," advised A-Kor. "At any minute a guard may come and discover you here. Go directly to the Avenue of Gates, which circles the city just within the outer wall. There you will find many places devoted to the lodging of strangers. You will know them by the thoat's head carved above the doors. Say that you are here from Manataj to witness the games. Take the name of U-Kal—it will arouse no suspicion, nor will you if you can avoid conversation. Early in the morning seek the keeper of The Towers of Jetan. May the strength and fortune of all your ancestors be with you!"

Bidding goodbye to Ghek and A-Kor, the panthan, following directions given him by A-Kor, set out to find his way to the Avenue of Gates, nor had he any great difficulty. On the way he met several warriors, but beyond a nod they gave him no heed. With ease he found a lodging place where there were many strangers from other cities of Manator. As he had had no sleep since the previous night he threw himself among the silks and furs of his couch to gain the rest which he must have, was he to give the best possible account of himself in the service of Tara of Helium the following day.

It was already morning when he awoke, and rising he paid for his lodgings, sought a place to eat, and a short time later was on his way toward The Towers of Jetan, which he had no difficulty in finding owing to the great crowds that were winding along the avenues toward the games. The new keeper of The Towers who had succeeded E-Med was too busy to scrutinize entries closely, for in addition to the many volunteer players there were scores of slaves and prisoners being forced into the games by their owners or the government. The name of each must be recorded as well as the position he was to play and the game or games in which he was to be entered, and then there were the substitutes for each that was entered in more than a single game—one for each additional game that an individual was entered for, that no succeeding game might be delayed by the death or disablement of a player.

"Your name?" asked a clerk as Turan presented himself.

"U-Kal," replied the panthan.

"Your city?"

"Manataj."

The keeper, who was standing beside the clerk, looked at Turan. "You have come a great way to play at jetan," he said. "It is seldom that the men of Manataj attend other than the decennial games. Tell me of O-Zar! Will he attend next year? Ah, but he was a noble fighter. If you be half the swordsman, U-Kal, the fame of Manataj will increase this day. But tell me, what of O-Zar?"

"He is well," replied Turan, glibly, "and he sent greetings to his friends in Manator."

"Good!" exclaimed the keeper, "and now in what game would you enter?"

"I would play for the Heliumetic princess, Tara," replied Turan.

"But man, she is to be the stake of a game for slaves and criminals," cried the keeper. "You would not volunteer for such a game!"

"But I would," replied Turan. "I saw here when she was brought into the city and even then I vowed to possess her."

"But you will have to share her with the survivors even if your color wins," objected the other.

"They may be brought to reason," insisted Turan.

"And you will chance incurring the wrath of O-Tar, who has no love for this savage barbarian," explained the keeper.

"And I win her O-Tar will be rid of her," said Turan.

The keeper of The Towers of Jetan shook his head. "You are rash," he said. "I would that I might dissuade the friend of my friend O-Zar from such madness."

"Would you favor the friend of O-Zar?" asked Turan.

"Gladly!" exclaimed the other. "What may I do for him?"

"Make me chief of the Black and give me for my pieces all slaves from Gathol, for I understand that those be excellent warriors," replied the panthan.

"It is a strange request," said the keeper, "but for my friend O-Zar I would do even more, though of course—" he hesitated—"it is customary for one who would be chief to make some slight payment."

"Certainly," Turan hastened to assure him; "I had not forgotten that. I was about to ask you what the customary amount is."

"For the friend of my friend it shall be nominal," replied the keeper, naming a figure that Gahan, accustomed to the high price of wealthy Gathol, thought ridiculously low.

"Tell me," he said, handing the money to the keeper, "when the game for the Heliumite is to be played."

"It is the second in order of the day's games; and now if you will come with me you may select your pieces."

Turan followed the keeper to a large court which lay between the towers and the jetan field, where hundreds of warriors were assembled. Already chiefs for the games of the day were selecting their pieces and assigning them to positions, though for the principal games these matters had been arranged for weeks before. The keeper led Turan to a part of the courtyard where the majority of the slaves were assembled.

"Take your choice of those not assigned," said the keeper, "and when you have your quota conduct them to the field. Your place will be assigned you by an officer there, and there you will remain with your pieces until the second game is called. I wish you luck, U-Kal, though from what I have heard you will be more lucky to lose than to win the slave from Helium."

After the fellow had departed Turan approached the slaves. "I seek the best swordsmen for the second game," he announced. "Men from Gathol I wish, for I have heard that these be noble fighters."

A slave rose and approached him. "It is all the same in which game we die," he said. "I would fight for you as a panthan in the second game."

Another came. "I am not from Gathol," he said. "I am from

Helium, and I would fight for the honor of a princess of Helium."

"Good!" exclaimed Turan. "Art a swordsman of repute in Helium?"

"I was a dwar under the great Warlord, and I have fought at his side in a score of battles from The Golden Cliffs to The Carrion Caves. My name is Val Dor. Who knows Helium, knows my prowess."

The name was well known to Gahan, who had heard the man spoken of on his last visit to Helium, and his mysterious disappearance discussed as well as his renown as a fighter.

"How could I know aught of Helium?" asked Turan; "but if you be such a fighter as you say no position could suit you better than that of Flier. What say you?"

The man's eyes denoted sudden surprise. He looked keenly at Turan, his eyes running quickly over the other's harness. Then he stepped quite close so that his words might not be overheard.

"Methinks you may know more of Helium than of Manator," he whispered.

"What mean you, fellow?" demanded Turan, seeking to cudgel his brains for the source of this man's knowledge, guess, or inspiration.

"I mean," replied Val Dor, "that you are not of Manator and that if you wish to hide the fact it is well that you speak not to a Manatorian as you did just speak to me of—Fliers! There be no Fliers in Manator and no piece in their game of Jetan bearing that name. Instead they call him who stands next to the Chief or Princess, Odwar. The piece has the same moves and power that the Flier has in the game as played outside Manator. Remember this then and remember, too, that if you have a secret it be safe in the keeping of Val Dor of Helium."

Turan made no reply but turned to the task of selecting the remainder of his pieces. Val Dor, the Heliumite, and Floran, the volunteer from Gathol, were of great assistance to him, since one or the other of them knew most of the slaves from whom his selection was to be made. The pieces all chosen, Turan led them to the place beside the playing field where they were to wait their turn, and here he passed the word around that they were to fight for more than the stake he offered for the princess should they win. This stake they accepted, so that Turan was sure of possessing Tara if his side was victorious, but he knew that these men would fight even more valorously for chivalry than for money, nor was it difficult to enlist the interest even of the Gatholians in the service of the princess. And now he held out the possibility of a still further reward.

"I cannot promise you," he explained, "but I may say I have heard that this day which makes it possible that should we win this game we may even win your freedom!"

They leaped to their feet and crowded around him with many questions.

"It may not be spoken of aloud," he said; "but Floran and Val Dor know and they assure me that you may all be trusted. Listen! What I would tell you places my life in your hands, but you must know that every man will realize that he is fighting today the greatest battle of his life—for the honor and the freedom of Barsoom's most wondrous princess and for his own freedom as well—for the chance to return each to his own country and to the woman who awaits him there.

"First, then, is my secret. I am not of Manator. Like yourselves I am a slave, though for the moment disguised as a Manatorian from Mantaj. My country and my identity must remain undisclosed for reasons that have no bearing upon our game today. I, then, am one of you. I fight for the same things that you will fight for.

"And now for that which I have but just learned. U-Thor, the great jed of Manatos, quarreled with O-Tar in the palace the day before yesterday and their warriors set upon one another. U-Thor was driven as far as The Gate of Enemies, where he now lies encamped. At any moment the light may be renewed; but it is thought that U-Thor has sent to Manatos for reinforcements.

Now, men of Gathol, here is the thing that interests you. U-Thor has recently taken to wife the Princess Haja of Gathol, who was slave to O-Tar and whose son, A-Kor, was dwar of The Towers of Jetan. Haja's heart is filled with loyalty for Gathol and compassion for her sons who are here enslaved, and this latter sentiment she has to some extent transmitted to U-Thor. Aid me, therefore, in freeing the Princess Tara of Helium and I believe that I can aid you and her and myself to escape the city. Bend close your ears, slaves of O-Tar, that no cruel enemy may hear my words," and Gahan of Gathol whispered in low tones the daring plan he had conceived. "And now," he demanded, when he had finished, "let him who does not dare speak now." None replied. "Is there none?"

"And it would not betray you should I cast my sword at thy feet, it had been done ere this," said one in low tones pregnant with suppressed feeling.

"And I!" "And I!" "And I!" chorused the others in vibrant whispers.

XVII

A PLAY TO THE DEATH

lear and sweet a trumpet spoke across The Fields of Jetan. From The High Tower its cool voice floated across the city of Manator and above the babel of human discords rising from the crowded mass that filled the seats of the stadium below. It called the players for the first game, and simultaneously there fluttered to the peaks of a thousand staffs on tower and battlement and the great wall of the stadium the rich, gay pennons of the fighting chiefs of Manator. Thus was marked the opening of The Jeddak's Games, the most important of the year and second only to the Grand Decennial Games.

Gahan of Gathol watched every play with eagle eye. The match was an unimportant one, being but to settle some petty dispute between two chiefs, and was played with professional jetan players for points only. No one was killed and there was but little blood spilled. It lasted about an hour and was terminated by the chief of the losing side deliberately permitting himself to be out-pointed, that the game might be called a draw.

Again the trumpet sounded, this time announcing the second and last game of the afternoon. While this was not considered an important match, those being reserved for the fourth and fifth days of the games, it promised to afford sufficient excitement since it was a game to the death. The vital difference between the game played with living men and that in which inanimate pieces are used, lies in the fact that while in the latter the mere placing of a piece upon a square occupied by an opponent piece terminates the move, in the former the two pieces thus brought together engage in a duel for possession of the square. Therefore there enters into the former game not only the strategy of jetan but the personal prowess and bravery of each individual piece, so that a knowledge not only of one's own men but of each player upon the opposing side is of vast value to a chief.

In this respect was Gahan handicapped, though the loyalty of his players did much to offset his ignorance of them, since they aided him in arranging the board to the best advantage and told him honestly the faults and virtues of each. One fought best in a losing game; another was too slow; another too impetuous; this one had fire and a heart of steel, but lacked endurance. Of the opponents, though, they knew little or nothing, and now as the two sides took their places upon the black and orange squares of the great jetan board Gahan obtained, for the first time, a close view of those who opposed him. The Orange Chief had not yet entered the field, but his men were all in place. Val Dor turned to Gahan. "They are all criminals from the pits of Manator," he said. "There is no slave among them. We shall not have to fight against a single fellow-countryman and every life we take will be the life of an enemy."

"It is well," replied Gahan; "but where is their Chief, and where the two Princesses?"

"They are coming now, see?" and he pointed across the field to where two women could be seen approaching under guard.

As they came nearer Gahan saw that one was indeed Tara of Helium, but the other he did not recognize, and then they were brought to the center of the field midway between the two sides and there waited until the Orange Chief arrived.

Floran voiced an exclamation of surprise when he recognized him. "By my first ancestor if it is not one of their great chiefs," he said, "and we were told that slaves and criminals were to play for the stake of this game."

His words were interrupted by the keeper of The Towers whose duty it was not only to announce the games and the stakes, but to act as referee as well.

"Of this, the second game of the first day of the Jeddak's Games in the four hundred and thirty-third year of O-Tar, Jeddak of Manator, the Princesses of each side shall be the sole stakes and to the survivors of the winning side shall belong both the Princesses, to do with as they shall see fit. The Orange Princess is the slave woman Lan-O of Gathol; the Black Princess is the slave woman Tara, a princess of Helium. The Black Chief is U-Kal of Manataj, a volunteer player; the Orange Chief is the dwar U-Dor of the 8th Utan of the jeddak of Manator, also a volunteer player. The squares shall be contested to the death. Just are the laws of Manator! I have spoken."

The initial move was won by U-Dor, following which the two Chiefs escorted their respective Princesses to the square each was to occupy. It was the first time Gahan had been alone with Tara since she had been brought upon the field. He saw her scrutinizing him closely as he approached to lead her to her place and wondered if she recognized him: but if she did she gave no sign of it. He could not but remember her last words—"I hate you!" and her desertion of him when he had been locked in the room beneath the palace by I-Gos, the taxidermist, and so he did not seek to enlighten her as to his identity. He meant to fight for her—to die for her, if necessary— and if he did not die to go on fighting to the end for her love. Gahan of Gathol was not easily to be discouraged, but he was compelled to admit that his chances of winning the love of Tara of Helium were remote. Already had she repulsed him twice. Once as jed of Gathol and again as Turan the panthan. Before his love, however, came her safety and the former must be relegated to the background until the latter had been achieved.

Passing among the players already at their stations the two took their places upon their respective squares. At Tara's left was the Black Chief, Gahan of Gathol; directly in front of her the Princess' Panthan, Floran of Gathol; and at her right the Princess' Odwar, Val Dor of Helium. And each of these knew the part that he was to play, win or lose, as did each of the other Black players. As Tara took her place Val Dor bowed low. "My sword is at your feet, Tara of Helium," he said.

She turned and looked at him, an expression of surprise and incredulity upon her face. "Val Dor, the dwar!" she exclaimed. "Val Dor of Helium—one of my father's trusted captains! Can it be possible that my eyes speak the truth?"

"It is Val Dor, Princess," the warrior replied, "and here to die for you if need be, as is every wearer of the Black upon this field of jetan today. Know Princess," he whispered, "that upon this side is no man of Manator, but each and every is an enemy of Manator."

She cast a quick, meaning glance toward Gahan. "But what of him?" she whispered, and then she caught her breath quickly in surprise. "Shade of the first jeddak!" she exclaimed. "I did but just recognize him through his disguise."

"And you trust him?" asked Val Dor. "I know him not; but he spoke fairly, as an honorable warrior, and we have taken him at his word."

"You have made no mistake," replied Tara of Helium. "I would trust him with my life—with my soul; and you, too, may trust him."

Happy indeed would have been Gahan of Gathol could he have heard those words; but Fate, who is usually unkind to the lover in such matters, ordained it otherwise, and then the game was on.

U-Dor moved his Princess' Odwar three squares diagonally to the right, which placed the piece upon the Black Chief's Odwar's seventh. The move was indicative of the game that U-Dor intended playing—a game of blood, rather than of science—and evidenced his contempt for his opponents.

Gahan followed with his Odwar's Panthan one square straight forward, a more scientific move, which opened up an avenue for himself through his line of Panthans, as well as announcing to the players and spectators that he intended having a hand in the fighting himself even before the exigencies of the game forced it upon him. The move elicited a ripple of applause from those sections of seats reserved for the common warriors and their women, showing perhaps that U-Dor was none too popular with these, and, too, it had its effect upon the morale of Gahan's pieces. A Chief may, and often does, play almost an entire game without leaving his own square, where, mounted upon a thoat, he may overlook the entire field and direct each move, nor may he be reproached for lack of courage should he elect thus to play the game since, by the rules, were he to be slain or so badly wounded as to be compelled to withdraw, a game that might otherwise have been won by the science of his play and the prowess of his men would be drawn. To invite personal combat, therefore, denotes confidence in his own swordsmanship, and great courage, two attributes that were calculated to fill the Black players with hope and valor when evinced by their Chief thus early in the game.

U-Dor's next move placed Lan-O's Odwar upon Tara's Odwar's fourth—within striking distance of the Black Princess.

Another move and the game would be lost to Gahan unless the Orange Odwar was overthrown, or Tara moved to a position of safety; but to move his Princess now would be to admit his belief in the superiority of the Orange. In the three squares allowed him he could not place himself squarely upon the square occupied by the Odwar of U-Dor's Princess. There was only one player upon the Black side that might dispute the square with the enemy and that was the Chief's Odwar, who stood upon Gahan's left. Gahan turned upon his thoat and looked at the man. He was a splendid looking fellow, resplendent in the gorgeous trappings of an Odwar, the five brilliant feathers which denoted his position rising defiantly erect from his thick, black hair. In common with every player upon the field and every spectator in the crowded stands he knew what was passing in his Chief's mind. He dared not speak, the ethics of the game forbade it, but what his lips might not voice his eyes expressed in martial fire, and eloquently: "The honor of the Black and the safety of our Princess are secure with me!"

Gahan hesitated no longer. "Chief's Odwar to Princess' Odwar's fourth!" he commanded. It was the courageous move of a leader who had taken up the gauntlet thrown down by his opponent.

The warrior sprang forward and leaped into the square occupied by U-Dor's piece. It was the first disputed square of the game. The eyes of the players were fastened upon the contestants, the spectators leaned forward in their seats after the first applause that had greeted the move, and silence fell upon the vast assemblage. If the Black went down to defeat, U-Dor could move his victorious piece on to the square occupied by Tara of Helium and the game would be over— over in four moves and lost to Gahan of Gathol. If the Orange lost U-Dor would have sacrificed one of his most important pieces and more than lost what advantage the first move might have given him.

Physically the two men appeared perfectly matched and each was fighting for his life, but from the first it was apparent that the Black Odwar was the better swordsman, and Gahan knew that he had another and perhaps a greater advantage over his antagonist. The latter was fighting for his life only, without the spur of chivalry or loyalty. The Black Odwar had these to strengthen his arm, and besides these the knowledge of the thing that Gahan had whispered into the ears of his players before the game, and so he fought for what is more than life to the man of honor.

It was a duel that held those who witnessed it in spellbound silence. The weaving blades gleamed in the brilliant sunlight, ringing to the parries of cut and thrust. The barbaric harness of the duelists lent splendid color to the savage, martial scene. The Orange

Odwar, forced upon the defensive, was fighting madly for his life. The Black, with cool and terrible efficiency, was forcing him steadily, step by step, into a corner of the square—a position from which there could be no escape. To abandon the square was to lose it to his opponent and win for himself ignoble and immediate death before the jeering populace. Spurred on by the seeming hopelessness of his plight, the Orange Odwar burst into a sudden fury of offense that forced the Black back a half dozen steps, and then the sword of U-Dor's piece leaped in and drew first blood, from the shoulder of his merciless opponent. An ill-smothered cry of encouragement went up from U-Dor's men; the Orange Odwar, encouraged by his single success, sought to bear down the Black by the rapidity of his attack. There was a moment in which the swords moved with a rapidity that no man's eye might follow, and then the Black Odwar made a lightning parry of a vicious thrust, leaned quickly forward into the opening he had effected, and drove his sword through the heart of the Orange Odwar—to the hilt he drove it through the body of the Orange Odwar.

A shout arose from the stands, for wherever may have been the favor of the spectators, none there was who could say that it had not been a pretty fight, or that the better man had not won. And from the Black players came a sigh of relief as they relaxed from the tension of the past moments.

I shall not weary you with the details of the game—only the high features of it are necessary to your understanding of the outcome. The fourth move after the victory of the Black Odwar found Gahan upon U-Dor's fourth; an Orange Panthan was on the adjoining square diagonally to his right and the only opposing piece that could engage him other than U-Dor himself.

It had been apparent to both players and spectators for the past two moves, that Gahan was moving straight across the field into the enemy's country to seek personal combat with the Orange

Chief—that he was staking all upon his belief in the superiority of his own swordsmanship, since if the two Chiefs engage, the outcome decides the game. U-Dor could move out and engage Gahan, or he could move his Princess' Panthan upon the square occupied by Gahan in he hope that the former would defeat the Black Chief and thus draw the game, which is the outcome if any other than a Chief slays the opposing Chief, or he could move away and escape, temporarily, the necessity for personal combat, or at least that is evidently what he had in mind as was obvious to all who saw him scanning the board about him; and his disappointment was apparent when he finally discovered that Gahan had so placed himself that there was no square to which U-Dor could move that it was not within Gahan's power to reach at his own next move.

U-Dor had placed his own Princess four squares east of Gahan when her position had been threatened, and he had hoped to lure the Black Chief after her and away from U-Dor; but in that he had failed. He now discovered that he might play his own Odwar into personal combat with Gahan; but he had already lost one Odwar and could ill spare the other. His position was a delicate one, since he did not wish to engage Gahan personally, while it appeared that there was little likelihood of his being able to escape. There was just one hope and that lay in his Princess' Panthan, so, without more deliberation he ordered the piece onto the square occupied by the Black Chief.

The sympathies of the spectators were all with Gahan now. If he lost, the game would be declared a draw, nor do they think better of drawn games upon Barsoom than do Earth men. If he won, it would doubtless mean a duel between the two Chiefs, a development for which they all were hoping. The game already bade fair to be a short one and it would be an angry crowd should it be decided a draw with only two men slain. There were great, historic games on record where of the forty pieces on the field when the game opened only three survived—the two Princesses and the victorious Chief.

They blamed U-Dor, though in fact he was well within his rights in directing his play as he saw fit, nor was a refusal on his part to engage the Black Chief necessarily an imputation of cowardice. He was a great chief who had conceived a notion to possess the slave Tara. There was no honor that could accrue to him from engaging in combat with slaves and criminals, or an unknown warrior from Manataj, nor was the stake of sufficient import to warrant the risk.

But now the duel between Gahan and the Orange Panthan was on and the decision of the next move was no longer in other hands than theirs. It was the first time that these Mana-Atorians had seen Gahan of Gathol fight, but Tara of Helium knew that he was master of his sword. Could he have seen the proud light in her eyes as he crossed blades with the wearer of the Orange, he might easily have wondered if they were the same eyes that had flashed fire and hatred at him that time he had covered her lips with mad kisses, in the pits of the palace of O-Tar. As she watched him she could not but compare his swordplay with that of the greatest swordsman of two worlds— her father, John Carter, of Virginia, a Prince of Helium, Warlord of Barsoom—and she knew that the skill of the Black Chief suffered little by the comparison.

Short and to the point was the duel that decided possession of the Orange Chief's fourth. The spectators had settled themselves for an interesting engagement of at least average duration when they were brought almost standing by a brilliant flash of rapid swordplay that was over ere one could catch his breath. They saw the Black Chief step quickly back, his point upon the ground, while his opponent, his sword slipping from his fingers, clutched his breast, sank to his knees and then lunged forward upon his face.

And then Gahan of Gathol turned his eyes directly upon U-Dor of Manator, three squares away. Three squares is a Chief's move— three squares in any direction or combination of directions, only provided that he does not cross the same square twice in a given move. The people saw and guessed Gahan's intention. They rose and roared forth their approval as he moved deliberately across the intervening squares toward the Orange Chief.

O-Tar, in the royal enclosure, sat frowning upon the scene. O-Tar was angry. He was angry with U-Dor for having entered this game for possession of a slave, for whom it had been his wish only slaves and criminals should strive. He was angry with the warrior from Manataj for having so far out-generaled and outfought the men from Manator. He was angry with the populace because of their open hostility toward one who had basked in the sunshine of his favor for long years. O-Tar the jeddak had not enjoyed the afternoon. Those who surrounded him were equally glum—they, too, scowled upon the field, the players, and the people. Among them was a bent and wrinkled old man who gazed through weak and watery eyes upon the field and the players.

As Gahan entered his square, U-Dor leaped toward him with drawn sword with such fury as might have overborne a less skilled and powerful swordsman. For a minute the fighting was fast and furious and by comparison reducing to insignificance all that had gone before. Here indeed were two magnificent swordsmen, and here was to be a battle that bade fair to make up for whatever the people felt they had been defrauded of by the shortness of the game. Nor had it continued long before many there were who would have prophesied that they were witnessing a duel that was to become historic in the annals of jetan at Manator. Every trick, every subterfuge, known to the art of fence these men employed. Time and again each scored a point and brought blood to his opponent's copper hide until both were red with gore; but neither seemed able to administer the coup de grace.

From her position upon the opposite side of the field Tara of Helium watched the long-drawn battle. Always it seemed to her that the Black Chief fought upon the defensive, or when he assumed to push his opponent, he neglected a thousand openings that her practiced eye beheld. Never did he seem in real danger, nor never did he appear to exert himself to quite the pitch needful for victory. The duel already had been long contested and the day was drawing to a close. Presently the sudden transition from daylight to darkness which, owing to the tenuity of the air upon Barsoom, occurs almost without the warning twilight of Earth, would occur. Would the fight never end? Would the game be called a draw after all? What ailed the Black Chief?

Tara wished that she might answer at least the last of these questions for she was sure that Turan the panthan, as she knew him, while fighting brilliantly, was not giving of himself all that he might. She could not believe that fear was restraining his hand, but that there was something beside inability to push U-Dor more fiercely she was confident. What it was, however, she could not guess.

Once she saw Gahan glance quickly up toward the sinking sun. In thirty minutes it would be dark. And then she saw and all those others saw a strange transition steal over the swordplay of the Black Chief. It was as though he had been playing with the great dwar, U-Dor, all these hours, and now he still played with him but there was a difference. He played with him terribly as a carnivore plays with its victim in the instant before the kill. The Orange Chief was helpless now in the hands of a swordsman so superior that there could be no comparison, and the people sat in open-mouthed wonder and awe as Gahan of Gathol cut his foe to ribbons and then struck him down with a blow that cleft him to the chin.

In twenty minutes the sun would set. But what of that?

XVIII

A Task for Loyalty

ong and loud was the applause that rose above the Field of Jetan at Manator, as The Keeper of the Towers summoned the two Princesses and the victorious Chief to the center of the field and presented to the latter the fruits of his prowess, and then, as custom demanded, the victorious players, headed by Gahan and the two Princesses, formed in procession behind The Keeper of the Towers and were conducted to the place of victory before the royal enclosure that they might receive the commendation of the jeddak. Those who were mounted gave up their thoats to slaves as all must be on foot for this ceremony. Directly beneath the royal enclosure are the gates to one of the tunnels that, passing beneath the seats, give ingress or egress to or from the Field. Before this gate the party halted while O-Tar looked down upon them from above. Val Dor and Floran, passing quietly ahead of the others, went directly to the gates, where they were hidden from those who occupied the enclosure with O-Tar. The Keeper of the Towers may have noticed them, but so occupied was he with the formality of presenting the victorious Chief to the jeddak that he paid no attention to them.

"I bring you, O-Tar, Jeddak of Manator, U-Kal of Manataj," he cried in a loud voice that might be heard by as many as possible, "victor over the Orange in the second of the Jeddak's Games of the four hundred and thirty-third year of O-Tar, and the slave woman Tara and the slave woman Lan-O that you may bestow these, the stakes, upon U-Kal."

As he spoke, a little, wrinkled, old man peered over the rail of the enclosure down upon the three who stood directly behind The Keeper, and strained his weak and watery eyes in an effort to satisfy the curiosity of old age in a matter of no particular import, for what were two slaves and a common warrior from Manataj to any who sat with O-Tar the jeddak?

"U-Kal of Manataj," said O-Tar, "you have deserved the stakes. Seldom have we looked upon more noble swordplay. And you tire of Manataj there be always here in the city of Manator a place for you in The Jeddak's Guard."

While the jeddak was speaking the little, old man, failing clearly to discern the features of the Black Chief, reached into his pocket-pouch and drew forth a pair of thick-lensed spectacles, which he placed upon his nose. For a moment he scrutinized Gahan closely, then he leaped to his feet and addressing O-Tar pointed a shaking finger it Gahan. As he rose Tara of Helium clutched the Black Chief's arm.

"Turan!" she whispered. "It is I-Gos, whom I thought to have slain in the pits of O-Tar. It is I-Gos and he recognizes you and will—"

But what I-Gos would do was already transpiring. In his falsetto voice he fairly screamed; "It is the slave Turan who stole the woman Tara from your throne room, O-Tar. He desecrated the dead chief I-Mal and wears his harness now!"

Instantly all was pandemonium. Warriors drew their swords and leaped to their feet. Gahan's victorious players rushed forward in a body, sweeping The Keeper of the Towers from his feet. Val Dor and Floran threw open the gates beneath the royal enclosure, opening the tunnel that led to the avenue in the city beyond the Towers. Gahan, surrounded by his men, drew Tara and Lan-O into the passageway, and at a rapid pace the party sought to reach the opposite end of the tunnel before their escape could be cut off. They were successful and when they emerged into the city the sun had set and darkness had come, relieved only by an antiquated and ineffective lighting system, which cast but a pale glow over the shadowy streets.

Now it was that Tara of Helium guessed why the Black Chief had drawn out his duel with U-Dor and realized that he might have slain his man at almost any moment he had elected. The whole plan that Gahan had whispered to his players before the game was thoroughly understood. They were to make their way to The Gate of Enemies and there offer their services to U-Thor, the great Jed of Manatos. The fact that most of them were Gatholians and that Gahan could lead rescuers to the pit where A-Kor, the son of U-Thor's wife, was confined, convinced the Jed of Gathol that they would meet with no rebuff at the hands of U-Thor. But even should he refuse them, still were they bound together to go on toward freedom, if necessary cutting their way through the forces of U-Thor at The Gate of Enemies—twenty men against a small army; but of such stuff are the warriors of Barsoom.

They had covered a considerable distance along the almost deserted avenue before signs of pursuit developed and then there came upon them suddenly from behind a dozen warriors mounted on thoats—a detachment, evidently, from The Jeddak's Guard. Instantly the avenue was a pandemonium of clashing blades, cursing warriors, and squealing thoats. In the first onslaught life blood was spilled upon both sides. Two of Gahan's men went down, and upon the enemies' side three riderless thoats attested at least a portion of their casualties.

Gahan was engaged with a fellow who appeared to have been selected to account for him only, since he rode straight for him and sought to cut him down without giving the slightest heed to several who slashed at him as he passed them. The Gatholian, practiced in the art of combating a mounted warrior from the ground, sought to reach the left side of the fellow's thoat a little to the rider's rear, the only position in which he would have any advantage over his antagonist, or rather the position that would most greatly reduce the advantage of the mounted man, and, similarly, the Manatorian strove to thwart his design. And so the guardsman wheeled and turned his vicious, angry mount while Gahan leaped in and out in an effort to reach the coveted vantage point, but always seeking some other opening in his foe's defense.

And while they jockeyed for position a rider swept swiftly past them. As he passed behind Gahan the latter heard a cry of alarm.

"Turan, they have me!" came to his ears in the voice of Tara of Helium.

A quick glance across his shoulder showed him the galloping thoatman in the act of dragging Tara to the withers of the beast, and then, with the fury of a demon, Gahan of Gathol leaped for his own man, dragged him from his mount and as he fell smote his head from his shoulders with a single cut of his keen sword. Scarce had the body touched the pavement when the Gatholian was upon the back of the dead warrior's mount, and galloping swiftly down the avenue after the diminishing figures of Tara and her abductor, the sounds of the fight waning in the distance as he pursued his quarry along the avenue that passes the palace of O-Tar and leads to The Gate of Enemies.

Gahan's mount, carrying but a single rider, gained upon that of the Manatorian, so that as they neared the palace Gahan was scarce a hundred yards behind, and now, to his consternation, he saw the fellow turn into the great entrance-way. For a moment only was he halted by the guards and then he disappeared within. Gahan was almost upon him then, but evidently he had warned the guards, for they leaped out to intercept the Gatholian. But no! the fellow could not have known that he was pursued, since he had not seen Gahan seize a mount, nor would he have thought that pursuit would come so soon. If he had passed then, so could Gahan pass, for did he not wear the trappings of a Manatorian? The Gatholian thought quickly, and stopping his thoat called to the guardsmen to let him pass, "In the name of O-Tar!" They hesitated a moment.

"Aside!" cried Gahan. "Must the jeddak's messenger parley for the right to deliver his message?"

"To whom would you deliver it?" asked the padwar of the guard.

"Saw you not him who just entered?" cried Gahan, and without waiting for a reply urged his thoat straight past them into the palace, and while they were deliberating what was best to be done, it was too late to do anything—which is not unusual.

Along the marble corridors Gahan guided his thoat, and because he had gone that way before, rather than because he knew which way Tara had been taken, he followed the runways and passed through the chambers that led to the throne room of O-Tar. On the second level he met a slave.

"Which way went he who carried the woman before him?" he asked.

The slave pointed toward a nearby runway that led to the third level and Gahan dashed rapidly on in pursuit. At the same moment a thoatman, riding at a furious pace, approached the palace and halted his mount at the gate.

"Saw you aught of a warrior pursuing one who carried a woman before him on his thoat?" he shouted to the guard.

"He but just passed in," replied the padwar, "saying that he was O-Tar's messenger."

"He lied," cried the newcomer. "He was Turan, the slave, who stole the woman from the throne room two days since.

"Arouse the palace! He must be seized, and alive if possible It is O-Tar's command."

Instantly warriors were dispatched to search for the Gatholian and warn the inmates of the palace to do likewise. Owing to the games there were comparatively few retainers in the great building, but those whom they found were immediately enlisted in the search, so that presently at least fifty warriors were seeking through the countless chambers and corridors of the palace of O-Tar.

As Gahan's thoat bore him to the third Level the man glimpsed the hind quarters of another thoat disappearing at the turn of a corridor far ahead. Urging his own animal forward he raced swiftly in pursuit and making the turn discovered only an empty corridor ahead. Along this he hurried to discover near its farther end a runway to the fourth level, which he followed upward. Here he saw that he had gained upon his quarry who was just turning through a doorway fifty yards ahead. As Gahan reached the opening he saw that the warrior had dismounted and was dragging Tara toward a small door on the opposite side of the chamber. At the same instant the clank of harness to his rear caused him to cast a glance behind where, along the corridor he had just traversed, he saw three warriors approaching on foot at a run. Leaping from his thoat Gahan sprang into the chamber where Tara was struggling to free herself from the grasp of her captor, slammed the door behind him, shot the great bolt into its seat, and drawing his sword crossed the room at a run to engage the Manatorian. The fellow, thus menaced, called aloud to Gahan to halt, at the same time thrusting Tara at arm's length and threatening her heart with the point of his short-sword.

"Stay!" he cried, "or the woman dies, for such is the command of O-Tar, rather than that she again fall into your hands."

Gahan stopped. But a few feet separated him from Tara and her captor, yet he was helpless to aid her. Slowly the warrior backed toward the open doorway behind him, dragging Tara with him. The girl struggled and fought, but the warrior was a powerful man and having seized her by the harness from behind was able to hold her in a position of helplessness.

"Save me, Turan!" she cried. "Let them not drag me to a fate worse than death. Better that I die now while my eyes behold a brave friend than later, fighting alone among enemies in defense of my honor."

He took a step nearer. The warrior made a threatening gesture with his sword close to the soft, smooth skin of the princess, and Gahan halted.

"I cannot, Tara of Helium," he cried. "Think not ill of me that I am weak—that I cannot see you die. Too great is my love for you, daughter of Helium."

The Manatorian warrior, a derisive grin upon his lips, backed steadily away. He had almost reached the doorway when Gahan saw another warrior in the chamber toward which Tara was being borne—a fellow who moved silently, almost stealthily, across the marble floor as he approached Tara's captor from behind. In his right hand he grasped a long-sword.

"Two to one," thought Gahan, and a grim smile touched his lips, for he had no doubt that once they had Tara safely in the adjoining chamber the two would set upon him. If he could not save her, he could at least die for her.

And then, suddenly, Gahan's eyes fastened with amazement upon the figure of the warrior behind the grinning fellow who held Tara and was forcing her to the doorway. He saw the newcomer step almost within arm's reach of the other. He saw him stop, an expression of malevolent hatred upon his features. He saw the great sword swing through the arc of a great circle, gathering swift and terrific momentum from its own weight backed by the brawn of the steel thews that guided it; he saw it pass through the feathered skull of the Manatorian, splitting his sardonic grin in twain, and open him to the middle of his breast bone.

As the dead hand relaxed its grasp upon Tara's wrist the girl leaped forward, without a backward glance, to Gahan's side. His left arm encircled her, nor did she draw away, as with ready sword the Gatholian awaited Fate's next decree. Before them Tara's deliverer was wiping the blood from his sword upon the hair of his victim. He was evidently a Manatorian, his trappings those of the Jeddak's Guard, and so his act was inexplicable to Gahan and to Tara. Presently he sheathed his sword and approached them.

"When a man chooses to hide his identity behind an assumed name," he said, looking straight into Gahan's eyes, "whatever friend pierces the deception were no friend if he divulged the other's secret."

He paused as though awaiting a reply.

"Your integrity has perceived and your lips voiced an unalterable truth," replied Gahan, whose mind was filled with wonder if the implication could by any possibility be true—that this Manatorian had guessed his identity.

"We are thus agreed," continued the other, "and I may tell you that though I am here known as A-Sor, my real name is Tasor." He paused and watched Gahan's face intently for any sign of the effect of this knowledge and was rewarded with a quick, though guarded expression of recognition.

Tasor! Friend of his youth. The son of that great Gatholian noble who had given his life so gloriously, however futilely, in an attempt to defend Gahan's sire from the daggers of the assassins. Tasor an under-padwar in the guard of O-Tar, Jeddak of Manator! It was inconceivable—and yet it was he; there could be no doubt of it. "Tasor," Gahan repeated aloud. "But it is no Manatorian name." The statement was half interrogatory, for Gahan's curiosity was aroused. He would know how his friend and loyal subject had become a Manatorian. Long years had passed since Tasor had disappeared as mysteriously as the Princess Haja and many other of Gahan's subjects. The Jed of Gathol had long supposed him dead.

"No," replied Tasor, "nor is it a Manatorian name. Come, while I search for a hiding place for you in some forgotten chamber in one of the untenanted portions of the palace, and as we go I will tell you briefly how Tasor the Gatholian became A-Sor the Manatorian.

"It befell that as I rode with a dozen of my warriors along the western border of Gathol searching for zitidars that had strayed from my herds, we were set upon and surrounded by a great company of Manatorians. They overpowered us, though not before half our number was slain and the balance helpless from wounds. And so I was brought a prisoner to Manataj, a distant city of Manator, and there sold into slavery. A woman bought me—a princess of Manataj whose wealth and position were unequaled in the city of her birth. She loved me and when her husband discovered her infatuation she beseeched me to slay him, and when I refused she hired another to do it. Then she married me; but none would have aught to do with her in Manataj, for they suspected her guilty knowledge of her husband's murder. And so we set out from Manataj for Manatos accompanied by a great caravan bearing all her worldly goods and jewels and precious metals, and on the way she caused the rumor to be spread that she and I had died. Then we came to Manator instead, she taking a new name and I the name A-Sor, that we might not be traced through our names. With her great wealth she bought me a post in The Jeddak's Guard and none knows that I am not a Manatorian, for she is dead. She was beautiful, but she was a devil."

"And you never sought to return to your native city?" asked Gahan.

"Never has the hope been absent from my heart, or my mind empty of a plan," replied Tasor. "I dream of it by day and by night, but always must I return to the same conclusion—that there can be but a single means for escape. I must wait until Fortune favors me with a place in a raiding party to Gathol. Then, once within the boundaries of my own country, they shall see me no more."

"Perhaps your opportunity lies already within your grasp," said Gahan, "has not your fealty to your own Jed been undermined by years of association with the men of Manator." The statement was half challenge.

"And my Jed stood before me now," cried Tasor, "and my avowal could be made without violating his confidence, I should cast my sword at his feet and beg the high privilege of dying for him as my sire died for his sire."

There could be no doubt of his sincerity nor any that he was cognizant of Gahan's identity. The Jed of Gathol smiled. "And if your Jed were here there is little doubt but that he would command you to devote your talents and your prowess to the rescue of the Princess Tara of Helium," he said, meaningly. "And he possessed the knowledge I have gained during my captivity he would say to you, 'Go, Tasor, to the pit where A-kor, son of Haja of Gathol, is confined and set him free and with him arouse the slaves from Gathol and march to The Gate of Enemies and offer your services to U-Thor of Manataj, who is wed to Haja of Gathol, and ask of him in return that he attack the palace of O-Tar and rescue Tara of Helium and when that thing is accomplished that he free the slaves of Gathol and furnish them with the arms and the means to return to their own country.' That, Tasor of Gathol, is what Gahan your Jed would demand of you."

"And that, Turan the slave, is what I shall bend my every effort to accomplish after I have found a safe refuge for Tara of Helium and her panthan," replied Tasor.

Gahan's glance carried to Tasor an intimation of his Jed's gratification and filled him with a chivalrous determination to do the thing required of him, or die, for he considered that he had received from the lips of his beloved ruler a commission that placed upon his shoulders a responsibility that encompassed not alone the life of Gahan and Tara but the welfare, perhaps the whole future, of Gathol. And so he hastened them onward through the musty corridors of the old palace where the dust of ages lay undisturbed upon the marble tiles. Now and again he tried a door until he found one that was unlocked. Opening it he ushered them into a chamber, heavy with dust. Crumbling silks and furs adorned the walls, with ancient weapons, and great paintings whose colors were toned by age to wondrous softness.

"This be as good as any place," he said. "No one comes here. Never have I been here before, so I know no more of the other chambers than you; but this one, at least, I can find again when I bring you food and drink. O-Mai the Cruel occupied this portion of the palace during his reign, five thousand years before O-Tar. In one of these apartments he was found dead, his face contorted in an expression of fear so horrible that it drove to madness those who looked upon it; yet there was no mark of violence upon him Since then the quarters of O-Mai have been shunned for the legends have it that the ghosts of Corphals pursue the spirit of the wicked Jeddak nightly through these chambers, shrieking and moaning as they go. But," he added, as though to reassure himself as well as his companions, "such things may not be countenanced by the culture of Gathol or Helium."

Gahan laughed. "And if all who looked upon him were driven mad, who then was there to perform the last rites or prepare the body of the Jeddak for them?"

"There was none," replied Tasor. "Where they found him they left him and there to this very day his mouldering bones lie hid in some forgotten chamber of this forbidden suite."

Tasor left them then assuring them that he would seek the first opportunity to speak with A-Kor, and upon the following day he would bring them food and drink.

After Tasor had gone Tara turned to Gahan and approaching laid a hand upon his arm. "So swiftly have events transpired since I recognized you beneath your disguise," she said, "that I have had no opportunity to assure you of my gratitude and the high esteem that your valor has won for you in my consideration.Let me now acknowledge my indebtedness; and if promises be not vain from one whose life and liberty are in grave jeopardy, accept my assurance of the great reward that awaits you at the hand of my father in Helium."

"I desire no reward," he replied, "other than the happiness of knowing that the woman I love is happy."

For an instant the eyes of Tara of Helium blazed as she drew herself haughtily to her full height, and then they softened and her attitude relaxed as she shook her head sadly.

"I have it not in my heart to reprimand you, Turan," she said, "however great your fault, for you have been an honorable and a loyal friend to Tara of Helium; but you must not say what my ears must not hear."

"You mean," he asked, "that the ears of a Princess must not listen to words of love from a panthan?"

"It is not that, Turan," she replied; "but rather that I may not in honor listen to words of love from another than him to whom I am betrothed—a fellow countryman, Djor Kantos."

"You mean, Tara of Helium," he cried, "that were it not for that you would——"

"Stop!" she commanded. "You have no right to assume aught else than my lips testify."

"The eyes are ofttimes more eloquent than the lips, Tara," he replied; "and in yours I have read that which is neither hatred nor contempt for Turan the panthan, and my heart tells me that your lips bore false witness when they cried in anger: 'I hate you!'"

"I do not hate you, Turan, nor yet may I love you," said the girl, simply.

"When I broke my way out from the chamber of I-Gos I was indeed upon the verge of believing that you did hate me," he said, "for only hatred, it seemed to me, could account for the fact that you had gone without making an effort to liberate me; but presently both my heart and my judgment told me that Tara of Helium could not have deserted a companion in distress, and though I still am in ignorance of the facts I know that it was beyond your power to aid me."

"It was indeed," said the girl. "Scarce had I-Gos fallen at the bite of my dagger than I heard the approach of warriors. I ran then to hide until they had passed, thinking to return and liberate you; but in seeking to elude the party I had heard I ran full into the arms of another. They questioned me as to your whereabouts, and I told them that you had gone ahead and that I was following you and thus I led them from you."

"I knew," was Gahan's only comment, but his heart was glad with elation, as a lover's must be who has heard from the lips of his divinity an avowal of interest and loyalty, however little tinged by a suggestion of warmer regard it may be. To be abused, even, by the mistress of one's heart is better than to be ignored.

As the two conversed in the ill-lit chamber, the dim bulbs of which were encrusted with the accumulated dust of centuries, a bent and withered figure traversed slowly the gloomy corridors without, his weak and watery eyes peering through thick lenses at the signs of passage written upon the dusty floor.

XIX

The Menace of the Dead

he night was still young when there came one
to the entrance of the banquet hall where O-Tar
of Manator dined with his chiefs, and brushing
past the guards entered the great room with the
insolence of a privileged character, as in truth he
was. As he approached the head of the long board O-Tar took notice
of him.

"Well, hoary one!" he cried. "What brings you out of your
beloved and stinking burrow again this day. We thought that the sight
of the multitude of living men at the games would drive you back to
your corpses as quickly as you could go."

The cackling laugh of I-Gos acknowledged the royal sally. "Ey,
ey, O-Tar," squeaked the ancient one, "I-Gos goes out not upon pleasure bound; but when one does ruthlessly desecrate the dead of I-Gos,
vengeance must be had!"

"You refer to the act of the slave Turan?" demanded O-Tar.

"Turan, yes, and the slave Tara, who slipped beneath my hide
a murderous blade. Another fraction of an inch, O-Tar, and I-Gos'
ancient and wrinkled covering were even now in some apprentice
tanner's hands, ey, ey!"

"But they have again eluded us," cried O-Tar. "Even in the palace
of the great jeddak twice have they escaped the stupid knaves I call
The jeddak's Guard." O-Tar had risen and was angrily emphasizing
his words with heavy blows upon the table, dealt with a golden goblet.

"Ey, O-Tar, they elude thy guard but not the wise old calot, I-Gos."

"What mean you? Speak!" commanded O-Tar.

"I know where they are hid," said the ancient taxidermist. "In the dust of unused corridors their feet have betrayed them."

"You followed them? You have seen them?" demanded the jeddak.

"I followed them and I heard them speaking beyond a closed door," replied I-Gos; "but I did not see them."

"Where is that door?" cried O-Tar. "We will send at once and fetch them," he looked about the table as though to decide to whom he would entrust this duty. A dozen warrior chiefs arose and laid their hands upon their swords.

"To the chambers of O-Mai the Cruel I traced them," squeaked I-Gos. "There you will find them where the moaning Corphals pursue the shrieking ghost of O-Mai; ey!" and he turned his eyes from O-Tar toward the warriors who had arisen, only to discover that, to a man, they were hurriedly resuming their seats.

The cackling laughter of I-Gos broke derisively the hush that had fallen on the room. The warriors looked sheepishly at the food upon their plates of gold. O-Tar snapped his fingers impatiently.

"Be there only cravens among the chiefs of Manator?" he cried. "Repeatedly have these presumptuous slaves flouted the majesty of your jeddak. Must I command one to go and fetch them?"

Slowly a chief arose and two others followed his example, though with ill-concealed reluctance. "All, then, are not cowards," commented O-Tar. "The duty is distasteful. Therefore all three of you shall go, taking as many warriors as you wish."

"But do not ask for volunteers," interrupted I-Gos, "or you will go alone."

The three chiefs turned and left the banquet hall, walking slowly like doomed men to their fate.

Gahan and Tara remained in the chamber to which Tasor had led them, the man brushing away the dust from a deep and comfortable bench where they might rest in comparative comfort. He had found the ancient sleeping silks and furs too far gone to be of any service, crumbling to powder at a touch, thus removing any chance of making a comfortable bed for the girl, and so the two sat together, talking in low tones, of the adventures through which they already had passed and speculating upon the future; planning means of escape and hoping Tasor would not be long gone. They spoke of many things—of Hastor, and Helium, and Ptarth, and finally the conversation reminded Tara of Gathol.

"You have served there?" she asked.

"Yes," replied Turan.

"I met Gahan the Jed of Gathol at my father's palace," she said, "the very day before the storm snatched me from Helium—he was a presumptuous fellow, magnificently trapped in platinum and diamonds. Never in my life saw I so gorgeous a harness as his, and you must well know, Turan, that the splendor of all Barsoom passes through the court at Helium; but in my mind I could not see so resplendent a creature drawing that jeweled sword in mortal combat. I fear me that the Jed of Gathol, though a pretty picture of a man, is little else."

In the dim light Tara did not perceive the wry expression upon the half-averted face of her companion.

"You thought little then of the Jed of Gathol?" he asked.

"Then or now," she replied, and with a little laugh; "how it would pique his vanity to know, if he might, that a poor panthan had won a higher place in the regard of Tara of Helium," and she laid her fingers gently upon his knee.

He seized the fingers in his and carried them to his lips. "O, Tara of Helium," he cried. "Think you that I am a man of stone?" One arm slipped about her shoulders and drew the yielding body toward him.

"May my first ancestor forgive me my weakness," she cried, as her arms stole about his neck and she raised her panting lips to his. For long they clung there in love's first kiss and then she pushed him away, gently. "I love you, Turan," she half sobbed; "I love you so! It is my only poor excuse for having done this wrong to Djor Kantos, whom now I know I never loved, who knew not the meaning of love. And if you love me as you say, Turan, your love must protect me from greater dishonor, for I am but as clay in your hands."

Again he crushed her to him and then as suddenly released her, and rising, strode rapidly to and fro across the chamber as though he endeavored by violent exercise to master and subdue some evil spirit that had laid hold upon him. Ringing through his brain and heart and soul like some joyous paean were those words that had so altered the world for Gahan of Gathol: "I love you, Turan; I love you so!" And it had come so suddenly. He had thought that she felt for him only gratitude for his loyalty and then, in an instant, her barriers were all down, she was no longer a princess; but instead a—his reflections were interrupted by a sound from beyond the closed door. His sandals of zitidar hide had given forth no sound upon the marble floor he strode, and as his rapid pacing carried him past the entrance to the chamber there came faintly from the distance of the long corridor the sound of metal on metal—the unmistakable herald of the approach of armed men.

For a moment Gahan listened intently, close to the door, until there could be no doubt but that a party of warriors was approaching. From what Tasor had told him he guessed correctly that they would be coming to this portion of the palace but for a single purpose—to search for Tara and himself—and it behooved him therefore to seek immediate means for eluding them. The chamber in which they were had other doorways beside that at which they had entered, and to one of these he must look for some safer hiding place. Crossing to Tara he acquainted her with his suspicion, leading her to one of the doors which they found unsecured. Beyond it lay a dimly-lighted chamber at the threshold of which they halted in consternation, drawing back quickly into the chamber they had just quitted, for their first glance revealed four warriors seated around a jetan board.

That their entrance had not been noted was attributed by Gahan to the absorption of the two players and their friends in the game. Quietly closing the door the fugitives moved silently to the next, which they found locked. There was now but another door which they had not tried, and this they approached quickly as they knew that the searching party must be close to the chamber. To their chagrin they found this avenue of escape barred.

Now indeed were they in a sorry plight, for should the searchers have information leading them to this room they were lost. Again leading Tara to the door behind which were the jetan players Gahan drew his sword and waited, listening. The sound of the party in the corridor came distinctly to their ears—they must be quite close, and doubtless they were coming in force. Beyond the door were but four warriors who might be readily surprised. There could, then, be but one choice and acting upon it Gahan quietly opened the door again, stepped through into the adjoining chamber, Tara's hand in his, and closed the door behind them. The four at the jetan board evidently failed to hear them. One player had either just made or was contemplating a move, for his fingers grasped a piece that still rested upon the board. The other three were watching his move. For an instant Gahan looked at them, playing jetan there in the dim light of this forgotten and forbidden chamber, and then a slow smile of understanding lighted his face.

"Come!" he said to Tara. "We have nothing to fear from these. For more than five thousand years they have sat thus, a monument to the handiwork of some ancient taxidermist."

As they approached more closely they saw that the lifelike figures were coated with dust, but that otherwise the skin was in as fine a state of preservation as the most recent of I-Gos' groups, and then they heard the door of the chamber they had quitted open and knew that the searchers were close upon them. Across the room they saw the opening of what appeared to be a corridor and which investigation proved to be a short passageway, terminating in a chamber in the center of which was an ornate sleeping dais. This room, like the others, was but poorly lighted, time having dimmed the radiance of its bulbs and coated them with dust. A glance showed that it was hung with heavy goods and contained considerable massive furniture in addition to the sleeping platform, a second glance at which revealed what appeared to be the form of a man lying partially on the floor and partially on the dais. No doorways were visible other than that at which they had entered, though both knew that others might be concealed by the hangings.

Gahan, his curiosity aroused by the legends surrounding this portion of the palace, crossed to the dais to examine the figure that apparently had fallen from it, to find the dried and shrivelled corpse of a man lying upon his back on the floor with arms outstretched and fingers stiffly outspread. One of his feet was doubled partially beneath him, while the other was still entangled in the sleeping silks and furs upon the dais. After five thousand years the expression of the withered face and the eyeless sockets retained the aspect of horrid fear to such an extent, that Gahan knew that he was looking upon the body of O-Mai the Cruel.

Suddenly Tara, who stood close beside him, clutched his arm and pointed toward a far corner of the room. Gahan looked and looking felt the hairs upon his neck rising. He threw his left arm about the girl and with bared sword stood between her and the hangings that they watched, and then slowly Gahan of Gathol backed away, for in this grim and somber chamber, which no human foot had trod for five thousand years and to which no breath of wind might enter, the heavy hangings in the far corner had moved. Not gently had they moved as a draught might have moved them had there been a draught, but suddenly they had bulged out as though pushed against from behind. To the opposite corner backed Gahan until they stood with their backs against the hangings there, and then hearing the approach of their pursuers across the chamber beyond Gahan pushed Tara through the hangings and, following her, kept open with his left hand, which he had disengaged from the girl's grasp, a tiny opening through which he could view the apartment and the doorway upon the opposite side through which the pursuers would enter, if they came this far.

Behind the hangings there was a space of about three feet in width between them and the wall, making a passageway entirely around the room, broken only by the single entrance opposite them; this being a common arrangement especially in the sleeping apartments of the rich and powerful upon Barsoom. The purposes of this arrangement were several. The passageway afforded a station for guards in the same room with their master without intruding entirely upon his privacy; it concealed secret exits from the chamber; it permitted the occupant of the room to hide eavesdroppers and assassins for use against enemies that he might lure to his chamber.

The three chiefs with a dozen warriors had had no difficulty in following the tracks of the fugitives through the dust of the corridors and chambers they had traversed. To enter this portion of the palace at all had required all the courage they possessed, and now that they were within the very chambers of O-Mai their nerves were pitched to the highest key—another turn and they would snap; for the people of Manator are filled with weird superstitions. As they entered the outer chamber they moved slowly, with drawn swords, no one seeming anxious to take the lead, and the twelve warriors hanging back in unconcealed and shameless terror, while the three chiefs, spurred on by fear of O-Tar and by pride, pressed together for mutual encouragement as they slowly crossed the dimly-lighted room.

Following the tracks of Gahan and Tara they found that though each doorway had been approached only one threshold had been crossed and this door they gingerly opened, revealing to their astonished gaze the four warriors at the jetan table. For a moment they were on the verge of flight, for though they knew what they were, coming as they did upon them in this mysterious and haunted suite, they were as startled as though they had beheld the very ghosts of the departed. But they presently regained their courage sufficiently to cross this chamber too and enter the short passageway that led to the ancient sleeping apartment of O-Mai the Cruel. They did not know that this awful chamber lay just before them, or it were doubtful that they would have proceeded farther; but they saw that those they sought had come this way and so they followed, but within the gloomy interior of the chamber they halted, the three chiefs urging their followers, in low whispers, to close in behind them, and there just within the entrance they stood until, their eyes becoming accustomed to the dim light, one of them pointed suddenly to the thing lying upon the floor with one foot tangled in the coverings of the dais.

"Look!" he gasped. "It is the corpse of O-Mai! Ancestor of ancestors! we are in the forbidden chamber." Simultaneously there came from behind the hangings beyond the gruesome dead a hollow moan followed by a piercing scream, and the hangings shook and bellied before their eyes.

With one accord, chieftains and warriors, they turned and bolted for the doorway; a narrow doorway, where they jammed, fighting and screaming in an effort to escape. They threw away their swords and clawed at one another to make a passage for escape; those behind climbed upon the shoulders of those in front; and some fell and were trampled upon; but at last they all got through, and, the swiftest first, they bolted across the two intervening chambers to the outer corridor beyond, nor did they halt their mad retreat before they stumbled, weak and trembling, into the banquet hall of O-Tar. At sight of them the warriors who had remained with the jeddak leaped to their feet with drawn swords, thinking that their fellows were pursued by many enemies; but no one followed them into the room, and the three chieftains came and stood before O-Tar with bowed heads and trembling knees.

"Well?" demanded the jeddak. "What ails you? Speak!"

"O-Tar," cried one of them when at last he could master his voice. "When have we three failed you in battle or combat? Have our swords been not always among the foremost in defense of your safety and your honor?"

"Have I denied this?" demanded O-Tar.

"Listen, then, O Jeddak, and judge us with leniency. We followed the two slaves to the apartments of O-Mai the Cruel. We entered the accursed chambers and still we did not falter. We came at last to that horrid chamber no human eye had scanned before in fifty centuries and we looked upon the dead face of O-Mai lying as he has lain for all this time. To the very death chamber of O-Mai the Cruel we came and yet we were ready to go farther; when suddenly there broke upon our horrified ears the moans and the shrieking that mark these haunted chambers and the hangings moved and rustled in the dead air. O-Tar, it was more than human nerves could endure. We turned and fled. We threw away our swords and fought with one another to escape. With sorrow, but without shame, I tell it, for there be no man in all Manator that would not have done the same. If these slaves be Corphals they are safe among their fellow ghosts. If they be not Corphals, then already are they dead in the chambers of O-Mai, and there may they rot for all of me, for I would not return to that accursed spot for the harness of a jeddak and the half of Barsoom for an empire. I have spoken."

O-Tar knitted his scowling brows. "Are all my chieftains cowards and cravens?" he demanded presently in sneering tones.

From among those who had not been of the searching party a chieftain arose and turned a scowling face upon O-Tar.

"The jeddak knows," he said, "that in the annals of Manator her jeddaks have ever been accounted the bravest of her warriors. Where my jeddak leads I will follow, nor may any jeddak call me a coward or a craven unless I refuse to go where he dares to go. I have spoken."

After he had resumed his seat there was a painful silence, for all knew that the speaker had challenged the courage of O-Tar the Jeddak of Manator and all awaited the reply of their ruler. In every mind was the same thought—O-Tar must lead them at once to the chamber of O-Mai the Cruel, or accept forever the stigma of cowardice, and there could be no coward upon the throne of Manator. That they all knew and that O-Tar knew, as well.

But O-Tar hesitated. He looked about upon the faces of those around him at the banquet board; but he saw only the grim visages of relentless warriors. There was no trace of leniency in the face of any. And then his eyes wandered to a small entrance at one side of the great chamber. An expression of relief expunged the scowl of anxiety from his features.

"Look!" he exclaimed. "See who has come!"

XX

The Charge of Cowardice

ahan, watching through the aperture between the hangings, saw the frantic flight of their pursuers. A grim smile rested upon his lips as he viewed the mad scramble for safety and saw them throw away their swords and fight with one another to be first from the chamber of fear, and when they were all gone he turned back toward Tara, the smile still upon his lips; but the smile died the instant that he turned, for he saw that Tara had disappeared.

"Tara!" he called in a loud voice, for he knew that there was no danger that their pursuers would return; but there was no response, unless it was a faint sound as of cackling laughter from afar. Hurriedly he searched the passageway behind the hangings finding several doors, one of which was ajar. Through this he entered the adjoining chamber which was lighted more brilliantly for the moment by the soft rays of hurtling Thuria taking her mad way through the heavens. Here he found the dust upon the floor disturbed, and the imprint of sandals. They had come this way—Tara and whatever the creature was that had stolen her.

But what could it have been? Gahan, a man of culture and high intelligence, held few if any superstitions. In common with nearly all races of Barsoom he clung, more or less inherently, to a certain exalted form of ancestor worship, though it was rather the memory or legends of the virtues and heroic deeds of his forebears that he deified rather than themselves. He never expected any tangible evidence of their existence after death; he did not believe that they had the power either for good or for evil other than the effect that their example while living might have had upon following generations; he did not believe therefore in the materialization of dead spirits. If there was a life hereafter he knew nothing of it, for he knew that science had demonstrated the existence of some material cause for every seemingly supernatural phenomenon of ancient religions and superstitions. Yet he was at a loss to know what power might have removed Tara so suddenly and mysteriously from his side in a chamber that had not known the presence of man for five thousand years.

In the darkness he could not see whether there were the imprints of other sandals than Tara's—only that the dust was disturbed—and when it led him into gloomy corridors he lost the trail altogether. A perfect labyrinth of passages and apartments were now revealed to him as he hurried on through the deserted quarters of O-Mai. Here was an ancient bath—doubtless that of the jeddak himself, and again he passed through a room in which a meal had been laid upon a table five thousand years before—the untasted breakfast of O-Mai, perhaps. There passed before his eyes in the brief moments that he traversed the chambers, a wealth of ornaments and jewels and precious metals that surprised even the Jed of Gathol whose harness was of diamonds and platinum and whose riches were the envy of a world. But at last his search of OMai's chambers ended in a small closet in the floor of which was the opening to a spiral runway leading straight down into Stygian darkness. The dust at the entrance of the closet had been freshly disturbed, and as this was the only possible indication that Gahan had of the direction taken by the abductor of Tara it seemed as well to follow on as to search elsewhere. So, without hesitation, he descended into the utter darkness below. Feeling with a foot before taking a forward step his descent was necessarily slow, but Gahan was a Barsoomian and so knew the pitfalls that might await the unwary in such dark, forbidden portions of a jeddak's palace.

He had descended for what he judged might be three full levels and was pausing, as he occasionally did, to listen, when he distinctly heard a peculiar shuffling, scraping sound approaching him from below. Whatever the thing was it was ascending the runway at a steady pace and would soon be near him. Gahan laid his hand upon the hilt of his sword and drew it slowly from its scabbard that he might make no noise that would apprise the creature of his presence. He wished that there might be even the slightest lessening of the darkness. If he could see but the outline of the thing that approached him he would feel that he had a fairer chance in the meeting; but he could see nothing, and then because he could see nothing the end of his scabbard struck the stone side of the runway, giving off a sound that the stillness and the narrow confines of the passage and the darkness seemed to magnify to a terrific clatter.

Instantly the shuffling sound of approach ceased. For a moment Gahan stood in silent waiting, then casting aside discretion he moved on again down the spiral. The thing, whatever it might be, gave forth no sound now by which Gahan might locate it. At any moment it might be upon him and so he kept his sword in readiness. Down, ever downward the steep spiral led. The darkness and the silence of the tomb surrounded him, yet somewhere ahead was something. He was not alone in that horrid place—another presence that he could not hear or see hovered before him—of that he was positive. Perhaps it was the thing that had stolen Tara. Perhaps Tara herself, still in the clutches of some nameless horror, was just ahead of him. He quickened his pace—it became almost a ran at the thought of the danger that threatened the woman he loved, and then he collided with a wooden door that swung open to the impact. Before him was a lighted corridor. On either side were chambers. He had advanced but a short distance from the bottom of the spiral when he recognized that he was in the pits below the palace. A moment later he heard behind him the shuffling sound that had attracted his attention in the spiral runway. Wheeling about he saw the author of the sound emerging from a doorway he had just passed. It was Ghek the kaldane.

"Ghek!" exclaimed Gahan. "It was you in the runway? Have you seen Tara of Helium?"

"It was I in the spiral," replied the kaldane; "but I have not seen Tara of Helium. I have been searching for her. Where is she?"

"I do not know," replied the Gatholian; "but we must find her and take her from this place."

"We may find her," said Ghek; "but I doubt our ability to take her away. It is not so easy to leave Manator as it is to enter it. I may come and go at will, through the ancient burrows of the ulsios; but you are too large for that and your lungs need more air than may be found in some of the deeper runways."

"But U-Thor!" exclaimed Gahan. "Have you heard aught of him or his intentions?"

"I have heard much," replied Ghek. "He camps at The Gate of Enemies. That spot he holds and his warriors lie just beyond The Gate; but he has not sufficient force to enter the city and take the palace. An hour since and you might have made your way to him; but now every avenue is strongly guarded since O-Tar learned that A-Kor had escaped to U-Thor."

"A-Kor has escaped and joined U-Thor!" exclaimed Gahan.

"But little more than an hour since. I was with him when a warrior came—a man whose name is Tasor—who brought a message from you. It was decided that Tasor should accompany A-Kor in an attempt to reach the camp of U-Thor, the great jed of Manatos, and exact from him the assurances you required. Then U-Thor was to return and take food to you and the Princess of Helium. I accompanied them. We won through easily and found U-Thor more than willing to respect your every wish, but when Tasor would have returned to you the way was blocked by the warriors of O-Tar. Then it was that I volunteered to come to you and report and find food and drink and then go forth among the Gatholian slaves of Manator and prepare them for their part in the plan that U-Thor and Tasor conceived."

"And what was this plan?"

"U-Thor has sent for reinforcements. To Manatos he has sent and to all the outlying districts that are his. It will take a month to collect and bring them hither and in the meantime the slaves within the city are to organize secretly, stealing and hiding arms against the day that the reinforcements arrive. When that day comes the forces of U-Thor will enter the Gate of Enemies and as the warriors of O-Tar rush to repulse them the slaves from Gathol will fall upon them from the rear with the majority of their numbers, while the balance will assault the palace. They hope thus to divert so many from The Gate that U-Thor will have little difficulty in forcing an entrance to the city."

"Perhaps they will succeed," commented Gahan; "but the warriors of O-Tar are many, and those who fight in defense of their homes and their jeddak have always an advantage. Ah, Ghek, would that we had the great warships of Gathol or of Helium to pour their merciless fire into the streets of Manator while U-Thor marched to the palace over the corpses of the slain." He paused, deep in thought, and then turned his gaze again upon the kaldane. "Heard you aught of the party that escaped with me from The Field of Jetan—of Floran, Val Dor, and the others? What of them?"

"Ten of these won through to U-Thor at The Gate of Enemies and were well received by him. Eight fell in the fighting upon the way. Val Dor and Floran live, I believe, for I am sure that I heard U-Thor address two warriors by these names."

"Good!" exclaimed Gahan. "Go then, through the burrows of the ulsios, to The Gate of Enemies and carry to Floran the message that I shall write in his own language. Come, while I write the message."

In a nearby room they found a bench and table and there Gahan sat and wrote in the strange, stenographic characters of Martian script a message to Floran of Gathol. "Why," he asked, when he had finished it, "did you search for Tara through the spiral runway where we nearly met?"

"Tasor told me where you were to be found, and as I have explored the greater part of the palace by means of the ulsio runways and the darker and less frequented passages I knew precisely where you were and how to reach you. This secret spiral ascends from the pits to the roof of the loftiest of the palace towers. It has secret openings at every level; but there is no living Manatorian, I believe, who knows of its existence. At least never have I met one within it and I have used it many times. Thrice have I been in the chamber where O-Mai lies, though I knew nothing of his identity or the story of his death until Tasor told it to us in the camp of U-Thor."

"You know the palace thoroughly then?" Gahan interrupted.

"Better than O-Tar himself or any of his servants."

"Good! And you would serve the Princess Tara, Ghek, you may serve her best by accompanying Floran and following his instructions. I will write them here at the close of my message to him, for the walls have ears, Ghek, while none but a Gatholian may read what I have written to Floran. He will transmit it to you. Can I trust you?"

"I may never return to Bantoom," replied Ghek. "Therefore I have but two friends in all Barsoom. What better may I do than serve them faithfully? You may trust me, Gatholian, who with a woman of your kind has taught me that there be finer and nobler things than perfect mentality uninfluenced by the unreasoning tuitions of the heart. I go."

As O-Tar pointed to the little doorway all eyes turned in the direction he indicated and surprise was writ large upon the faces of the warriors when they recognized the two who had entered the banquet hall. There was I-Gos, and he dragged behind him one who was gagged and whose hands were fastened behind with a ribbon of tough silk. It was the slave girl. I-Gos' cackling laughter rose above the silence of the room.

"Ey, ey!" he shrilled. "What the young warriors of O-Tar cannot do, old I-Gos does alone."

"Only a Corphal may capture a Corphal," growled one of the chiefs who had fled from the chambers of O-Mai.

I-Gos laughed. "Terror turned your heart to water," he replied; "and shame your tongue to libel. This be no Corphal, but only a woman of Helium; her companion a warrior who can match blades with the best of you and cut your putrid hearts. Not so in the days of I-Gos' youth. Ah, then were there men in Manator. Well do I recall that day that I——"

"Peace, doddering fool!" commanded O-Tar. "Where is the man?"

"Where I found the woman—in the death chamber of O-Mai. Let your wise and brave chieftains go thither and fetch him. I am an old man, and could bring but one."

"You have done well, I-Gos," O-Tar hastened to assure him, for when he learned that Gahan might still be in the haunted chambers he wished to appease the wrath of I-Gos, knowing well the vitriolic tongue and temper of the ancient one. "You think she is no Corphal, then, I-Gos?" he asked, wishing to carry the subject from the man who was still at large.

"No more than you," replied the ancient taxidermist.

O-Tar looked long and searchingly at Tara of Helium. All the beauty that was hers seemed suddenly to be carried to every fibre of his consciousness. She was still garbed in the rich harness of a Black Princess of Jetan, and as O-Tar the Jeddak gazed upon her he realized that never before had his eyes rested upon a more perfect figure—a more beautiful face.

"She is no Corphal," he murmured to himself. "She is no Corphal and she is a princess—a princess of Helium, and, by the golden hair of the Holy Hekkador, she is beautiful. Take the gag from her mouth and release her hands," he commanded aloud. "Make room for the Princess Tara of Helium at the side of O-Tar of Manator. She shall dine as becomes a princess."

Slaves did as O-Tar bid and Tara of Helium stood with flashing eyes behind the chair that was offered her. "Sit!" commanded O-Tar.

The girl sank into the chair. "I sit as a prisoner," she said; "not as a guest at the board of my enemy, O-Tar of Manator."

O-Tar motioned his followers from the room. "I would speak alone with the Princess of Helium," he said. The company and the slaves withdrew and once more the Jeddak of Manator turned toward the girl. "O-Tar of Manator would be your friend," he said.

Tara of Helium sat with arms folded upon her small, firm breasts, her eyes flashing from behind narrowed lids, nor did she deign to answer his overture. O-Tar leaned closer to her. He noted the hostility of her bearing and he recalled his first encounter with her. She was a she-banth, but she was beautiful. She was by far the most desirable woman that O-Tar had ever looked upon and he was determined to possess her. He told her so.

"I could take you as my slave," he said to her; "but it pleases me to make you my wife. You shall be Jeddara of Manator. You shall have seven days in which to prepare for the great honor that O-Tar is conferring upon you, and at this hour of the seventh day you shall become an empress and the wife of O-Tar in the throne room of the jeddaks of Manator." He struck a gong that stood beside him upon the table and when a slave appeared he bade him recall the company. Slowly the chiefs filed in and took their places at the table. Their faces were grim and scowling, for there was still unanswered the question of their jeddak's courage. If O-Tar had hoped they would forget he had been mistaken in his men.

O-Tar arose. "In seven days," he announced, "there will be a great feast in honor of the new Jeddara of Manator," and he waved his hand toward Tara of Helium. "The ceremony will occur at the beginning of the seventh zodein the throne room. In the meantime the Princess of Helium will be cared for in the tower of the women's quarters of the palace. Conduct her thither, E-Thas, with a suitable guard of honor and see to it that slaves and eunuchs be placed at her disposal, who shall attend upon all her wants and guard her carefully from harm."

Now E-Thas knew that the real meaning concealed in these fine words was that he should conduct the prisoner under a strong guard to the women's quarters and confine her there in the tower for seven days, placing about her trustworthy guards who would prevent her escape or frustrate any attempted rescue.

As Tara was departing from the chamber with E-Thas and the guard, O-Tar leaned close to her ear and whispered: "Consider well during these seven days the high honor I have offered you, and—its sole alternative." As though she had not heard him the girl passed out of the banquet hall, her head high and her eyes straight to the front.

After Ghek had left him Gahan roamed the pits and the ancient corridors of the deserted portions of the palace seeking some clue to the whereabouts or the fate of Tara of Helium. He utilized the spiral runway in passing from level to level until he knew every foot of it from the pits to the summit of the high tower, and into what apartments it opened at the various levels as well as the ingenious and hidden mechanism that operated the locks of the cleverly concealed doors leading to it. For food he drew upon the stores he found in the pits and when he slept he lay upon the royal couch of O-Mai in the forbidden chamber sharing the dais with the dead foot of the ancient jeddak.

In the palace about him seethed, all unknown to Gahan, a vast unrest. Warriors and chieftains pursued the duties of their vocations with dour faces, and little knots of them were collecting here and there and with frowns of anger discussing some subject that was uppermost in the minds of all. It was upon the fourth day following Tara's incarceration in the tower that E-Thas, the major-domo of the palace and one of O-Tar's creatures, came to his master upon some trivial errand. O-Tar was alone in one of the smaller chambers of his personal suite when the major-domo was announced, and after the matter upon which E-Thas had come was disposed of the jeddak signed him to remain.

"From the position of an obscure warrior I have elevated you, E-Thas, to the honors of a chief. Within the confines of the palace your word is second only to mine. You are not loved for this, E-Thas, and should another jeddak ascend the throne of Manator what would become of you, whose enemies are among the most powerful of Manator?"

"Speak not of it, O-Tar," begged E-Thas. "These last few days I have thought upon it much and I would forget it; but I have sought to appease the wrath of my worst enemies. I have been very kind and indulgent with them."

"You, too, read the voiceless message in the air?" demanded the jeddak.

E-Thas was palpably uneasy and he did not reply.

"Why did you not come to me with your apprehensions?" demanded O-Tar. "Be this loyalty?"

"I feared, O mighty jeddak!" replied E-Thas. "I feared that you would not understand and that you would be angry."

"What know you? Speak the whole truth!" commanded O-Tar.

"There is much unrest among the chieftains and the warriors," replied E-Thas. "Even those who were your friends fear the power of those who speak against you."

"What say they?" growled the jeddak.

"They say that you are afraid to enter the apartments of O-Mai in search of the slave Turan—oh, do not be angry with me, Jeddak; it is but what they say that I repeat. I, your loyal E-Thas, believe no such foul slander."

"No, no; why should I fear?" demanded O-Tar. "We do not know that he is there. Did not my chiefs go thither and see nothing of him?"

"But they say that you did not go," pursued E-Thas, "and that they will have none of a coward upon the throne of Manator."

"They said that treason?" O-Tar almost shouted.

"They said that and more, great jeddak," answered the major-domo. "They said that not only did you fear to enter the chambers of O-Mai, but that you feared the slave Turan, and they blame you for your treatment of A-Kor, whom they all believe to have been murdered at your command. They were fond of A-Kor and there are many now who say aloud that A-Kor would have made a wondrous jeddak."

"They dare?" screamed O-Tar. "They dare suggest the name of a slave's bastard for the throne of O-Tar!"

"He is your son, O-Tar," E-Thas reminded him, "nor is there a more beloved man in Manator—I but speak to you of facts which may not be ignored, and I dare do so because only when you realize the truth may you seek a cure for the ills that draw about your throne."

O-Tar had slumped down upon his bench—suddenly he looked shrunken and tired and old. "Cursed be the day," he cried, "that saw those three strangers enter the city of Manator. Would that U-Dor had been spared to me. He was strong—my enemies feared him; but he is gone—dead at the hands of that hateful slave, Turan; may the curse of Issus be upon him!"

"My jeddak, what shall we do?" begged E-Thas. "Cursing the slave will not solve your problems."

"But the great feast and the marriage is but three days off," plead O-Tar. "It shall be a great gala occasion. The warriors and the chiefs all know that—it is the custom. Upon that day gifts and honors shall be bestowed. Tell me, who are most bitter against me? I will send you among them and let it be known that I am planning rewards for their past services to the throne. We will make jeds of chiefs and chiefs of warriors, and grant them palaces and slaves. Eh, E-Thas?"

The other shook his head. "It will not do, O-Tar. They will have nothing of your gifts or honors. I have heard them say as much."

"What do they want?" demanded O-Tar.

"They want a jeddak as brave as the bravest," replied E-Thas, though his knees shook as he said it.

"They think I am a coward?" cried the jeddak.

"They say you are afraid to go to the apartments of O-Mai the Cruel."

For a long time O-Tar sat, his head sunk upon his breast, staring blankly at the floor.

"Tell them," he said at last in a hollow voice that sounded not at all like the voice of a great jeddak; "tell them that I will go to the chambers of O-Mai and search for Turan the slave."

XXI

A Risk for Love

y, ey, he is a craven and he called me 'doddering fool'!" The speaker was I-Gos and he addressed a knot of chieftains in one of the chambers of the palace of O-Tar, Jeddak of Manator: "If A-Kor was alive there were a jeddak for us!"

"Who says that A-Kor is dead?" demanded one of the chiefs.

"Where is he then?" asked I-Gos. "Have not others disappeared whom O-Tar thought too well beloved for men so near the throne as they?"

The chief shook his head. "And I thought that, or knew it, rather; I'd join U-Thor at The Gate of Enemies."

"S-s-st," cautioned one; "here comes the licker of feet," and all eyes were turned upon the approaching E-Thas.

"Kaor, friends!" he exclaimed as he stopped among them, but his friendly greeting elicited naught but a few surly nods. "Have you heard the news?" he continued, unabashed by treatment to which he was becoming accustomed.

"What—has O-Tar seen an ulsio and fainted?" demanded I-Gos with broad sarcasm.

"Men have died for less than that, ancient one," E-Thas reminded him.

"I am safe," retorted I-Gos, "for I am not a brave and popular son of the jeddak of Manator."

This was indeed open treason, but E-Thas feigned not to hear it.

He ignored I-Gos and turned to the others. "O-Tar goes to the chamber of O-Mai this night in search of Turan the slave," he said. "He sorrows that his warriors have not the courage for so mean a duty and that their jeddak is thus compelled to arrest a common slave," with which taunt E-Thas passed on to spread the word in other parts of the palace. As a matter of fact the latter part of his message was purely original with himself, and he took great delight in delivering it to the discomfiture of his enemies. As he was leaving the little group of men I-Gos called after him. "At what hour does O-Tar intend visiting the chambers of O-Mai?" he asked.

"Toward the end of the eighth zode," replied the major-domo, and went his way.

"We shall see," stated I-Gos.

"What shall we see?" asked a warrior.

"We shall see whether O-Tar visits the chamber of O-Mai."

"How?"

"I shall be there myself and if I see him I will know that he has been there. If I don't see him I will know that he has not," explained the old taxidermist.

"Is there anything there to fill an honest man with fear?" asked a chieftain. "What have you seen?"

"It was not so much what I saw, though that was bad enough, as what I heard," said I-Gos.

"Tell us! What heard and saw you?"

"I saw the dead O-Mai," said I-Gos. The others shuddered.

"And you went not mad?" they asked.

"Am I mad?" retorted I-Gos.

"And you will go again?"

"Yes."

"Then indeed you are mad," cried one.

"You saw the dead O-Mai; but what heard you that was worse?" whispered another.

"I saw the dead O-Mai lying upon the floor of his sleeping chamber with one foot tangled in the sleeping silks and furs upon his couch. I heard horrid moans and frightful screams."

"And you are not afraid to go there again?" demanded several.

"The dead cannot harm me," said I-Gos. "He has lain thus for five thousand years. Nor can a sound harm me. I heard it once and live—I can hear it again. It came from almost at my side where I hid behind the hangings and watched the slave Turan before I snatched the woman away from him."

"I-Gos, you are a very brave man," said a chieftain.

"O-Tar called me 'doddering fool' and I would face worse dangers than lie in the forbidden chambers of O-Mai to know it if he does not visit the chamber of O-Mai. Then indeed shall O-Tar fall!"

The night came and the zodes dragged and the time approached when O-Tar, Jeddak of Manator, was to visit the chamber of O-Mai in search of the slave Turan. To us, who may doubt the existence of malignant spirits, his fear may seem unbelievable, for he was a strong man, an excellent swordsman, and a warrior of great repute; but the fact remained that O-Tar of Manator was nervous with apprehension as he strode the corridors of his palace toward the deserted halls of O-Mai and when he stood at last with his hand upon the door that opened from the dusty corridor to the very apartments themselves he was almost paralyzed with terror. He had come alone for two very excellent reasons, the first of which was that thus none might note his terror-stricken state nor his defection should he fail at the last moment, and the other was that should he accomplish the thing alone or be able to make his chiefs believe that he had, the credit would be far greater than were he to be accompanied by warriors.

But though he had started alone he had become aware that he was being followed, and he knew that it was because his people had no faith in either his courage or his veracity. He did not believe that he would find the slave Turan. He did not very much want to find him, for though O-Tar was an excellent swordsman and a brave warrior in physical combat, he had seen how Turan had played with U-Dor and he had no stomach for a passage at arms with one whom he knew outclassed him.

And so O-Tar stood with his hand upon the door—afraid to enter; afraid not to. But at last his fear of his own warriors, watching behind him, grew greater than the fear of the unknown behind the ancient door and he pushed the heavy skeel aside and entered.

Silence and gloom and the dust of centuries lay heavy upon the chamber. From his warriors he knew the route that he must take to the horrid chamber of O-Mai and so he forced his unwilling feet across the room before him, across the room where the jetan players sat at their eternal game, and came to the short corridor that led into the room of O-Mai. His naked sword trembled in his grasp. He paused after each forward step to listen and when he was almost at the door of the ghost-haunted chamber, his heart stood still within his breast and the cold sweat broke from the clammy skin of his forehead, for from within there came to his affrighted ears the sound of muffled breathing. Then it was that O-Tar of Manator came near to fleeing from the nameless horror that he could not see, but that he knew lay waiting for him in that chamber just ahead. But again came the fear of the wrath and contempt of his warriors and his chiefs. They would degrade him and they would slay him into the bargain. There was no doubt of what his fate would be should he flee the apartments of O-Mai in terror. His only hope, therefore, lay in daring the unknown in preference to the known.

He moved forward. A few steps took him to the doorway. The chamber before him was darker than the corridor, so that he could just indistinctly make out the objects in the room. He saw a sleeping dais near the center, with a darker blotch of something lying on the marble floor beside it. He moved a step farther into the doorway and the scabbard of his sword scraped against the stone frame. To his horror he saw the sleeping silks and furs upon the central dais move. He saw a figure slowly arising to a sitting posture from the death bed of O-Mai the Cruel. His knees shook, but he gathered all his moral forces, and gripping his sword more tightly in his trembling fingers prepared to leap across the chamber upon the horrid apparition. He hesitated just a moment. He felt eyes upon him—ghoulish eyes that bored through the darkness into his withering heart—eyes that he could not see. He gathered himself for the rush—and then there broke from the thing upon the couch an awful shriek, and O-Tar sank senseless to the floor.

Gahan rose from the couch of O-Mai, smiling, only to swing quickly about with drawn sword as the shadow of a noise impinged upon his keen ears from the shadows behind him. Between the parted hangings he saw a bent and wrinkled figure. It was I-Gos.

"Sheathe your sword, Turan," said the old man. "You have naught to fear from I-Gos."

"What do you here?" demanded Gahan.

"I came to make sure that the great coward did not cheat us. Ey, and he called me 'doddering fool'; but look at him now! Stricken insensible by terror, but, ey, one might forgive him that who had heard your uncanny scream. It all but blasted my own courage. And it was you, then, who moaned and screamed when the chiefs came the day that I stole Tara from you?"

"It was you, then, old scoundrel?" demanded Gahan, moving threateningly toward I-Gos.

"Come, come!" expostulated the old man; "it was I, but then I was your enemy. I would not do it now. Conditions have changed."

"How have they changed? What has changed them?" asked Gahan.

"Then I did not fully realize the cowardice of my jeddak, or the bravery of you and the girl. I am an old man from another age and I love courage. At first I resented the girl's attack upon me, but later I came to see the bravery of it and it won my admiration, as have all her acts. She feared not O-Tar, she feared not me, she feared not all the warriors of Manator. And you! Blood of a million sires! how you fight! I am sorry that I exposed you at The Fields of Jetan. I am sorry that I dragged the girl Tara back to O-Tar. I would make amends. I would be your friend. Here is my sword at your feet," and drawing his weapon I-Gos cast it to the floor in front of Gahan.

The Gatholian knew that scarce the most abandoned of knaves would repudiate this solemn pledge, and so he stooped, and picking up the old man's sword returned it to him, hilt first, in acceptance of his friendship.

"Where is the Princess Tara of Helium?" asked Gahan. "Is she safe?"

"She is confined in the tower of the women's quarters awaiting the ceremony that is to make her Jeddara of Manator," replied I-Gos.

"This thing dared think that Tara of Helium would mate with him?" growled Gahan. "I will make short work of him if he is not already dead from fright," and he stepped toward the fallen O-Tar to run his sword through the jeddak's heart.

"No!" cried I-Gos. "Slay him not and pray that he be not dead if you would save your princess."

"How is that?" asked Gahan.

"If word of O-Tar's death reached the quarters of the women the Princess Tara would be lost. They know O-Tar's intention of taking her to wife and making her Jeddara of Manator, so you may rest assured that they all hate her with the hate of jealous women. Only O-Tar's power protects her now from harm. Should O-Tar die they would turn her over to the warriors and the male slaves, for there would be none to avenge her."

Gahan sheathed his sword. "Your point is well taken; but what shall we do with him?"

"Leave him where he lies," counseled I-Gos. "He is not dead. When he revives he will return to his quarters with a fine tale of his bravery and there will be none to impugn his boasts—none but I-Gos. Come! he may revive at any moment and he must not find us here."

I-Gos crossed to the body of his jeddak, knelt beside it for an instant, and then returned past the couch to Gahan. The two quit the chamber of O-Mai and took their way toward the spiral runway. Here I-Gos led Gahan to a higher level and out upon the roof of that portion of the palace from where he pointed to a high tower quite close by. "There," he said, "lies the Princess of Helium, and quite safe she will be until the time of the ceremony."

"Safe, possibly, from other hands, but not from her own," said Gahan. "She will never become Jeddara of Manator—first will she destroy herself."

"She would do that?" asked I-Gos.

"She will, unless you can get word to her that I still live and that there is yet hope," replied Gahan.

"I cannot get word to her," said I-Gos. "The quarters of his women O-Tar guards with jealous hand. Here are his most trusted slaves and warriors, yet even so, thick among them are countless spies, so that no man knows which be which. No shadow falls within those chambers that is not marked by a hundred eyes."

Gahan stood gazing at the lighted windows of the high tower in the upper chambers of which Tara of Helium was confined. "I will find a way, I-Gos," he said.

"There is no way," replied the old man.

For sometime they stood upon the roof beneath the brilliant stars and hurtling moons of dying Mars, laying their plans against the time that Tara of Helium should be brought from the high tower to the throne room of O-Tar. It was then, and then alone, argued I-Gos, that any hope of rescuing her might be entertained. Just how far he might trust the other Gahan did not know, and so he kept to himself the knowledge of the plan that he had forwarded to Floran and Val Dor by Ghek, but he assured the ancient taxidermist that if he were sincere in his oft-repeated declaration that O-Tar should be denounced and superseded he would have his opportunity on the night that the jeddak sought to wed the Heliumetic princess.

"Your time shall come then, I-Gos," Gahan assured the other, "and if you have any party that thinks as you do, prepare them for the eventuality that will succeed O-Tar's presumptuous attempt to wed the daughter of The Warlord. Where shall I see you again, and when? I go now to speak with Tara, Princess of Helium."

"I like your boldness," said I-Gos; "but it will avail you naught. You will not speak with Tara, Princess of Helium, though doubtless the blood of many Manatorians will drench the floors of the women's quarters before you are slain."

Gahan smiled. "I shall not be slain. Where and when shall we meet? But you may find me in O-Mai's chamber at night. That seems the safest retreat in all Manator for an enemy of the jeddak in whose palace it lies. I go!"

"And may the spirits of your ancestors surround you," said I-Gos.

After the old man had left him Gahan made his way across the roof to the high tower, which appeared to have been constructed of concrete and afterward elaborately carved, its entire surface being covered with intricate designs cut deep into the stone-like material of which it was composed. Though wrought ages since, it was but little weather-worn owing to the aridity of the Martian atmosphere, the infrequency of rains, and the rarity of dust storms. To scale it, though, presented difficulties and danger that might have deterred the bravest of men—that would, doubtless, have deterred Gahan, had he not felt that the life of the woman he loved depended upon his accomplishing the hazardous feat.

Removing his sandals and laying aside all of his harness and weapons other than a single belt supporting a dagger, the Gatholian essayed the dangerous ascent. Clinging to the carvings with hands and feet he worked himself slowly aloft, avoiding the windows and keeping upon the shadowy side of the tower, away from the light of Thuria and Cluros. The tower rose some fifty feet above the roof of the adjacent part of the palace, comprising five levels or floors with windows looking in every direction. A few of the windows were balconied, and these more than the others he sought to avoid, although, it being now near the close of the ninth zode, there was little likelihood that many were awake within the tower.

His progress was noiseless and he came at last, undetected, to the windows of the upper level. These, like several of the others he had passed at lower levels, were heavily barred, so that there was no possibility of his gaining ingress to the apartment where Tara was confined. Darkness hid the interior behind the first window that he approached. The second opened upon a lighted chamber where he could see a guard sleeping at his post outside a door. Here also was the top of the runway leading to the next level below. Passing still farther around the tower Gahan approached another window, but now he clung to that side of the tower which ended in a courtyard a hundred feet below and in a short time the light of Thuria would reach him. He realized that he must hasten and he prayed that behind the window he now approached he would find Tara of Helium.

Coming to the opening he looked in upon a small chamber dimly lighted. In the center was a sleeping dais upon which a human form lay beneath silks and furs. A bare arm, protruding from the coverings, lay exposed against a black and yellow striped orluk skin—an arm of wondrous beauty about which was clasped an armlet that Gahan knew. No other creature was visible within the chamber, all of which was exposed to Gahan's view. Pressing his face to the bars the Gatholian whispered her dear name. The girl stirred, but did not awaken. Again he called, but this time louder. Tara sat up and looked about and at the same instant a huge eunuch leaped to his feet from where he had been lying on the floor close by that side of the dais farthest from Gahan. Simultaneously the brilliant light of Thuria flashed full upon the window where Gahan clung silhouetting him plainly to the two within.

Both sprang to their feet. The eunuch drew his sword and leaped for the window where the helpless Gahan would have fallen an easy victim to a single thrust of the murderous weapon the fellow bore, had not Tara of Helium leaped upon her guard dragging him back. At the same time she drew the slim dagger from its hiding place in her harness and even as the eunuch sought to hurl her aside its keen point found his heart. Without a sound he died and lunged forward to the floor. Then Tara ran to the window.

"Turan, my chief!" she cried. "What awful risk is this you take to seek me here, where even your brave heart is powerless to aid me."

"Be not so sure of that, heart of my heart," he replied. "While I bring but words to my love, they be the forerunner of deeds, I hope, that will give her back to me forever. I feared that you might destroy yourself, Tara of Helium, to escape the dishonor that O-Tar would do you, and so I came to give you new hope and to beg that you live for me through whatever may transpire, in the knowledge that there is yet a way and that if all goes well we shall be freed at last. Look for me in the throne room of O-Tar the night that he would wed you. And now, how may we dispose of this fellow?" He pointed to the dead eunuch upon the floor.

"We need not concern ourselves about that," she replied. "None dares harm me for fear of the wrath of O-Tar—otherwise I should have been dead so soon as ever I entered this portion of the palace, for the women hate me. O-Tar alone may punish me, and what cares

O-Tar for the life of a eunuch? No, fear not upon this score."

Their hands were clasped between the bars and now Gahan drew her nearer to him.

"One kiss," he said, "before I go, my princess," and the proud daughter of Dejah Thoris, Princess of Helium, and The Warlord of Barsoom whispered: "My chieftain!" and pressed her lips to the lips of Turan, the common panthan.

XXII

At the Moment of Marriage

he silence of the tomb lay heavy about him as O-Tar, Jeddak of Manator, opened his eyes in the chamber of O-Mai. Recollection of the frightful apparition that had confronted him swept to his consciousness. He listened, but heard naught. Within the range of his vision there was nothing apparent that might cause alarm. Slowly he lifted his head and looked about. Upon the floor beside the couch lay the thing that had at first attracted his attention and his eyes closed in terror as he recognized it for what it was; but it moved not, nor spoke. O-Tar opened his eyes again and rose to his feet. He was trembling in every limb. There was nothing on the dais from which he had seen the thing arise.

O-Tar backed slowly from the room. At last he gained the outer corridor. It was empty. He did not know that it had emptied rapidly as the loud scream with which his own had mingled had broken upon the startled ears of the warriors who had been sent to spy upon him. He looked at the timepiece set in a massive bracelet upon his left forearm. The ninth zode was nearly half gone. O-Tar had lain for an hour unconscious. He had spent an hour in the chamber of O-Mai and he was not dead! He had looked upon the face of his predecessor and was still sane! He shook himself and smiled. Rapidly he subdued his rebelliously shaking nerves, so that by the time he reached the tenanted portion of the palace he had gained control of himself. He walked with chin high and something of a swagger. To the banquet hall he went, knowing that his chiefs awaited him there and as he entered they arose and upon the faces of many were incredulity and amaze, for they had not thought to see O-Tar the jeddak again after what the spies had told them of the horrid sounds issuing from the chamber of O-Mai. Thankful was O-Tar that he had gone alone to that chamber of fright, for now no one could deny the tale that he should tell.

E-Thas rushed forward to greet him, for E-Thas had seen black looks directed toward him as the tals slipped by and his benefactor failed to return.

"O brave and glorious jeddak!" cried the major-domo. "We rejoice at your safe return and beg of you the story of your adventure."

"It was naught," exclaimed O-Tar. "I searched the chambers carefully and waited in hiding for the return of the slave, Turan, if he were temporarily away; but he came not. He is not there and I doubt if he ever goes there. Few men would choose to remain long in such a dismal place."

"You were not attacked?" asked E-Thas. "You heard no screams, nor moans?"

"I heard hideous noises and saw phantom figures; but they fled before me so that never could I lay hold of one, and I looked upon the face of O-Mai and I am not mad. I even rested in the chamber beside his corpse."

In a far corner of the room a bent and wrinkled old man hid a smile behind a golden goblet of strong brew.

"Come! Let us drink!" cried O-Tar and reached for the dagger, the pommel of which he was accustomed to use to strike the gong which summoned slaves, but the dagger was not in its scabbard. O-Tar was puzzled. He knew that it had been there just before he entered the chamber of O-Mai, for he had carefully felt of all his weapons to make sure that none was missing. He seized instead a table utensil and struck the gong, and when the slaves came bade them bring the strongest brew for O-Tar and his chiefs. Before the dawn broke many were the expressions of admiration bellowed from drunken lips—admiration for the courage of their jeddak; but some there were who still looked glum.

Came at last the day that O-Tar would take the Princess Tara of Helium to wife. For hours slaves prepared the unwilling bride. Seven perfumed baths occupied three long and weary hours, then her whole body was anointed with the oil of pimalia blossoms and massaged by the deft fingers of a slave from distant Dusar. Her harness, all new and wrought for the occasion was of the white hide of the great white apes of Barsoom, hung heavily with platinum and diamonds—fairly encrusted with them. The glossy mass of her jet hair had been built into a coiffure of stately and becoming grandeur, into which diamond-headed pins were stuck until the whole scintillated as the stars in heaven upon a moonless night.

But it was a sullen and defiant bride that they led from the high tower toward the throne room of O-Tar. The corridors were filled with slaves and warriors, and the women of the palace and the city who had been commanded to attend the ceremony. All the power and pride, wealth and beauty of Manator were there.

Slowly Tara, surrounded by a heavy guard of honor, moved along the marble corridors filled with people. At the entrance to The Hall of Chiefs E-Thas, the major-domo, received her. The Hall was empty except for its ranks of dead chieftains upon their dead mounts. Through this long chamber E-Thas escorted her to the throne room which also was empty, the marriage ceremony in Manator differing from that of other countries of Barsoom. Here the bride would await the groom at the foot of the steps leading to the throne. The guests followed her in and took their places, leaving the central aisle from The Hall of Chiefs to the throne clear, for up this O-Tar would approach his bride alone after a short solitary communion with the dead behind closed doors in The Hall of Chiefs. It was the custom.

The guests had all filed through The Hall of Chiefs; the doors at both ends had been closed. Presently those at the lower end of the hall opened and O-Tar entered. His black harness was ornamented with rubies and gold; his face was covered by a grotesque mask of the precious metal in which two enormous rubies were set for eyes, though below them were narrow slits through which the wearer could see. His crown was a fillet supporting carved feathers of the same metal as the mask. To the least detail his regalia was that demanded of a royal bridegroom by the customs of Manator, and now in accordance with that same custom he came alone to The Hall of Chiefs to receive the blessings and the council of the great ones of Manator who had preceded him.

As the doors at the lower end of the Hall closed behind him O-Tar the Jeddak stood alone with the great dead. By the dictates of ages no mortal eye might look upon the scene enacted within that sacred chamber. As the mighty of Manator respected the traditions of Manator, let us, too, respect those traditions of a proud and sensitive people. Of what concern to us the happenings in that solemn chamber of the dead?

Five minutes passed. The bride stood silently at the foot of the throne. The guests spoke together in low whispers until the room was filled with the hum of many voices. At length the doors leading into The Hall of Chiefs swung open, and the resplendent bridegroom stood framed for a moment in the massive opening. A hush fell upon the wedding guests. With measured and impressive step the groom approached the bride. Tara felt the muscles of her heart contract with the apprehension that had been growing upon her as the coils of Fate settled more closely about her and no sign came from Turan. Where was he? What, indeed, could he accomplish now to save her? Surrounded by the power of O-Tar with never a friend among them, her position seemed at last without vestige of hope.

"I still live!" she whispered inwardly in a last brave attempt to combat the terrible hopelessness that was overwhelming her, but her fingers stole for reassurance to the slim blade that she had managed to transfer, undetected, from her old harness to the new. And now the groom was at her side and taking her hand was leading her up the steps to the throne, before which they halted and stood facing the gathering below. Came then, from the back of the room a procession headed by the high dignitary whose office it was to make these two man and wife, and directly behind him a richly-clad youth bearing a silken pillow on which lay the golden handcuffs connected by a short length of chain-of-gold with which the ceremony would be concluded when the dignitary clasped a handcuff about the wrist of each symbolizing their indissoluble union in the holy bonds of wedlock.

Would Turan's promised succor come too late? Tara listened to the long, monotonous intonation of the wedding service. She heard the virtues of O-Tar extolled and the beauties of the bride. The moment was approaching and still no sign of Turan. But what could he accomplish should he succeed in reaching the throne room, other than to die with her? There could be no hope of rescue.

The dignitary lifted the golden handcuffs from the pillow upon which they reposed. He blessed them and reached for Tara's wrist. The time had come! The thing could go no further, for alive or dead, by all the laws of Barsoom she would be the wife of O-Tar of Manator the instant the two were locked together. Even should rescue come then or later she could never dissolve those bonds and Turan would be lost to her as surely as though death separated them.

Her hand stole toward the hidden blade, but instantly the hand of the groom shot out and seized her wrist. He had guessed her intention. Through the slits in the grotesque mask she could see his eyes upon her and she guessed the sardonic smile that the mask hid. For a tense moment the two stood thus. The people below them kept breathless silence for the play before the throne had not passed un-noticed.

Dramatic as was the moment it was suddenly rendered trebly so by the noisy opening of the doors leading to The Hall of Chiefs. All eyes turned in the direction of the interruption to see another figure framed in the massive opening—a half-clad figure buckling the half-adjusted harness hurriedly in place—the figure of O-Tar, Jeddak of Manator.

"Stop!" he screamed, springing forward along the aisle toward the throne. "Seize the impostor!"

All eyes shot to the figure of the groom before the throne. They saw him raise his hand and snatch off the golden mask, and Tara of Helium in wide-eyed incredulity looked up into the face of Turan the panthan.

"Turan the slave," they cried then. "Death to him! Death to him!"

"Wait!" shouted Turan, drawing his sword, as a dozen warriors leaped forward.

"Wait!" screamed another voice, old and cracked, as I-Gos, the ancient taxidermist, sprang from among the guests and reached the throne steps ahead of the foremost warriors.

At sight of the old man the warriors paused, for age is held in great veneration among the peoples of Barsoom, as is true, perhaps, of all peoples whose religion is based to any extent upon ancestor worship. But O-Tar gave no heed to him, leaping instead swiftly toward the throne. "Stop, coward!" cried I-Gos.

The people looked at the little old man in amazement. "Men of Manator," he cackled in his thin, shrill voice, "wouldst be ruled by a coward and a liar?"

"Down with him!" shouted O-Tar.

"Not until I have spoken," retorted I-Gos. "It is my right. If I fail my life is forfeit—that you all know and I know. I demand therefore to be heard. It is my right!"

"It is his right," echoed the voices of a score of warriors in various parts of the chamber.

"That O-Tar is a coward and a liar I can prove," continued I-Gos. "He said that he faced bravely the horrors of the chamber of O-Mai and saw nothing of the slave Turan. I was there, hiding behind the hangings, and I saw all that transpired. Turan had been hiding in the chamber and was even then lying upon the couch of O-Mai when O-Tar, trembling with fear, entered the room. Turan, disturbed, arose to a sitting position at the same time voicing a piercing shriek. O-Tar screamed and swooned."

"It is a lie! "cried O-Tar.

"It is *not* a lie and I can prove it," retorted I-Gos. "Didst notice the night that he returned from the chambers of O-Mai and was boasting of his exploit, that when he would summon slaves to bring wine he reached for his dagger to strike the gong with its pommel as is always his custom? Didst note that, any of you? And that he had no dagger? O-Tar, where is the dagger that you carried into the chamber of O-Mai? You do not know; but I know. While you lay in the swoon of terror I took it from your harness and hid it among the sleeping silks upon the couch of O-Mai. There it is even now, and if any doubt it let them go thither and there they will find it and know the cowardice of their jeddak."

"But what of this impostor?" demanded one. "Shall he stand with impunity upon the throne of Manator whilst we squabble about our ruler?"

"It is through his bravery that you have learned the cowardice of O-Tar," replied I-Gos, "and through him you will be given a greater jeddak."

"We will choose our own jeddak. Seize and slay the slave!" There were cries of approval from all parts of the room. Gahan was listening intently, as though for some hoped-for sound. He saw the warriors approaching the dais, where he now stood with drawn sword and with one arm about Tara of Helium. He wondered if his plans had miscarried after all. If they had it would mean death for him, and he knew that Tara would take her life if he fell. Had he, then, served her so futilely after all his efforts?

Several warriors were urging the necessity for sending at once to the chamber of O-Mai to search for the dagger that would prove, if found, the cowardice of O-Tar. At last three consented to go. "You need not fear," I-Gos assured them. "There is naught there to harm you. I have been there often of late and Turan the slave has slept there for these many nights. The screams and moans that frightened you and O-Tar were voiced by Turan to drive you away from his hiding place." Shamefacedly the three left the apartment to search for O-Tar's dagger.

And now the others turned their attention once more to Gahan. They approached the throne with bared swords, but they came slowly for they had seen this slave upon the Field of Jetan and they knew the prowess of his arm. They had reached the foot of the steps when from far above there sounded a deep boom, and another, and another, and Turan smiled and breathed a sigh of relief. Perhaps, after all, it had not come too late. The warriors stopped and listened as did the others in the chamber. Now there broke upon their ears a loud rattle of musketry and it all came from above as though men were fighting upon the roofs of the palace.

"What is it?" they demanded, one of the other.

"A great storm has broken over Manator," said one.

"Mind not the storm until you have slain the creature who dares stand upon the throne of your jeddak," demanded O-Tar. "Seize him!"

Even as he ceased speaking the arras behind the throne parted and a warrior stepped forth upon the dais. An exclamation of surprise and dismay broke from the lips of the warriors of O-Tar. "U-Thor!" they cried. "What treason is this?"

"It is no treason," said U-Thor in his deep voice. "I bring you a new jeddak for all of Manator. No lying poltroon, but a courageous man whom you all love."

He stepped aside then and another emerged from the corridor hidden by the arras. It was A-Kor, and at sight of him there rose exclamations of surprise, of pleasure, and of anger, as the various factions recognized the coup d'etat that had been arranged so cunningly. Behind A-Kor came other warriors until the dais was crowded with them—all men of Manator from the city of Manatos.

O-Tar was exhorting his warriors to attack, when a bloody and disheveled padwar burst into the chamber through a side entrance. "The city has fallen!" he cried aloud. "The hordes of Manatos pour through The Gate of Enemies. The slaves from Gathol have arisen and destroyed the palace guards. Great ships are landing warriors upon the palace roof and in the Fields of Jetan. The men of Helium and Gathol are marching through Manator. They cry aloud for the Princess of Helium and swear to leave Manator a blazing funeral pyre consuming the bodies of all our people. The skies are black with ships. They come in great processions from the east and from the south."

And then once more the doors from The Hall of Chiefs swung wide and the men of Manator turned to see another figure standing upon the threshold—a mighty figure of a man with white skin, and black hair, and gray eyes that glittered now like points of steel and behind him The Hall of Chiefs was filled with fighting men wearing the harness of far countries. Tara of Helium saw him and her heart leaped in exultation, for it was John Carter, Warlord of Barsoom, come at the head of a victorious host to the rescue of his daughter, and at his side was Djor Kantos to whom she had been betrothed.

The Warlord eyed the assemblage for a moment before he spoke. "Lay down your arms, men of Manator," he said. "I see my daughter and that she lives, and if no harm has befallen her no blood need be shed. Your city is filled with the fighting men of U-Thor, and those from Gathol and from Helium. The palace is in the hands of the slaves from Gathol, beside a thousand of my own warriors who fill the halls and chambers surrounding this room. The fate of your jeddak lies in your own hands. I have no wish to interfere. I come only for my daughter and to free the slaves from Gathol. I have spoken!" and without waiting for a reply and as though the room had been filled with his own people rather than a hostile band he strode up the broad main aisle toward Tara of Helium.

The chiefs of Manator were stunned. They looked to O-Tar; but he could only gaze helplessly about him as the enemy entered from The Hall of Chiefs and circled the throne room until they had surrounded the entire company. And then a dwar of the army of Helium entered.

"We have captured three chiefs," he reported to The Warlord, "who beg that they be permitted to enter the throne room and report to their fellows some matter which they say will decide the fate of Manator."

"Fetch them," ordered The Warlord.

They came, heavily guarded, to the foot of the steps leading to the throne and there they stopped and the leader turned toward the others of Manator and raising high his right hand displayed a jeweled dagger. "We found it," he said, "even where I-Gos said that we would find it," and he looked menacingly upon O-Tar.

"A-Kor, jeddak of Manator!" cried a voice, and the cry was taken up by a hundred hoarse-throated warriors.

"There can be but one jeddak in Manator," said the chief who held the dagger; his eyes still fixed upon the hapless O-Tar he crossed to where the latter stood and holding the dagger upon an outstretched palm proffered it to the discredited ruler. "There can be but one jeddak in Manator," he repeated meaningly.

O-Tar took the proffered blade and drawing himself to his full height plunged it to the guard into his breast, in that single act redeeming himself in the esteem of his people and winning an eternal place in The Hall of Chiefs.

As he fell all was silence in the great room, to be broken presently by the voice of U-Thor. "O-Tar is dead!" he cried. "Let A-Kor rule until the chiefs of all Manator may be summoned to choose a new jeddak. What is your answer?"

"Let A-Kor rule! A-Kor, Jeddak of Manator!" The cries filled the room and there was no dissenting voice.

A-Kor raised his sword for silence. "It is the will of A-Kor," he said, "and that of the Great Jed of Manatos, and the commander of the fleet from Gathol, and of the illustrious John Carter, Warlord of Barsoom, that peace lie upon the city of Manator and so I decree that the men of Manator go forth and welcome the fighting men of these our allies as guests and friends and show them the wonders of our ancient city and the hospitality of Manator. I have spoken." And U-Thor and John Carter dismissed their warriors and bade them accept the hospitality of Manator. As the room emptied Djor Kantos reached the side of Tara of Helium. The girl's happiness at rescue had been blighted by sight of this man whom her virtuous heart told her she had wronged. She dreaded the ordeal that lay before her and the dishonor that she must admit before she could hope to be freed from the understanding that had for long existed between them. And now Djor Kantos approached and kneeling raised her fingers to his lips.

"Beautiful daughter of Helium," he said, "how may I tell you the thing that I must tell you—of the dishonor that I have all unwittingly done you? I can but throw myself upon your generosity for forgiveness; but if you demand it I can receive the dagger as honorably as did O-Tar."

"What do you mean?" asked Tara of Helium. "What are you talking about—why speak thus in riddles to one whose heart is already breaking?"

Her heart already breaking! The outlook was anything but promising, and the young padwar wished that he had died before ever he had had to speak the words he now must speak.

"Tara of Helium," he continued, "we all thought you dead. For a long year have you been gone from Helium. I mourned you truly and then, less than a moon since, I wed with Olvia Marthis." He stopped and looked at her with eyes that might have said: "Now, strike me dead!"

"Oh, foolish man!" cried Tara. "Nothing you could have done could have pleased me more. Djor Kantos, I could kiss you!"

"I do not think that Olvia Marthis would mind," he said, his face now wreathed with smiles. As they spoke a body of men had entered the throne room and approached the dais. They were tall men trapped in plain harness, absolutely without ornamentation. Just as their leader reached the dais Tara had turned to Gahan, motioning him to join them.

"Djor Kantos," she said, "I bring you Turan the panthan, whose loyalty and bravery have won my love."

John Carter and the leader of the new come warriors, who were standing near, looked quickly at the little group. The former smiled an inscrutable smile, the latter addressed the Princess of Helium. "Turan the panthan!" he cried. "Know you not, fair daughter of Helium, that this man you call panthan is Gahan, Jed of Gathol?"

For just a moment Tara of Helium looked her surprise; and then she shrugged her beautiful shoulders as she turned her head to cast her eyes over one of them at Gahan of Gathol.

"Jed or panthan," she said; "what difference does it make what one's slave has been?" and she laughed roguishly into the smiling face of her lover.

His story finished, John Carter rose from the chair opposite me, stretching his giant frame like some great forest-bred lion.

"You must go?" I cried, for I hated to see him leave and it seemed that he had been with me but a moment.

"The sky is already red beyond those beautiful hills of yours," he replied, "and it will soon be day."

"Just one question before you go," I begged.

"Well?" he assented, good-naturedly.

"How was Gahan able to enter the throne room garbed in O-Tar's trappings?" I asked.

"It was simple—for Gahan of Gathol," replied The Warlord. "With the assistance of I-Gos he crept into The Hall of Chiefs before the ceremony, while the throne room and Hall of Chiefs were vacated to receive the bride. He came from the pits through the corridor that opened behind the arras at the rear of the throne, and passing into The Hall of Chiefs took his place upon the back of a riderless thoat, whose warrior was in I-Gos' repair room. When O-Tar entered and came near him Gahan fell upon him and struck him with the butt of a heavy spear. He thought that he had killed him and was surprised when O-Tar appeared to denounce him."

"And Ghek? What became of Ghek?" I insisted.

"After leading Val Dor and Floran to Tara's disabled flier which they repaired, he accompanied them to Gathol from where a message was sent to me in Helium. He then led a large party including A-Kor and U-Thor from the roof, where our ships landed them, down a spiral runway into the palace and guided them to the throne room. We took him back to Helium with us, where he still lives, with his single rykor which we found all but starved to death in the pits of Manator. But come! No more questions now."

I accompanied him to the east arcade where the red dawn was glowing beyond the arches.

"Goodbye!" he said.

"I can scarce believe that it is really you," I exclaimed. "Tomorrow I will be sure that I have dreamed all this."

He laughed and drawing his sword scratched a rude cross upon the concrete of one of the arches.

"If you are in doubt tomorrow," he said, "come and see if you dreamed this."

A moment later he was gone.

Appendix

Jetan or Martian Chess

For those who care for such things, and would like to try the game, I give the rules of Jetan as they were given me by John Carter. By writing the names and moves of the various pieces on bits of paper and pasting them on ordinary checker-men the game may be played quite as well as with the ornate pieces used upon Mars.

THE BOARD: Square board consisting of one hundred alternate black and orange squares.

THE PIECES: In order, as they stand upon the board in the first row, from left to right of each player.

Warrior: 2 feathers; 2 spaces straight in any direction or combination.

Padwar: 2 feathers; 2 spaces diagonal in any direction or combination.

Dwar: 3 feathers; 3 spaces straight in any direction or combination.

Flier: 3 bladed propellor; 3 spaces diagonal in any direction or combination; and may jump intervening pieces.

Chief: Diadem with ten jewels; 3 spaces in any direction; straight or diagonal or combination.

Princess: Diadem with one jewel: same as Chief, except may jump intervening pieces.

Flier: See above.

Dwar: See above.

Padwar: See above.

Warrior: See above.

And in the second row from left to right:

Thoat: Mounted warrior 2 feathers; 2 spaces, one straight and one diagonal in any direction.

Panthans: (8 of them): 1 feather; 1 space, forward, side, or diagonal, but not backward.

Thoat: See above.

The game is played with twenty black pieces by one player and twenty orange by his opponent, and is presumed to have originally represented a battle between the Black race of the south and the Yellow race of the north. On Mars the board is usually arranged so that the Black pieces are played from the south and the Orange from the north.

The game is won when any piece is placed on the same square with the opponent's Princess, or a Chief takes a Chief.

The game is drawn when either Chief is taken by a piece other than the opposing Chief, or when both sides are reduced to three pieces, or less, of equal value and the game is not won in the ensuing ten moves, five apiece.

The Princess may not move onto a threatened square, nor may she take an opposing piece. She is entitled to one ten-space move at any time during the game. This move is called the escape.

Two pieces may not occupy the same square except in the final move of a game where the Princess is taken.

When a player, moving properly and in order, places one of his pieces upon a square occupied by an opponent piece, the opponent piece is considered to have been killed and is removed from the game.

The moves explained. Straight moves mean due north, south, east, or west; diagonal moves mean northeast, southeast, southwest, or northwest. A Dwar might move straight north three spaces, or north one space and east two spaces, or any similar combination of straight moves, so long as he did not cross the same square twice in a single move. This example explains combination moves.

The first move may be decided in any way that is agreeable to both players; after the first game the winner of the preceding game moves first if he chooses, or may instruct his opponent to make the first move.

Gambling: The Martians gamble at Jetan in several ways. Of course the outcome of the game indicates to whom the main stake belongs; but they also put a price upon the head of each piece, according to its value, and for each piece that a player loses he pays its value to his opponent.

GLOSSARY

Comprising people, places, and things referenced in the first five novels of the John Carter of Mars series: A Princess of Mars, The Gods of Mars, The Warlord of Mars, Thuvia, Maid of Mars, *and* The Chessmen of Mars.

PEOPLE *and* TITLES

A-Kor: Prince of Manator; son of O-Tar and Haja of Gathol; dwar of the Towers of Jetan and later Jeddak.

A-Sor: Tasor's name in Manator.

Astok: Prince of Dusar.

Bar Comas: Jeddak of Warhoon.

Black Pirates: The First Born of Barsoom. They are more than six-feet tall with handsome features and dark, ebony skin.

Carthoris: John Carter's son by Dejah Thoris; Prince of Helium.

Dak Kova: A Warhoon Jed who later becomes Jeddak.

Dator: Title bestowed on a Black Pirate prince or chief.

Dejah Thoris: Daughter of Mors Kajak; Princess of Helium; wife of John Carter; mother of Carthoris and Tara of Helium.

Djor Kantos: Son of Kantos Kan; padwar in the Fifth Utan.

Dotar Sojat: John Carter's Tharkish name, from the names of the first two warriors he killed. (See *John Carter*.)

Dwar: Captain.

E-Med: A Manator warrior who becomes dwar of the Towers of Jetan after A-Kor.

E-Thas: Major-domo of the palace of Manator.

Father of Therns: Title of the High Priest and ruler of the Therns; also known as Hekkador.

First Born: The Black Pirates.

Floran: A Gatholian warrior enslaved in Manator.

Gahan: Jed of Gathol; Husband of Tara of Helium.

Ghek: A kaldane; the third foreman of the fields of Luud.

Gozava: Wife of Tars Tarkas who was killed by order of Tal Hajus.

Green Men (Martians): Six-limbed, fifteen-foot tall nomads. Enemy to all other Martian races.

Gur Tus: An officer in the Helium navy; dwar of the Tenth Utan.

Haja: Princess of Gathol who was enslaved in Manator; mother or A-Kor.

Hal Vas: Son of Vas Kor the Dusarian noble.

Hekkador: Title of the High Priest and king of Therns. (See *Father of Therns*.)

Holy Therns: Members of the primary religious cult of Barsoom.

Hortan Gur: Jeddak of Torquas.

Hor Vastus: A padwar in the Helium navy.

I-Gos: A taxidermist in Manator.

I-Mal: Dead chief of Manator.

I-Zav: A warrior of Manator

Issus: Goddess of Life Eternal and Death. Her temple is on the banks of the Lost Sea of Korus.

James K. Powell: John Carter's companion while prospecting in Arizona. Killed by Apache Indians.

Jav: A Lotharian.

Jed: Prince or king.

Jeddak: Emperor.

Jeddara: Empress.

John Carter: A human from post-Civil War U.S. who is transported to Mars where he becomes Prince of Helium, Warlord of Mars, and eventually, Jeddak of Jeddaks.

John A. Shea: Edgar Rice Burroughs's secretary.

Kab Kadja: Jeddak of the Warhoons of the South.

Kadar: Guard.

Kaldanes: Beings that resemble human heads with six spiderlike legs and two stout chelae that grow in front of the legs.

Kantos Kan: An officer in the Helium navy.

Kar Komak: Odwar of the bowmen of Lothar.

Kulan Tith: Jeddak of Kaol.

Lakor: A Holy Thern in the guard of Matai Shang.

Lan-O: A slave girl of Manator; Princess of Gathol.

Larok: A warrior of Dusar.

Lorquas Ptomel: A Jed among the Tharks.

Luud: A Kaldanes community.

Matai Shang: The Father of Therns.

Moak: A Kaldanes community.

Mors Kajak: Crown Prince of Helium, Jed of Lesser Helium, and father of Dejah Thoris.

Ninth Cycle: A Thern that's one rank below the Holy Therns.

Nolach: A Kaldanes community; also a Kaldanes leader.

Notan: The Royal Psychologist of Zodanga.

Nutus: The Jeddak of Dusar.

Odwar: A commander or general.

Olvia Marthis: Daughter of the Jed of Hastor.

O-Mai the Cruel: Jeddak of Manator 5,000 years ago.

O-Tar: Jeddak of Manator.

O-Zar: A warrior from Manataj.

Padwar: Lieutenant.

Panthan: A soldier of fortune.

Parthak: A Zodangan who brought food to John Carter in the pits of Zat Arrras.

Phaidor: Daughter of Matai Shang.

Plant Men: A manlike race that inhabits the Valley of Dor. They are around twelve feet tall with arms resembling elephant trunks, a single eye, a long tail, hairless bodies, and thick black hair (that writhes) on their heads.

Ptor: Family name of three Zodangan brothers.

Red Men: The dominant, human-like race on Mars. Their skin is reddish copper.

Sab Than: Prince of Zodanga.

Salensus Oll: Jeddak of Okar.

San Tothis: An officer of Gathol.

Saran Tal: Carthoris's major-domo.

Sarkoja: An older Thark woman who was one of Tars Tarkas's attendants.

Sator Throg: A Holy Thern of the Tenth Cycle.

Sept: A Kaldane of Luud.

Sola: Daughter of Tars Tarkas.

Solan: A master swordsman and operator of the great magnet in Kadabra.

Sorav: Commander of Salensus Oll's palace force.

Sovan: Prince of the Ptarth navy.

Tal Hajus: Jeddak of Thark; killed by Tars Tarkas.

Talu: Rebel prince of Marentina and nephew of Salensus Oll; Jeddak of Okar; later Jeddak of Jeddaks of the North.

Tan Gama: A Warhoon warrior.

Tanus: Warrior of Gathol.

Tara of Helium: Daughter of John Carter and Dejah; wife of Gahan.

Tardos Mors: Jeddak of Helium; grandfather of Dejah Thoris.

Tario: Jeddak of Lothar.

Tars Tarkas: A Thark warrior; later Jeddak of Thark.

Tasor: A noble of Gathol, known as A-Sor in Manator.

Tenth Cycle: A rank among the Holy Therns.

Thabis: Issus's chief.

Than Kosis: Jeddak of Zodanga.

Thar Ban: A Jed among the hordes of Torquas.

Tharks: The green men of Thark.

Therns: The remnant of the white race at the South Pole. They are priests who are bald from birth and wear auburn wigs.

Thorian: Chief of the lesser Therns.

Thurds: Green men; enemies to Torquas.

Thurid: A Black Pirate dator.

Thuvan Dihn: Jeddak of Ptarth; father of Thuvia.

Thuvia: Princess of Ptarth; daughter of Thuvan Dihn; wife of Carthoris.

Torith: An officer among the Black Pirates; guard at the submarine pool in Omean.

Torkar Bar: Dwar of the Kaolian Road.

Turan: Gahan's alias.

Turjun: Carthoris of Helium's alias.

U-Dor: Dwar of the 8th Utan of O-Tar; Jeddak of Manator.

U-Kal: Gahan's alias in Manator.

Uncle Ben: The author's African-American servant; also known as Old Ben.

Uthia: Tara of Helium's slave girl.

U-Thor: Jed of Manatos.

U-Van: Warrior of Manator.

Val Dor: Warrior of Helium; enslaved in Manator.

Vas Kor: A noble of Dusar.

Warhoon: The green men in the southern hemisphere.

Xodar: A dator among the Black Pirates; later Jeddak of the First Born of the Valley of Dor.

Yersted: Commander of the Black Pirates' submarine.

Zad: A Thark warrior.

Zat Arras: Jed of Zodanga.

Zithad: A Black pirate; dator of the Guards of Issus.

GLOSSARY

PLACES

Aaanthor: A dead city of ancient Mars.

Atmosphere Plant: A huge building that is the source of the artificial atmosphere of Mars.

Avenue of Ancestors: A street in Helium that leads from the Gate of Jeddaks to the Temple of Reward.

Avenue of Gates: The street that circles Manator just inside the outer wall.

Avenue of Quays: A street in Aaanthor.

Barsoom: Mars.

Carrion Caves: A series of caverns connecting the cities of the north pole with the outside world.

Cluros (Deimos): The further moon.

Dusar: Martian kingdom of red men.

Fields of Jetan: A court in Manator that's laid out like a Jetan board.

Garden of the Jeddaks: A garden in the inner courtyard of the Palace of Kadabra.

Gate of Enemies: A gate in Manator.

Gate of Jeddaks: A gate in Helium.

Gathol: The nation of red men. Known for its ancient and seemingly inexhaustible diamond mines.

Golden Cliffs: The cliffs surrounding the Valley of Dor. The caves of the Therns are found here.

Golden Temple of Issus: The shrine and palace of Issus; on the shore of the Lost Sea of Korus in the Land of the First Born.

Greater Helium: Capital of the Empire of Helium.

Guardian of the North: The great magnet of Kadabra, located at the north magnetic pole.

Hall of Chiefs: The great hall in Manator.

Hastor: A city of the empire of Helium, far to the southwest of Greater Helium.

Helium: The empire of red men in the southeastern quadrant.

Holy Land: Name given by the Black Pirates to their subterranean domain on the shores of Omean.

Horz: An ancient deserted city; where Barsoomian culture first blossomed.

Hotel Raleigh: A hotel in Richmond, Virginia, where the author met with John Carter upon Carter's second return to Earth.

Illall: A city in Okar.

Iss: The River of Death.

Kadabra: The capital city of Okar.

Kaol: A city and empire of red men that lies along the equator almost halfway around the planet from Helium.

Korad: An ancient, dead city.

Korus: The lost sea in the Valley of Dor. On the shore stands the Golden Temple of Issus.

Lesser Helium: The second city of Helium, situated about seventy-five miles from Greater Helium.

Lothar: The forgotten city; inhabited by a race of auburn-haired, fair-skinned people.

Manataj: The farthest city of Manator.

Manator: The city of red men.

Manatos: Second city of Manator.

Marentina: A city in Okar.

Mountains of Torquas: Mountain range that guards the borders to Torquas.

Okar: Land of the yellow men.

Omean: The buried sea—harbor of the Black Pirates.

Otz Mountains: These surround the inner Valley of Dor and the Lost Sea of Korus.

Otz Valley: Lies in a mighty depression at the south pole, sunk hundreds of feet below the level of the surrounding country.

Pit of Plenty: A torture chamber near the center of the palace in Kadabra.

Polodona: Martian equator.

Ptarth: A kingdom of red men, one of the three major powers of the eastern hemisphere.

Shador: The prison isle in the sea of Omean.

Temple of Beauty: Art gallery in Greater Helium.

Temple of Reward: A giant domed coliseum that acts as the supreme courtroom of Helium.

Thark: The ancient city and empire of the green men.

Throxus (also Throxeus): Mightiest of the five Martian oceans.

Thuria: The nearer of the two moons of Barsoom (Phobos).

Thurian Tower: One of the Towers of Jetan.

Torquas: City of the green men.

Towers of Jetan: Prison buildings in Manator.

Twin Cities: Greater and Lesser Helium.

Valley of Dor: A valley located near the south pole; the Martian heaven.

Valley of Lost Souls: A section of the Otz Valley, around the canyon of the Iss, inhabited by those who turned aside at the last minute from their pilgrimage to the Valley of Dor and cannot return to the outside world.

Warhoon: An ancient city of green men.

Zitidar: The city and empire of red men, 1,900 miles east of Helium.

FLORA *and* FAUNA

Apt: A huge Arctic monster with six limbs, head and mouth similar to a hippopotamus, and two huge eyes with thousands of ocelli (facets) each.

Banth: A fierce lion-like creature that roams the low hills surrounding the dead seas. It has ten legs and several rows of fangs in its enormous jaws. It is hairless, except for a mane around its neck.

Calot: A dog-like creature about the size of a small pony. It has ten short legs and a frog-like head. Its jaws have three rows of long tusks. It is the fastest animal on Barsoom.

Calot Tree: This carnivorous plant is about the size of a large sagebrush. Each branch ends in a set of strong jaws, which have been known to drag down and devour large beasts.

Corphals: Legendary evil spirits that could allegedly enter the bodies of criminals and gain mastery over them.

Darseen: A chameleon-like creature.

Komal: The Lotharian banth-god.

Man-Flower: A plant whose blooms have eyes and hands with which to see and seize the insects that form its diet.

Orluk: A huge arctic beast that's hunted for its black-and-yellow striped pelt.

Pimalia: A gorgeous flowering plant.

Rykor: The headless bodies used by the Kaldanes.

Silian: A slimy aquatic reptile inhabiting the lost sea of Korus.

Sith: A six-legged, hornet-like beast about the size of a bull. It has dangerous jaws and a mighty, poisoned stinger. The eyes cover three fourths of the head, permitting the creature to see in all directions at once.

Sompus: A kind of tree.

Sorak: A small, six-legged animal about the size of a hand. It's kept as a house pet by the red men.

Sorapus: A hardwood tree that bears large nuts, about a foot in diameter.

Thoat: A green-man mount, ten feet high at the shoulder, with four legs on either side and a broad, flat tail.

Ulsio: Martian rat with many legs; comparable in size to a large Airedale terrier.

Usa: Fruit tree that bears tasteless fruit.

White Apes: A manlike creature that's ten to fifteen feet tall with an intermediary set of arms or legs midway between its upper and lower limbs. It is white and hairless except for an enormous shock of bristly hair on the head.

Woola: John Carter's calot.

OTHER BARSOOMIAN TERMS

Ad: Unit of measurement equal to 11.694 inches.

Destination Control Compass: A mechanical steering device that keeps a flier pointed toward a set of coordinates (aka Controlling Destination Compass).

Eighth Ray: The ray of propulsion. It is an inherent property of all light.

Ersite: A Martian building stone.

Flier: What John Carter calls any small Barsoomian aircraft.

Great Games: Contests in which men fight until the death. The survivor of each battle fights new contestants until ultimately, only one survivor is left.

Ground Flier: A vehicle with wide tires. It is willed with the Eight Ray, giving it just enough buoyancy to give traction for steering. Used only on the streets in the cities of Okar.

Haad: Unit of measurement equal to 2,000 ads.

Jetan: Martian game that's similar to chess; played on a board with 100 alternating black and orange squares.

Kalksus: Cruiser; transport commanded by Vas Kor.

Kaor: A Martian greeting.

Karad: Unit of measurement equal to 100 haads.

Ninth Ray: Ray used in manufacturing the artificial atmosphere of Barsoom.

Radium Bulb: Glass bowl filled with radium powder, which gives a clear light that lasts nearly indefinitely. The major means of artificial lighting on Barsoom.

Sak: Martian word for "jump."

Sofad: Unit of measurement equal to 1/10 of an ad.

Tal: A unit of time. 1/200 of a xat, or a little less than one second.

Utan: A military unit of 100 men, commanded by a dwar.

Vanator: Gahan's cruiser.

Xat: A Martian unit of time, equal to 1/50 of a zode, or about three minutes.

Xavarian: A Helium battleship.

Zode: A Martian unit of time, equal to 1/10 of a day, or about two hours and twenty-eight minutes.

About the Author

orn on September 1, 1875, into a well-to-do-family in Chicago, Edgar Rice Burroughs enjoyed a privileged upbringing and education. He tried his hand at several business ventures, but found himself drawn more to an itinerant life of adventure than to a life in the boardroom.

In 1912, after many failed business ventures, the thirty-six-year-old Burroughs published his first story, "Under the Moons of Mars," in the pulp magazine *All-Story*. It was so successful that he turned soon thereafter to writing full time. He would write nearly 70 novels and numerous short stories before his death in 1950. Although best known for his immensely popular *Tarzan* novels—he later bought an estate near where the films were shot in Southern California that he named Tarzana—Burroughs didn't confine himself to a single genre, and also wrote medieval romances, westerns, and mainstream novels.

Among his many science-fiction works, Burroughs wrote eleven novels in the John Carter of Mars series, the titular final installment of which was published fourteen years after his death.